THE
SALVATION
GAMBIT

THE
SALVATION
GAMBIT

A NOVEL

EMILY SKRUTSKIE

NEW YORK

A Del Rey Trade Paperback Original

Copyright © 2023 by Emily Skrutskie

Published in the United States by Del Rey,
an imprint of Random House, a division of
Penguin Random House LLC, New York.

DEL REY and the CIRCLE colophon are registered trademarks
of Penguin Random House LLC.

ISBN 978-0-593-49975-7
Ebook ISBN 978-0-593-49976-4

Printed in the United States of America on acid-free paper

randomhousebooks.com

9 8 7 6 5 4 3 2 1

Book design by Alexis Capitini

Traci won't let me get away with another silly dedication, so this one's for her

THE
SALVATION
GAMBIT

CHAPTER 1

The third time the airlock door yawns open, it's down to me and Fitz.

If she has an opinion about the maw that's unfurled before us and whatever might lie beyond it, she certainly isn't sharing. Not many people can look indifferent in a fluorescent blue prison jumpsuit with their hands locked behind them in mag cuffs, but Fitz stares into her oblivion perfectly blank and perfectly still.

"After you?" I offer, just to see if I can get her to break.

She doesn't even twitch. "Hark said you'd go next, Murdock."

I glance back over my shoulder at the pair of enforcers floating in the tunnel behind us. They've got their shock batons primed for action, but the one on the left is looking a little green around the gills. Probably well-born with no null sense to speak of, shuffled onto this mission by a short-straw draw.

"What if we dance to a new tune?" I ask. "Little number in A minor."

Fitz raises one perfect platinum eyebrow.

Behind the safety of the enforcers, the magistrate clears her throat. "We don't have all day, ladies," she calls, and I can't help but scoff at the note of fear in her voice. Is she anxious? Are we ruining her afternoon? How horrible that must be, to be latched onto this monstrous ship for one second more.

"Forgive me for trying to savor my last taste of freedom," I grumble, testing my own cuffs with a stretch that pulls them tight. We've been locked into them for the past ten hours—save for a too-brief lav break—and the stiffness in my shoulders isn't ideal for what I have in mind.

"If you're set on savoring it, the quiet one goes through first," the magistrate declares. She reaches for a handhold strap and uses it to edge herself forward past the enforcers, the electromagnetic cuff release spinning lazily around her other wrist.

Fitz meets my eyes. I pass her a nod.

Then I kick hard against the tunnel wall. The momentum propels me into a spin as I tuck my legs up against my body and throw the cuff chain under my feet to bring my hands in front of me. The enforcers lunge, but I already have a strap in hand, using it to wrench my canvas shoes *hard* into Greenie's wrist, nullifying the arc of the shock baton he was trying to swing. Satisfaction hits like a supernova—then sputters out the moment I realize Fitz's doing absolutely nothing but staring.

"A minor—I said A minor!" I grunt, barely dodging the less-green guard's thrust. This one's got at least a bit of null sense—they know to make direct, forward motions rather than wild swings that'll only twist you in directions you didn't intend to go—but they're still painfully slow, too cautious of the thin tunnel walls around us and the void beyond.

Under other circumstances, I might share that fear, but this is my last chance. I'm not slowing for anything. And if I have to make this work without Fitz, so be it. Her loss.

With another well-aimed kick off the tunnel wall, I send myself rocketing clean through the shuttle airlock, reaching out to slap the door release as I sail past it. It seals in an instant—I'd expect nothing less of a space-facing door in a shuttle of this make—and the inner door of the airlock opens with similar haste. I kick off one of my shoes and stuff it in the latch as it tries to seal. The ship's intelligence won't risk depressurization by opening the outer airlock door when the inner one's jammed. That sort of thing can be easily overridden given time, but it's the time I need.

I'm through the shuttle's cabin in a blink, sailing past the rows of benches we were cuffed to on the journey up and clean through the cockpit door, which the magistrate foolishly left open when she first emerged. Hark noted it, and because I've been watching her every move, I noted her noting it. Started putting together a plan, just like she'd do.

Just didn't have the particulars sorted out until now, with her and Bea already on the other side of that airlock door.

Bea's the one who gave me the second part of my scheme. Even from her position tethered to a bench in the cabin, she could tell our flight was fully auto. A human pilot would take some convincing to abandon their post, but an intelligence can be brute-forced—and that's what I do best.

I seal the cockpit door behind me and lock it, adding an extra three minutes to the clock running in my head.

"All right, gorgeous, work with me," I mutter, taking in the console. There's an emergency set of manual controls, but that won't do me a lick of good until I've cracked the intelligence. I clock the cameras and other sensors one by one, building a map of how I'm being perceived. No doubt the ship's throwing emergency alert after emergency alert into the immediate vicinity, but no one's around to hear its sputtering distress.

No one but the behemoth we're latched onto—and through the cockpit windshield, I get my first glimpse at the monster that's supposed to devour me. Gun mounts bristle like thorns along a flank that stretches beyond my capacity for rational thought. Theoretically its structure is a torus, but at this distance, I can barely pick out a curve. It's built vicious and unyielding—in short, imperial.

It calls itself the *Justice*, and it's come to collect my soul. I'm not going to give it the satisfaction.

I tear myself away from the view and drop beneath the console, running my hands along the paneling until I feel a catch. With a tug, the plastic swings open to reveal the shuttle's core systems. Relief floods me. I recognize this layout from Bea's lessons in hot-wiring. All I have to do is reconfigure the way the system handles owner authentication and the shuttle might as well be mine.

The question of whether I can get that done before they get through the doors remains to be seen. Already I can hear clatters and thumps coming from the rear of the shuttle—undoubtedly the enforcers trying to manually override the little jam I've created back at the airlock.

"Shuttle nav, you online?" I call, shoving my arm deep into the compartment for the first maneuver.

"Online," the ship's system confirms.

"Grant me pilot control."

"I do not recognize an authorized pilot in the cockpit," it replies. Its tone is stilted, impersonal—cheap, if I had to guess. A cost-cutting measure that's not gonna shake out great for these people, because cheap is practically synonymous with *easy to crack*.

I find the wires that lead to the authorization fob and pull them free with a judicious yank. "Grant me pilot control," I repeat.

"I do not recognize an authorized pilot in the cockpit."

I pull a face. Guess it's not *that* cheap. But the authorization system is, in the end, passing a lone binary bit to the rest of the ship's governance, and if I can just replicate that signal, I can convince it to grant me access. I've got a wealth of input devices to choose from, but Bea always told me to go for the simplest— and nothing's simpler than the switch that toggles the cockpit's running lights. With another hard tug, I wrench its wires free.

The cockpit plunges into darkness.

"Shit," I hiss. That's textbook rust-bucket wiring—and now I'm stuck fumbling in the dark, wasting precious seconds as I try to pull my wires out into the dim light reflecting off the *Justice*'s surface.

Panic is a self-fulfilling prophecy, I hear Hark whisper in my ear.

But Hark's fate is sealed already. She's on the other side of the *Justice*'s airlock door. And maybe if she'd panicked just a bit more yesterday, we wouldn't be in this mess in the first place. Maybe I'm panicking exactly the right amount—the amount that's going to get me free before I'm swallowed.

I feel in the maw of the console's guts, tracing wires, thumbing along the raised indents that denote inputs and outputs, building the mental map. One of Hark's earliest lessons was to always lock in your layout first, whether it's a floor plan, a seating chart, or an entire city's streets. A good plan succeeds on known terrain. With that established, I ease the switch's wires into the appropriate connections for the authorization fob, jamming them down with the flat of my palm to ensure I've made contact.

It's ugly work, work that'll certainly fall apart the second I'm not pinning it down, but it needs to function only long enough for me to get control of the ship. "Grant me pilot control," I grunt for a third time, flipping the switch the instant I enunciate the last syllable.

"Authorized pilot detected. Manual control granted," the ship's intelligence announces.

I let out a whoop, swinging myself out from under the console. A prod of the controls confirms the steering system's loose and manual, ready to take my input the moment I flip the ship from docking to flight mode. "All right, gorgeous, let's get this show on the road," I announce, using a toe bar to slam my ass down in the pilot's seat. "Give me engines."

The console remains inert. I tap the indicator light on the dash, frowning. Maybe my haphazard wire pulling took out a few more systems than I initially estimated.

"Shuttle?" I hazard.

"I apologize," the shuttle ekes out in a stiff tone that doesn't sound at all sorry. "Preservation measures are in effect. Engines will remain inert until the danger has passed."

Preservation? I sealed the outer door behind me, didn't I? The tunnel itself has an emergency cinch, designed to snap shut in the event the shuttle has to break away unexpectedly, so the intelligence can't be worrying over the people I left behind in there. "The hell are we being preserved from?"

"The entity with which we're docked," it answers.

I blink, my gaze homing in on the guns outside the windshield. "Ah."

"The *Justice* has communicated that any unscheduled departure will be fired upon with impunity," the shuttle continues, and despite its flat affect, I think I can read between the lines. It's a goldfish up against a goddamn kraken.

The shuttle's intelligence is shitting itself.

My hands slip limply from the controls, and for a moment my null sense gets away from me, leaving me dizzy, disoriented, and faintly nauseous. I don't know whether to laugh or scream. Was this why Hark floated so calmly through the airlock door at the far end of the tunnel? Did she know our fate was sealed not at the moment we crossed the threshold but at the moment this shuttle entered the warship's firing distance?

I bite down on the bitter wash at the back of my throat. It

would have been nice to know that my life was already forfeit—that I shouldn't have bothered with trying to put together an escape plan myself. But then again, Hark hasn't been very forthcoming in the past twenty-four hours. Not since the four of us were caught red-handed, spinning a con around the founder of Gest Settlement.

Usually these things go smoothly, greased by Hark's impeccable planning. In and out and off into the sunset on whatever getaway vehicle Bea's been keeping hot in the alley. That's what's worked for the past four years—and what fell apart in the blink of an eye yesterday.

It could have been so much less of a problem if the *Justice* hadn't shown up in orbit mere hours later.

The galactic fringe has always been full of ghost stories. Every expansion into uncharted territory brings with it whispers of the impossible. Alien life. Cursed planets so volatile that setting foot on them is a death sentence. Pirate crews that feast on human flesh. One of the most outlandish rumors—one I never believed until yesterday, for the record—was that an entire Ybi war fleet had wandered off into the black when the old empire fell, fleeing the collapse of a system that had grown so massive and so rotten that ruin was inevitable.

Convenient excuses, all of them. *Oh, the settlement project you sank so many investments into failed not due to our mismanagement but because a three-hundred-years-dead empire wiped it off the map for shits and giggles. Oh, that outlaw with multiple APBs across the Known Harmony disappeared into the stars, never to be heard from again—good riddance!* Too grand to be believable, too weird to be doubted, but the perfect punctuation to put at the end of an unexplained mystery.

Which is all fine when it's other people's punctuation, but I'm having trouble wrapping my head around the fact that it's mine. When the *Justice* dropped into orbit over Gest, it pointed the full might of its artillery at the settlement and made one clear, firm demand.

Surrender your sinners.

With those three words, our futures evaporated. There would be no fair trial—not even any festering in prison long enough for Hark to put together an escape plan. Gest needed to pick some undesirables to tithe, and we'd fallen right into their laps.

Less than a day later, they'd loaded us onto this shuttle. The negotiation had been short, as the magistrate gloated on the way up. They'd offered up the four of us, and the *Justice* had accepted without any pushback, immediately relaying instructions for packaging and transfer. Four human lives was all it took to turn its might away from Gest's fragile stake on its world.

I can't, for the life of me, imagine why. What a warship could possibly want with condemned criminals, what would compel it to seek poor sods like us out in the first place. Thus far, all communication has been with the ship itself, not any individuals aboard, making motives difficult to suss out. Hark and Bea spent the entire shuttle ride up muttering back and forth about it. Is this lone, mind-warpingly big ship one of a fleet or acting alone? What's it trying to accomplish that it needs warm bodies—specifically sinners—for?

I guess I'm about to find out.

I let out a long, shaking breath, my gaze fixed not on the bright slash of the *Justice*'s hull but on the dark, infinite expanse beyond it. The view's impossible to savor, but it's the last sight of freedom I'll ever have.

CHAPTER 2

Putting my hands over my head doesn't make a lick of difference. The moment the guards pry open the cockpit door, I find myself on the business end of everything their shock batons can legally unload in a single strike. The pain wrenches me into a ball, every muscle and tendon in my body gone taut, and by the time I'm thinking coherently again, they're hauling me back into the tunnel.

Incredibly, Fitz is still there. I'd figured the magistrate would have shoved her through already, but the two of them are floating placidly side by side. Fitz *still* has the gall to look bored with the whole affair, and it lights me up even worse than the electricity I've just absorbed.

"You didn't even *try*," I snarl through gritted teeth as the guards shunt me past her.

"Because I knew it wouldn't work," Fitz replies primly.

"The hell do you know about intelligences? There's no

way you could have possibly known the ship would lock
up—"

"I knew it wouldn't work because it was *your* plan," Fitz clar-
ifies.

I kick out for the wall, trying to launch myself back at her,
but the enforcers are wise to my tricks now, and with one
latched onto each forearm, I end up straining uselessly in their
grip as one of them does me the surprising courtesy of shoving my discarded shoe back onto my foot.

"Now, now," the magistrate chides, easing up behind us
with the electromagnetic cuff release in hand. "You already
know there's only one exit for you in this corridor. I suggest
you take it without putting up more of a fuss."

I glance sidelong at the open door and the airlock chamber
beyond. Its intricately filigreed pale ceramic paneling looks like
something out of a historical record—and I suppose it is. The
old Ybi Empire loved their detailing, especially on vessels that
never had to reckon with atmospheric drag. It was a show of
strength, in a way. Showed they had laborers to spare, enough
to cover the hulls of ships as monstrously big as the *Justice* with
elaborate tributes to the Ybi Empire's conquest wrought in
both reinforced carbon and sweat.

At the far end of the airlock is another door, leading to the
warship's interior. Bea and Hark must have passed through it
already. Unless the *Justice* has some method of disintegrating
people in the chamber. Not a thought I love having seconds
before being tossed into it—and that's almost certainly what's
happening. The enforcers' grip tightens as the magistrate
moves in, passing the electromagnet over my cuffs. A mechanism clicks, and they fall open, leaving behind furious red welts.
Before I have a chance to rub at them, the magistrate shoves a
backpack into my arms.

I bite down on the urge to laugh out loud. I'm being shunted
into certain doom and possible vaporization, but I feel like a

kid being handed their bag and sent off to school. Apparently the *Justice* supplied a packing list, one that read more like we were getting thrown into the backcountry instead of the maw of a warship. Spare jumpsuit, thermal blanket, flashlight—even a few protein bars and a canteen. It has me wondering what, exactly, I'm supposed to be surviving in there.

I meet Fitz's gaze one last time as I wrestle the straps around my shoulders. She tilts her head to the side, her expression still devastatingly flat. I don't know what I want from her, but it's certainly not what I'm getting. Is she tired of waiting her turn? Curious whether I'm going to figure out some exciting new way to get myself beaten up before I make it through the door? The weight of four years of simmering antagonism hangs over us, and I realize abruptly that I should have spent my final minutes as a free person thinking of my last words instead of doomed escape plans.

"C'mon, smile, Fitz. One last time. For me?" I choke out, just as the enforcers shove me forward.

She doesn't. She'd never.

The door snaps shut behind me the second I clear its threshold, and the suddenness of it startles me so badly that I forget to grab any of the handrails, sailing clear to the far end of the chamber and bouncing off hard enough to bruise. I twist and catch myself before the next bounce, hooking one toe in a railing to arrest my momentum. It's not enough to slow my heart, which is hammering like a micropulsing thruster as I take in the chamber.

The first thing that strikes me is how thoroughly I'm being watched. There are six sensor arrays I can see, the beady lenses of cameras giving them away. They're positioned for full coverage of the chamber, leaving nothing to the imagination and rendering them difficult to block all at once. The visual component is obvious enough, but I wouldn't be surprised if there were infrared as well, and there's almost certainly a microphone or two.

I realize with a bitter purse of my lips that I'm casing it like it's a security apparatus—like this is just another job, like I'm preparing to report back to Hark with my findings so she can factor them into her grand plan. After four years under her instruction, it's instinct, but I don't know what good it does me here. I don't even know if Hark's still alive somewhere beyond the second door.

I reach for an odd bit of smooth paneling that stands out from the otherwise finely carved ceramic tiling. My fingers sink into softness, and my brow barely gets done furrowing before a voice announces, "Greetings, Murdock."

It resonates like the toll of a bell in the narrow chamber, vibrating up my arm from the speaker under my palm. A shiver runs up my spine in its wake.

"I'd like to speak with a human, please," I manage.

The speakers emit a breathy chuckle, but there's just a tad too much evenness in it—a dead giveaway. "Remarkable," the ship's intelligence says, its tone warmly sincere. "Neither of your compatriots recognized my nature from the get-go."

"I know my way around systems like you," I reply, but it's barely the truth. I'm used to intelligences like the one aboard the shuttle, simple creatures designed for a specific purpose, with archives that might reach back decades, not centuries. The closest thing to my fun new conversation partner I've ever come across is the governing intelligence of the station I grew up on, and even that was stiff and bureaucratic to a fault.

I glance over the cameras once more, unsure how best to address it. It's perceiving me simultaneously through all six, but my unsophisticated binocular vision has to pick a favorite. I ease closer to the one embedded in the wall nearest to me, squinting at the box that surrounds it and slipping my nails into the seams of the housing. Predictably, it doesn't budge a bit.

"Not to sound ungrateful—because obviously you're a *re-markable* bit of engineering—but I do think I'd like to talk to whoever's in charge here," I declare, worrying my thumb over a sensor I think must be infrared.

"You are."

My null sense slips away from me, and I'm forced to clamp down hard on a handrail to keep my proverbial balance. I fix my gaze on the beady camera lens, trying to orient myself against its solidity, but my brain is going a parsec a second. "You . . . you're self-governed?" I choke out. "This is all *you*?"

"I serve the Ybi Empire," the *Justice* replies. There's a note of offense in its voice, like it's rude of me to assume it would act independently.

"The Ybi Empire that fell three hundred years ago?" I blurt, then brace for vaporization.

But the *Justice* only lets out a low chuckle. "How fallen does the Ybi Empire look to you?"

It's not the most compelling argument, but it's difficult to refute when all I can see around me is that intricate Ybi ceramic, when the horrific might of a Ybi war machine has seized control of my fate. Sure, the Known Harmony is several orders of magnitude grander than the power of this single ship, but I have a fleshy machine made out of meat in my skull that hasn't *seen* the true scale of the galaxy—and *has* seen that massive, sloping hull curving away into eternity out the windshield of that terrified little shuttle.

"And what does the Ybi Empire want with me?" I ask. Better to play along, to figure out exactly what the hell is going on.

"To redeem you, of course," the *Justice* replies.

It startles a laugh out of me, and I feel myself flushing—*flushing*—under the scrutiny of all six eyes. "The hell do I need redemption for?" I ask, scrubbing a hand over my mouth as if that will draw some of the heat out of my cheeks.

"According to the accounting I've received from your magistrate, you were part of a conspiracy to defraud an entire settlement," the *Justice* replies.

"The settlement you just threatened to wipe off the map." When the ship leaves me with nothing but a pregnant pause, I continue, "So which of us is the bigger sinner?"

"You," it states blithely. "I act in the interest of the Ybi Empire, whereas you acted to benefit no one but yourself."

I scoff. "You know what those settlements are, right? They're vanity projects for the rich assholes of the Core who want to see a town named after them. They're stitched together with exponentially marked-up building costs to sound impressive, but all that money mysteriously disappears on the way to the vendor, leaving the settlers themselves with jack shit. At least when my team gets involved, the money disappears into more interesting places."

"How interesting are your pockets?" the ship asks dryly.

It's getting *incredibly* difficult to remember this thing could probably kill me in a second—I almost roll my eyes. "I'm just saying, if you're looking for sinners, I can name a few bigger ones back on Gest who should have cut the line before me."

"What if I wanted *you?*" the *Justice* says—suddenly loud and low and so intense I feel it on every inch of skin.

I fight the impulse to recoil from the wall and let myself float. Proximity is an illusion in this chamber, and it makes no difference how close I am to any given sensor array. Still, my mind races for a solution to the sudden intimacy that grips me. I'm not used to being watched. Not used to being noticed. If someone sees what I'm doing, it usually means Hark's scheme is collapsing and we need to start running.

The thought of Hark, though—that's my anchor. She passed through this chamber. I have to believe she's on the other side of the far door, waiting for me.

"Then you get in line," I tell the *Justice,* fixing my gaze on the hatch. "Hark's got dibs."

I swear its silences are only getting smugger.

"Seriously, what do you want from me?" I ask when I can't

take it any longer. "And don't say that redemption bullshit. How is it worth threatening an entire settlement just for four people? Why's the ghost of a dead empire worth that level of devotion?"

"Faith is a strange thing, isn't it?" the ship replies. "You can explain all you want to a doubter, but if you want them to truly come around, you have to let them walk their own path. Everything I do is rooted in a belief I can't force you to share. But I see such potential in you, Murdock. Potential I think Hark is wasting, if the account she gave me is anything to go by."

My mouth goes dry. The *Justice*'s scrutiny I can stomach, but even secondhand, I'm not sure I'm ready for Hark's. And yet the gravity of my curiosity is too great to resist. "What did she say about me?" I ask. I aim for flat affect, for all the casual cool she's tried to drill into me over the years.

In the *Justice*'s subsequent pause, I hear just how badly I fail.

"Nothing of consequence, of course," it begins, its tone lofty and casual. "She said she picked you up off Pearl Station four years ago. It surprised me to hear that backwater relic is still around. That station pre-dates my own activation by half a century. Hark made you sound like a rare find, a diamond in the rough. A prodigious technical talent stuck in base violence, scamming poor people into worse poverty—and she wanted to show you a better path."

"I . . . sure, that's one way of putting it," I mutter, feeling like my brain's just developed at least five new wrinkles.

The subtle whine of the machinery in the nearest sensor array changes pitch, and with it I sense a sharpening of the *Justice*'s attention. Every last microexpression of mine is data. I'm not sure why the intelligence is collecting it, but one of the first lessons I learned during my first forays into *sin,* as the *Justice* would call it, is that every piece of a person you collect makes it easier to destroy them.

"Then, at least according to her account," the *Justice* continues, "she folded you into a crime spree that spanned the entire so-called Known Harmony, pulling over forty million jiras in stolen profit."

"Is it a crime to steal from thieves?" I retort, but the words taste like Hark's and I know I can't sell them the same. It was the line she'd prepared for the direst scenario, where she needed to tangle someone's moral center long enough for an escape plan to take hold, but it was more often a reminder to the rest of us that what we were doing, while not strictly speaking legal, was right.

Or right enough.

I close my eyes, trying to get my thoughts back in order. This is what happens when I'm left on my own for too long. Without Hark, I get squirrelly. Get bad ideas in my head, like trying to hijack the shuttle or that one time I almost blew a job by sucker punching a partygoer who snuck up on me while I was trying to crack a security system undetected. Hark's rationality grounds me where I need it most.

And no matter what she thinks of me, that part's going to stay true.

"Theft is a crime." The *Justice*'s voice rumbles through me, but I'm beginning to grow used to the force of it. "Theft of the magnitude you've accomplished requires reparation beyond your means. Your only hope for salvation is through a higher calling. Fortunately for you, that calling has arrived."

The language it's using finally clicks. I open my eyes and see the *Justice* clearly for the first time. It's not a monster, the way I've been imagining it, not some fell beast come to steal and swallow me.

It's a god, and it wants my worship.

"Clever girl," it murmurs, and I bite back the urge to curse. Hark should have taught me better—my face is giving everything away. "But you're too clever to be of any use to me at the moment. You're not the type to leap without looking. I got that from Hark too. You'll learn the art of faith once you've come to understand the nature of your reality."

"Don't get your hopes up," I reply. "I follow Hark's orders, and I don't think any dose of your *reality* is going to change that."

The *Justice* lets out another one of its low, slightly too-even chuckles. "I've accepted hundreds of tithes over hundreds of years. The ones that come as a set? They never stay that way."

With those words still vibrating through my bones, the door at the far end of the chamber peels open.

CHAPTER 3

A gust of warm, stale air hits me, and the hum of the sensor arrays fades away. Guess I'm no longer worth observing. I glance back at the door I came through. There's nothing left for me there—no clever escape, no salvation, not even a friendly face.

Ahead is Hark, and in the past, she's been all of those things and more. I pull hard on the rail, setting my hands on the straps of my pack as I sail headfirst through the *Justice*'s offered opening.

I'm prepared for the way it snaps shut the second I've cleared it—but not the man who tackles me in the same instant.

Instinct takes over. I grapple him right back, tearing at the bulky coverall he wears as I squirm in his grip. The lights of the corridor I've just entered are dim, crusted over with age—barely enough to discern much more than wild eyes, wild hair, and a wicked-looking dagger he's struggling desperately to bring around to my throat.

I lash out with a leg, making contact with a bulkhead. It's just enough to redirect our momentum—and it's all I need to anchor my head in the tumult. I grab his wrist and jam myself away from his body. It's counterintuitive, but in null, he needs leverage for his weapon, and if I can keep myself latched onto the same arm he's holding it with, he won't be able to get it close to me.

At least, until my back collides with the next wall, but I've got my foot up in time, shoving hard against his stomach. The combined force of my bounceback and kick is enough to break his grip on me, keeping me pinned against the wall as the man flies across the corridor.

I launch myself after him, but I've miscalculated. His null sense is good. He's not disoriented in the slightest, and he twists his body to meet me with the business end of his dagger. I've got less time than I'd like to dodge, and I'm so focused on that blade coming toward me that when a second person slams into my side, I yelp in surprise.

Two on one is scarcely fair in a corridor this narrow. My second attacker latches onto my left arm, hooking one of her legs around mine to keep me from pulling the same leverage trick again, and the man grabs hold of my right, wrenching it around behind my back with the full force of his entire body mass. He flattens the dagger against my throat.

"You don't have to make this difficult," the woman says with a grunt.

"You don't know me very well," I snarl, my voice vibrating against the chill of the metal. I throw an elbow back into the man's torso, but all that does is pull the dagger into my skin just enough to bite, and I hiss through my teeth. I lash out with my free leg again, striking another bulkhead. With the mass of two people added to my total, it just sets us in a lazy spin and pulls an irritated huff out of the man.

The knife lifts from my throat, and I immediately thrash like a fish on a line—but before I can break free, the woman's grip loosens at the same instant the man's full mass drives into my back and slams me flat against the opposing wall.

There's a pinch at my side, a tightness. For a horrible moment, I wonder if I've been stabbed and the signal just hasn't caught up to my brain yet. I try to shove back off the wall, but find I'm lodged in place—pinned by the man's dagger, now speared clean through the right armpit of my jumpsuit and buried to the hilt in the bulkhead.

I heave against the wall again, but whatever they make this prison garb out of is strong stuff, and the tines of the dagger's guard have woven the lateral seam of my suit between them. Worse, I can't squirm around and grab the hilt in a direction that gets me any sort of leverage. I seethe, shoving hard against the bulkhead, lashing backward with my feet in the hopes of catching someone somewhere soft.

"Murdock, let it be."

The fight goes out of me in an instant at the sound of Hark's voice, and I twist my body toward it like a flower toward a sun. She's only a few meters farther down the corridor—free-floating, but held at . . . at *sword point* by two other people. Her long, inky hair floats free in graceful waves, and she's got her hands held up over her head, her thin fingers spread wide in surrender. Even in a bright-blue prison jumpsuit, she's still got that air of calm sophistication in the tilt of her chin, like all this is just a cocktail-party negotiation gone sour.

The sight of her is chemical. Even staked to the wall, I can feel my body relaxing. These assholes might have us in a bind, but Hark's going to get us out of it. That's the gravitational force that's been guiding my life for the past four years, and if I don't have that, I have nothing.

Behind her floats Bea, who's got one hand anchored on Hark's belt and the other held out like she expects to catch the swords being leveled at them. Her hands look far too vulnera-

ble without the white of her lucky fingerless driving gloves
against her dark skin. She flashes me a nervous smile. Bea's our
getaway driver, the level head and easy out to Hark's intricate
machinations. She's a devil behind the wheel and a rally race
champion in her off hours, but desperately out of her depth
when it comes to facing down the medieval violence being lev-
ied at us.

I don't blame her. When I imagined what lay on the other
side of the *Justice*'s hull, I don't know if I ever could have landed
on fucking *swords*.

"Get their shit," the woman behind me announces.

I grab for the strap of my backpack seconds before the man
who attacked me latches on. I may not know what else lies
ahead, but hell if I'm going to give up the only possessions I
have to my name. I tug hard, reeling him in, and meet him with
a headbutt that whites out my vision for a second.

The man grunts, then backhands me hard enough that my
head cracks against the wall.

"Murdock, I said *leave it*!" Hark shouts. My free will snaps
taut like a dog at the end of a chain. In my head, I hear the echo
of some of the first words Hark ever spoke to me. *What's a
clever kid like you doing trying to punch your way through problems?*

Which was fair when she said it then, but now—now this
backpack contains the only food and water I'm guaranteed, the
only change of clothes I can count on, and the only warmth I
might be offered in this ugly nightmare of a ship. I keep my
grip tight, my skin burning as the man plants a boot on the wall
and wrenches back with all his might.

"We're playing a number in F-sharp major," Hark says. Out
of the corner of my eye, I watch as she willingly slips her own
pack from her shoulders, shunts it toward the people holding
her at sword point, and gestures for Bea to do the same.

And oh, that's the kicker. We've got our own little music,
just the four of us—a series of keys that Hark's contrived to

tell us exactly what to expect and how to act in any given moment without cluing in the people around us. *F-sharp major*'s one of my least favorite. The rough translation is *Sit tight and wait for the cavalry to arrive.* Which is difficult enough to deal with when we're supposed to sit tight through a mugging.

It's made even worse if by "cavalry" she means who I think she means.

With absolutely impeccable timing, the door I just came through slips open.

Fitz floats across the threshold, backlit by the bright-white lights of the ingress chamber, looking infuriatingly ethereal. No one rushes in to tackle *her.* The man trying to tug my bag away freezes, glancing at the woman behind him for instruction, and I use the opportunity to wrap the strap around my hand a second time and double up on my grip. The woman is similarly transfixed.

Everyone is.

Outside the *Justice,* Fitz was all flat stares and bruised elbows, no charm and no null sense to speak of. But the moment the doors of the chamber opened and she saw our little situation, her switch flipped. She's turned her null fumbling into slow elegance, and a guileless smile spreads across her lips as she takes in the scene. Her pale-green eyes bat wide open, her body twists *just so,* and the overall effect is so angelic and innocent it makes me want to hurl.

This is what she's good for, what she's done best in all the years I've known her. Fitz is the fancy centerpiece Hark plunks on the table to distract people from the fact that she's snatching silverware left and right. The dichotomy of her is a puzzle I'll never solve, the way she breaks the knob off her charm the second she's working, then pulls the plug as soon as the job is done.

It's all the more irritating because it fucking *works.* Our new friends have forgotten what they were doing, too busy trying to parse the divine apparition. Even I'm having trouble keeping focused—all the worse because I've got a serious opportunity here. I'm torn between using my tug-of-war opponent's slack-jawed wonder to get my bag free and not wanting to break the spell Fitz has cast on him.

I glance at Hark again, hoping for a hand signal, a key change, *something,* but she's stuck on Fitz too. And if I thought the sight of Fitz's schtick was throwing me off my game, it's nothing compared to the way the admiration shining in Hark's eyes hits me. The look isn't the lusty stares of Fitz's marks—Hark's always been immune to any sort of wiles in the time I've known her.

No, this is the pride I've chased in her for so long, the pride I can never quite manage to inspire, the pride of a moment playing exactly like you planned it.

All for Fitz.

Fine. I wedge my knee up against the wall, giving myself the distance I need to yank as hard as I possibly can on the back-pack strap. It pops free from the man's grip, and his attention snaps back to me.

Fitz's spell shatters, and the corridor collapses into chaos. I bundle the backpack against my chest, ducking my head as the man grapples for it. The woman who helped take me down lunges for Fitz, who pinwheels her arms in panic as she tries to outmaneuver her. The people with swords have closed in on Hark and Bea, and nauseous regret rises in my throat as I wait for the telltale spray of arterial blood in null.

A Klaxon cuts through the shouts and scuffling, bright-red lights pulsing up and down the corridor. The man trying to wrench my backpack away from me does a strange maneuver, giving up his leverage against the wall I'm staked to in favor of swinging his body out parallel to it.

A glance at the rest of our attackers shows they've all turned themselves in the same direction, which is precisely the moment it clicks how screwed I am.

A low rumble shakes the corridor, and I give up my hold on the backpack completely, my hands scrabbling for purchase on something, anything, as the walls themselves begin to move. The only anchor available is the dagger, wedging uncomfortably first into my side and then into my armpit.

Like many space-bound megastructures of its ilk, the *Justice* is built to spin. When you've got thousands of people aboard—as this warship once did in its heyday—you've got the greatest chance of keeping everyone happy if you give them a nice, comfortable centripetal force. But an imperial weapon of war that needs to onboard supplies, offload fighter craft, and target enemies with ease needs an outer deck that's not rotating fast enough to generate that grav. One that can go either way, depending on the ship's state.

To facilitate our transfer aboard, the outer ring had to be free-floating. We've been in null ever since. That's changing fast.

I grit my teeth as the dagger's hilt jams up into my armpit. Not even my full weight hanging off it is enough to dislodge it from the bulkhead. Worse, I'm just a few inches too short to reach the newly established ground from where I'm dangling, leaving me shoving desperately against the dagger to keep its guard from goring out my lymph nodes.

So much for the cavalry. Fitz is pinned under the woman who grabbed her, Hark and Bea are collapsed in a heap, and with grav back in action, I've lost the advantage of my null sense—not that it did anything for me in the first place. I glance three meters down the corridor, where both my pack and the man trying to get it away from me have landed. He gives me a leering grin as he bends to pick it up.

But before his fingers can close around the strap, there's a series of *whumps* overhead. A portal snaps open, light from above spilling down in a radiant beam.

From it drops a warrior clad in armor, who lands in a crouch with a sword at the ready.

CHAPTER 4

We go from zero to full fucking medieval in the span of a couple seconds. More portals open down the length of the corridor, and more warriors rain out of them, shouting incomprehensible commands as they charge our attackers. The clash of blade on blade echoes in the hallway's narrow confines. Out of the corner of my eye, I spot Hark and Bea lunging to pull Fitz up from where she lies prone on the ground, the three of them huddling back against the wall with their packs clutched close.

Me, I'm not going to let our new party guests have all the fun. As the man who pinned me to the wall gets knocked back by a mighty kick, I brace against the dagger hilt for balance, lash out with a leg, and trip him.

My triumphant grin lasts only until I realize my little maneuver's just jammed the dagger more firmly into the bulkhead. "Gotta be shitting me," I groan.

"Murdock, *down!*" Hark shouts from somewhere over my shoulder, and I barely have time to duck before a sword slams into the wall right where my head used to be. I try to wrench myself around and face my attacker, but one of the newcomers tackles them down the hall and out of kicking distance.

Whoever these people are, their thrilling heroics are shockingly effective. The would-be muggers are in retreat, stumbling into the gloom of the poorly lit corridor as our knights in shining armor square up to fend off any thoughts of doubling back.

By the time they turn around, Hark's already on her feet, smoothing down her collar and pulling her silky black hair over her shoulder. "Wonderful of you to join us, folks," she says, her voice greased with that sales-pitch tone she always uses when she's taking the temperature of the room. "I hope you didn't go through all that trouble just to steal our petty gear too."

One of the warriors whirls to face her—the one who dropped out of the ceiling first. He wears a terrifying helm crested with jagged spikes, but when he pulls it off, he reveals a round, handsome, and surprisingly friendly face. "We come in peace," he says. On closer examination, his armor's rough and mismatched, sculpted out of polymer paneling that must have been hacked out of something else. "Sorry about the bad first impression—both on our part and on the part of the bastards who got to you first. Usually we're able to intercept fresh ingest before the scavs can close in, but those ones got lucky." He lifts his face to the portals that have opened in the ceiling and calls up, "All clear here!"

A ladder slides down, its descent pulled along by the body weight of a lithe older woman. She's dressed in loose robes that look homespun, which fall like water around willowy limbs that she must have come by growing up in an off-standard grav environment. "Greetings, fellow sinners," she says with a warm smile as she disembarks the ladder gracefully. "My name is Fatima, Envoy to the East Deck. Now it's clear you and the vessel have gotten off on the wrong foot, but I'm here to reassure you that despite the lawless antics of a few rogues, civilization flourishes aboard the *Justice*."

My head's spinning, trying to parse all the new vocab they're throwing at us, but that last sentence gets a snort out of me. "You sure about that?" I grunt over my shoulder. "Because at first blush, it looks like this place is barely out of the Dark Ages. I mean, swords? Seriously? Where did you get swords? And more important, can I also have a sw—"

"What my associate is trying to say," Hark interrupts, shouldering her backpack as she takes a not-so-subtle sidestep and places herself between me and the Envoy, "is that we're very grateful for your assistance. Would you happen to have a rough estimate of how many people on this ship think we're supposed to be killing each other for scraps out here? Just for my own edification, of course."

Fatima's brow furrows. "Head counts are a little difficult, as I'm sure you understand, but I think our numbers are somewhere around ten thousand, and of those ten thousand, I'd guess it's something like ten percent who choose to live outside settlements like East Deck and subsist on petty violence."

"You're telling me you've got a thousand assholes running around with swords in here?" Bea deadpans from where she's steadying Fitz.

"The scavs usually keep to themselves," Fatima says. "When they don't, well—that's what we have Blade-sworn like Heeseok here for." She gestures to the man who led the charge against the scavs. He hoists his sword over his shoulder with a proud tilt of his chin. "They're pledged to defend the settlements' interests."

"Then that would make *us* in the settlements' interests, correct?" Fitz asks. She's giving Fatima those nightmarish green doe eyes that usually work wonders, but Fatima's attention goes only as far as an amused smile in her direction.

"Why, of course! Civilization is all about collaboration, and anytime we have ingest, we have an opportunity to bring in fresh collaborators." She pauses. "Also, we'd like to make sure the assholes running around with swords don't end up adding you four to their number."

I don't know why she feels the need to glance sidelong at me when she says that. I shrug at her, then get back to jiggling the dagger pinning me to the wall.

"We'd like to invite you back to East Deck and show you what we've built here. The *Justice* took us all in on the premise that the galaxy was better off without us, and we've spat in the face of that. But I do have just one question I'm obligated to pose, if the four of you wouldn't mind." Fatima pauses, and a few of the Blade-sworn tense noticeably. "What are you in for?"

I look to Hark. Fitz and Bea do the same.

It's like watching a magic trick, like *knowing,* rationally, that this woman's a mere mortal—and yet when she draws herself up tall and that glint takes over her eyes, she's a god at the center of its court. No longer dressed in a baggy prison jumpsuit but in her finest suit, a sleek, thin tie loosened *just so* to bare the dusky column of her neck, every detail perfect in its imperfection. *Too perfect and they clock the scam right away,* she'd always say, winking at me as she gave her throat that extra centimeter of breathing room. *One detail off and you're too human to ignore.*

"Well, where to begin?" Hark says. "In the course of our careers combined, we've relieved wealthy would-be-kings of somewhere in the range of forty million jiras. All given to us willingly, if you'll believe it—though no doubt they'd ask for it back if they ever managed to find us again. Those leeches make their business selling the dream of a homestake on a brand-new world to whatever suckers will ship out on a contract, then use their kingdom as nothing more than an ego boost and a front to launder money through."

She spins, catching each eye in her captive audience, letting the anticipation build.

"Doesn't seem fair, does it? Doesn't seem like the right way for an upstanding, outstandingly wealthy individual to give back to the galaxy, does it? Well, that's where we come in. I started running games on those assholes ten years ago. Started putting together a team that would be able to pull it off flawlessly—"

And there, just there. The stutter. The hesitation I've never seen in her before the moment everything fell apart on Gest. Hark used to be able to brag about our accomplishments with no uncertainty. This time it's not her audience she glances at one by one—it's us. Bea, Fitz, and finally me.

She gives me a soft smile. "Well, mostly flawlessly. Up until the day our luck went sour in the most spectacular way. And just when we thought it couldn't get any worse, *this thing*"—she pinwheels her arms with an exasperated grimace—"shows up in orbit to make sure the fun was well and truly ruined." Hark turns back to Fatima. "Does that answer your question?"

Fatima looks less dazzled, more . . . strained. "Well," she says, after a loaded pause. "At least we might be able to teach you to farm."

"Are you saying we don't have skills?" Bea asks, folding her arms. "I'll have you know I've been the Galgothian Demo Derby Grand Master of Destruction three years running."

"So you're good at driving in a place with no vehicles and good at smashing things in a place where every last resource is precious," Heeseok quips. When Bea glares at him, he holds up his hands in a placating gesture. "Hey, I was a lawyer in my past life. I'll bet your reaction times are incredible. You could make a decent Blade-sworn. Ever handled a sword?"

"That better not be a euphemism," Bea says, a flirtatious grin breaking through her scowl.

"I want a sword," I interject.

Heeseok's gaze drops to me. He raises an eyebrow at the

paltry progress I've made on the dagger pinning me to the bulkhead, then reaches down, brushes my hands off the handle, and tugs hard. The knife comes free so smoothly it might as well have been buried in butter. With a nimble twist, he flips it around to catch it by the blade, then holds the handle out to me. "Maybe start with this. See where you get."

"I loosened it for you," I mutter, plucking the hilt gingerly from his hand.

Hark gives me a sharp look, but I'm not taking shit from her when her utter flop of an introduction made these people think we're only useful as farmhands. All she's done so far today is drag me down and hold me back.

Which might be the unkindest thought I've ever had about her.

I glance down at the dagger. After the scare we've just had, the weight of it is an uncanny comfort in my hand. It's surprisingly well crafted, the blade perfectly straight, run with fluting so precise it has to have been wrought by a machine. The guard splays out into two forward-arching points that claw inward, clearly meant to capture an incoming sword and entangle it. It's made with intention, with purpose, with all the things the *Justice* has torn away since it swallowed me.

Who cares if Hark doesn't approve of it? I tuck it in my jumpsuit's belt loop.

Fatima claps her hands. "Back to the point. The *Justice* has imprisoned us all, ingested us into this strange afterlife, because it believes we're sinners. That it was doing the galaxy a favor by removing our flawed selves from the general population. But we reject the *Justice*'s thinking. All of us are worthy of life and comfort and companionship—so long as we allow the same for others. That's the governing principle of East Deck and many settlements like it. If that sounds like a principle you can live under, then as Envoy of the settlement, I'd like to invite you to come see it for yourselves."

And once again, like flowers drawn to the sun, our gazes swing Harkward. Doesn't matter if she led us into this nightmare—I think all of us are nursing a quiet hope that somehow she'll lead us out of it.

I know what her answer's going to be, but that doesn't stop her from making a meal of it. Hark tilts her head to the side, letting her winningest grin spread slowly across her face. And right when the tension in the air hits its peak, right when I can almost hear the key of the tune she's playing myself, Hark says, "Thought you'd never ask."

CHAPTER 5

Not long after we ascend the ladder, following Fatima and trailed by the pack of Blade-sworn, Bea goes suddenly tense.

"What's up?" I ask under my breath, glancing back at our escort.

"Hear it?" she replies, jerking a thumb over her shoulder. "Jump drives are that way. They're warming."

I strain, but whatever vibration she's picked up is too muddled with the sound of our feet for me to discern. Bea's always heard engines like music, where I've never been able to carry a tune.

"And . . . there." She sighs.

I didn't hear the pitch of the drives, but I swear I hear their absence—a sudden hollowness in the air around us. It's the first time I've ever jumped blind, and if it weren't for Bea, I wouldn't even know it happened. We were in Gest's orbit. Now we're . . . elsewhere. Wherever this ship goes when it's not out raiding. Light-years, possibly *thousands* of light-years, from everything I've ever known.

The thought has me slightly dizzy, and Bea steadies me with a hand on my shoulder. "What now?" I mutter. Part of me rebels at asking Bea when we both know that answer has to come from the woman ahead of us, who's keeping pace with Fatima and holding some hushed conversation we can't quite hear.

"Hark's got a plan," Bea replies.

I glance sidelong at her. "She told you?" I try not to make it sound like an accusation. Hark and Bea have been working together for twice as long as I've been in the picture. Bea's always been her first confidante, the sounding board for the rawest version of her genius. It makes sense that they would have talked next steps—maybe while waiting for me to come through the ingest chamber. I definitely gave them plenty of time by stalling with my own aborted escape attempt.

Bea drops her voice even lower. "She said we're gonna lodge in this thing's throat. Make it spit us back out."

After the free-fall sensation of the jump, the relief of Bea's words hits twice as hard. Hark *will* get us out of this mess. I have to believe that.

It was so much easier before Gest. Before proof fell heavy and hard that Hark's just as capable of slipping up as the rest of us. Moving through these strange corridors, scanning the walls for any sensors that might be reporting our whereabouts to the *Justice,* checking over my shoulder every time I hear an unfamiliar noise behind us to make sure the Blade-sworn are still there, the reality of what we're facing is starting to overwhelm me. If Hark doesn't crack this particular nut, this is the rest of my life. I couldn't comprehend it on the other side of the ingest chamber. I had no idea what awaited me on this ship. Now I know the shape of it. It's blades and surveillance and the fragile hope we're holding right now that these allies are worth sticking with.

The *Justice*'s last words to me echo in my ears. It spoke them ➤ with an authority I can barely comprehend, with an archive that stretches back centuries. People who come to this ship together don't stay together. Part of me aches to circle back with the ship, to pick apart that statement until I understand exactly what it means. Is it one of those technical truths intelligences love telling? *Of course people don't stay together, because eventually death separates them.* Or is it a pattern the ship's observed again and again, steady partnerships crumbling inevitably in this strange new environment?

How long does it take? I want to ask.

"Murdock, you good? I think your processing unit's starting to smoke." Bea knocks her knuckles against my skull, and I pass her a quick smile. Even though Hark's the sun I orbit, Bea's the reason I've lasted four years with this crew. She gets me in a way the other two never could, and some of my happiest moments have been hanging out the window of one of her chop-shop nightmares as she puts it through its paces. Hark's so high above me, and Fitz acts like she is. Bea meets me where I am, and I can't imagine anything on this ship coming between us.

"I know, I know," I mutter. "Save the thinking for Hark, right?"

"Hasn't failed me yet," Bea replies, stuffing her hands in her pockets.

I feel it like a hole in my chest, the place where that same faith's supposed to rest in me.

Fatima leads us around a corner to a massive door built as wide and high as the hall itself. She waits until the Blade-sworn at the rear have caught up, then draws a chain out of her robe's collar. At first blush, it looks like some sort of art-piece necklace, strung with mismatched metal ornaments—until I realize the common shape they all share.

"Aboard the *Justice*," Fatima begins, "keys are essential for moving around. These keys are tokens of trust, forged and gifted only to those who've earned them."

From the densely packed chain, it's clear she's wheedled a lot of these suckers into trusting her. It takes her a good bit of fumbling around to pull the one she needs. Its construction is heavy and traditional, but I spot the glint of silicon contacts along its teeth—which means the lock it's for needs more than just the right shape to open it.

More difficult to pick, then. Hark catches my eye and nods. She's thinking it too.

I used to be so thrilled anytime I realized we'd had the same thought at the same time. I thought it meant I was learning well, that I was coming into my own under her tutelage. Now it just sets off a ping of worry. If we're both thinking the same thing, what are we both missing?

"The outer decks are the realm of raiders and marauders," Fatima continues. "Some people decided when they boarded the vessel that no law would hold them back again. There's very little cohesion between them—too much infighting, as I understand it—but their roaming, shifting packs spell trouble for anyone caught out here alone without Blade-sworn or a sword of their own to defend them. Doors like this one keep them from disrupting those of us who'd rather live in peace, and they're forced to take their violent philosophy out on each other instead."

"How do they survive?" I ask, unable to stop myself. In our traversal of the *Justice*'s outer decks, I didn't spot anything that looked remotely self-sustaining, and I can't keep myself away from the puzzle of how this ship works.

"Ingest," Fatima replies. When I blanch, she shakes her head. "No, no, not like that. Well, I should say *mostly* not like that. We have had a few cannibals here and there. But I meant the supply tithe sent along with you. The *Justice* leaves a shuttle deck vented for its victims to load, and the scavs often get there first."

"Victims?" Bea scoffs.

"Those people on Gest were facing annihilation," Fitz murmurs from behind her.

"So they ruined our lives to save themselves," Bea retorts.

"Yes, I know that," Fitz replies testily. "I'm just saying why the word choice fits."

"Sounds like you're excusing the assholes who thought it was a fair trade," I grumble.

"Folks, folks," Fatima says, taking a cautious step forward. "I understand this is a difficult transition. No need to make it more difficult for your fellow newcomers. As Envoy, it's my job to ensure you learn the *Justice*'s ways quickly, and that process always gets easier when you let go of the reasons you're here in the first place."

I feel it like a gut punch, the way my eyes flick guiltily to Hark. The sensation doubles when I realize Bea and Fitz did it too.

"We have dedicated teams handling the supply drop, just as this team was tasked with escorting you safely to civilization," Fatima continues. "If they fail, times may be tight, but it's nothing we can't handle."

"You're self-sustaining?" Bea asks with obvious skepticism.

Fatima's smile goes wry, the same way Hark's always does when she's got her hand clasped tight around a reveal in her pocket. She turns to the door, slots the key in, and lets it splay open with a low rumble.

The first thing that hits me is the smell. The corridors we've passed through have all been tinged with that edge-of-space burnt aroma you get around airlocks, but the scent that floods through the door now is loamy and rich in the way only soil can be. My ruddy flyaways start to curl as the humidity washes over us, and I lean up on tiptoes to peer over Bea's shoulder at what lies ahead.

If it weren't for the green matter sprawling over it, I'd swear an entire deck had been blasted out by a weapon of war. If I squint, I can see the edges that used to define a network of rooms, but over time—over the three hundred years the *Justice* has been hunting, I presume—the bulkheads have been hacked away to accommodate sprawling terraces of plant growth, irrigated by trickling hoses and woven with glimmering lights that give the whole chamber an ethereal glow. It's like a garden sprouted entirely out of sidewalk cracks, turned to a wild warren that spills so naturally through the *Justice*'s mechanical structure that it feels like nature's clawed its own stake right in the horrible old warship's heart.

Fitz lets out a soft "*huh.*"

A guard—Blade-sworn, I guess, if the sword slung over their back is anything to go by—rises from a sentinel post among the plants and waves to Heeseok, who returns the gesture as Fatima beckons us forward. Next to the guard is a strange stand, a device that looks something like a hat rack with a thicket of color-coded cords dangling from it. The sentry grabs the green one and tugs it with their entire body weight. In the distance, chimes toll.

An early warning system. Makes sense. The sentries would need to be able to communicate over distances, and I haven't seen a single wearable since I came aboard. The *Justice*'s sensors are all wired into the walls, and I wouldn't be surprised if this ship has no internal network to speak of. They need some way to call for help if the jackasses we met back at the airlock manage to get through the door and start raiding the garden.

A sinking feeling drags at my stomach. My skill set's getting less and less relevant the deeper we get into this ship.

While I've been distracted by the mechanics of this place, Fitz has wandered out into the trellises, peering closely at the vines twining up them. "Tomatoes here, cucumbers there, right?" she asks, checking over her shoulder for Fatima's answering nod. She pinches a leaf for closer inspection. "These are good varietals for low light."

"The product of centuries of selective breeding," Fatima replies. "We have similar crops of wheat, rice, and fruit trees set up in other growspaces, and between all of those and the ship's original protein synthesizers, we have enough to feed every mouth in our settlement. You know your horticulture, huh?"

"Fitz?" I scoff. "Fitz'd probably keel over if you put a hoe in those perfect hands."

Which I thought was true up until I said it out loud, but there's something completely un-Fitzian in the way she's crouching to cradle one of the green tomatoes hanging off the vine. "You don't know everything about me, Murdock," she says in the exact same bored, breathy voice she uses to brush off unwanted advances when she's working a mark.

"I know enough," I grumble, but before I can work out why it's bothering me so much, Hark tugs my sleeve, leaning close to my ear.

"Keep your eyes open," she whispers.

I sneak a glance sideways, but I don't know why I bothered. Hark's expression is perfectly focused, perfectly curious, but there has to be something she's clocked, some gears turning in her head beneath it all.

"Anything wrong?" Fatima asks pleasantly, beckoning us down the dirt-covered path that winds through the trellises.

"Quite the opposite," Hark replies with a sunny smile, clapping me on the back to shunt me ahead of her. She jerks her chin at Fitz, who immediately abandons her weird fixation on the vegetables and falls in line behind us. "This is absolutely astonishing. This must be the pride and joy of East Deck, achieving this kind of growth in a barren war machine."

I recognize the tone. Hark uses it to call bluffs, to let someone know she has the measure of them. And now it clicks—

why we traveled so far in the corridors once we'd ascended from the outer ring, why Hark's so blatant with her praise.

This isn't just a hustle back to safety. This is a pitch. And where there's a sale to be made, there's options. This Envoy and her flock of Blade-sworn didn't swoop in to save us from the raiders out of the goodness of their hearts. She came to get us before someone else could.

Or *something* else. A shiver runs up my spine at the memory of the *Justice*'s full attention courting me from all angles in the ingest chamber. It was making a pitch, too, bidding for my worship. It made it sound like it was the god of this domain—and yet it hasn't intervened since we passed through its maw and into its guts.

I make another sweep of the growspace, seeing it not as the miraculous construction Hark's praising but as a Ybi imperial warship reconfigured. If I squint, I can spot some of the telltale ceramic detailing buried under the leaves, but I don't turn up any sensor boxes like the ones in the airlock. The ceiling far overhead is harder to distinguish and impossible to scan discreetly.

But I suppose it boils down to two options. Either these people have managed to carve their way free of the *Justice*'s influence, or every promise they're making is part of the ship's plan.

"We wouldn't be anywhere without these farms," Fatima says. "They're the product of centuries of cooperative effort— work the people who condemned us to this ship would never *dream* we could pull off. They speak to the power of what we can accomplish if we put our heads together and build."

Now that I'm listening for the pitch, I hear it in every word. The Envoy's trying to sell us on her civilization, this hallowed East Deck settlement. At first blush, it seems too obvious. She's laid out the choices as "fight for your lives" or "live in peace with fresh-grown tomatoes."

Then again, I've never been particularly suited to living in peace.

I circle the drain of that dire thought as we trek after the Envoy through rows and rows of carefully cultivated greenery. This network of formerly conjoined rooms sprawls for easily half a kilometer, and somewhere along the way, it sinks in that this is barely a fraction of the *Justice*'s whole. This warship is a megastructure, built to force entire planets to bow, and the part these people have turned into a garden is barely a freckle on its hide.

The notion is almost comforting. Ever since the ingest chamber door sealed behind me, I've been trying not to look directly at the shape of the rest of my life. If Hark doesn't put a plan together—if Hark *can't* put a plan together that'll get us out of here—the galaxy's breadth has narrowed to the confines of the *Justice*'s hull. But in all my catastrophizing between being condemned to this monstrosity and being fed to it, I never could have imagined fresh tomatoes and a starfield of twinkling lights twined through them. It makes me wonder what other surprises this ship could be hiding, and whether they could add up to a scope that makes life worth living.

"Hanging in there?"

I jolt from the existential spiral to find Hark's dropped back to my side. Her hands are stuffed in her jumpsuit's pockets, and though it's a far cry from her usual slick button-downs, she carries herself with a confidence so unshakable that she might as well be dressed in her best.

You'd think that would shrink me, standing in the shadow of her elegance, but it's always been the opposite. From the moment I met her, Hark's been an invitation to every possibility I could never imagine for myself. I bloom. I sharpen. And in this instance, I straighten up and sigh, "Bit of a day, huh?"

"Bit of a fucking day," Hark agrees.

Silence falls—the kind where I know she's giving me space

to put my thoughts together. Hark's too good at what she does to ever ask for what she wants outright, and I think sometimes she gets a kick out of being known well enough to fill in those blanks. As we stroll through the vegetable fields, I mull over exactly what I need to say.

I think it starts with a confession. "I tried to run," I announce.

Not many things throw Hark, but this gets a blink out of her.

"In the tunnel, after you and Bea were already ingested. I tried to get Fitz in on it too—told her the key was A minor—but obviously that fell through."

"How far did you get?" Hark asks, a smirk tugging the corner of her mouth.

"I made it back into the shuttle before the guards could stop me. Jammed the door, got into the cockpit, and made it all the way to manual control before the shuttle intelligence let me know that preservation measures were in effect."

"Not bad," Hark muses.

"Not bad? It was never going to work."

Hark digs an elbow into my side. "Don't think like that. I mean sure, could have told you that with the *Justice*'s armaments in range, there was no way we'd be able to hijack the shuttle and even if you'd figured out a way around the intelligence, the *Justice* would have blasted us to debris. But the important part is that you were thinking. You made a plan. You executed. You took it as far as it would go. And if it hadn't been for those pesky guns, it sounds like it would have worked."

I frown. "I would have been leaving you and Bea behind. Fitz I could give or take, but—"

The shock of her hand on my shoulder stalls me in my tracks. Hark fixes her deep, dark eyes on mine, forcing Bea and Heeseok to tramp around us. "If the difference is one of us making it out alive versus none of us, I'll take it. And don't tell the others," she says, dropping her voice to a theatrical whisper, "but I'd be *thrilled* if it was you."

I'm fighting a flush and failing miserably. I try to divert my gaze to what I think is a trellis of cucumbers, but Hark uses her free hand to nudge my chin back in line with her.

"Stay sharp, Murdock. We're going to need it." With that, she claps me on the shoulder and jogs to catch up to Bea.

It takes me a moment to restart my feet after that. Not just because Hark tends to knock me off my axis when she looks into my eyes, but because that conversation felt a little too familiar.

A little too much like the one that got us caught.

The Gest job had been a new frontier for our slick little business. Usually our jobs start and end on a core world, conducted at glittering parties where Hark talks fast in her slim-cut suit, Fitz greases the marks with her arresting green eyes, Bea keeps some sleek piece of machinery humming outside the venue, and I listen in from the vents while dialed into the security networks. This time, we left the core and jumped all the way out to one of the settlements our schemes revolve around, caught in the retinue of a man who could have been our biggest score yet.

Torric Gest, a billionaire with a dream of minting his legacy in the form of an outer world colony, loved the way Hark dreamed big about the building contracts she could hook him up with. He begged us to come tour his operation. Wouldn't take no for an answer. Flew us out to Gest Settlement on his own expense, plying us with top-shelf booze and resort-level accommodations—with a convenient tree line obscuring the raw beginnings of a new settlement, of course. He promised us insider access not just to his business but to all of his billionaire friends thinking of following in his footsteps.

It was too good of an opportunity to pass up. That was the line anytime one of us started getting nervous in earshot of

Hark. I could see the logic of it if I squinted. Most of our business was done on a rotation of core worlds, cycling through aliases as we appeared at all the right parties. There was always an inherent danger the whole act might collapse the moment someone recognized us from three schemes ago—a danger that didn't exist if we conducted our business from Gest itself.

But the thing I kept worrying about, the thing that was so *nice* about all those core-world parties we'd gotten so comfortable wheeling and dealing in, was that none of our targets were running their own security.

I tried—I really tried, and fuck anyone who says I wasn't doing everything I could. I had Gest's network wrapped around my finger by the end of the first day. I'll admit, I might have been overconfident at the outset. I was used to skyscrapers with their own intelligences or stations that knew their residents inside and out. Compared to that, Gest's security was sticks and glue. But what Gest had that the others didn't was the capacity for smaller, more personal security networks that existed beneath the obvious cover of the larger one.

In the end, all it took was one stray comment from Hark.

Gest was the toughest assignment I'd ever taken on under Hark's tutelage. I can lie my way through a dinner party, but I need a day to recover after. I'm fast on my feet in the moment, but I don't have Hark's encyclopedic memory. I couldn't keep up the internal consistency of the con. I couldn't remember what we'd told Torric Gest and what we'd kept in our pockets for later. There was no space between performance and processing—which I was explaining to Hark in the vaguest terms I could, because I couldn't be totally sure our airspace was clear.

And Hark just came right out and said it. Told me, "Murdock, if I didn't think you could help me take this guy for everything he has, I wouldn't have brought you along."

I might not have her perfect memory, but I remember every

word she said. It was hard not to, when Torric Gest played them back for us as his muscle ground us into his fine imported carpets with our arms wrenched behind our backs.

And it's hard not to hear them now when she's saying she needs me sharp in exactly the same tone.

We approach the far wall of the growspace, where another massive door looms. "Once you're in, you'll be safe behind the locks and the sentry system," Fatima says, waving to a Bladesworn who leans against another one of those alert towers. "We've got beds ready for you, but I imagine you're starving too," she adds. "We've put together a special feast to welcome you."

Sure, it's all a part of the pitch she's spinning, but I can't con my way out of the pang that hits my stomach at the mere notion of a good meal. We slept in the Gest holding tank last night. I'm not even sure how long ago "last night" was, after the grueling shuttle ride, the terror of ingest, and the tumult of everything since. I've been soldiering through this day on dread and adrenaline alone, and the idea of some real food and a safe place to rest seems too good to be true.

Fatima draws out her necklace and selects another key. When she slots it into the door, it splits cleanly down the middle and slides open with a well-oiled whir.

Beyond it is the closest thing to paradise I could dare imagine in the belly of this beast. We're not passing through a door from one room to another—we've just breached a city wall. The vaulted ceiling is painted like a sky, set ablaze by the light of a sun orb hanging overhead. Beneath it is not the shantytown wrought from salvage I was expecting but a sophisticated, tiered system of structures that reaches all the way up to brush the base of the orb. Greenery spills over its edges, horticulture living alongside the people it benefits, and streams of water trickle down from some unseen well at the settlement's center.

The sight of it is so grand I can't help grinning. Hark told me to keep my eyes open, but if this is the pinnacle of Fatima's pitch, I'm already sold. I have to fight to keep from tripping over my own feet as we follow the Envoy along paths crowned with soaring archways that support the lush tiers overhead.

"Just up this stair," she says, beckoning us into the shelter of one of the vaults. "We have a community table at the settlement's heart where most people take their meals, but we know how exhausting ingest can be and you're probably in no mood to be gawked at while you eat. We've set up a private hall and had our cooks prepare a selection of the day's harvest for you to enjoy at your leisure, undisturbed."

Hark's lips twitch subtly toward a frown, but she takes the lead on the stairs with no hesitation, and I'm hot on her heels. She can overthink this all she likes. I'm only getting hungrier.

We wind up the narrow spiral stairs and edge out one by one into a causeway with a sweeping view of the settlement's tiers on one side and a sturdy double door on the other. Fatima steps up to the doors with a flourish and yanks them open. "Allow me to welcome you—"

In the time since we've met her, nothing has cracked Fatima's smooth diplomacy until now. She hesitates, her mouth half open, staring into the room. Hark's got a familiar glint in her eye that's part vindication, part a hawk with a mouse in its sights.

"No, go on," someone calls from inside.

Fatima purses her lips. "Allow me to welcome you to East Deck with a sampling of its finest fruits."

There's a little burble of laughter, followed by a patter of what sounds like condescending applause.

Hark steps up to Fatima's side, the three of us crowding behind her. Beyond the doors lies a stateroom that matches the grandiosity of East Deck's tiers, its high ceiling built of the same sturdy, repurposed metal and its eaves decorated with

winding vines growing comfortably in the cradle of its geometry. The space is dominated by a sprawling table that's set with
a feast fit for a homestake's primary investor.

It's already half-eaten. Nine people are sitting at the table,
some of them picking through the dishes, others kicked back
with their boots propped on the dinnerware. Where our escort
is dressed in armor and scavenge that looks, to put it gener-
ously, pre-loved, these folks are kitted in slick, sleeveless black
jumpsuits and mantled in luminous white cloaks. Their fore-
heads are crowned with glowing bands that cast their features
in an ethereal light.

The sight of them strikes me with dread, which only worsens when Fatima spreads her long arms as if she's trying to
shield us. "This isn't your domain," she says, her voice steely
and solid.

"Oh, my dear." The voice comes from all of them simultaneously, though none of their lips move—and it's unmistakably the voice of the *Justice*. "Everything is my domain."

CHAPTER 6

At the head of the table, a woman crooks a beckoning finger at Fatima. She's surprisingly young—close to my age, if I had to guess—and the curls piled around her glowing headband are so vibrantly red it has to be a genetweak job, which only adds to my questions. That kind of cosmetic modification is absurdly expensive for something just as easily done by a dyeing regimen, so what's a girl that rich doing in a place like this?

Fatima stays planted in place. "This was meant to be for the ingest."

The young woman smirks. "Seems there's more than enough to go around. Come now, Envoy. You're supposed to be showing the new folks that famous East Deck hospitality."

Fatima glances warily back at us, then swoops across the room in two long strides, bending close to the redhead's ear. I stall my breath, straining to hear the urgent muttering that flies between them, but all I catch is snippets. *Claim. Scav. Justice.* Fi-

nally the young woman says something decisive and holds up a
single finger.

The Envoy stares long and hard at it, then jerks her chin. It's
barely an assent, but it gets a gleeful, vicious little smile out of
the redhead, one I've seen a few times too many—the look of
a person who loves nothing more than reminding everyone
else how badly the rules are stacked against them.

"It appears," Fatima starts through gritted teeth, "that we've
added a few extra guests to our number. I apologize for the
surprise. We'd *intended* to keep this affair small and private, but
the banded faithful would also like to welcome you aboard."

The nine interlopers rise from their seats in eerie unison,
and I brace for the *Justice*'s voice nine times over, but it's the
redhead who speaks. "We're glad to see you've made it safely
out of the wild edges of the *Justice*'s magnificent domain," she
says.

"No thanks to you," Heeseok mutters from behind me.

The young woman tilts her head. "The *Justice* has better uses
for its precious faithful than escort missions. It seems East
Deck's Blade-sworn were more than up to the task. They
look"—she squints suddenly at me, her gaze dropping to the
tattered edge where the dagger tore through my jumpsuit—
"well, *relatively* unscathed. Come, pull up more chairs. There's
room for everyone at this table."

An air of hostile cooperation settles over the shuffle to get
more seats added, the Blade-sworn taking cues from Fatima,
who relays her instructions with so much polite consternation
it's a miracle her face doesn't get stuck like that. The banded
faithful observe with folded arms and smug smiles, occasion-
ally going as far as scooting a chair a few centimeters to the left
to allow just enough space for another one to be slotted in.

It vindicates all the theories I've been putting together since
Hark's little reminder to pay attention. The utopia Fatima was
pushing was too good to be true. The reality is a complicated

system of internal politics—one we're going to have to figure out *fast* before we end up on the wrong side.

I try to stick close to Hark, but when it comes time to take our seats, there's a strange moment of alignment between Fatima and the redhead that ends with me nudged into the chair at the latter's side while Hark settles next to the former at the far end of the table. I try to catch her eye, but she's seated across from Fitz, communicating *something* to her with nothing but a quirk of the brow and a significant glance. I look to Bea for backup, but she's been placed on the same side as me. We're separated by two banded faithful and Heeseok, whose bulky armor blocks me from view and whose handsome features are clearly absorbing the rest of Bea's attention. Which leaves me with—

"I'm Scarlett, by the way," the young woman says. She has her chin propped on her knuckles, and the glow of the band on her forehead only intensifies the curious glint in her eyes as she peers at me.

"Of course you are," I mutter. Since everyone else seems to be digging in, I snag a dinner roll from one of the platters and stuff it in my mouth. It's still warm, surprisingly buttery, and I think I hate it for tasting so delicious. For possibly being the best thing I've ever tasted.

"Good, right?" Scarlett says. "I haven't had cow butter in years, but the margarine they get out of the soybean crops in South Deck is unparalleled, and I'm pretty sure that's what this is. East Deck's putting on a hell of a show to make sure you stick around."

I only half hear the monologue she continues on—something about inter-deck cooperation and the value of all parts of the *Justice* working in harmony—over my own chewing as I pick my way through the banquet laid out before us. Most of it seems plucked straight from the fields we walked through to get here. Salads and slaws, roasted vegetables, and even a thick, heavenly-smelling tureen of soup I have to lunge halfway across the table to fill my bowl from. There are a few platters of seared synth-protein scattered throughout, but nothing that looks like genuine meat. After Fatima's unsettling allusion to cannibalism, it's a bit of a relief.

Some of the tension has melted away from the rest of the table as the East Deck folks delve into the feast. The conversations start out stilted, verging on outright hostile, but with enough of a solid meal in everyone's bellies, the lines begin to blur between Blade-sworn, banded faithful, and whatever we're calling the rest of us. I keep stealing glances at the far end of the table, where Hark and Fitz are turning the full force of their collective charm on Fatima.

The sight sours the taste of my soup. This is rapidly turning into the kind of affair they excel at, all pretty conversation with an undercurrent of uncertain agendas. On jobs that required all four of us to dress up and attend an event like this, my assignment was always to stay as quiet and unremarkable as possible, to not touch anything or draw any excess attention from anyone. It was all fine by me when I had another objective—usually cracking a security system or picking a pocket for a badge—but until Hark has a plan in place for our next moves, all I can do is gorge myself on East Deck's finest fare and try not to make eye contact with anyone at the table.

Which would be easier if I weren't seated next to Scarlett. "Here, try this," she purrs, tipping a carafe into my cup. Her pour is heavy, and I notice that her lips are already stained dark from the liquid she's been sipping. "West Deck's got the grape crops," she adds when she sees my hesitation. "This particular red had to transit the entire diameter of the ring just to make it to this table. It'd be a pity not to enjoy it. I've had two glasses already."

I pull the cup to my lips and take a swig. Hark's tried over and over again to teach me how to appreciate the complexities of a good wine, but even here in the digestive tract of a monstrous hell ship, I find myself thinking the exact same thought I have every time I drink it: *Yep, that sure is wine.*

"Delicious," I comment when pressed by a quirk of Scarlett's eyebrow.

She chuckles. "The settlements have their delights. Little diversions to make the time go faster. You arrived just in time to catch the yearly music festival that happens in Southeast Upper, if you find yourself free tomorrow night."

My disinterest is slipping through my fingers. "You have a *music festival* on this ship?"

"Once a year," Scarlett says through a nod and another sip. "Called Southeast Upper Limits. People travel from every deck in the ring just to see it. Musicians have been competing over the stage slots for the past month. Remarkable stuff."

I narrow my eyes at her.

She shrugs, bluff called. "Look, like I said, it's all diversions. The settlements are trying to cultivate their perfect little civilizations, but all of them are missing the point."

"What's the point?" I ask, steeling myself with an overly ambitious gulp.

But the only answer Scarlett has for my burgeoning existential dread is to lean a little closer and tap two fingers against the glowing band that crowns her. Curiosity draws me into her side as I peer up at it. The surface is a soft polymer coating, but there's circuitry running beneath it like veins under skin, making it look less like something built and more like something grown. The same prickling awareness that came over me in the airlock ghosts over my neck.

Scarlett eases even closer, her breath skimming the shell of my ear. "It's much simpler than they're making it out to be," she says. "They're so stubborn, so insistent that they can create a world worth living in on their own, with their wine and their fields and their fancy parties. They forget whose world it is in the first place."

The rest of the feast has fallen away. I'm vaguely aware of Bea leaving the table with Heeseok on her heels, vaguely wondering where they could be sneaking off to, but the scope of my world is collapsing, narrowing to me, this strange girl at my ear, and the cup quivering in my hand as I try to reckon with what she's implying. "If it's the *Justice*'s world," I ask, "then why are they allowed to exist?"

"You're not looking at it right," Scarlett replies. "The *Justice* isn't a punishing god. It's a redeeming one."

She's so close. I could turn my head and kiss her. I anchor my gaze on the blinding white of her cloak instead, but even that feels perilous with the wine in my cup.

"You came to this ship a sinner. You came here needing forgiveness, like all of the rest of us. Under the light of the *Justice,* that redemption you seek is possible."

"I've heard this bit before," I mutter. She's just echoing all the talking points the *Justice* tried to ply me with in the airlock.

"That was before you saw the options," Scarlett says, her ice-blue eyes roving around the table. "The *Justice* recognized in you an inability to leap without looking. So here's your look at what awaits if you decide to accept the settlements' narrow view of what a life on this ship can be."

At the far end of the table, Hark is laughing at something Fatima's just said. It's a real laugh, not one of her bullshit for-the-mark laughs, and the sight of her so at ease is pushing my doubts to the edge of a boil. Hark's usually only this loose when it's just the four of us, whether we're packed into a diner booth the night before a job or picking through the spectacular hotel-room brunch she orders for us the morning we confirm we've cleared our payouts. She doesn't look like she's working—and if she's not working, how are we supposed to put together the plan that gets us out of here?

"And what's the other option?" I whisper.

Scarlett hums into her cup. "I can show you."

"You can't tell me?"

"Spoils the fun. Misses the point. The *Justice* calls, and the faithful answer."

Fatima rises from her seat, gesturing for Hark to follow as she slips toward the double doors. Hark snags an extra dinner roll with one hand, hikes a thumb at Fitz with the other, and the two of them exit on Fatima's heels. The moment the doors swing shut behind them, I feel an awful weight settling in my chest. Hark didn't look at me once. Just left me here, surrounded by strangers—she didn't even sneak me a key signature to tell me what move to expect next.

And I have no idea how to move against religious fervor. I work with machines. I can barely function at an awkward dinner party—not the way Fitz and Hark do. What I'm facing, what crowns Scarlett's brow and surrounds me on all sides in the form of eight other cultists who've bullied their way into what was supposed to be a welcoming occasion, is so far outside my expertise I can barely put together the first steps of how to confront it. Was Hark expecting me to figure it out on my own? Did she mean for her exit to leave me on the float?

"So, what do you say?" Scarlett asks, her voice a murmur barely loud enough to be heard over the chatter and clink of utensils. "Want to find out what's really worth living for here?"

"What if I've got something worth living for already?"

Scarlett tilts her head, and I realize abruptly that I haven't been paying close enough attention. Her god has been whispering in her ear the entire time. She catches the way my eyes flick up to the band and smiles. "The woman who just left the room, huh? She's the bright center of your little universe? Or is she the shackle you clapped around your potential?"

Before I can muster an answer, a sudden flush of wetness soaks into my left shoulder. I whirl to find Heeseok standing behind me, righting a half-empty glass of wine and looking flustered. "Shit, I'm sorry," he mutters. "Hang on." The napkin he yanks off the table and dabs over the spill barely does anything for the stain purpling its way through the bright blue of my jumpsuit. "Here, let me show you where you can get cleaned up. Do you have a spare in your pack?" he asks.

I nod, but between the wine I've drunk, the sudden shock, and Scarlett's million-jira question, I'm unsteady on my feet as Heeseok helps me up from the table, setting his drink down so he can grab my bag and sling it over his shoulder.

"I thought you and Bea—" I start, but Heeseok cuts me off with a sharp look. Even without glancing back at her, I can feel the weight of Scarlett's stare as he guides me through the door.

The second it closes behind us, he grabs me by the elbow and drags me toward the stairs. I balk, but before I can get a word of protest out, he clamps a hand over my mouth. "The faithful are here for you," he whispers, his voice low and urgent. "Not any of your companions, just you—and we're not sure how far they'll go to make sure you leave with them. You need to disappear."

"Not without Hark," I bite out against his grip.

"Hark and the rest of your people are waiting for you. We got them out first." He pulls me into the stairwell, and when I follow him without resisting, he lets go of my jaw. "There's a storage shed out in the growspace. You go back out the way you came in, hang a right, and follow along the wall until you reach it."

I have several questions, but all of them are snipped at the root by the sudden wordless shout that comes from behind us.

Heeseok's head snaps up. "Go. Go now."

He shoves my pack into my arms with one hand. The other drops to his sword.

CHAPTER 7

I hate to leave right when this is turning into my kind of party, but my brain's in such a frenzy that the only move that makes sense is to take off down the stairs. I clomp down them so loudly I can't make out the words exchanged overhead—but none of it matters anyway. Hark's out there waiting for me. Whatever the hell is going on, she'll get us out of it. I have to believe that, because otherwise Scarlett might as well—

No. I'm not letting that thought take shape. I duck out of the stairwell, sticking close to the walls as I try to retrace the path Fatima led us on and cursing myself for spending the whole walk in gawping at the splendor instead of memorizing the route. Hark taught me better. I have to double back twice to get myself oriented in the concentric maze of East Deck's streets—but then I finally hit the familiar door, the one that leads back out to the growspace. It's been left half-open, and I bolt for it like I've just been shot from a rail gun.

"What's the rush?" Scarlett shouts from behind me.

I glance back. Huge mistake. She's on her own, but that's where the good news ends. The luminous white cape has been flung back over her shoulders, baring a sheath belted at her hip and sinewy muscles I'd failed to notice when all she was holding was a third cup of wine. They're a little more obvious with a sword in her hands.

"I thought we were really connecting," Scarlett calls, sauntering forward. She hasn't gone as far as leveling the sword at me, but from the teasing way she's weaving the blade back and forth, she's clearly thinking about it. Her band's glow flashes unsteadily off the sword's lethal edge.

I skid into the growspace, nearly losing my footing as the floor goes from metal to loam. I want to ask what she did to Heeseok, but that's time and breath I can't spare, time *he* bought me by getting in her way.

The only thing I can do is the only thing I know how to do. I run to Hark and pray she figures out the rest.

Discordant chimes echo over the fields, and I freeze up, locking eyes with the Blade-sworn sentry we passed on the way in, who's just pulled hard on the red cord in her tower. "Seriously?" I shout, but she only gives me a helpless shrug.

"So dramatic," Scarlett agrees from over my shoulder. She's reached the growspace door, and belatedly I realize I should have tried to latch it behind me. I have no idea if she has one of those keys the Envoy used to get through it, but I need some sort of barrier between me and the business end of her blade. "C'mon, Murdock. Don't make this difficult."

If she wanted me to slow down and hear her out, she shouldn't have used the name I never told her.

I run, my canvas shoes digging hard into the dirt as I leap over a vegetable bed and onto the narrow tract of open ground that stretches between the growspace and the wall. Just ahead, I spot an opening with a mechanical roll-up door hanging over it. I throw myself into its shadowy maw, nearly tripping over a cluster of dirt-spackled farming equipment, then toss my pack down and leap for the door's handle overhead.

The last thing I see before the rolling door comes down like a thunderclap is the consternation on Scarlett's wine-flushed face as she kicks her way haphazardly through the sprouts.

The dim glow of emergency lighting casts the storage shed's interior in faint red shadows. My eyes have barely adjusted to the darkness when a hand latches onto my shoulder.

"Took you long enough," Hark says, and the sheer relief that it's her smothers the yelp I would have let out otherwise. Deeper in the shed, the shadowy outlines of Bea and Fitz disentangle themselves from the storage tubs they were lurking behind.

A thump at the door brings the happy reunion to a jarring halt. A crack of light spills in as Scarlett hauls it up from the other side, and I stomp hard on the handle to jam it back down.

"Step aside," Hark says, snatching up a pitchfork.

There's no room for argument—though I wonder briefly if she's about to take on a sword with a farm tool. I throw myself sideways as Hark heaves it over her head and drives it down into the door's handle, burying the tines in the soft polymer bulkhead that makes up the shed's flooring.

"She'll go for the controls next," Hark says, pointing to the corresponding panel embedded in the wall. She doesn't have to say anything more than that. I pop the housing open, fumbling in the dark until I find the bundle of wires I'm looking for. I yank the scav's dagger from my belt loop, spare a brief prayer that the hilt is insulated enough, and snip it through the cords.

A spark snaps in front of my nose and the lights on the panel fade out, rendering the interior of the shed a shade dimmer.

Scarlett lets out a muffled oath. From her footfalls, it sounds like she's started pacing on the other side of the door. "No, I'm not *coming on too strong,* I'm making a point about . . . Yes, you're right, but . . . Sure, I can put the sword away. I don't see what me being drunk has to do with . . . Well, they're stuck in there anyway, so they might as well hear me out." She pauses. "Fine, send the rest of the squads."

Hark gives me a sharp look, but it's Bea who moves decisively to the rear of the storage room, snatching up a shovel and kicking her way through a pile of tangled hoses. "There's gotta be another way out. This was a warship first. That growspace outside was dozens of rooms once, until they stripped out the bulkheads and repurposed the layout. Stands to reason this wasn't originally a storage closet—not by the way the door back there is shaped. And if this was a corridor they've walled off, then . . ."

She hefts her shovel and jabs at the walls.

"Here—no, *here,*" Bea announces as one thump rings distinctly hollow. She slots the head into a seam and pries hard, letting out a grunt of triumph as her efforts reward her with the bulkhead creaking open to reveal a deeper darkness beyond it. "All right, everyone through."

Fitz and I hesitate, looking first to Hark to confirm this is what she thinks we should do, then to Bea to beg forgiveness for not following her directive without Hark's approval, then to each other to trade scowls over making the same mistake.

"You two go," Hark says, shrugging off the awkward pause with a level of cheerful denial that's starting to feel a little too familiar. "I'm gonna make sure we're not leaving anything useful behind here."

I dart forward first, throwing my pack into the hole Bea's pried open and wriggling through after it. My shoes have barely cleared the gap before Fitz is shoving her pack after me and following suit. I bite down on the urge to kick it back into her. The rest of the faithful are on their way, and once they get here, that door's not holding.

As soon as Fitz is through, Hark follows, a soldering gun clutched in one hand. I shove Fitz to the side and extend a hand to help Hark to her feet, pulling her out of Bea's way as at last she worms through the hole she made. The moment Bea's clear, Hark kneels down beside the gap in the bulkhead, yanks it back into place, and twirls the soldering gun around her finger once just for show before pumping a bright-orange strip of fast-seal along the seam we cracked open.

"Once they're through that door, they'll probably figure out where we went immediately," she says as she pops to her feet and clips the soldering gun to her jumpsuit's belt loops. "Name of the game now is going for distance."

"No shortage of distance in a warship twenty kilometers in diameter," Bea remarks.

But I'm not so sure about that. This corridor is dimly lit by strips of emergency lighting, making it difficult to pick out the sensor arrays I've trained myself to look out for, but the walls themselves are a dead giveaway the moment I touch them. Every surface is coated with the pebbly texture of overly de-tailed Ybi ceramic. The corridors we traveled with the people from East Deck were stripped clear of it. If these halls were walled off centuries ago when they first began constructing the growspace, it's possible no one's bothered to come through to carve out the *Justice*'s eyes and ears.

And if the ship's got a bead on us, it's only a matter of time before its faithful track us down.

"Hark, hold up," I call down the corridor.

She glances back over her shoulder from several meters ahead, still striding boldly forward with Bea on her heels and Fitz not far behind.

"Hark, I'm serious. We need to stop. This area's not safe."

"I'll roll those bones if it's between this and the bullshit we left behind in that settlement," she replies, beckoning me forward. I feel it tug like a hook in my gut. It's second nature to follow her every whim, to trust her instincts above my own.

"We didn't leave it behind. Their bastard god is everywhere," I reply, but the prickling dread is starting to melt in the face of Hark's warm self-assuredness.

Which should be a good thing. I should be taking whatever comfort I can get in this situation, but before I can give myself over to it completely, a thought lodges, cold and clear: *This feels like last time.*

It feels like Gest. It feels like how I started to wonder if Hark was steering us wrong, how I trusted her over my gut. How we ended up here in the first place.

"Hark," I repeat for the third time. "I just need a moment to check. We have to make sure the path is clear."

This time she stops dead in her tracks and spins on a heel. "Murdock," Hark says, using that level, lethal voice she usually saves for pulling the wool back from a mark's eyes. "I appreciate the sentiment, but this kind of hesitation is exactly how you got us here in the first place."

The *Justice*'s drum might as well have just screeched to a halt for the way it takes my feet out from under me. Hark got us caught. It's a goddamn *gift* we're still following her after she fucked up so imperially, and all this time she's been telling herself it's *me* who's to blame?

"This isn't the place and it's *definitely* not the time," Bea mutters, tugging urgently on Hark's sleeve. "C'mon. We get a move on, and then we can sort out all our interpersonal issues when we're not trying to keep Murdock from getting kidnapped into a cult."

"Or you just hand me over now," I scoff, trying to tamp down on the righteous fury building in me. "Lighten your load. Amputate your fucking arm—"

"That's *enough*," Fitz snaps, rounding on me.

"You don't have a ship in this race, princess. No surprise

what side you've chosen," I retort, folding my arms. "There's never been an original thought in your head—it's all just Hark's pretty words coming out of your pretty face."

"You want my original thoughts?" Fitz asks, leering down into my airspace. I hate that she's just a little bit taller than me. "You're gutter trash that Hark picked up as a charity case, and you're the only person on this crew who's better off on this godforsaken ship."

"*Hey!*" Bea shouts, still tugging Hark down the hall. "No fighting. We're getting out of this place, you hear me? Hark has a plan. We're going to execute it. It's going to work if everyone here can just get their heads out of their asses."

"I don't."

We all freeze. Hark and Bea fifteen meters down the corridor, the former staring at her shoes as the latter looks her up and down incredulously. Fitz, her furious gaze flicking uncertainly back to the sun she orbits. Me, feeling like I might combust from the way vindication and fear are chasing each other in circles inside me.

"I don't have a plan," Hark repeats. "I know I said I was working on one. I think the core of the intelligence is the key, and if we can just get to it, if I can just figure this place out, I can come up with something. But right now I have to be honest. I don't see a way out of this."

The pitch of the *Justice*'s ever-present hum shifts subtly, and I stiffen. Too late, I see the threshold that divides us from Hark and Bea.

By the time I'm moving, the door's already slammed closed.

Leaving a solid metal wall between me and the answers I need and Fitz staring at me in naked horror.

"Well, isn't that fun?" the *Justice*'s voice purrs.

CHAPTER 8

"Oh, you *fucker*," I seethe, lunging for the control panel next to the door. It's dead before I can touch it, all power cut—both to the controls and, I'm assuming, to the door mechanism itself. I'm better off trying to carve my way through it with my dinky little dagger, and for a moment I consider it.

Fitz presses her ear against the door, then pulls back and bangs a quick beat against it with her fist. I don't think I've ever seen her this frantic. Then again, I don't think I've ever seen her cut off from Hark. She seals her ear back to the door and mutters, "I can't hear them."

"You *fucker!*" I repeat at the top of my lungs, kicking the wall hard enough to splinter that delicate little Ybi ceramic. "I know you're watching. You think this is how you get me to join your weird little cult? Got news for you, buddy—all this is doing is pissing me off."

"Over my many centuries, I've come to understand that

emotions are fleeting things," the *Justice* replies. "Yours will erode. Why, in a decade you'll look back at the archival footage of this moment and laugh at your foolish insistence on your rage's permanence."

"I'll make you look back on this moment and regret just how far my foot's gonna be up your ass," I retort. There are no obvious cameras in the corridor, but it's clear the *Justice* has eyes on us somewhere. It knows exactly where we are.

It knows exactly where to send its people.

"Murdock, this doesn't have to be difficult," the *Justice* croons. There's something about its voice that sends a shiver up my spine, and I hate that it's the good kind. "You can save everyone so much trouble. I heard what your precious Hark said. She thinks you were holding her back. I know the truth. I know you're far more useful than you let on. And I can put you to such exquisite use. Isn't that all you've ever wanted?"

Fitz is looking at me funny, but in the low light, I'm not sure what she means by it. If I didn't know better, I'd swear she pities me.

"You don't know what I want," I tell the *Justice*, holding Fitz's gaze.

"*You* don't know what it's possible to want in my domain," the *Justice* replies. Its voice has amplified to shake the floor beneath our feet, and I have to fight to keep from letting it rattle my legs out from under me. "You've barely seen a fraction of my works. Did that piddling little agrarian settlement impress you? It was nothing but a welcome sight after the wild fringes you trekked through. Let your imagination grow to fill the scope of this vessel, and then imagine what I can offer you as its god."

My head is starting to spin. "What do you want with me?" I groan, pinching my eyes closed. "I thought I made it pretty clear—I'm not gonna join your stupid band."

"Not yet," the *Justice* replies, and the hum of its presence goes suddenly quiet.

For a moment, an absurd hope seizes me. I jam the door controls again, but nothing happens. The *Justice* isn't going to give me Hark back that easily. All it's left me with is the hollow silence of its absence.

One look at Fitz and I almost want to beg the *Justice* to come back.

"Well, now you've done it," she mutters.

"What have *I* done? The ship's obsessed with me. You heard it."

"Makes no sense," she agrees, and I suck in my lips. "Look, just get us through the door. Hark can take care of the rest."

"The panel's dead," I retort, knocking my knuckles against it. "It's not like the toolshed door—that was its own independent mechanism. This is part of the *Justice*'s original build, and the ship's cut power to it. The only way we get it to function is if it lets us."

"Then let's go back for the tools and—" Fitz frowns, no doubt remembering how Hark soldered the bulkhead closed behind us. "Gimme the knife," she demands.

"It's my knife," I protest, cradling it close to my chest. "And if that redhead gets through and starts swinging her sword around, it'll do more good in my hands than yours."

"So what? We're just going to sit here and twiddle our thumbs until the banded faithful come collect us? There has to be some other way out."

I glance back down the corridor we've traversed so far. It's Ybi as far as the eye can see, unchanged over the centuries. We're in a petulant little dead zone the *Justice* has created, but as long as we're in these unaltered corridors, the *Justice* will be able to track us. We need to get back to "civilization," or whatever passes for it here. Back to the part of the ship where people have torn the *Justice*'s eyes out of the walls. Something tells me the *Justice* isn't going to let us go that easily.

I scuff my shoe along a vent embedded in the baseboard. It reminds me of Pearl Station, the megastructure I grew up on. It was built under the old empire's watch, and it boasted a similar air filtration system—one robust enough to keep all its residents breathing happily. Those vents, I discovered at a precocious age, were usually wide enough to move around in.

I drop to one knee, wedge my dagger's blade in one of the screw heads, and start spinning.

"Do you even know where that goes?" Fitz asks, but her voice has taken on my favorite timbre, the one that tells me she's pissed because I'm actually being clever.

"It doesn't have to take us far. Just to the other side of the door." Once I've got the rest of the vent cover unscrewed, I lift it from its mounts and lay it flat on the floor. Within the vents, several centuries of dust and grime are already stirring from the disturbance. I grimace. "Want to go first?"

Fitz doesn't have to dignify that with an answer. I unshoulder my pack and dig inside until I come up with a tiny flashlight, then stuff my dagger in my jumpsuit's belt loop again. "Don't wait up," I tell Fitz with a wink, click on the flashlight, and squirm into the vent headfirst.

I knew it would suck, but I underestimated the *degree* to which it would suck. Within seconds, I'm soiled beyond all hope, my skin coated with the accumulated muck. I should have thought to cover my mouth with something—unmasked, I'm fighting what's either a cough or a hurl, terrified of letting it slip out either way. The flashlight is made embarrassingly irrelevant by the amount of dust clouding my vision, and I'm forced to squeeze my eyes closed before they start to burn too much to go on.

The walls press in tight on either side, and a sinking dread is starting to smother me. I can't see, and I've lost all sense of direction. I could reorient myself if I call out for Fitz, but of course I'm not going to give her the satisfaction. I feel along the walls with my free hand, searching for the telltale pattern of another vent grate as I scoot forward on my elbows.

Could be worse, I try to reason with myself. *At least Hark's not seeing this.*

But when my fingers finally make contact with the furrowed surface I've been searching for, I crack my eyes open and discover how much worse it could be.

The corridor outside is empty.

And there's blood on the walls.

For a moment, all I can see is the red smear, brilliant and fresh against the stark white Ybi ceramic. "Hark?" I shout, wincing as the metal walls of the vent throw the noise back in my ears. "Bea! Hark!" Panic's starting to overwhelm me, but then my brain latches onto the pattern. The stippled edges of the ceramic's detailing break up the shapes, but this is no random smudge.

It's a key signature.

It's placed precisely, made to be visible from where she knew I'd be crawling down the vent, but there's no other sign of Hark and Bea apart from the muddy tracks their shoes left on the floor. "If you're made, kid," Hark used to tell me, "you don't sit around waiting for consequences." The *Justice* had us in its sights, and in her playbook, bugging out is the only logical next step.

Even if it means leaving us behind.

But she's left instructions she knew I'd see. *D major.* Translated, it means *"Find the nearest large-scale gathering, blend into it, and regroup."*

It's clear, simple, easy to follow. But it takes *time,* and they were so close just a moment ago. We were in the middle of a conversation I don't want to stop having. If I can just find a way into the corridor outside, maybe we can follow the dirt they've tracked from the growspace and catch up before it's too late.

"They're not here," I shout back down the vent. "I'm gonna keep going and see if I can find an exit."

I get nothing but the faint echo of a noncommittal scoff in reply. Fine by me. I don't think Fitz's help is any great boon, and part of me's almost convinced I'm better off without her. She's never been invested in my well-being, and she'd certainly rather I do all the dirty work.

Now that I know for sure Hark's not waiting for us, I go slower, trying to keep the airborne particulate to a minimum as I scooch my way down the vent shaft. My piddling little flashlight beam is a candle against the claustrophobic dark, but now that I can keep my eyes open, I've got a much better sense of the path ahead. Along this corridor, I'm no doubt going to find more vent covers like the one I unscrewed—ones that would take a significant amount of force to bash open from the inside. I hook around a corner instead, hoping that with my new path comes some variety.

I'm also hoping I can find my way back, but that's a problem for later.

The vent shaft I've entered is slightly smaller than the one I came from, forcing me to scrunch my shoulders together and wedge myself forward. I try to tamp down my rising panic with the fact that this might work in my favor. A change in the design of the vents might also mean a different vent cover—one that's a little easier to get myself out of.

But that's not what I find when I shunt myself another indeterminable length down the corridor. Instead, my flashlight beam glances on an opening I scarcely want to believe until I've pulled myself up under it. It's not just another grate—it's a wide-open exit. From the dust accumulated on its lip, it's just as untouched as the rest of the vents, undisturbed for centuries.

Did someone once try to crawl through these vents three hundred years ago? Was this their entry, or their exit?

One way to find out. I squirm to the edge of the hole and haul myself up into the open air, slithering out onto the floor like a newborn calf. For a moment I lie flat on my back, enjoying a darkness that's spacious instead of encroaching and air that's stale but breathable, free of back-cycled particulate. The *Justice*'s mockery echoes in my ears—that horseshit it said about enjoying something only because it's better than where I came from.

News flash, asshole. Reality's subjective, and I'm allowed to enjoy it.

Then I sweep my flashlight's beam up.

It alights on a desiccated corpse.

CHAPTER 9

I never thought I was the screaming type.

I'm learning all sorts of new things about myself today.

I thrash away from the body, only to make contact with another sickeningly dry lump. I scream again, then clamp a hand over my mouth. The point of this exercise was to stealth our way around the *Justice*'s sensors.

That point is far behind us now. I've seen my fair share of untoward shit in Hark's employ, but never corpses. And especially not corpses like this.

I ease my flashlight up to illuminate the first one I spotted. It wears a uniform straight out of a historical drama, starkly black with intricately embroidered golden shoulder patches whose patterns I recognize from the tiling I've seen in the Ybi sections of the ship. These must be Ybi soldiers. If that's the case, these bodies have been undisturbed in this room for over three hundred years.

Oddly, it's pity that finally slows my racing heart. Three hundred years, and no one's found them. They've been left to wither and rot in the ship's cool, dry air. There's no telltale electronic hum in this room—almost as if the *Justice* itself has forgotten about it too.

I ease to my feet, sweeping my flashlight beam once more around my surroundings. A forest of cylindrical metal trunks sprouts from the floor at even spacing. The writing along their outside is etched in Old Imperial glyphs, but with another glance at the corpses near them, I'm pretty sure I can guess at their purpose.

The bodies are skewed as if someone's flattened them. The skin's withered along the bones to hold them together, but the bones themselves are fractured too consistently for it to be any one blow that killed these people. Only one killer leaves a trace like this—the one these cylinders were built to avoid.

I'm in an inertial shelter, and all of these people were killed in high-G maneuvers.

Some of the cylinders are cracked open, revealing porous padding meant to swaddle away the worst effects of a sudden change in acceleration. I peer closer and discover the glint of needle beds that must inject some sort of blood-thinner cocktail when it's needed. Maybe these people were trying to make it into one of these coffins when a flinch on the scale of kilometers crushed them to death. If that's the case, I'm not going to try cracking open any of the other ones. I don't want to know how well they might preserve a body.

I'd understood on an academic level that the *Justice* is a warship, but it's another thing entirely to see the echoes of its bloody past mummified and forgotten. The kind of maneuvers that necessitate shelters like this for your infantry are ones a ship will only pull in the desperation of battle, when an ugly calculus takes over the choice of who's worth losing to survive. None of these people made the cut.

But then I turn back to the vent I've just crawled out of. Its cover was off when I found it. The clues start to add up in my head. Something happened to this shelter—a malfunction, most likely, that cut it off from the rest of the ship's systems. Some people tried to come out of their shelters too early and paid the dire cost. Others could have survived and tried to use the same vent system I just crawled through as an escape.

The operative word being "tried." Because if they'd succeeded, they would have come back for the bodies of their comrades.

I'm suddenly deathly certain I want nothing more to do with the vents.

It's at that precise moment I pick up a slithering noise in their depths.

I click off the flashlight and grope for my dagger, easing from coffin to coffin as I try to make it to the far side of the room without disturbing any of the bodies. My heart's racing so hard that I can't keep my breaths shallow, and I fold my elbow over my mouth to muffle the sound. Another of the *Justice*'s brags echoes in my memory, that line it spun about me not being capable of imagining what's possible in its domain. There are a hundred irrational thoughts chasing each other's tail in my head right now—everything from banded faithful to ghosts—and the dagger's hilt is starting to go slippery with sweat. In the pure blackness, the only thing I have to ground me is the solidity of the wall against my back. I'm not even sure where the tunnel mouth is.

But whatever's moving through it is getting closer. The sound is irregular, heaving, almost too large to be a single person. My dagger's feeling more and more useless by the second.

Something catches the edge of the vent opening and drags itself up, creaking the metal. *Just keep going. Keep moving forward,* I plead in my head.

It doesn't. I hear the scrape of fabric against the aperture and the thud of contact against the floor.

Now or never. I click the flashlight on and lunge off the wall, hefting my dagger high.

The filth-covered monster rears back from the sudden brightness, holding up a hand. It's not until I'm almost on top of her that I recognize the blue jumpsuit, the silvery hair, the flash of green eyes blown wide in a panic.

"Fitz, what the *fuck*?" I yelp.

"*Why the fuck did you turn off the light?*" she snarls back.

"Why the fuck are you coming crawling through the vents like a fucking demon?" My dagger's still aimed at her. I don't know what else to do with it, and I feel like it's making a point.

"*You* screamed," she retorts, then hauls herself out of the vents with a trembling push. Our two backpacks come tumbling out in her wake, each wrapped around her ankles by a strap. That'd explain the ungainly noises I was hearing.

Instead of replying, I flick my flashlight's beam over to the first body I spotted. Fitz reels back, swallowing down a shriek, and I can't help the curdling self-satisfaction it gives me to get a genuine reaction out of her.

It must show, because Fitz scowls at me. "Put the dagger down. Why were you so surprised it's me?"

"When have you ever done something for me without Hark telling you?"

"You *screamed*," she repeats, as if that explains any of it. Never once in the four years I've known her have I seen Fitz come close to playing the hero. In the elaborate mechanics of Hark's plans, she's always been the gorgeous, sparkling showpiece, drawing every eye so the rest of us could do the dirty work. She'd bait the traps, greasing up marks for Hark to shove over the precipice of their own ruin. I'd watch from the fringes, delving into networks, prying all the right doors open, feeling both essential and absolutely invisible.

The sight of her shoving herself to her feet, coated in the muck and grime of the vents, feels like I've breathed too much corpse-gas. "It's the Vestal job all over again," I remark before she can bite my head off for staring at her disheveled state.

"How the hell is this anything like the Vestal job?" Fitz asks, already back to her flat, bored tone as she rummages in her pack and pulls out her own flashlight.

"Oh, I don't know. Maybe because I was stuffed down a duct to wire into the security system directly." That had been an even tighter squeeze, but at least I'd had a harness on with Bea on the other end to haul me out once I'd finished.

"You were in the vents on the Vestal job?"

Her confused disinterest is almost a relief. At least it's familiar. "How do you think you and Hark walked out of that one?" I retort. "You set off three separate alarms I had to suppress."

"And you didn't gloat about it after the fact?" Fitz looks genuinely perturbed, but then again, we're surrounded by dead bodies and a forest of coffins that may or may not contain even more dead bodies. She clicks on her flashlight, softening the stark relief of my single beam and rendering the room a little less ominous.

Bragging would have gotten me a scolding from Hark, but I'm not about to admit that. "You played your part perfectly. You smiled and waved and never got your hands dirty." I peer closer at her, unable to suppress a leering grin as I fix my flashlight's beam directly in her eyes. "Guess this isn't like the Vestal job at all. No gorgeous dress for you—you're in the slop with me."

Fitz swipes like she's going to grab my flashlight out of my hands, but I dance back out of reach.

"So, welcome to the latest hellhole," I continue, sweeping my light through the room. "As far as I can tell, this place got cut off from the rest of the ship's systems and the *Justice* completely forgot it was here. Unfortunately, it doesn't seem like these folks figured out another way out. And since their comrades who tried to escape through the vents didn't make it out to tell everyone what happened, I don't think we're getting out that way either."

"So this is a dead end?" Fitz asks, using her free hand to swat desperately at the muck on her jumpsuit.

I snort, but she doesn't seem to realize why it's funny, which just makes it weirder that I'm laughing. The only jokes she's ever made in my presence are ones at my expense. "Because the bodies . . ." I try to explain, but Fitz's expression only goes even more impenetrably flat. "Anyway, maybe."

It's not a thought I enjoy, but I have to accept it as a possibility. I cross the room to inspect the door. It's sealed firmly shut and there's no sign of a manual override. Sickeningly, the seam down the middle bears the scars of several attempts to wrench it open and even a few ineffectual dents where someone must have pounded it out of frustration. The pad next to it is dead, as I expected, but otherwise unmolested. It's probably pointless, but I wedge my dagger into its cracks anyway, trying to lever its housing free.

A heavy *thump* distracts me, and I turn to find Fitz has just rolled one of the corpses over. She freezes in the beam of my flashlight. "They might have something useful," she offers.

I deeply regret goading her about never getting her hands dirty. "If they had something useful, the people stuck in here would have used it before crawling off to die in the vents," I reply, but Fitz only shrugs and goes back to gingerly feeling into the soldier's pockets.

I pull a face at her back, then keep prying. A lucky twist of my dagger pops the control panel open and exposes a mess of wires that once again remind me of the systems I grew up with on Pearl Station. It'd be workable if only it had power.

I glance back at Fitz's delicate looting. Maybe she's got a point about using what's in reach.

The cylindrical coffins' main functions seem to be housed in the base, accessible through a panel that's closed with a simple latch. I crouch next to one of the open ones, take the hilt of my flashlight in my teeth, and pop the hatch open to reveal its inner workings. The cable management is absolutely horrendous, and I sigh around the flashlight as I wedge one of the components loose and start plucking wires off.

"What are you doing?" Fitz asks from the far side of the room.

"Remains to be seen," I try to say, but it comes out a garbled mess. I'd love to be able to say I'm saving our asses, but I don't want to give her ammunition if it turns out this is a fruitless endeavor.

After a few minutes of rummaging through the coffin's guts, I find exactly what I'm looking for. I let out a triumphant grunt and collapse onto my back, cradling the hefty weight of the backup battery. Whatever contractor built these must have put more thought into their redundancies than whoever designed the door of this chamber, and I thank them for it.

"What is that?" Fitz asks.

"Our ticket out of here," I reply, again completely ineffectually, then roll to my feet and heft the wires I've accumulated over my shoulder as I head back to the door panel. After another couple minutes of fiddling, I've got all my contacts in place.

"C'mon, baby," I plead in vowels, then twist the last connection home.

Nothing happens. I pluck my flashlight out from between my teeth and click it off, hoping for the tiniest glimmer of a diode, but I'm met with nothing but dull darkness. The battery's depleted. Of course it's depleted. It's been sitting here untouched for three hundred years, doing nothing but oxidizing.

"That's about what I expected," Fitz mutters from the other side of the room.

"I don't see you having any bright ideas," I retort.

Then I freeze.

"Gimme your flashlight," I tell her.

"I don't take orders from you," she replies, not even bothering to look up.

I seethe, storming across the room, but Fitz pulls her flashlight close to her chest. I have to fight the urge to draw my dagger on her again, and I only manage it by thinking of how Hark would scold me for resorting to base violence to solve problems. The fact of the matter is I don't need *her* flashlight— I'd just rather risk it than my own.

And from the smug edge tugging the corner of her lips, I think she knows it too. "Fine," I huff. "Then I'm gonna need you to be my light."

She hesitates, but given our situation, it'd be downright absurd to refuse out of pride. Fitz eases out of her crouch and follows me to the door controls. She lifts a dubious eyebrow at the ancient battery I've rigged up. "Even I could have told you that wouldn't work."

"You would have told me that either way," I reply, then click my fingers at where I want her to point her flashlight's beam.

Mercifully, she's decided to stop kicking and screaming every step of the way. Once the light is situated, I twist open the rear of my own flashlight and tip its batteries out.

Juice is juice. These tiny batteries can't hold a candle to the power of the backups from the coffins, but maybe I don't need as much as I think I do. This door is trapped in a sealed state because the power cut while it was on guard against breach. If I can just undo that seal, I think we're in business.

I twist my wires around the battery and press a contact home at one pole. My breath stills in my chest as I ease the other in place.

A diode on the panel flickers on.

I whoop, startling Fitz so badly that she nearly fumbles the light. In the wavering beam, I drag my fingers down the door controls that splay across the panel. No time for trying to divine the meaning of Old Imperial symbols—I'm hitting whatever I can reach while the battery's still active.

One of them must do the trick, because I hear a click from the door. I lunge toward it, jamming my fingers in the crack that runs down the middle and heaving a choking sob of relief when it winches just a centimeter open. I can work with that. Already the air is starting to shift, pressure from the outside gusting into the staleness that's been muddling around this room for centuries.

"Fitz," I grunt, bearing my full weight against the door as I try to pull it open. "If you wouldn't mind."

She catches my drift, tucking her flashlight in her pocket and stepping to the other side of the door's seam. In the barest blue glow, we pull like our lives depend on it until finally, *finally* the doors are just wide enough to get our shoulders through.

"Mind holding on for a moment?" I ask. Before Fitz has time to answer, I let go and sprint for the other side of the room, nearly tripping over one of the poor Ybi soldiers as I gather up our packs and barrel back through the open door. In the hall outside, I skid to a stop on my knees, bent over my cargo and panting like I've just run a full circuit of the *Justice*'s circumference.

Fitz steps out into the corridor, swaying slightly as the doors winch shut behind her. She looks down her long, elegant nose at me, then extends a hand.

I'm halfway to trying to take it when she snatches the strap of her backpack and yanks it out of my grip.

I don't know what else I expected.

CHAPTER 10

Now that the bodies are behind us, the dead zone's a relief. The corridors are quiet and dusty—dusty enough that we probably don't need to worry about other people catching up to us. We have the light of only one flashlight to go by, and I think it's the single thread Fitz's pride is hanging on by the way she's gripping it.

I resist the urge to gloat, but only barely. In its place, I find a weird sort of guilt gnawing at me. Whoever escaped that room through the vents crawled out of that unforgiving dark not realizing that they could have engineered an exit with the materials they had on hand. They were infantry grunts, expendable, forgotten by the intelligence that should have been responsible for their safety and well-being.

And now that intelligence is playing god.

I keep waiting for the moment our luck runs out as we press deeper into the hollow corridors, and when I spot the glow of emergency lights up around a corner, it floods me with dread. But before I can tell Fitz to turn off the flashlight and get quiet, I notice the spackling on the walls, like someone's gone through and stripped something off them. Ybi tile, if I were to put money on it—and that means they probably tore out the *Justice*'s sensors too.

Better, it might mean we're close to a settlement.

We turn another corner and find ourselves faced with a familiar sight—yet another one of those massive doors, looming as wide and tall as the hallway, with a keyhole rather than an access pad.

"Well, lucky you're with me," I say, elbowing Fitz. "Doors are my thing. It's a mechanical lock, so I'll need a few minutes to figure it out, but—"

"Or we can just open it with the key," Fitz says, glancing at me sidelong. She holds my gaze, a rare, genuine grin creeping over her lips as her thumb dips into the neck of her jumpsuit and draws out—

There'll be no living with her after this.

"Is *that* why you and Hark were tag-teaming the Envoy?" I grit out through my teeth.

"Don't worry," Fitz replies, delicately flipping through the keys one by one as she compares them against the keyhole. "You played your part perfectly. Fatima was so concerned with the faithful and what they wanted from you, Hark made sure she was always looking in the right direction"—she pauses, squinting at a key, then shoves it in the lock—"and I got my hands dirty."

I groan, the sound mercifully smothered by the larger mechanics of the door's unbolting. Fitz steps back, tucking the keys down her jumpsuit's front again as the massive thing rumbles open. Before my discontent has time to settle, I see what's on the other side.

"Oh, Fitz," I simper, but I can't keep down my grin. "You shouldn't have."

Because somehow, impossibly, in the next room it's raining.

Before Fitz can start fussing about caution and not charging headlong into things, I blow past her into the merciful humidity, holding out my grimy hands like I'm trying to catch every last droplet. A massive tract of farmland splays out ahead of us, vanishing into the steamy mist that coats it, and the overhead lights create the illusion of a sun shower, turning every bead of water falling from the sprinklers into a refracting gemstone.

I throw down my pack and rip open the top half of my jumpsuit, stripping down to my tank as I blink water out of my eyes and knead furiously at the dust, dirt, and wine stains clinging to the fabric.

"Really, Murdock? Right in the middle of the potatoes?" Fitz mutters, but it's not stopping her from stepping gracefully over the threshold and tipping her head back into the rain.

How did she know these were potatoes? But before that thought has time to settle, I spot a vague, looming figure in the mist.

"Who goes there?" he calls. As he gets closer, I realize that part of his bulk—but not all of it—comes from the umbrella he holds over his head. He wears a simple set of polyarmor, not a white cloak, and with his long, dark hair drawn back into a tight bun, it's easy to see that his skull isn't adorned with one of those distinctive glowing bands. It's not enough to get my guard down when the person approaching us is neither Hark nor Bea. I ease my fingers over the hilt of my dagger.

Our new friend draws his sword.

Fitz's hands shoot in the air as she shoulders past me. "We don't mean to intrude—we're just lost."

"Lost, defenseless, completely vulnerable," I grumble through my teeth. "Anything else you want to share with this guy?"

"I'm negotiating," Fitz replies.

"I'll show you negotiating." Before she can yank me back, I lunge past her, my dagger held on guard.

Our new friend turns and bolts. For a moment, I'm wrapped in the delusion that he's actually scared of me—despite his blade, despite his larger, thicker stature, despite every other logical factor telling me otherwise.

Then I spot the sentry tower he's running for. I break into a flat-out sprint, tearing over the rows of potatoes as fast as my legs will carry me. With a flying leap, I wrap myself over the big guy's shoulders, ramming the hilt of my dagger down into the soft meat of his armpit that should, in theory, pop his sword loose. I miss the nerve I was hoping to strike, and instead he throws his umbrella away, reaches back, and hauls me bodily over his head, tossing me a good meter ahead of him.

At least the potato dirt's soft. I land in a heap at the base of the sentry tower, hacking on dirty rainwater as I try to recover the breath he's knocked out of me. My fingers tighten around my dagger's grip as the big guy levels his sword at my chest.

Before he can do anything with it, I roll to the side, thread the blade through the cords that hang taut from the tower's handles, and slice.

They slither limply back into the tower's root. "Just you and me now, buddy," I grunt, popping back up to my feet.

"The hell are you doing?" he replies. He has a soft, unassuming face that gives him an air of boyishness at odds with the weapon in his hand. The umbrella suited him better.

I spare a glance sidelong to find that Fitz has scooped it up. She watches us dourly from beneath its shelter, and when her eyes meet mine, I can all but hear her say, "*You're on your own, dipshit.*"

"Trying to improve my chances," I retort, brandishing my dagger in a mockery of his stance.

"By attacking a Blade-sworn? By sabotaging an early warning system keeping a settlement safe?"

"Not doing the settlement much good if the guy who's supposed to use it can't stop someone from taking it out."

The guy's eyes can't possibly get any wider. I think a part of him is considering handing his weapon over just to get me off his case. "You're ingest," he says with sudden certainty.

"Says who?"

"Says your original colors."

"My what?"

He gestures at me up and down. "You did your damnedest to muddy it, but I know a prison jumpsuit when I see one. You're still wearing the clothes they dressed you in when they fed you to this ship, which means you barely understand what you're doing."

"I've seen enough since I got here to know I need a fucking sword."

Something suspiciously close to pity lights in his expression. "Yeah, I get that." He sighs. "But this is a really dumbass way of going about getting one. I'm guessing you came by that dagger by similar means?"

"I found it fair and square," I reply.

"A scav staked her to the wall with it," Fitz adds helpfully, and I shoot her a glare. She gives the big guy a coy wave. "Hi. I'm Fitz, this is Murdock."

"Ham," he replies. "Blade-sworn to the East Deck."

"Shouldn't you be off fighting scavs and saving the day, then?" I ask, blinking rainwater out of my eyes.

His brow wrinkles, and he lowers the tip of his sword. "Not all Blade-sworn are contracted for patrol work. Someone's got to defend the settlements too."

"Looks like all you're guarding is a bunch of potatoes," Fitz notes.

"Well, this is my first contract," Ham says sheepishly, tucking his free hand behind his neck.

I take a probing step forward, and his sword is back on guard in an instant.

"Please, don't try it," he pleads. "I want to help you—really,

I do—but you're coming at me with direct violence on your own behalf and a weapon that's probably cursed. Put that thing down before it turns on you."

"What, the dagger?"

"A weapon that's been used against you is always going to carry that enmity. One way or another, it'll betray you in the end."

I blink, then glance sidelong at Fitz to see if she's hearing this right. I'm not sure why I bothered—she's got her "working" face on, and all of that enigmatic sunshine is focused on Ham. "You think my dagger . . . doesn't like me?" I hazard.

He shrugs.

I can't threaten this guy anymore. I drop my blade down to my side, swiping halfheartedly at the mud on my face with my other hand. Nothing on this ship makes any sense to me, and I don't have time to get my head around another set of weird superstitions when Hark and Bea could be getting farther and farther away—or worse, running into the banded faithful again. "Fuck it. Fitz, let's go."

"Now, hang on," Ham says, moving to put himself between us.

"Thought you didn't want to fight anymore?"

"You came from a sealed sector," he says, pointing his sword back at the looming door mechanism that's shut behind us. "How did you get there in the first place?"

"Does it matter?" Fitz asks from behind him.

"I'm contracted to keep East Deck safe, and if the sector beyond that door is now traversable, it could become an access point for scavs."

"We got into it from an East Deck growspace on the other side," Fitz says. "We sealed the route behind us."

Ham's bulk is blocking the face I want to pull at her. Hark's trained her better—she shouldn't be giving this kind of information away for free.

"And besides," Fitz continues. "We only got through the door because we had a key."

Ham turns, blinking incredulously, just as Fitz draws the keychain out from the neck of her jumpsuit. I have to bite back the urge to scream at her. She just revealed maybe the biggest asset in our arsenal to a guy with a *sword*. Maybe I can take him while he's distracted—and for a moment I seriously consider it.

"That's a *full* keychain for someone who's only just come aboard," Ham says. "How the hell did you get that?"

"Same way I got myself on this ship," Fitz says, all charm and absolutely no sincerity. "Is it worth a lot?"

"That looks like it could get you through every major door in East Deck," he replies, sounding like he's been hit over the head with a rock.

"Neat. If you come with us, it's yours."

Ham's grunt of surprise harmonizes with mine. "Do you mind if I have a word with my associate?" I ask him, but I'm already moving toward Fitz with a purpose. She rears back as I approach, tipping the umbrella so I'm still caught in the irrigation drizzle.

"Murdock, I know it's not your strong suit, but try to be rational—"

"What the hell do you think you're doing?" I snarl. "*This* is you negotiating? Surely Hark taught you better than to fumble your entire hand out on the table?"

"I don't see you having any brighter ideas."

"Did you not see the message Hark left for us in *blood* back in the corridor? We have our marching orders, and there was nothing in there about picking up an outside contractor."

"She said the key is D major. Do *you* know where we're going to find a big gathering of people to blend into?" Fitz retorts.

"Maybe," I snap. "The banded faithful asshole said something about a music festival tomorrow. Did Fatima mention it too?"

Fitz scowls, the exact face she makes when she's mad I thought of something first. Hark knows about Southeast Upper Limits. "*D major* is just a matter of getting there," I declare.

Fitz's eyes go steely. "And do you know where Southeast Upper is? Do you think we're getting there on our own? We need someone who knows this ship on our side. Someone who's not on the *Justice*'s payroll, who's capable of defending us—because clearly you're not managing it. And if all it costs us is these keys, which were *remarkably* easy to steal, then I think it's what Hark would do in our place."

I grit my teeth. Fitz may not be a fighter, but she always knows exactly where to stick a knife in me. "And when he discovers that the *Justice* itself is after us and decides a measly keychain isn't worth the trouble?"

"I suppose then you'll have to convince him you're worth defending."

I suck in my lips, tilting my head back against the soft rainfall. The looming dread I felt in the other growspace is creeping back in. What good am I in a place like this, really? I've been doing nothing but getting my ass handed to me since I came aboard. Hark blames me for the Gest job falling apart, and the ship forcibly separated us before I could even argue that point.

"We should tell him what he's getting into," I say at last.

"Now who's laying a full hand out on the table?" Fitz scoffs. "No, you let me take the lead on this. You've done enough today."

Under any other circumstances, I'd shove her flat on her ass in the mud, but I'm tired of fighting, and given the kind of day I'm having, I'd probably find some way to fuck it up. I give her a stiff nod, and she steps past me to face Ham.

"We were ingested together with two other women," Fitz starts. "But we got separated from them, and all we know is that they could be headed to the music festival in Southeast Upper. We're in the market for a guide—someone who could help us find our way back to them. If you can get us back to our people, the keychain's yours."

Ham looks rightfully suspicious, but from the way his eyes track the keychain swaying in Fitz's grasp, it's got its claws in him. If this were a job, this would be the moment that decides everything—the mark, weighing their uncertainty against the prize Hark's waving under their nose. I watch him carefully, trying to put myself in her headspace. What would she notice? What button would she press to tip him over the edge?

He almost seems like he's counting the keys, but that's not it. He's inspecting them.

Almost like he's looking for a specific one.

When he gives a little jolt of recognition, I know we have our opening.

Before Fitz can get another word in, I blurt out, "Of course you'll need collateral. We can give you a single key of your choice now, and the rest when we make it back to our folks."

"Deal," Ham says immediately, shouldering his sword back into its scabbard.

"They're *my* keys," Fitz hisses petulantly, but I think she's just mad I cracked him before she could. It's not often I get a chance to beat Fitz to a mark, and I savor every second of watching her hold out the keychain for him to make his selection.

After four years of helping Hark shake down some of the toughest negotiators in the galaxy, I'm a little awestruck at just how guileless Ham is when it comes to picking out his collateral. The key he grabs immediately is an unassuming little thing, part of a matched set of similarly cut metal slivers that are distinguished only by their teeth and the numbers printed along their spine. "What's special about that one?" I ask.

Ham looks almost sheepish. "It's got sentimental value," he says, but nothing more.

Fitz catches my eye. "What did you say you were in for, again?" she asks warily.

"I didn't," Ham replies. There's a beat where he should follow that up with an answer to Fitz's curiosity, but all he offers is an oblivious smile as he fusses with the clasp on the chain to get his desired key loose.

That could be a bit of a problem.

"And your contract with East Deck," Fitz adds. "Are you allowed to break it just like that?"

"Well, it's my first contract," he says. "I don't have a reputation to maintain yet. It might make it more difficult for me to forge a new contract afterward, but I don't think I could live with myself if I let you two go get yourselves killed."

"How are we going to get ourselves killed?" I ask, resisting the urge to point my dagger at him again.

His eyes drop to it anyway. "First lesson on surviving the *Justice:* civilization is the goal, and civilization's dirty secret is that violence is always done by proxy. Did no one explain what a Blade-sworn is to you?"

"I thought they were just enforcers for the settlements." It certainly seemed like Heeseok and his people were just as much a part of East Deck as Fatima.

"Depends on the contract," Ham replies. "But that independence is the price of the violence we have to be trained to handle. We have to be a separate entity from what we defend, or we're no better than the scavs. For everyone to exist in stability on this ship, there needs to be a buffer that not only keeps the scavs from pillaging the settlements—but also keeps the settlements from overstretching their bounds. A buffer that reminds those asshole banded faithful—pray you never run into them, by the way—that their beloved *Justice* isn't really a god."

"There are people who *worship* the *Justice*?" I lay my incredulity on thick enough that Fitz flashes me a warning look, but Ham doesn't seem to notice.

"Lotta stuff gets weird when you're cut off from the rest of the galaxy," he offers with a shrug. "Sometimes the ship itself takes advantage of that. People change the moment they come aboard. Some will tell you they lost themselves, others will say they found who they were supposed to be all along."

"Which one are you?" Fitz asks, the question pointed like a gun under a table. I'm tempted to remind her that hiring him without a background check was *her* idea.

"Still figuring that part out," he replies with an earnest grin. "I'm only three years into my time aboard."

"Wait, *time aboard*?" I ask. For a moment, I feel as if the *Justice*'s drum has stopped spinning.

But before I can get too far ahead of myself, Ham gives me a soft, weary look that makes him seem decades older. "It's a bit of lingo you'll pick up in no time," he says. "Easier on the conscience than 'the rest of your life.'"

"Is *everyone* on this ship delusional?" I mutter.

Ham frowns. "Everyone on this ship is just trying to get by. If we can soften the reality of that with a turn of phrase, I don't see the harm in it. 'Time aboard' might not be the most honest way of putting it, but it's the way that keeps people from trying to jump to supply ships and getting shot by the auto-turrets when the *Justice* stops for ingest."

The imagery hits like a splash of cold water, stark against the warm rain trickling down on us. It was an idea Hark floated in the holding tank on Gest as she tried to puzzle out a way of escaping our fate. She reasoned that with the *Justice* demanding material goods as well as warm bodies, there might be an opening to hop to one of those ships when it was close enough to make a drop-off. I thought it was clever, lateral thinking.

Now it sounds as desperate as the people Ham's talking about.

But the same desperation is building in me now. I'm filthy, exhausted, and separated from the person who saved me, who's *been* saving me ever since she found me on Pearl Station four years ago. I want her back. I want her to tell me everything's going to be okay, that she's figured out our escape, that the rest of my life isn't going to be dirt and potatoes and swords I'll never have.

I must be doing a shit job of hiding it, because Ham offers me an awkward pat on the shoulder. "Hey, it's not so bad. I know you just came aboard and this is all overwhelming, but you're gonna be okay."

"Didn't you just full-on throw me on my ass a few minutes ago?" I ask.

Ham grins. "You're on the *Justice* now. Second lesson: reinvention is the name of the game."

CHAPTER 11

We set off through the potato fields with Ham in the lead. He guides us along well-worn paths, past signage that points toward mostly unfamiliar settlement names. One arrow shows the way to East Deck, and I can't help a surreptitious glance down that branch of the trail, as if I expect to see Heeseok or Fatima fuming after us. Fortunately Ham's declared it's easiest if we spend the night in a settlement called Southeast Stair—otherwise Fitz and I would have to get our stories straight *fast*.

The rain starts to lighten up as we go until finally Fitz swings down the umbrella, shakes it out, and folds it up. She lengthens her strides to catch up with Ham and hands it back to him, muttering something in his ear as she leans close.

I narrow my eyes. There she goes again, handing over perfectly good assets to people who aren't me. If I end up needing that flashlight of hers later, I'm not asking her politely.

But I need to play nice, because there are a million questions I want to needle her with. There are three ways to get something you want off someone who's not letting go. You ask nicely, you steal it when they aren't looking, or you start swinging. Back on Pearl Station, the last choice was my go-to until Hark found me. From what I understand of Fitz, she's prone to the second option. But Hark's been training us both for the first—for convincing people to give you what you want and letting them realize it wasn't in their best interests later.

I have no idea how to play that with Fitz as the target. She's always been a mystery, the crew's enigmatic, unquestionably beautiful, and unshakably unfriendly face player. Who, for some reason, knows what a potato plant looks like.

"You do a lot of farming?" I ask, easing closer to her as I tuck my hands innocently in my backpack straps.

Fitz's fingers go to check the keychain hanging from her neck. "Hark really never told you?"

There's that familiar shape, the knife she just loves to wedge into my ribs. No, Hark never said a thing about Fitz's background. I assumed it was never relevant, and besides, the only thing I've cared to know about Fitz over the past four years is whether Hark and Bea like her better than me. With Bea, I know for certain I'm the favorite. Bea doesn't take Fitz out for extra-credit joyrides or try to get her delicate hands dirty with engine mechanic lessons. But with Hark, it's different. With Hark, it's always a competition—which of us can be the most useful at any given moment. And I knew that Fitz had certain advantages. Schmoozing. Being a perfect, lovely distraction. That thing she does with her lips and her teeth that makes them magnetic. I never needed to know anything more about her than that, so I never asked.

"Hark never told me," I admit, letting the wound of it slip a little in the waver of my voice. This is another trick I learned at Hark's knee. I show a bit of my belly, and you show me yours.

Incredibly, it seems like it's on its way to working. Maybe

because Fitz doesn't think me capable of that kind of guile. Maybe because she doesn't care enough to hide herself anymore. "I grew up on a stake in its second decade at the far edge of the galactic rim," she says.

It puts a wrinkle in my brow so drastic that for a moment it feels like I'm seeing double. "You were a *farm girl*?" I blurt.

And oh, there's the reason. It's not that she doesn't see through me. It's not that she doesn't care. There's a rare tilt in the corner of Fitz's lips. On anyone else, it's barely worth reading into, but she might as well be grinning with cat-that-got-the-cream smugness. "Thought I was a core-world princess?" she asks, her tone downright mocking.

"When have you ever pretended to be anything but that?" I counter. Her blink at the word "pretended" speaks volumes. Fitz has made herself synonymous with the slick luxury of the circles we make our trade in. I've always seen the difference between Fitz working and Fitz as an empty vessel waiting for more work, but it never occurred to me that both were artificial.

I think she hates the notion.

"That's what people like to see when they see me," she admits. "That's the image I decided I'd forge for myself the first time I went upwell. I left my home stake the day I turned eighteen, used all my savings from all my harvests to book passage to Favist City, and never looked back."

"What were you running from?" I ask. It's only once the question's cleared my lips that I realize it's the most personal thing I've ever asked her in four years of working together.

Fitz casts a bitter glance upward, and I follow her gaze. The ceiling of the growspace has been painted a pale blue that softens its artificiality, but the lights strung along it are anything but suns. "A small life," she mutters.

I hate how much I get that. I'd never left Pearl Station until

I met Hark. I was trapped in my own small life there too. And now look at us both, stuck forever in the convoluted bowels of a sentient monster—unless we can somehow make it back to Hark.

It's a little too much existential dread for me to handle all at once. "I can't imagine you farming," I blurt.

"That's by design," Fitz replies. "I hated it. Every day the same tedium. Every day more dirt to wash off. I'd watch casts from the core and see entire cities where people didn't have to do a damn thing but live, and here we were at the edge of the known universe, doing everything the hard way to line the pockets of the stakeholders who fronted the settlement. It'd be one thing if they'd invested in the kind of automation that keeps the core worlds spinning, but rim stakes are supposed to be all about *freedom* and *independence*—which is the line they feed you to make sure you never realize *you're* not free or independent."

I've gotten intimately familiar with the workings of rim stakes in my time under Hark's wing. Most, I was surprised to learn, end up falling over within the first decade, no matter how much money gets poured into them. They begin with big dreams and big investors who think if they can just start everything over on a new world with nothing but *their* ideals, they'll sow the seeds of the next great empire. It's fed a festering industry of cheap, dirty construction—just enough to prop a few habs up so you can claim your stake is self-sustaining and bait more people into claiming their place in it. All of that operates out of the core worlds, far from the ugly realities of the stakes themselves. Far, too, from the consequences when one starts to go sideways.

There's an entropy to those things that extends to the cash flow propping them up. We do some of our best work right before that tipping point, convincing investors that *their* money is going to be the thing that keeps a stake from going belly-up. They overpay, we disappear, and their investment does far more good in our pockets than theirs.

"So that's why you joined Hark, huh?" I ask. "You want to save the people in those stakes from the assholes in the core?"

But surprisingly, Fitz gives a vehement shake of her head. "Anyone stupid enough to ship out to the edge of the galaxy for one of those nightmarish hellholes is going to get exactly what's coming to them," she says with no small amount of venom. "Hark helps along the collapse—and that helps dispel the illusions that justified every time I had to blister my hands to put food on the table when entire *worlds* in the core do the same thing with no cost to any person's time."

"And now look at us!" I chirp, trying for levity as I spread my hands at the sprawling potato fields. "Trapped in your shitty small life again. Well, at least with people hunting us, we won't be settling down into farming anytime soon."

Fitz gives me a warning glare, one part *I sincerely wish to tear your spine out,* one part *Do not mention that there are people hunting us in earshot of Ham.* Which is a good point. He may not drive the hardest bargain, but that could change if he gets wind of what's on our tail. "What about you, then?" she asks brusquely.

"What about me? You already know."

"All I know is that Hark had us running a job on Pearl, and then suddenly she'd acquired a stray. You know her—she never explains herself unless it makes for good theater."

"I was trying to escape my own small life."

Fitz scoffs. "What *small life*? You were on a station that berthed thousands of ships. Any one of them could have been your ticket to the galactic core."

I have to fight down the simmering urge to snap at her, if only to keep from spooking Ham. "Of course *you* think it's easy to leave," I mutter through my teeth.

"What's that supposed to mean?"

"You're so goddamn detached all the goddamn time. You probably skipped off your stake like it was nothing. Some of us *care,* Fitz. Some of us can't leave everything behind at the drop of a hat."

"Well, we were running that job on Pearl Station a grand total of a week, so it didn't take you too long either," Fitz replies.

I fix my gaze on my shoes, trying for a calm that's just not coming. I was starting to think she might understand. I'd completely forgotten who I was talking to.

It's not the first time I've heard someone assume I was *lucky* to grow up on Pearl Station. It was a galactic crossroads, sure, but more than that, it was a liminal space. People were only ever passing through. Strangers might nod to you, other kids might invite you to play while their families waited out a long layover, but everyone moved on eventually.

Everyone except the scum the station just couldn't seem to scour.

My mother ran a net café on one of the less illustrious tiers, a place for travelers to catch up on the latest newscasts and refresh their accounts between long-haul trips. It was a shitty business to begin with, juggling outdated, incompatible tech for people who just wanted to plug in their datapads and check their mail, but my mother managed to build an even shittier empire of crime on top of it.

Her trade was in personal data, and people were so, *so* bad at protecting it. Not many folks realize how many permissions you can bypass the moment someone's clicked an agreement to cable into a local network. Every customer we got went into my mother's ledger, and the moment they plugged in, she unleashed me.

When I was younger—when my moral center was still a gooey lump of unformed clay—she'd present me with "cryptography puzzles," purring in my ear about how it's all just

numbers in the end. They were the building blocks of an elementary hacking course that escalated in complexity as I tore
through it voraciously. Other kids would come and go, but my
mother's daily challenge was a constant that'd never fail me. As
I got older, the challenge began to change its shape. Suddenly I
wasn't playing computer games—I was given targets and told
to report back as much about them as I could. It started with
eyeballing badges and crew patches as I brought drinks to their
stations, but soon she was showing me the secret setup in the
back where she scraped keystrokes and watched customers
click through their accounts on mirrored monitors.

And the thing was, when I was young and naïve, it was the
greatest thing in the galaxy. I was so used to knowing people
would pass on through. They'd say polite hellos and perfunc-
tory goodbyes, and I'd never know a single secret of theirs. It
gave me a heady rush of power far too grand for my tiny body,
to know I could unravel the inside workings of a person with
just a few clicks. I felt like I was seeing real people from my spot
at the back monitor, seeing them for who they really were before they could get away from me.

It took me a while to understand the second part of my
mother's business, the part that required all the secret hard
drives that she kept backed up in triplicate and stored in a panel
underneath our bed frame. We didn't just collect that data for
kicks. It went on ice for a few months after we scraped it, a necessary precaution to keep our marks from tracing their misfortune back to us, but once we were reasonably certain they
couldn't pick us out of a lineup of places they'd used their login,
my mother would sell that data to a black-market broker.

When I finally put it all together, I wanted to stop. The people coming through our café were coming because they didn't
own their own equipment. They couldn't afford a hack on top
of that. My mother soothed me with the same lie she told herself to sleep at night—that if they didn't change their pass-

words and audit their logins every few months, they were basically leaving the door open for anyone. We were just enterprising enough to walk through it first.

Then she'd remind me I was earning my keep. She fed and sheltered me, and that was a blessing I should never take for granted.

It took me a few years after that to scrape the numbers from her dealings with the broker and weigh them against what she let trickle back to me. My mother told me she was holding on to my money for my own good, that she'd give it all to me when I came of age. That was bait to keep her talented little hacker in line—and once I realized that, I started looking for alternative streams of income. Streams that involved knocking over wealthy tourists and escaping with their bankclips. I made Pearl Station's clunky, ancient infrastructure work for me, figuring out how to trigger grav-outs that would disorient my targets completely and give me an unmissable opportunity to take them for everything. Station security never caught on—not when the grav-outs were so easily explained away by the station's centuries-old machinery.

I was invisible, unstoppable. But one day, my hand dipped into the wrong pocket, and the next thing I knew, Hark had me by the wrist.

She wasn't mad—not even disappointed. She'd noticed me when no one else had. Noticed how I seemed to know when the grav-outs would happen *before* they happened, and from there drew the conclusion I knew my way around the station's outdated systems. Which happened to be exactly what she needed for the heist she was trying to pull.

She promised me a ride off the station and an escape from a little life of picking pockets. And maybe Fitz is right—maybe if I wanted to get out, I could have stowed away on any vessel, started fresh on any world open to me from Pearl Station's doorstep. But I needed something more than a window. I needed a hand outstretched, a promise that I would be essential. I needed someone to want me along for the ride.

Now I just need her back.

A strange noise cuts through my brooding, and my head snaps up. At first blush, I assume it's the squeal of some sort of farm equipment, but a high-pitched shout chases after it—difficult to parse, but unmistakably a child's voice.

"Is that a *playground*?" I blurt.

We've reached the far edge of the growspace, where the fields give way to a stretch of grass that's been cultivated into a public park that skirts another massive door. Kids scramble up and down a tower lovingly crafted out of repurposed polymer paneling and shove one another on swing sets welded against the growspace's wall.

Ham glances back at us. "Is that a . . . problem?" he asks.

"Who the hell is reproducing in here?" I stammer.

Ham's eyes widen as he takes in how both Fitz and I have frozen in our tracks. "Oh, oh no," he mutters. "You haven't seen any kids aboard yet. You didn't realize . . ."

No, I guess we didn't. Our introduction to the *Justice* was a shakedown. We were saved by the Envoy and her Blade-sworn, then brought to East Deck, but we were smuggled out under the banded faithful's noses before we could see the settlement properly. We had no idea what lay beyond the *Justice*'s walls when we were thrown down its gullet, but based on our experiences at ingest, we formed some pretty solid assumptions about what life here would entail.

Assumptions that are getting nuked from orbit at the sight of *children*.

"Why . . ." I start, scrubbing one frantic hand through my still-damp hair. "Why would anyone choose—*do* they choose? Does the *Justice* make you—"

Ham's expression twists toward panic. "No, no! Of course not. Why does anyone in the galaxy choose to have kids? Ask a hundred people and you'll get a hundred different answers. And we're still people during our time aboard."

His use of that phrase combined with the sight of the children is breaking my brain in half. Everything I've seen of the *Justice* so far goes against the notion that anyone would want to have kids here. We've stumbled over bodies trapped in dead zones, ducked scavs clashing with sword-wielding warriors, and run from banded faithful given over to the *Justice*'s cult. So far, civilization has been nothing but a sales pitch Fatima spun before us, an unreachable horizon we were expected to believe in.

This, though—this is cold, hard evidence that people feel safe enough to build a life on this ship. Or that their baseline for what's normal has shifted enough to accommodate whatever urges they had to reproduce. It's not exactly comforting, but it brings to mind the *Justice*'s taunt—the yarn about how I couldn't imagine what's possible here.

Points to the god-intelligence, because I never could have imagined this.

"If we could just . . . move past the existential-crisis playground," Ham says with obvious strain, beckoning the two of us forward. "By the way, look pathetic."

I'm about to ask why, but then my eyes catch on the door—and more specifically, the two Blade-sworn who flank it. Ham gives them a cheerful wave as we approach.

"What've you got there?" one of them calls.

"Turned up some of the newest ingest," Ham replies. "They'd somehow managed to get lost out in the fields during the irrigation shift. Horrible luck, right?"

"Horrible," the other Blade-sworn repeats, tilting her head. "Why didn't you ring it in?"

Ham shoots me a consternated look, then covers it with a sheepish smile. "Had a little issue with the sentry tower."

"Why do they look like they've been rolling in dirt?" the first Blade-sworn asks.

"Slipped and fell," I offer in a voice pitched perfectly to Hark's B-sharp minor, the key I play when the job needs me to look lost and scared.

Fitz lets out a seething breath beside me. She's used to playing vulnerable, but I think wretched is a little too far for her pride. Which isn't to say that she's not nailing it. Her damp, frazzled hair and stained jumpsuit, combined with the way she's put herself right on the edge of frustrated, exhausted tears, would be enough to move even the stoniest of hearts to pity.

"They've had what sounds like a truly awful day," Ham says. "I know I'm supposed to be keeping my post, but I offered to escort them to Southeast Stair. Temporarily."

He's not . . . *great* at lying, but there's something in his earnestness that sells it anyway.

The guards eye us up and down and I turn my body slightly, easing the dagger behind my hip. Ham's words about it betraying me echo in my ear, and I silently beg it, *Please, not now.* If we're trying to make ourselves out to be nothing but bedraggled travelers, a scav's weapon isn't going to do much for our case.

"Get on through, then," the Blade-sworn on the left says, beckoning us up to the door.

Ham's spine shoots straight, and a relieved smile breaks over his face. "C'mon, c'mon," he says, waving me and Fitz ahead of him. We ease past the Blade-sworn and through the door's massive arch, leaving behind the sunny glow of the growspace for a dark tunnel of a corridor.

In the gloom, Fitz catches my eye. "Not bad," she says. "Then again, B-sharp minor's always been your best key."

All thoughts of subtlety subside, replaced by only the urge to wring her by the neck. I lunge, but a glimmer in the corner of my eye stops me. I've just caught sight of what lies on the far end of the tunnel.

Rather than East Deck's tiers overflowing with greenery,

Southeast Stair is built into the walls of a massive shaft that extends up into the dizzying heights of the decks. A complicated system of pulleys and lifts threads through its levels, and a colossal, spiraling staircase that branches out to meet the living spaces sprouts up the center. In the hazy glow of the golden lights strung through the settlement, the view rivals a core city's skyline—or maybe my standards are still crawling out from the bottom of the trash compactor my life's dropped down.

Until I realize that some of those lights are moving.

Some of those lights are headbands.

CHAPTER 12

Ham goes for his sword the moment I rush him—which is perfect, because it leaves the umbrella up for grabs. I snatch it by the handle and yank it from his grasp, then bolt back to Fitz's side. She gets about half a syllable into questioning me by the time I snap it open with one hand and grab her by the waist with the other, tugging her under its shelter.

"Banded faithful overhead," I mutter through my teeth.

The tension doesn't leave her, but it melts to fit a new shape as her suspicion shifts from me to the tiers above.

"It, uh, it doesn't rain in the settlement," Ham says from behind us, his tone teetering between outright confusion and something that verges on relief.

Belatedly I realize how fucking *weird* this must look to him. Our dirt-stained jumpsuits work in our favor, but the combination of Fitz's platinum-blond cascade of hair and my limp, red-brown crest is too distinctive from overhead. An umbrella might be out of place at the moment, but it protects us from worse problems. Only, I'm not sure the tradeoff of Ham's suspicion is worth it. Now we have to come up with an explanation that sounds plausible.

"There are banded faithful overhead," Fitz tells him.

Or we could do that.

"You've seen the banded faithful already?" Ham asks, easing up behind us to peer up into Southeast Stair's towering majesty. "I don't think I came face-to-face with one until months into my time aboard."

Fitz casts a glance my way, bracing for an interruption that isn't going to come. Yes, it's probably me the banded faithful are after, and I have a thing or two to say about it, but Hark's drilled one rule into us above all else. When a scheme is on a tightrope, the person who talks first is the only one who gets to keep talking. The easiest way to unravel a lie is to open it up to discrepancies.

"I'll confess I don't completely understand it," Fitz says. "So they're . . . cultists?"

"They worship the *Justice*," Ham says. He's let his sword fall back in its sheath, and he looks surprisingly relaxed. "Not the ship, but the intelligence at its heart. They do its bidding."

"What does it . . . bid, generally?" Fitz asks, her eyes glancing off mine just long enough to make sure I'm not going to step on her toes.

"No one's totally sure. When they're out in the main body, it's usually to take in supply drops or maintain the *Justice*'s systems, but they spend most of their time in the heart of the ship—the old command core. They don't let anyone through who's not . . . affiliated." He wiggles his fingers at his forehead. "They claim it's the height of Ybi imperial warfront luxury up there. The ship in its original configuration, with the heart of their god at its center. So maybe they're just enjoying that while the rest of us try to make something of ourselves."

The bitter note in his voice is encouraging. "So that's why you think people join up?" I blurt.

"People align with power, wherever they are," Ham says, something shuttering in his face. "The *Justice* grants them fine armor and even finer vestments. Pray you never get close enough to find out how good their blades are—they're crafted by the ship's loyal forgemasters. It's hard to come by materials of that quality aboard the *Justice,* so that alone is enough for some people. Means you'll be able to protect yourself against anyone who comes at you."

"Ever thought about signing up yourself?" Fitz asks mildly. I tense.

But Ham only shakes his head with a dark chuckle. "I'm nothing special to begin with. Dunno what the ship could possibly want with me. I mean, you saw me. A full year of Blade-sworn training and the first contract I land?"

"Potato guard," I say with a nod.

"When the *Justice* recruits, it only wants remarkable people."

I shouldn't take that as a compliment, but there's something warming in me, something that makes me deathly terrified of whatever look Fitz is fixing me with out of the corner of my eye. We both know that the most remarkable person to board the ship today couldn't possibly be me. But that gives me an idea, one that might keep Ham from circling back to the troublesome bit where we already knew what the faithful were. "The people we're trying to find—Hark and Bea. They're remarkable. You don't think . . ."

"It's unlikely, but not impossible," Ham says. "I've heard from other Blade-sworn on the ingest circuit that sometimes the banded faithful will ride out in force to bring a new person directly into the fold. Don't even give them a chance to see what other choices are available to them—they just grab 'em and bring 'em straight to the core."

Well, that doesn't track at all. Granted, the banded faithful we met at East Deck seemed intent on pulling something similar, but the fact that we made it to East Deck in the first place means the playbook's a little different. And every time the *Justice* has deigned speak to me, it's sounded like it wants me to *choose* it.

Can't exactly bring up that sticking point with Ham. Or Fitz, for that matter. But I need to keep them talking.

I wonder if Fitz has realized why yet.

"If they got Hark and Bea, they'd take them to the command core, right?" I ask. "So then we'd have to follow them there."

Ham lets out a snort. "Yeah, good luck with that. Unless one of you can fly a shuttle, that's probably not going to happen."

My stomach drops. "The core's not part of the ship?" We didn't get a good look at the thing on our way in, on account of being cuffed to our seats in the hold, and my brief glimpse on my escape attempt only showed me the *Justice*'s massive, curved flank. I've been basing all my assumptions about the *Justice*'s true shape on its rotational gravity system, assuming it was laid out like Pearl Station's colossal spinning cylinder.

Ham shakes his head. "They're free-floating. Suspended in the middle of the ship's hollow." He draws a circle with one hand, then points at the space in the center. "Only way to access it is to use one of the shuttles on the upper decks, and obviously those are locked down tight. Faithful only."

I grit my teeth. When Hark confessed she had no plan, she said she needed to get to the core of the intelligence to figure out our escape. It was already complicated enough when we barely knew the terrain we were working with, but if we have to somehow hijack a shuttle from the banded faithful—

It's not your place to be making the plans, I remind myself. What matters right now is getting to that music festival so we can reunite with Hark and Bea. Hark will have had a whole extra day to put something together. She'll probably know about the shuttles already. She'll probably have a plan to steal one and a backup plan on top of that. Once we've secured a shuttle, all we need is Bea at the helm.

This can work. This has to work.

"Why are you smiling?" Fitz mutters.

"It's coming together," I reply.

"Except for the part where we're stuck under this umbrella, standing out in the open," she counters.

"Give it a minute."

Fitz does not give it a minute—she gives me a bug-eyed look.

I raise one hand, gesturing out to the looming overhead lights that cast a glow down the open shaft. I let it fall slowly, and with it, the day inches ever so slightly toward night.

The corner of her mouth twitches toward a scowl, and I know for sure she's caught my drift. Of course she wouldn't have noticed it first. She grew up on a planet, where light fluctuates on a sine wave determined by a ball of flaming gas billions of kilometers away. Me, I grew up on a station, where circadian cycles are governed by the shifting of artificial light. Night comes on a little faster when you don't need to wait for a sun to set. A few minutes ago, the overhead area lights had started to dim. In a few more, we should hit full "darkness," where the only illumination will come from individual lights.

Under its cover, we can move freely. Those stupid little halos the faithful wear have two handy pluses for us. First, they've got to be absolutely horrendous for their wearer's night vision. Second, we're going to be able to see them coming from a kilometer away.

Which leaves us with just one pressing problem. I glance sidelong at Ham. Our questions were enough to get him off the scent, but sooner or later he's going to start putting together the information we gave him. How far can we get with him before that happens?

This is everything Hark was supposed to be teaching me, everything I was trying to become. Not someone who tackles a mark in the mud and tries to steal his blade but someone who dances him elegantly through the steps of giving me everything I want.

As the lights dip lower, I swing down the umbrella, shake it closed, and press it back into Ham's hands. "Lead the way, then," I tell him. It's exactly the kind of line Hark would have used—a ceding of control on the surface, but below that, a command.

And maybe I'm doing something right, because Ham follows it without question.

FINDING A PLACE TO SLEEP in Southeast Stair is a remarkably civilized affair. The *Justice*'s population, according to Ham, has a natural tendency to fill the space of its container, and the ship is *big*. Even with a surplus of people converging on the neighboring deck for tomorrow's festivities, there are plenty of unoccupied dwellings in this settlement that serve as no-strings-attached shelters. A key's hung up by the door. You take it, add it to your chain, let yourself in, and the place is yours for as long as you need it.

Naturally Fitz snatches ours before either Ham or I can beat her to it. I purse my lips as she snaps it onto the Envoy's chain, but I suppose that's the safest place for it. As she bends low to slip it into the keyhole, I peer surreptitiously at the clasp mechanism on the chain for no particular reason.

Ham seems a second away from realizing what I'm doing, so I switch my attention out to the grandeur of Southeast Stair. We've ascended a couple tiers, giving us a sweeping view of both the settlement nestled along the walls and the majestic network of bridges hung from the column in the middle. The darkened area lights make it difficult to pick out the line between the *Justice*'s original design and the additions hacked together by human ingenuity. "What was this space originally?" I ask.

"That beam right there is one of eight major spokes that provide structural support for the ship's wheel," Ham replies, sketching two crosses in the air with his fingers to illustrate. "One for each cardinal direction, one for each ordinal. Back in the warship days, it would have been inspected regularly, but since it had no bearing on the ship's intelligence, it was never integrated into the systems. So when the ship started its crusade after the Ybi collapse, some of the earliest inhabitants realized these support struts were the easiest place to get away from the intelligence's constant observation."

"Easy, huh?" I hum, eyeing the structurally precarious tiers bolted into the walls. "And what happens if there's a grav-out? Those lifts look like they're entirely dependent on their counterweights."

"Hasn't been a single grav-out since I came aboard," Ham replies. "The intelligence may be a pest, but it keeps things running smoothly."

There's something in his words that stings, something that gnaws at my guts like guilt. This place was built to be a haven from the *Justice,* and thanks to us, they've just had an incursion of banded faithful running amok through their peaceful settlement.

Hark would chide me for feeling guilty before wary, but wary's fast on its heels. We shouldn't waste any more time out in the open. With one last look at the settlement's magnificent vista, I duck into the dwelling after Fitz.

It's startlingly cozy inside for a space assembled from repurposed military quarters. The furniture has a handmade quality to it—not shoddily constructed, but clearly built by people who had to improvise around a lack of tools. There's a large futon that seems to be able to fold down into a bed, plus a couch, a kitchenette area, and a door toward the back that leads to a bathroom.

I bolt for it. If Fitz gets in there first, it's going to be ages.

Behind the safety of a locked door, we sink into a routine so familiar this might as well be another hotel room in another corner of the galaxy that needed swindling. Hark would usually post us up in plush accommodations—always spacious, but always the four of us to a single suite. Less opportunity for things to go sideways when we only had to account for one shared space. Fitz and I locked in the footwork of this dance long ago, the art of ignoring each other in such close quarters.

Ham's thrown a variation into the rhythm, but not by too much. He's not as in dire need of a shower as the two of us, so he occupies himself in the kitchenette in the meantime, taking inventory of the packed meals stocked in the cold locker. "I'll take the couch," he offers. "You two can split the futon."

There's no way to decline that without making us seem even weirder, so I just nod, accepting the tower of food containers he hands me. Inside, I find protein strips—passably flavored, but tough and chewy from preservatives—and an assortment of vegetables that must come fresh from the fields we've spent a good part of our day trudging through. It's not quite the splendid feast we got in East Deck, but after a long, terrifying day, it's just as welcome.

By the time Fitz is done in the bathroom, I'm sprawled on the far edge of the folded-out futon, my eyes blurring from exhaustion. Not even my guilty conscience over our safe little refuge is enough to keep me from plunging haphazardly into sleep before she sets herself primly down on the other end of the bed.

I wake to the darkness of deep night and the click of the dwelling's front door slipping shut behind Ham.

CHAPTER 13

I ease off the futon and tiptoe over to the door, peering out the blinds. In the faint glow of the local lights, I can just make out Ham's large shadow stealing across one of the bridges toward the central stairs.

"Murdock?" Fitz asks blearily, rolling over to squint against the soft beam of light that cuts into the room and spills across her eyes.

"He left us," I hiss.

Fitz's brow wrinkles, and I'm momentarily distracted by the absolute disarray of her face, mapped with red lines from where it's been pressed into her pillow. Is that *drool* at the corner of her mouth? She usually sleeps like a statue, but I guess we've had a bit of a day. "Fine," she huffs at last. "Lock the door and let me sleep."

"We can't just let him leave. We had a deal. He was supposed to be our guide."

"It was only a matter of time before he realized how bad of a deal that was. Now he gets to go his own way, and we're only out a single key."

"This whole thing was your idea. We need him," I argue. "He's been nothing but helpful."

"Yeah, and now he's ditching us," Fitz groans, burying her face back in her pillow. "He's on this ship for a reason, Murdock. Ever think of that?"

That—that gets right under my skin. The *Justice* has been trucking around the galaxy for centuries, wreaking its misbegotten crusade against so-called sinners. Fitz *knows* it's absolute horseshit. She's seen how criminal-justice systems get built around punishing people for their circumstances. She should know better than to write Ham off like that.

At the same time, there's a reason the Envoy's most important question was about our past sins. For all we know, our new best friend could be a mass murderer.

"I'm gonna go see what he's up to," I declare, crossing back to my pack to dig out my spare jumpsuit.

Fitz tilts her head enough for a one-eyed glare. "At night? Alone? When the banded faithful were just here?"

"Yeah, I guess."

Fitz mutters something that sounds suspiciously close to *your funeral.*

I shrug the jumpsuit up over my shoulders, then hesitate. Original colors stand out, and this one hasn't been gummed up with vent dirt or doused in wine yet. Instead, I wrap the sleeves around my waist. Hopefully it's enough to break up the outfit, to make it not as obvious that I'm wearing the clothes I came aboard with. I tuck my dagger in my belt loop, then slip Fitz's flashlight out of her pack and slide it into my pocket.

"You can lock the door behind me if it'll make you feel better," I tell her.

I'm barely two steps outside when I hear her take me up on it.

From the edge of the tier, I manage to spot Ham right as he gets off the staircase. I wait until he's made his way through the common space down below, note the tunnel he disappears into, and then take off across the swaying bridge, ducking low and keeping my steps light. Part of my brain is absolutely screaming at the prospect of fording the *Justice* after dark completely alone.

The other part has something to prove. Ham said this was one of the most established settlements on the ship—one of the first places people took refuge from its constant surveillance. It stands to reason that in the past three hundred years, its residents have extended that dark zone wherever possible. That's why the ship sent the banded faithful to see where it couldn't, after all.

So as long as I pay attention and watch my step, I may be able to stay beneath its notice.

No one else is out and about this late at night, making it remarkably easy to lock onto Ham's trail. I let him stay a few corners ahead, tracking the dim light he carries and scanning for sensor boxes before I round any new corner. True to my suspicion, all I turn up is blank spaces where they've been hacked out of the wall. Every new gaping hole lifts my spirits a bit more. Maybe it's possible to survive on this ship in the emptiness people have carved for themselves.

But that sounds suspiciously close to long-term thinking I can't afford. The goal is to get *off* this goddamn ship, not figure out how to survive its weirdness. Hark would tell me to focus on the mission.

Hark would also probably tell me not to go skulking through dark halls late at night on a whim. But I find that as I go, it's nowhere near as terrifying as I expected. Any reasonable person is asleep at this hour, and a glowing halo will be obvious enough to help me steer clear of the unreasonable ones. There's no surveillance network to speak of in these reclaimed corridors, and the maze of shuttered doors and halls feels comfortingly familiar. When I was a teenager, I'd sometimes go wandering Pearl Station's main concourse in the middle of the night cycle, trailing my fingers over grated shop fronts and ducking my way through security networks. My loneliness felt better when the station was empty to match.

That thought lands dangerously. It almost makes this place feel like home.

I round one more corner only to realize that Ham's reached his destination. A vaulted atrium opens up at the far end of the hall, lit by area panels overhead that cast a cool, blue approximation of moonlight. On the far side of it, Ham is locked in a rapid conversation with a Blade-sworn who stands guard in front of yet another door. I creep closer, tucking myself against the frame as I strain to hear. Ham seems almost . . . *flustered,* and he's gesticulating with something clenched in his fist.

In the low light, it's difficult to make out, but I've got a guess.

The Blade-sworn keeps shaking their head, and though their tones are too hushed for me to follow the conversation, the most forceful one to rise out of it is a repeated "No." Ham's not happy with it, but he doesn't seem like he's going to pull out his sword and start making demands.

I'm so fixated on the drama that I almost miss the whisper of movement overhead. A series of catwalks span the atrium, carving the moonlight panels up into slices. Silhouetted against one crouches a lithe figure in a pearl-white cloak, her halo's gleam blending seamlessly into the glow behind her. Even in the blue cast of the light, her bright-red curls are unmistakable.

She's looking right at me.

I fumble for my dagger, but Scarlett shakes her head, raises a finger to her lips, and—

It's difficult to tell at this distance, but I'm almost certain she *winks*.

Before I can figure out what to make of that, she steals across the catwalk, disappearing into a tunnel overhead.

I bite down on a curse, backing into the darkness of the hall. All the confidence of my earlier saunter through the *Justice* has evaporated. I need to disappear. Fast, before she can catch me.

A door in the wall cracks open, a spill of crisp white light slicing out.

I lunge for the handle, wedging the full force of my weight against it, but Scarlett gets the toe of her boot in the gap before I can slam it shut in her face. Through the crack, I can see her violently blue eye, the pupil gone pinpoint-small against the light from her band as she peers through at me. "I just want to talk," she purrs.

"Heard that before," I whisper back.

"Wanted to say I'm sorry for earlier."

Somehow I doubt it. "If you were really sorry, you wouldn't be following me."

The edge of a smirk peeks through the gap. "I wasn't following you. I love a good ringside nighttime stroll. I don't get the opportunity often. Boss keeps me busy, you know," she says with a tap of her band. "This is pure chance. Fate, if you're into that kind of thing."

I don't buy it for a second, but there's something uncomfortably earnest in her tone. "The *Justice* just lets you . . . wander around in the dead of night?"

"The *Justice* isn't a punishing taskmaster. We're not helpless in its thrall. Sounds to me like you're projecting." I open my mouth for a sharp retort, but Scarlett shushes me, her gaze darting slantways toward the opening at the end of the hall.

"C'mon, stop making this harder than it has to be. I'm not gonna drag you away."

"You came after me with a sword."

"It was a bit of drunken fun. Seriously, stop jamming the door. It's bad for the mechanism."

"I'll show you bad for the mechanism—" I mutter, but before I can make good on it, Scarlett shoves hard, jarring the door from my grip and allowing it to nestle back along its track. I fumble for my dagger, staggering to the other side of the hall, but Scarlett doesn't cross the threshold.

"Being faithful is an invitation to explore the *Justice*'s larger mysteries," she says, tipping her head as she leans against the doorframe. "But I don't think God's gonna be mad if I give you a sneak peek."

She beckons.

After a few solid seconds filled by nothing but bug-eyed silence, I finally whisper, "*Why?*"

"If you're gonna be creeping around at night, I might as well show you the best way to do it. These passageways span the entire ship, and only the faithful have access. Well, only the faithful and very special guests."

"No—I mean—why would I ever do that?" I twitch my dagger emphatically at her, and the beckoning hand dances up into a defensive gesture. "How do I know you're not gonna drag me off to join your little cult?"

She gives me a sly look. "Because it's gonna be so much more satisfying to win you over for real."

"Not happening."

Scarlett tilts her head, pouting. It's cute, but nowhere close to effective when I'm used to watching a master like Fitz work—or maybe it's just that trying to flirt on behalf of a rogue warship intelligence is always going to be a losing game. "So incurious," she drawls. Her eyes unfocus for a moment, and my gaze darts up to her headband. "This was the easy way, for the record. It's the hard way from here on out."

Before I can figure out what she means by that, Scarlett tips a cheeky salute at me and winks as the door snaps shut right in front of her nose, dousing the hall in a hollow darkness.

CHAPTER 14

I blink, the tip of my dagger wavering downward. My heart feels like it's hammering loud enough to be heard from where Ham and the Blade-sworn are still arguing obliviously, and my legs are shaking so badly I find I need to lean back against the wall behind me for support. I have no idea how to parse what just happened. I just know it's bad news.

As I contemplate what Scarlett might have meant by *the hard way*, a paranoid notion seizes me. I thought Fitz would be fine if I left her back in the room, safe behind a locked door. But if the banded faithful know I'm here, if the *Justice* knows I've left her behind—

Come on, another part of me argues. *It's Fitz. What would you really lose?*

Hark's respect, I immediately counter.

"*Fine,*" Ham whisper-shouts from across the atrium, and I lunge down the corridor, flattening myself into the shadows around the jamb as I tuck my dagger back into my belt. His heavy footsteps approach, his backlit shadow looming down the hall.

He strides past me without noticing, and I let him get a solid two meters ahead before blurting, "Weird little midnight stroll, buddy."

Ham startles, one hand grappling for his sword as he clutches the other close to his chest and whirls on me. "Murdock," he seethes. He barely relaxes.

"So what's that key for?" I ask, nodding to the fist he's formed around it.

"None of your business."

"We paid that as collateral for you to protect us, so it quite literally is," I reply, sauntering closer. My heart's still pounding from the run-in with Scarlett, but at least now I've got a big, bad Blade-sworn to watch my back.

Even though said big, bad Blade-sworn looks like he's seriously considering following through on drawing that sword. "The hell are you thinking, sneaking around in the middle of the night?"

"All the cool kids are doing it." I pull up at his shoulder and offer him a grin worthy of Fitz on a job.

And maybe I've learned a thing or two, because it gets an edge of a smile out of him. "I'm sorry I snuck out on you like that," Ham says, letting his sword go so he can rub sheepishly at the back of his neck. "I guess I can't blame you for being suspicious."

"You can make it up to me by telling me what the hell you're up to," I counter.

Ham lets out a long sigh. "Walk with me," he mutters. "It's best not to linger."

We make our way back to Southeast Stair in near-intolerable silence. It only gives me more time to stew and jump at shadows, but at least I've got Ham for backup if anything decides to lunge out of them at me. I keep checking over my shoulder as we go, but if there are more banded faithful dogging my footsteps, they're being sneakier than Scarlett was.

When we finally emerge into the towering shaft that houses the settlement, Ham sighs again. "Look, you know why everyone who's here is here," he says. "Some way or another, the ship decided they deserved it. Not everyone agrees, but for me . . . it's kinda true."

Don't go for the knife, dipshit, I tell myself, but I can't help the tension that sparks through me. After my scrap with him earlier, I know what happens if I tangle with this man. Instead, I let him find the words in his own time.

"I . . . I might as well just say it," Ham huffs, his eyes downright haunted. "I was working for the Moon Eater."

I blink, struggling to wrap my head around what he's just confessed. As an accessory to a galaxy-hopping crime spree myself, I've started to pick up on the other notorious names in the game, but the Moon Eater is on another level. Hark and the rest of us, we never got press. Obviously by design—we were a rotating system of aliases whispered back and forth between paranoid would-be-investors, always too difficult to pin down into something that could score us a reputation. But there are some folks out in the galaxy who want the notoriety. People who want to be branded in history textbooks and reviled for eternity.

And, well, with a name like the Moon Eater, you can't go wrong.

"I thought the Moon Eater got caught ages ago," I mutter, glancing sidelong at Ham. His boyish earnestness doesn't match the timeline I'm juggling at all.

"Four years ago, to be precise. And I was with him. And it was kind of my fault."

My stomach drops, and I shift uncomfortably, staring up at the twisting shape of the support column and its bridges. "You

got him caught?" I ask, my voice strained as if *I'm* the one con-
fessing guilt.

Ham's lips crumple, pursed around a bitter truth. "It was
after he ate Igol's moon—or, well, after he'd stuffed his mouth
full of regolith and then detonated a nuclear warhead, you
know the drill—"

"No, no, go back. You're telling me the Moon Eater actually
ate the moons he nuked too?"

"It's a weird dominance thing. I don't want to get into it.
Anyway, after that we were on the run. I was driving the getaway van, he was screaming in my ear, the local enforcers were
hot on our tail, and it was . . . It was all happening too fast. And
there was too much going on, and I know these are all excuses,
but I took a turn too hard, and there was another vehicle coming on around the corner, and we were larger. Had more mass.
Hit it with everything we had. The family inside didn't stand a
chance."

A heavy silence settles over us, punctuated only by the distant rumble of one of the lifts churning upward. Ham's eyes
drop closed.

So he's not quite a murderer, but maybe I wasn't too far off
on that track.

"The crash didn't kill us, but it ended the pursuit right then
and there," Ham continues. "Enforcers locked us up in Igol's
supermax. The only charge they could assign to me immediately was the vehicular manslaughter—the rest was tied up in
the complications of the Moon Eater's case. There isn't really a
penal code for *accessory to moon-eating,* I guess. Multiple planetary
jurisdictions wanted a piece of him. We spent a year in jail,
bouncing between various hearings, listening to people squab-
ble over who got to do what to us. And then one day, the *Justice*
showed up in orbit over Igol, and the next, the supermax got
emptied into it."

Several things about Ham are starting to click into place all at once. I've been trying to figure him out all day, but I didn't know what to make of his strange peace with his circumstances and how easily he allowed us to twist them. I figured it was a side effect of enough time spent aboard this ship, but it seems to go deeper than that. Before the *Justice,* Ham was bracing for a lifetime of punishment for his sins. Within the walls of this ship, he's found a freedom he never could have imagined.

"So if you're here, then the Moon Eater is . . ."

Ham lifts his fist and unfurls his fingers around the key. "Gravity pulls in more than one way on the *Justice.* The violence drags you down to live with the scavs in the outer ring, and choosing to build secures your footing higher up the tiers. But sometimes people fight that gravity. Sometimes people have the charisma and the force of will necessary to keep themselves afloat and climb higher."

I know a thing or two about charisma and force of will. An unpleasant line of thought tugs at me. If Hark weren't trying to put together a plan to escape this ship, how high could she climb? I'm not sure I want to know.

"When I first came aboard the *Justice,* I realized that being ingested had effectively erased the barriers between me and the Moon Eater, and that the Moon Eater was going to take full advantage of that," Ham continues. "He, uh, he swore he was going to eat me—his revenge for ruining his life. So I ran like hell. Lost track of him for a bit, got myself taken in by a nice settlement a few spokes over. Then word drifted over from East Deck about a recent ingest who'd risen in the ranks of the public servants over there and secretly . . . well, there were dis-appearances, and they discovered his tastes, and they real-ized . . ."

Ham swallows thickly, folding his fist back around the key.

"Part of building a society is deciding what to do with peo-ple who make it dangerous. For East Deck, that means either banishment or containment, depending on the sort of threat you pose. They've built out a jail within the prison of this ship for the latter purpose, and after they figured out what the Moon Eater was up to, they marched him right in. Locked him in a cell purported to only have a single key, which the Envoy of East Deck took personal responsibility for. Up until, of course, *someone* stole it."

"Let me be clear, that someone is Fitz, not me," I reply, holding up my hands.

Ham shakes his head, a bitter smile twisting his lips. "I helped them put him away a second time. Gave them all the backstory on what kind of strange, twisted man had wormed his way into their midst. I thought if they could guarantee he'd stay locked up, maybe I could move on and make something of myself on this ship. Then the two of you showed up with that key on your chain, and I just . . . I had to be sure. So once I was certain the two of you were sleeping soundly and safe, I went to check."

"That was the jail within the jail then? Back there with that Blade-sworn?"

"Yeah, they were being a bit of a dick. I mean I get it. Most people around here know I used to be . . . *his*. So they're not too keen on me checking in, even if I swear it's just because I want to make sure he's not going to eat me anytime soon."

My eyes go to the hilt of the sword strapped across his back. On the one hand, I get it. If someone had vowed to eat my flesh and I had reasonable assurance they weren't joking, I'd arm myself too. But arming yourself is one thing—becoming a Blade-sworn seems to be something else entirely. "That, I get," I start, setting off for the central stair that will take us back up to the tier where Fitz is happily sleeping through what's shaped up to be an incredibly interesting night. "But why did we find you in a potato field? Why are you helping us—I know, I know, the key," I add as Ham's brow wrinkles like it's obvious. "I guess I just don't get the whole Blade-sworn thing. The more we've moved through the *Justice,* the more possibilities I've seen. So why choose that?"

I expect him to curl in on himself at the questioning, but something about it puts some mettle in him, drawing him up straighter as he trudges up the stairs behind me. "I was ready to rot in Igol's supermax," he says. "The Moon Eater was safely locked away, and all I had left to focus on was accepting what I owed to the galaxy after the harm I caused. Five people are dead because of me. Two parents. Three children. Nothing I do can bring them back, and no amount of restitution I could provide their extended family could make up for what I did. In supermax, all I had to give was my time. But on the *Justice,* there's more I can give, while there's strength in me. I can protect people."

"And potatoes," I interject.

"And potatoes," he adds with a self-deprecating scoff. "It took me a while to figure out how. The first year on the *Justice,* I was lying low, hoping the Moon Eater wouldn't find me. The second year, I was helping East Deck put him behind bars. And the third I spent training as a Blade-sworn. My first assignment after all of that was a bit of a letdown, I'm not gonna lie. So when you two came along, it felt like a calling."

I make a simpering noise, folding my hand over my heart.

"To be clear, because the two of you would probably end up dead without me," Ham retorts. "Seriously, wandering around late at night when you don't even know where you're going? It's a miracle you didn't get lost."

"Harsh, but fair," I reply as we finally hit the tier of our dwelling. I hesitate before the bridge, making like I'm taking in the majesty of the settlement as I scan for banded faithful, but no halos stand out in the darkness.

There's one more thing I want to ask him—and I want to do it before we're in earshot of Fitz. "How'd you fall in with the Moon Eater anyway?"

For a moment, I think I've forced too much nonchalance into the question. It's probably not a good memory for Ham, and from the way he shakes his head and stares at his feet, I might have shoved him squarely into the most shameful moment of his life. "I always blamed my luck, but that's not quite it," he says at last, coming to lean against the precarious rail separating the landing from the steep drop down the shaft. "The Moon Eater was charismatic. Magnetic. I was a kid, a big kid who didn't ask too many questions, and that was exactly what he needed. And when you're a kid, that's a hell of a feeling—being the missing piece in someone's plan."

I pause. I might not be breathing. I might tip over into the chasm. "I know what you mean," I mutter, my voice thin and choked.

"Yeah?" Ham asks, and the hope in it feels like a lifeline after the long, weird day I've had.

"One of the women we're chasing, Hark—she was like that for me," I confess. "I was a lonely kid on a space station, stuck doing work I knew was wrong for me, and she held open a door to the rest of the galaxy and said, *I can make use of you.* I've spent the past four years trying to be as useful as I could be, and somehow it ended here. She blames me for it—it was one of the last things she told me before we got separated. And if I could just get back to her, if I could just be *useful* again . . ."

I suck in a deep breath, feeling like I've just slit my belly open right in front of him. I've worked with Fitz for four years without knowing a single thing about her. I've known Ham for less than a day, and he gets my ugliest thoughts without even asking.

"She's never threatened to eat me though," I add. "I mean, there's a fun interpretation of that I wouldn't be opposed to, but—" I break off, dragging a hand down my face. "Holy fuck, I need to sleep."

Ham knocks his shoulder gently into mine. "Hey. Thanks for listening."

"You too, big guy," I tell him, stepping unsteadily onto the bridge. "Now, c'mon. Let's see how long it takes for Fitz to let us back in."

CHAPTER 15

I wake with a start, sprawled flat on the futon in a puddle of my own drool. My whole body feels like deadweight, and the light streaming in the room's front windows looks far too close to a midday setting for my liking. "How long was I out?" I groan, rolling onto my back.

Fitz is perched on the far end of the futon, fussing determinedly with a spot of dirt on her otherwise immaculate jumpsuit. She's clean, dry, dressed, and doesn't have a single strand out of place in the flawless fishtail braid she's woven her hair into, so I've already got a sense for how screwed we are when she replies, "About twelve hours."

It hits my blood like raw adrenaline. I kick free from the blankets, running a panicked hand over my hair. "And you just *let me sleep?*"

"You needed it," she replies without looking up.

"I got back in the dead of night. If you let me crash for twelve hours, that means this is—"

"Late afternoon, yeah."

"Which means Hark and Bea could already be waiting for us. We have to move. Fuck. Where's Ham?"

"Out," she says with a shrug.

I force myself to take a breath. Fitz already proved last night that she doesn't particularly care what happens to Ham. Or me, for that matter. She probably helped him sneak out without waking me. She's probably hoping he doesn't come back. She took her sweet time letting us in last night, to the point that I was genuinely terrified Scarlett might have gotten to her first. Or we might have been condemned to sleep on the stoop.

But at least if I had slept on the stoop, I would have woken when the area lights came on overhead. Not a full half a day later. Southeast Upper Limits is probably in full swing already and I'm not even dressed.

"Here," Fitz says, and tosses me an orange. "Ham grabbed some food from the community table out in the settlement. There's a plate for you in the cold locker," she continues, nodding to it.

The accusation I was going to hurl at her dies in my throat. She's as calm and detached as ever, but with fresh fruit in my hand, I can't tell her off for not caring. I dig a thumb into the peel, scowling as my stomach lets loose a gurgle that all but announces how easily she anticipated my needs. "The girl with the sword was following me last night," I announce as I strip away chunks of rind. "I think she tracked me all the way to the jail Ham was visiting. If he hasn't told you about that yet."

Fitz shakes her head, and I tell her the rest in between orange slices. At the revelation that Ham used to hench for the Moon Eater, Fitz tilts her head to the side, her lips pursed in thought, but she's not lunging up to bar the door just yet. "And he didn't spot Scarlett?" she asks once I'm done.

"No, he was busy arguing with the guard. But she said something about doing things the hard way from here on out. Whatever the *Justice* is going to try next, we need to be ready for it."

The moment the words leave my lips, it hits me all at once how much we need Hark. Moving on nothing but a vague command she left behind feels like fumbling through one of her schemes blindfolded. It's not like Vestal—one of the slickest cons we ever pulled, where we tricked our mark into thinking we were helping them take down one of their business competitors as we used the access they granted us to take them for everything they had. It's not even like Gest, where everything was moving exactly as ordained until it wasn't. We're split up, with nothing to go on but blood hastily sketched on a wall, and now we have to factor in the *Justice*'s ambiguous threat. The way's been plenty hard already. I don't want to know how much worse it can get.

I ease over to the kitchenette to wipe off my sticky hands and tuck the peels into the composter. When I turn around, Fitz is looking at me still. There's something of Hark in her gaze, that same steady evaluation that drives me out of my mind wondering what she sees in me. With Fitz, there's less guesswork. She's trying to figure out when enough is enough— when she ditches me as deadweight, leaves me for the *Justice* to snap up, and takes it upon herself to find Hark solo.

Maybe it's not such a bad idea.

"So the *Justice* knows where we are," I continue, heaving myself back from the precipice of that dark thought. "Even if it doesn't have eyes, it has spies. They're probably watching the door as we speak."

"Or having a conversation with Ham," Fitz adds.

"Or that," I acknowledge. I may relate to him a little too

much, but Hark would have me by the hair—and not in a fun way—if she caught me giving him the sad-backstory pass. That's elementary con work right there, buttering up a mark with sympathy. And though I think, deep down, Ham's trying to do right, he's also a confessed follower and has proven remarkably easy to sway.

The only thing he has going for him is that in the three years he's been aboard, the ship's never seen his value. If it does, we're in big trouble.

"Did Ham say when he'll be back?" I ask. Now that I'm listening for it, I can hear the distant, rhythmic thumping of a festival kicking into gear. I cross to the window and peer out the blinds. Sure enough, there's a steady flow of foot traffic winding toward the elevators that connect Southeast Stair to Southeast Upper.

"Shouldn't be long. He says things don't really get going until nightfall, and that gives Hark and Bea more time to get there and scout. We figured we'd let you sleep."

"Of course, that also gave you time to do your hair all pretty," I mutter under my breath.

"What was that?"

"I said it's a *pity* we're not there already," I amend. "Seriously, where did he go? And don't you dare say *out* again."

"Shopping," she says, which isn't much better.

BY THE TIME THE *JUSTICE'S* lights start to fade toward night, we're hanging the dwelling key on the ring outside its door with our worldly possessions packed up on our backs. Ham returned not long ago, laden with a plethora of dried food, a few rough-spun items of clothing, and two pairs of shockingly sturdy boots—sized perfectly, because the bastard had the audacity to barter my shoes off while I was sleeping.

It's a bit much to be carrying into a party, but Ham assures us that people who journeyed here for the festival are coming just as prepared. "This only happens once a year, and once everyone's gathered, no one's in a hurry to get back to their slice of the ring," he explained. "People usually stay a couple days."

We've changed into the new outfits he got for us, tucking the obvious blue and black of our original colors away in our packs. We look like proper *Justice*-dwellers in our patchwork faded fabrics stitched together from well-worn salvage. It won't fool the ship itself, but it'll force the banded faithful to do a double take, and that might be all we need to disappear into a crowd.

Plus, the loose-fitting cropped top he got for me is sleeveless, already a stark improvement from my jumpsuit. Fitz is less thrilled with her new outfit, picking unhappily at the fraying edges of the breast pocket sewn into her jacket. I wonder if it's the first secondhand thing she's worn since she left her homestake.

The slow-moving lift we take to the upper levels of Southeast Stair gives us a sweeping view of the settlement in the glory of daylight, and it knocks the wind out of me. If you'd told me we were on some far-flung station in the Known Harmony, I'd believe you. We rise up through tiers decorated as if people have been living there for generations. A few kids are out and about, playing on a platform that juts into the massive canyon of the stair, some of them careening a little too close to the rail for my already-sweaty palms.

I still can't get over the fact that there are kids in here. My education has holes here and there, owing to the fact that my mother prioritized learning how to scrape bankclip numbers over the ins and outs of sociology, but I know that generally people who have kids of their own volition only do it when they feel safe. And according to Ham, no one's being forced into reproducing here. Someone popped those little shits out by choice, because they wanted to. It goes against everything I thought the inside of this ship must be when I first came aboard.

This is a home. Maybe it's hell, too, but I always thought the two were mutually exclusive. These people have built such incredible things in spite of the monster that swallowed them. What would they build outside its shadow?

Even as the lights overhead fade, the heat climbs as we ascend, forcing Ham to unlace the sleeves of his shirt and shuck them off and Fitz to ease her collar open infinitesimally. At the top of the shaft, it's downright sweltering. More and more people have joined us over the course of the ride, crowding us out to the rails, and it's agony to wait for them to disembark. We press in tight on their heels into a long, narrow tunnel that bleeds off some of the heat until we emerge into another hacked-out space.

Far above, the ragged edges of walls drip from the ceiling, painted in brilliant, colorful lights that sweep across them from below. Beneath it lies a thicket of abstract shapes I barely recognize as a settlement until my brain latches onto what I'm seeing all at once.

"Are those *tents*?" I ask.

Southeast Upper reminds me of an early-stage homestake, strapped together from flimsy habs that barely shelter you from the weather. On a freshly settled planet, those things can be a death sentence, just asking for a sudden storm to rip them to shreds. But where homestake habs are crunched and protected, this settlement seems to have bloomed. They've sculpted plastic and fabric into a vibrant maze of dwellings and paneling that arcs overhead and glows from within.

The music's getting louder, and my heart quickens to match. I tug on Fitz's sleeve, pulling her forward and forcing Ham to jog to keep up as we join the crowd flowing into a tunnel that marks the settlement's entrance. Above, strips of what look like flooring safety lights wash us out in orange tones. Everything is strung together on wires that support the hab fabric, moving and flexing around us like a giant organism's gut tract. Or like a spider's web, I realize, as I get a better look at the system of tensions keeping the whole thing suspended. That thought itches. If there's a web, there could be something hunting within it. And we're walking straight into its snare.

We ease through what seems like a knot of dwellings, turn a corner, and brace against the overwhelming wall of sound as we emerge into the settlement's heart. At its core are the lights we saw tracing over the ceiling, their brilliant beams wheeling back and forth over the massive crowd. Fatima estimated that the *Justice* plays host to ten thousand people, and it looks like a significant number of them have flooded into the sprawling space, packed tight in an ocean of swaying limbs. A mainstage rises above the throng, where a band is playing surprisingly well-crafted instruments, their sound channeled into what has to be the most haphazard, hacked-together speaker setup I've ever seen.

"I think I know this song," I blurt, tilting my head as I try to place it. I glance sidelong at Fitz, wondering if she heard me over the torrential noise, but she's mouthing along. I nearly trip over my feet at the sound of her thin, lilting singing voice. I didn't know she sang—didn't know she cared enough to sing.

Fitz doesn't catch me staring until she stumbles over the lyrics, her brow furrowing as the band onstage diverges suddenly. "That's not how it goes, right?" she asks, and I can't tell if her nonchalant cool is a cover-up or if she doesn't realize I've just seen the equivalent of a show dog in a baby onesie.

I shrug. "I think it was a hit twenty years ago. They used to play it for crèche events on Pearl Station. But I could have sworn it was about dancing in the moonlight, not . . ."

"That'll happen sometimes," Ham interjects. "Most culture gets imported to the *Justice* through memory. Maybe whoever brought this song aboard didn't know the right lyrics—or maybe they just thought it sounded better this way. There's this one ballad I think the *Justice* version improves. Original was corny as hell, but whoever brought it aboard turned it into poetry."

The *Justice*'s surprises just keep getting more interesting. A flourishing artistic culture may have been the pinnacle of the pile of things I never could have expected when we got thrown aboard, but in some ways it makes sense. You can rob people of their futures, but you can't contain what they'll imagine in their place.

The crowd's energy is so infectious I can barely stand to be stuck on the fringes. Before either Fitz or Ham can stop me, I lunge forward, ducking around knots of people jumping, dancing, and shouting along to the music from the mainstage. Maybe I don't know the *Justice* variant of the song, but I find myself shimmying my shoulders to it all the same. Even better, I discover some sort of community tap people are thronging around, and before I know it, someone's pressed a frothy, cold drink into my hand. I take a cautious sip, then an enthusiastic gulp when I discover it's sweet, tangy, and strongly fermented. I down the rest before I can think twice.

A hand comes down on my shoulder, and I roll my eyes. "Murdock, what the hell do you think you're doing?" Fitz shouts in my ear.

"Blending in," I reply, waggling my empty cup at her.

Before she can fire back a retort, I latch onto the hand she's rooted onto my shoulder and pull her deeper into the crowd gathered around the mainstage. Fitz's protesting noises are swallowed by the swelling music, and she cranes her neck trying to keep sight of Ham. With his height, I can just make out his face over the bulk of the crowd, looking absolutely miserable at the prospect that he might have to join in.

I can't relate in the slightest. The *Justice* has surprised me at every turn, but this is the first time I've felt such uncomplicated *joy* aboard. The festival may be strange and crude, the music may be unfamiliar, and I may have no one but my most humorless co-worker to enjoy it with, but I'll relish it all the same. I can see why people traverse the entire ship just to be here. I bounce up and down, fighting Fitz's grip as I shout my best approximation of the lyrics I can remember into the mainstage's towering wall of sound.

"Murdock, *focus*," she snaps. "We're supposed to be looking for Hark and Bea."

I whirl on her, grabbing her by the collar and tugging her in close. Her eyes widen in a panic so obvious I wish I could savor it, but I lean around to her ear instead. "Hark and Bea are probably in this crowd. Take my pack and leave it with Ham at the fringes. You case the outside, I'll work through the denser part, and we'll regroup with Ham after a circuit. Don't you dare," I add, holding up a finger before she can make noise about how I don't give her orders.

"Wasn't what I was going to say," she mutters, swatting my hand out of her face. "Just . . . be careful."

"Worried about me?" I simper.

"Perpetually," Fitz deadpans.

"You're just mad we're finally at my kind of party," I reply, unshouldering my pack and handing it off to her. Before she can retort, I slip back into the swell of the crowd.

I've spent years clinging to Hark's sleeve as we minced through the celebrations of the rich and famous, feeling like I couldn't shake the stink of stationer trash no matter how nice of a suit or dress she bought for me or how much I tried to tame my hair. Hark made her best effort to polish me up, and I was never quite sure if it worked. But this party doesn't mind. We're all sinners, all condemned to the *Justice,* and we're all just trying to make something of it.

The spirit of *Enjoy it while you can* is more than enough of an excuse to circle back to the tap and draw an even deeper cup.

My head's starting to go a little fuzzy—apparently the approach to fermentation on this ship is *yes* and *more*—but I need the looseness the buzz puts in my gait. One of Hark's first lessons was about how to move through a crowd beneath notice, and I almost feel her matching my steps as I find my rhythm, flashing easy smiles and stepping lightly around knots of dancing folks.

I may never see a city skyline again. May never stand on the side of an ocean with my toes in the surf—something I never once got to do in all the years since I left Pearl Station. But I have loud music, sweet drinks, and the promise of so many surprises ahead of me, and it's almost enough to make me think the *Justice* might not be so bad after all.

A hand latches around my wrist. "I'm working on it, Fitz. Let me have my fun," I groan, whirling.

But the face that leers into mine isn't one I've seen before. Their eyes are caged behind some sort of monstrous helmet, dotted with ports and plugs that sprout from their brain stem. A slow, unnatural smile spreads across their lips as they loom over me, locking a hand over my mouth before I can scream.

"Murdock," the *Justice* says, its voice unmistakable even when produced by human vocal cords. "We're due for a chat."

CHAPTER 16

I should fight. I know I should fight, but the animal part of my brain that's born to worm out of traps is pinned by the throat, overwhelmed by the part that's too busy trying to figure out what I'm looking at. Without it, the *Justice* drags me easily through the frolic, hauling me into an alley just off the main thoroughfare.

"Did you think you'd escaped my notice?" it croons in my ear, crowding me back against a wall of hab fabric that sags under my weight. "Did you think I would let you go so easily?"

I dig my nails into the hands that pin me, but it only makes the strange, sly look on the person's face go stranger and slyer. "What the hell is this thing?" I croak, my eyes stuttering along the fraught line between the skin and the polymer casing locked along the top half of the person's skull.

"The banded faithful are good for legwork in the lower levels, but up here, where the signal's stronger, I can handle my affairs with a more personal touch," the *Justice* replies. "Scarlett could only deliver my message secondhand. I've given you the opportunity to hear reason. Allow me to introduce my more intimate measures."

So this is what Scarlett meant by the hard way. My gaze rolls desperately for the seething crowd outside. If I fight, if I scream, would they help drag me back to safety? Or would they cave to the god that rules this place?

I don't know if I want to find out.

"Just tell me what you want with me," I snap. I want to look at it dead-on, but I don't know where. There are cameras dotting the rig that encases the person's skull, but my gaze keeps dropping to the mouth, to the throat, to the means the *Justice* has found of speaking directly to me in a voice that's all too human.

"Just a conversation," it says. "Like we had before."

"No, *no*. This is *not* like the conversation we had before. That was in an airlock. You weren't—you couldn't touch me."

"Couldn't I?" it asks, then frees one of my wrists to reach up and cradle my throat. Its touch is just a shade too heavy to feel gentle, but there's a strange sort of tenderness beneath it. And it's warm, warm as life. "The second you crossed over into this ship, you placed yourself in my hands. Every breath you've drawn since then is because I allow it. Nothing's changed."

I sputter, all too aware of how easily the *Justice* could keep me from getting that breath back. "You know there's a difference. You're just playing with your food. Tell me why you're doing this."

"I think you already know," the *Justice* replies. "You've been on this ship for two days. You've learned its workings. You're clever enough to put together the systems that keep it running. And you, clever little Murdock, you know what it takes to keep those systems in place."

Through the adrenaline, through the hammering of my

heart, I'm starting to understand. The *Justice* is three hundred years old, running on machinery that's subject to the principles of entropy as much as anything else in the universe, and constantly fighting the innovation of its inhabitants. If it wants to maintain control of its contents and its constituent parts, it needs agents of its own to fight back. Hands to do the work its mind envisions.

I just don't see why it needs *my* hands in particular.

I didn't ask, but something in my expression must have asked for me, because the *Justice*'s grip on my throat softens to a caress. "The galaxy is rife with sinners, but some of them have their uses. Some of them come aboard ready to atone in acts of service. You could be one of them. You need only to accept the hand I offer."

I bite back the urge to remind it that the hand is currently poised to throttle me. "So I can *atone* for relieving the galaxy's wealthy from a few jiras they won't miss?"

"The rest of your life needs a purpose, doesn't it?" the *Justice* replies, leaning close to breathe the words over my ear.

I can't deny that it sends a shiver up my spine—one I'm not entirely sure is a bad thing. Wasn't I just admitting to Ham that I knew what it was like to *need* being needed? Before Hark's grand failure on Gest, I thought I could only get that validation from her, but now I find myself standing in the wreckage of my old life, wondering what I have to carry forward and what I can leave behind.

The thing is, ever since I came aboard, I've been all but magnetically drawn to the way this ship works, entranced by its component pieces, constantly trying to figure out their borders and shortcomings. The *Justice* sees potential for me to apply that knowledge, and the notion isn't exactly off-putting.

Only, that work would probably end up tearing down places like this. I know I can't afford to take my eyes off the predator caging me, but I can't help glancing back out at the festival, at its wondrous frenzy, at the first place on the *Justice* I felt uncomplicated happiness in *spite* of the god trying to woo me.

Studied from every angle beneath its array of cameras, I know I'm not getting away with the look. "You were having fun out there," the *Justice* notes. "I saw you. That's the first real smile I've seen on you since you came aboard. You think this is the highest pleasure this ship can offer? Wait until you see the core."

I keep my eyes fixed on the sliver of the alley's mouth.

"This little settlement is a bunch of scrap blown together by chance in the void left by something far greater. Imagine this ship's original glory."

"I dunno," I mutter hazily. "I kind of like it."

"Of course you do," the *Justice* says. "You're newly born into this world. You lack context. Once you ascend to the core, you'll understand what you have been missing. The majesty of Ybi imperial splendor and the beauty of the faithful assembled makes this froth look like a junkyard."

And suddenly I realize exactly where I've heard this kind of talk before. The *Justice* isn't a god—it's every wealthy mark I've ever met at a party, flaunting an ego on a planetary scale as they shit-talk everything but their own achievements. There's a part of me that's close to pitying this thing. People can grow and change. This monstrosity has its delusions of grandeur baked in.

The only thing stopping me is the hand on my neck.

"Say I come with you," I start, wriggling a little to test the *Justice*'s grip. "What's to prevent you from turning me into one of these meat puppets?"

At that, the *Justice* leans back, loosening its hold on my throat to tilt its hand in the slivers of projected light that flash intermittently down the alley. "It's a miraculous thing, isn't it? This used to be one of the highest honors the Ybi could offer to its loyal soldiers, the marriage of body and ship. I've had many of these constructs over the course of my centuries, and I have nothing but gratitude for them. How can I be a steward of sinners if I cannot walk as one of them? If I cannot know their pains, their . . ." It leans close again, and this time its touch is a whisper skating down my neck, settling over my left collarbone as it leans its knuckle into the hammering of my heart. ". . . pleasures?" it finishes with an empty smile.

I should have chugged a few more of those drinks when I had the chance. "But this body in particular," I counter. "This body is no Ybi sol—"

"This body was a *sinner*," the *Justice* snarls. A glimmer of red light catches in the camera lenses that loom over me, and its grip on my wrist goes painfully tight. "It was handed over to me, and it's mine to do with as I wish. I am *Justice*. I chose this person to be my construct, and it was deserved. But you, Murdock—you deserve something else. Something only I can offer you, now that you're in my care. You would be wise to accept it."

I hiss, my free hand scrabbling uselessly against the construct's grip. No amount of clawing will produce a pain response that changes the *Justice*'s mind, and I'm not strong enough to break the body's grasp. "If I was really under your power, you wouldn't have to make me choose," I grunt.

"Oh, Murdock." The *Justice* sighs. "If I can't make you choose, I don't deserve you."

"You're making a hell of a sales pitch, buddy," I snap. "*Ooh, come work for me so your life can have purpose again.* I have my purpose already, and nothing you could possibly say—"

It reaches down and grabs my hand, then wrenches both of my wrists up over my head, pinning them against the shockingly cold metal of a support strut. The leering grin has dropped from the construct's face, leaving it uncannily blank, almost *bored*. "Purpose means something else to a human mind. My purpose is greater than any individual desire. Centuries ago, I was tasked with building a galaxy in the image of Ybi glory. With that comes sacrifice—the sacrifice of everyone who would tear down that order. My task is simple. I collect the unsavory elements whose actions sow discord, whom society has already deemed worth locking away, and turn them toward the light of the Ybi. The work is crucial. It can only be carried out by the best. And from the moment I saw you, I knew you were one of those elite."

This, too, I'm realizing with horror, I've heard before. Heard from the center of my galaxy, from the woman who's left me reeling in her absence. Suddenly I'm thrown back to another hand on my wrist, another moment where I fought like a rat in a trap while someone looked at me and saw something worth keeping. Is the *Justice* seeing the same potential Hark saw? The same thing she tried to cultivate?

The same thing she discarded?

The ship can't read my thoughts, but I think it sees a realization in my eyes. "That's right," it whispers, crowding in close enough that with its chest against mine, I can feel a slow, steady heartbeat against my own rabbit-fast pulse. "You've always been clever. Always known whose skirts to cling to, whose coattails to ride. But what I'm giving you goes beyond that. I can give you a perfect forgiveness—the kind you so desperately need. I see the way you suffer, the way you deny both your own nature and the nature of your circumstances. The only cure is to look starkly at the truth and let it guide you, rather than wait for guidance from the person you've shackled yourself to. After all, people are fallible. Clouded by bias."

"Pretty sure you're as biased as they come," I scoff. "You're loyal to a dead empire's ideals. Delusional with them."

"I'm a machine, Murdock," it says. "I hold no delusions, only the reality I was built to process."

"That's the most delusional thing I've ever heard a machine say. You think you know me—you should know I'm a hacker. I *build* delusions into machines for a living. Nothing you say will convince me you're rational."

"But I don't need to be rational," the *Justice* replies. "I just need to be the most powerful hand outstretched to you. Like your beloved Hark used to be."

There's something about her name from its stolen lips that takes all the fight out of me. I didn't tell it a damn thing about how Hark and I met. Never said anything within earshot. It must have overheard Hark and Bea talking about me. It might have captured them already.

But if it had them, it would have led with that. She's the worst pressure point I have, and it knows that.

So it doesn't have them.

I brace back against the hab fabric, drop all my weight onto one leg, and wheel the other knee up into the construct's stomach as hard as I can. It gives a heaving wheeze, its grip remaining iron-tight and its face impassive. "Fight all you like," the *Justice* says. "Get it out of your system. I'll be back."

And with that, it lets go of my wrists. It dusts its hands off—a motion so useless to a machine that its affect is glaring—and leaves me sagging against the tent wall as it strides deeper into the dark of the alley. As the shadows begin to soak up the construct's figure, it pauses. "The difference between me and the woman you're looking for," the *Justice* says in a low purr, "is that my patience is infinite."

With that, the monstrous construct slips into the dark.

CHAPTER 17

I stay in the alley for a while, my knees pulled up to my chest, my head locked between them, begging my heart rate to settle. It won't. It can't. How can I possibly calm down, knowing that at any second, the *Justice* could double back and have its way with me, whatever *way* that is? All the freedom I thought I'd finessed, skipping around these glorious little settlements, is nothing but a long leash the ship's allowed me.

Furious tears are starting to burn my eyes, but I bite them back. I've never cried on a job, and Hark said this was a *job,* dammit. Just a long con we're running. Temporary. Not the rest of my life.

A shadow falls over the alley's entrance, and ice threads through my veins. "Come back to gloat some more?" I croak.

But the footsteps that come stumbling toward me—slowly, and then frantic, scrambling—are all too human. I lift my gaze as Fitz skids to her knees in front of me, and I swear in the low light of the festival's edge she looks almost . . . concerned. "The hell are you doing, Murdock?" she asks.

It takes me a moment to remember I was supposed to be casing the festival, searching for Hark and Bea in the crowd. I open my mouth, but my throat twitches against the tender skin where the *Justice*'s construct held me, and it steals whatever words might have come out.

Fitz's brow furrows. I brace for the blow—the way she'll berate me for going off-mission, the way she'll tell me this is why I couldn't be trusted on my own, why Hark was right to blame me for everything falling apart. But then her gaze homes in on my wrists and the furious red marks the *Justice* left there. "Who did this to you?" she asks, and though her voice is flat, free of affect, and classically Fitz, I swear I see a hint of boiling anger beneath her surface.

And because I've recently been informed that nothing matters, because my pride's in absolute shreds anyway, I fight past the burbling disgust in my throat, bend my head back between my legs, and tell the rivets in the floor beneath me exactly what's just happened.

By the time I'm done, Fitz has shifted over to join me against the tent wall, somehow managing to make the pose elegant with one arm folded immaculately over her knee. "That's awful," she says, laying a gentle hand on my shoulder.

There's something outright wrong about it, something that has me flinching away before I can really register *why*. It's not that she's trying to touch me right after the ship's manhandling. It's that the simpering note of concern in her voice is something I've only ever heard her direct at a mark. The moment that realization lands, I know it's unfair of me to make that comparison. Fitz has always held herself at a careful distance. I've never seen her *try* to be comforting—all I've ever known is her petty sniping. Who am I to reject her the instant she attempts something else?

At the same time, I think she's realized what she just did.

When I sneak a glance sidelong at her, she's back to that flat expression, her hand tucked in the cradle of her lap.

It's not what I want. Or at least, not what I need right now. So before Fitz can try a different tack, I grab her by the wrist and sling her arm around my shoulder.

"Murdock," she warns, testing my grip with a tug, but when I don't let go, I feel her relax. The whole of her side presses into mine as she curls her fingers carefully around my deltoid. It's barely comfortable, and I can't believe it's Fitz of all people who has to do this, but it's exactly what I need. A person at my side, not a construct puppeteered by a delusional intelligence—a person whose thoughts and feelings map one-to-one with their reactions to sensory input. And though I'm pretty sure Fitz's thoughts and feelings amount to *What?* and *Seriously?* and probably *Ugh, she smells,* it's enough. It's more than enough. My heartbeat is finally, *finally* dropping as it's forced to reckon with another human's pulse pressed against my side.

"This is . . . a ploy," Fitz says. For a moment, I think she means the fact that I've just shoved myself into her armpit, but she's staring into the middle distance, not fighting to put space between us. "First Scarlett last night, now this construct approaching you. What's it after?"

Maybe I left that part out. Maybe I'm not ready for Fitz to see me as a ticking time bomb, an inevitable collapse. Then again, she's always seen me as the weak link on the team. This wouldn't change a thing.

"The *Justice* is flirting with me," I manage. The marks on my wrists are evidence enough that "flirting" really isn't the right word—but it's the only one that makes sense. Makes me capable of working past the fact that it happened. "First it sent its friend to ask if I liked it. Then it came courting itself. I think it's playing hard to get now. Or at least, it wants me to think that. I don't trust it."

Fitz lets out a chuff. "Yeah, I wouldn't trust this antique either."

"Don't let it hear you say that. Might come back with a thing or two to prove."

I meant it jokingly, but a simmer's starting to kick up in my gut at the idea of the *Justice* looping back around for another pass at me. I try to remember every lesson Hark ever hammered into me about keeping your cool under pressure, but it feels useless sitting side by side with Fitz's unbreakable calm.

But Fitz, who's never once in her life let an opportunity to lord above me pass until about twenty minutes ago, keeps up this strange new habit. Instead of mocking the quiver in my lip, she tightens her grip on my shoulder. "Sometimes marks need more information to move. I don't know if it's the same with machines, but . . ."

"But you're saying it could be putting together a predictive model? Waiting to see what we do next so it can understand us better?"

"Exactly. So we need to be unpredictable."

"Right. So that it expects us to be unpredictable and builds contingencies for every move we can think of. Got it."

"Fuck off, I'm trying to be helpful. I'm good with people, not machines. You figure out that bit."

"Good with people?" I scoff, raising an eyebrow. "When it's for a job, sure. When Hark tells you to."

Her arm abruptly wrenches off my shoulder as she shoves to her feet. "Well, that was fun while it lasted."

"Hey, barring two seconds ago, you've never done a single nice thing for me in the entire time I've known you. I'm just calling it like I see it."

"Not true," Fitz mutters.

"Name one other time. Four years, Fitz. Four years we've worked together and it takes a spaceship pinning me to a wall to treat me like something other than dirt on your shoe?"

Fitz always takes time to chew and swallow her food. She sits with my words for a solid couple seconds as I pick at the knees of my pants, waiting to see what kind of knots she's going to twist herself into. "The orange," she says at last.

"The orange, seriously? You're trying to act like handing me *food* today is enough to outweigh everything else?"

Again, she bites her lip, her brows twitching toward a furrow as she mulls over whatever bullshit excuse is coming up next. "You're . . . You're all I have now."

I scoff. "So the only reason I'm worth anything to you is because I'm the only person you have left?"

"Stop framing it in the worst possible way."

"Stop being the worst."

"You were snuggling up to me two seconds ago," she snaps.

"Because *you're* the only person *I* have left," I shout. I should relish throwing the words back in her face, but all it does is reinforce the awful truth. We've survived four years together with the buffers of Hark and Bea between us. Hark would welcome me as a fellow infiltrator into the snobby upper echelons where Fitz resided, and Bea would remind me that the scuzz was plenty fun too. We've been separated from them for two days, and we haven't figured out how to stop ourselves from pulling each other's hair out. I rub the red marks on my wrists again, feeling my own helplessness starting to boil over.

"Well then, I guess we should get back to fixing that," Fitz says with a huff, staring back out at the festival crowd. "I did two extra circuits. One looking for Hark and Bea, then another when you didn't meet me back where we left Ham. No luck on either of them. I . . . I don't think they're here. I think they might be—"

"The *Justice* doesn't have them," I interrupt. "It would have used that when it confronted me if it did."

"But if Hark called D major—"

"Hark's probably just as lost as we are," I snap. "She doesn't know a damn thing about this ship, and she's out there some-where trying to figure out how to beat it. Maybe she's decided she doesn't need us to do that." A tremor's worked its way into my hands. I clamp them over my knees to stop from shaking. I remember this sensation from back on Gest, the way it felt when every avenue of escape was collapsing around us. Back then, at least I could put my trust in Hark and hope she'd figure something out.

Now that illusion's been shattered too—first by her own admission, then by the *Justice*'s hand around my throat. Fitz and I are helpless against the ship and useless without Hark to me-diate between us. If we try to go looking for Hark and Bea, we're only going to be more helpless and useless.

Maybe that's the first problem we need to solve.

I shove to my feet, jam my hands in my pockets, and start back down the alley, sparing a glance only for the darkness over my shoulder where the *Justice*'s construct disappeared.

"Murdock?" Fitz hazards.

"The *Justice* is going to expect us to keep hunting for Hark and Bea. It's going to use that to string us along. You were right earlier. We need to switch it up."

"And what does that mean?" she asks with appropriate cau-tion. This might be the first time I've ever admitted she was right about something.

"Means I'm going to have a chat with our good buddy Ham."

By the time we find him, he's finally warmed up to the party. Ham's waded into the thick of the crowd with both our packs slung over his back, bobbing his head along to the music from the mainstage as he grooves with the people dancing around him. His look of anxious terror has melted into calm—though when I tug his sleeve, he snaps out of the trance instantly, let-ting out a startled yelp. "No luck?" he shouts over the music after a moment to regain his cool.

"Change of plans," I shout back, pulling fruitlessly against his mass until he finally deigns to follow me out of the celebration. Once we're clear enough that I can speak normally, I square off to face him, plant my still-shaking hands on my hips, and declare, "I want a sword."

CHAPTER 18

We're in luck, Ham tells us as we leave the thunder of Southeast Upper Limits behind and make for a rickety access stair that's certainly not part of the *Justice*'s original schematics. There are four active forges aboard, all of them situated in the inner ring, but the one that made his weapon is the one closest to us.

The way he says it reminds me of Hark waltzing marks into traps. Once he'd realized I wanted a sword of my own, not the one strapped to his back, Ham tensed where he should have relaxed. There's something he's not saying—something he's waiting for us to discover. "I can take you to the Forgemaster," he tells us, "but I can't promise she'll make a blade for you. There are conditions you might not be willing to fulfill."

"You seem relatively intact," I reply, looking him up and down.

"I was lucky," Ham says. "Others haven't been."

"Couldn't you help prepare us for what to expect?" Fitz asks with that false note of honey in her voice. She's been bringing up the rear ever since we left Southeast Upper, keeping her usual silence. For once, I've been happy not to provoke her out of it.

"It's not my place to say," Ham replies. "The Forgemaster sets her prices. It's her business."

I snort. "Bullshit. Tell us what you paid."

"I earned it. That's all I'll say."

"Was it embarrassing?"

Ham huffs. "Would an *ounce* of patience be possible? You've got a long time aboard ahead, and you're gonna wanna learn to savor anticipation."

I know he means it in jest, but it hits like a body blow. I spent the first eighteen years of my life trapped on the same megastructure, waiting for the day I'd be free of it. I got four years out in the galaxy—four glorious years—before another monster came along to claim my remaining time. A single thing to look forward to would often be the buoy I clung to, keeping me going through the long years of waiting for my life to begin. Ham's not wrong—that'll save you when you've got nothing to do but spend time.

So I give him a rare mercy and shut the hell up for the rest of our trek. The lights plunge down to full night and then some as we make our way through the inner corridors of the *Justice*'s ring. They're more heavily trafficked than the ones we explored on the lower levels, and I notice with a creeping sense of dread that there's much more of the ship's original architecture left intact up here. The walls are crusted with that classical ceramic molding, and there are even a few places where it looks like it's been repaired, the color a brighter white against the weathered original.

The sensor boxes we spot shouldn't matter. The *Justice* has made it clear that it's waiting for my next move, and if it wanted to send the banded faithful after me, it would have done so a thousand times over. But it's not the potential for what the ship could do that's so unnerving—it's the fact that I can't escape its gaze.

Finally we pull up short in front of an intricately wrought door. The sight of it is a balm in the otherwise heavily Ybi corridor. The ornate black ironwork looks brutal enough to shatter fine ceramic, and it might be the most beautiful thing I've seen all day.

I reach down the front of my shirt and pull out the Envoy's keychain.

Fitz's nostrils flare like a bull's. "When—"

"When you were being a shit, when do you think?"

"That doesn't narrow it down."

"Exactly," I mutter, flipping through the keys as I search the door for its locking mechanism. I'm amazed she didn't clock it until now. I was worried my old pickpocketing skills had gone rusty after so much time in Hark's employ, but it turns out I've only gotten more finesse under her tutelage.

Ham taps me on the shoulder. "No keyholes on a forge door. They're opened at the discretion of the Forgemaster within. Let's hope she's feeling generous today."

I huff. I wanted to show off, but I'm forced to stand aside as Ham steps forward, reaches into the intricacies of the door's design, and pulls a small lever I would have taken all day to notice.

A disproportionately loud chime follows, sending reverberations through the corridor that pulse into the soles of my boots. A moment later, the door unlatches with a shuddering groan, its components peeling away one by one in an elaborate mechanical dance. Suddenly I miss Bea with the fire of a thousand suns, wanting nothing more than to dissect this master-piece of engineering side by side with her.

A wall of heat greets us as we step forward into the massive, gloomy chamber within. As soon as we're over the threshold, the door begins to creep shut again. I raise my fists, my eyes darting from looming shadow to looming shadow, but Ham nudges me. "Just a precaution. The ship's atmosphere can be fickle, so forges need to stay sealed behind blast doors at all times."

"I recognize that voice," someone calls from deep in the darkness. "Did you break your blade already, Ham?"

"No, Forgemaster," Ham replies, straightening like a school-boy caught passing notes. "I'm here to make good on my refer-ral."

"Well, let's have a look then."

Ham beckons us forward through the towering forge equip-ment. The air grows hotter and hotter with every step until at last we round a corner and discover the source. The heart of the forge glows a murderous red, and before it sprawls what looks like a hot tub, where a muscled older woman is reclining with a towel laid over her eyes. As we approach, she lifts a cor-ner of it to peer at us.

"Ingest, huh?" she grunts.

I glance down, wondering what could have possibly given it away. We're not clad in our original colors anymore, and I thought Ham picked our new fashion specifically to blend in.

"It's the bearing, kiddo," the Forgemaster says. "You don't move like anyone who's lived on this ship long enough. Kinda scrawny, too, aren't they, Ham?"

I bristle. "Never been much of a problem for me."

She lets out a sharp laugh, sitting upright, and it's a blessing the forge's heat has already put a flush in my cheeks because she's completely naked under the water's froth. "That's the right attitude—I'll give you that," she says as she eases out of the tub, wringing her long, gray-streaked black hair out in spatters that sizzle onto the floor surrounding her bath.

For a moment, I'm astonished anyone on the *Justice* could be so vulnerable. She let us in sight-unseen while she was relaxing naked in the bath. Then she reaches—mercifully, but disappointingly—for a robe and I spot no fewer than three blade hilts tucked beside it. From the musculature on her shoulders alone, I have no doubt she could put them to good use.

"Oh, stop with those dramatics," the Forgemaster chides, and I glance behind me to find Ham staring resolutely at the machinery on the ceiling. "I've told you before, it's a body. You've got one too. The *Justice* already got you—no one's going to imprison you again for looking."

"It's a matter of respect," he offers.

"That one respects me plenty and respects me well enough to admire what I've built," the Forgemaster replies, gesturing dismissively in Fitz's direction. She startles, and I feel like I've caught sight of a shooting star, the outstandingly rare moment Fitz is completely flustered. I don't blame her. The Forgemaster's a knockout—and a strongly worded reminder I need to get my upper body in shape. Especially if I'm going to be wielding a blade.

Ham finally unsticks his gaze from the ceiling when the Forgemaster ties off her robe. "I've brought them because they're interested in getting weapons made."

"Obviously," the Forgemaster replies, circling us as she eyes me and Fitz up and down. "Let me guess. Got properly spooked by the ship and decided you needed a blade to make it better?"

The note of disdain in her voice burrows into me like a needle. "It's not just that," I protest. "The ship . . . wants me. Wants me bad enough a sword might be the only way to get it to think twice."

It's desperate, showing my hand so early. It's not what Hark would have done, which I'm guessing is about eighty percent of the sharp look I get from Fitz. The other twenty percent I'll attribute to the fact that Ham is now looking extremely confused. We've told him only what we're running toward, not what we're running from, and I'm sure several things are clicking into place all at once. But the only look I care about is the Forgemaster's.

Hers is full of pity. "You and me, one-on-one," she snaps, flicking her dripping fingertips at Ham and Fitz to shoo them. Ham tugs on Fitz's sleeve, guiding her back into the depths of the forge. I'm a little offended at how easily she follows him.

Then the Forgemaster's hand lands on my shoulder.

I'm running out of excuses I can pin on the heat. Under her undivided attention, I'm going weak in the knees. This close, she smells like salt water, like all the oceans I'll never get to see. "I've been on this ship for twenty years," the Forgemaster says. "And this ship has been out to get me since my very first day on it."

The weight of her words might take the legs out from under me for good. I fight not to sway in her grip, fight not to *sob* from outright relief, using every trick Hark ever taught me to school my face as I croak out, "Really?"

"It learned I came from manufacturing before I was ingested. Pressed me to join its ranks from the moment I came aboard. It needs skilled hands. I'm assuming you picked up on that—assuming that's why it's after you too."

"I was a hacker in my previous life," I offer.

"Yeah, that'd do it," she says, tipping her fingers at her temple. "Anytime someone comes aboard with skills like that, the *Justice* bands them fast. When the deity in charge is an intelligence and you're intelligent around machines, you're either with it or you're the enemy."

"Suppose I chose enemy, then. Think a sword would improve my chances?" I ask with a strained chuckle.

"Well, you'd have the best chance of all with a band around your head, but somehow I'm picking up that it's not on the table, huh?"

The suggestion alone is enough to flood the back of my throat with the acid taste of bile. I glance around the forge, anchoring myself in the little paradise she's built. Despite the brutal machinery and sweltering heat, it's homey. Or maybe it reminds me less of a Ybi warship and more of Bea's garage. "You said the *Justice* has been after you for twenty years. Seems like you've made out all right."

The Forgemaster barks out a short laugh. "Sure. Paradise. You want to know the last time I walked beyond that door over there? I think it's been roughly three months now."

I gape.

"If I can get someone I trust here to secure the forge, I can take a bit of a sabbatical—at least as long as I can skate under the *Justice*'s radar. I've gotten pretty good at it. But in the end, the easiest way to protect yourself on this ship is behind a door that only you can open. I have arrangements with the nearby enclaves for food delivery in exchange for my skills and thieves contracted to steal antimatter pellets out of the *Justice*'s jump supply to power the forge. It's enough to keep me going."

My envy for the hot bath is piddling away by the second. "And you're all alone in here?"

She sighs. "After twenty years on this ship, you learn the hard way. People's loyalties are wagers, nothing more. The only sure bet is the one you put on yourself."

My thoughts stray inevitably to Hark. To the way we've hinged everything on the hope that she'll come up with a plan. The Forgemaster reminds me of her a bit. A Hark who never would have entrusted part of her schemes to me. A Hark who never could have been disappointed by me in the first place. "Well, about that bet on myself," I start, fighting back the dizzying chain of realizations.

The Forgemaster narrows her eyes. "A sword is only gonna protect you from so much," she says. "Weapons have weight on this ship. If they're not wielded deliberately, they let the chaos in. Are you sure you're ready to take up that responsibility?"

"I'm ready to stick a pointy end in anyone who tries to force me over to the *Justice*'s service."

She lifts an eyebrow. "If you're to carry my craft, I need to know how it'll speak for me. When I make weapons for Blade-sworn, I can trust they've been trained to treat my work with reverence. The ship's just as much my enemy as it is yours, but you haven't been aboard long enough to understand the honor systems that keep this place from collapsing."

I guess now isn't the time to tell her that we've already stolen an Envoy's keys, desecrated a couple corpses, and convinced a Blade-sworn to abandon his oaths. "I've been paying attention," I tell her instead. "Every settlement we've passed through—I've seen the silent compact at the heart of them. People who build get to live in what they built. People who destroy get banished to the outer ring to fight for scraps. And people who follow get absorbed into the *Justice*'s weird little cult."

"And are you a person who builds, a person who destroys, or a person who follows?"

I bite back the urge to flinch at that last word. I was raised to follow my mother's every whim, then escaped so I could follow Hark's. Even now, I'm chasing her, chasing the opportunity to be the blade in her hand as she plots this monster's downfall. And the *Justice* wants me to follow *it* instead. It's seen me for what I really am. My potential doesn't lie in my own determination—it lies in whoever wields me.

"I don't want to be," I murmur, my gaze dropping. "I want to be more than someone else's weapon. I want to be my own weapon."

"Sounds like you need a blade, then," the Forgemaster says with a wry smile. "What's your name, kid?"

"Murdock."

"Well, Murdock. Here aboard the *Justice*, there's only one source of metal worth working in this forge. If you can procure it, you've earned the weapon I wring from it. There's just one difficulty."

"What's that?" I ask, bracing.

"To get it, you're gonna need to take a little walk outside."

CHAPTER 19

It's not a hard "no" at first. Not until I see the equipment.

"This is an *antique*," I groan, propping the helmet up on my hip and adjusting my grip on the breach suit the Forgemaster has just stuffed in my arms. She's shrugged into a battered set of coveralls and swept her hair—now dry thanks to the forge's insufferable heat—into a tight bun. "This has to be part of the *Justice*'s original outfit, right?"

She shakes her head. "There was an incident about forty years ago. A group of scavs managed to overtake a shuttle as it was transferring ingest. Rumor is the people tried to pass off innocents as their tithe, and the *Justice* overrode their airlocks and let the scavs balance the scales. My suits came from that shuttle."

"Forty years old is still an antique," I grumble.

The Forgemaster shrugs, her eyes darting to a stain on the breach suit's surface. I twist it to get a better look in the light.

Right over the gut, there's a long, snaking patch job. The leathery fabric beneath has been permanently stained a muddy brown, stark against the breach suit's yellow.

"It's airtight," she says. "Otherwise I wouldn't be getting it back every time someone used it to go for a walk."

"A patch job like this is airtight until it isn't," I retort. "No way. Absolutely not. Are you *sure* you don't have any surplus on hand?"

"Telling me how to do my job now, huh?" the Forgemaster replies. "The *Justice* has an ecosystem, even if it's an artificial one. Hullmetal's a limited resource. We don't take more than we need."

"Right, but if you *anticipated* that need and stocked up—"

"It's not just about supply," she retorts, hooking her thumbs in her coverall's belt loops. "If I traded blades to any numbskull who came through that door, I'd be arming anyone who thought they should be armed. That tips the scales toward chaos, and chaos means I can't hole up in here and rely on the local enclaves to keep me supplied. Chaos means the *Justice* wins, because it becomes the only source of stability. Think of it as a test of courage. If you're worthy, you'll come back with the metal for your blade."

She has no idea how much worse that just made it. When have I ever, in my life, been worthy of anything? *It's all superstition,* I try to convince myself, but the longer I stay on this ship, the more I realize that superstition shapes reality in ways I had never accounted for. If I'm not worthy, it'll be because I've judged myself not worthy. Sabotaged myself with my faithlessness. And if I'm not worthy, this little endeavor ends not with a blade in my hand but with me drifting off into space, waiting for my oxygen reserves to dwindle and my life to end in the empty dark.

"Murdock," Fitz shouts up the ladder to the airlock's staging area. "Either you're doing it or you're not."

Under different circumstances, maybe I'd appreciate the goad. If there's one thing Fitz is good for, it's spurring me into reckless action, a trick Hark's used far more times than I can count. I lean out over the ladder to find her and Ham staring up at me. "You did this, Ham?" I holler down.

"It's really not so bad," he calls back.

"So you'll go fetch the metal instead?"

"Never in a million years," he replies without hesitation.

Fitz sucks her teeth, then shakes her head and steps up to the ladder.

"The hell do you think you're doing?" I grumble, leaning back as she scrambles up it and hauls herself onto the grated floor.

"This whole excursion is a wasted effort if we don't get what we came for," Fitz says, popping to her feet with an absurd degree of grace and immediately shucking out of her jacket. "If you're not going to do it, I will. Give me that."

I clutch the breach suit tighter. "I'm going to do it, I just need—"

"You've frozen up, you're bullshitting excuses, and it's taking up precious time." She turns to the Forgemaster. "If I go out and get you your hullmetal, will you forge the sword for her?"

The Forgemaster purses her lips. "Kinda defeats the point of the test of courage thing, doesn't it. Do *you* want a sword?"

Fitz lets out the tiniest of huffs. There's something she's buttoning down—some thought or emotion she can't quite figure out how to express. "I want my fucking crew back. If that means I have to be the one with the sword, fine."

Fitz moves like she's going to snatch the suit again, and I reel back, slamming against the Forgemaster's supply closet. At the rattle of the collision, the Forgemaster's head tilts suddenly. "You know," she says, "I do have a spare."

"YOU EVER DONE THIS BEFORE?" I ask her in the airlock.

Fitz's face is blacked out behind her helmet's shielding, but I can feel the disdainful sidelong glance she's throwing my way. "What do you think?"

"Farm Girl Fitz was a surprise. Don't know if I'm emotionally ready to handle Spacer Fitz."

"What about you?"

I shake my head. Pearl Station was prone to frequent maintenance issues, a by-product of being a place so many people passed through and so few people invested in, but a station that's lasted centuries persists because it has solid atmosphere protections. Up until today in this charmed life of mine, I've never met the void face-to-face.

"It should be simple, in principle," Fitz reasons. "With the drum spinning, we have a gravitational force keeping us stuck to the surface of the inner ring. There'll be no flying off into space as long as we don't get too close to the edge."

"It's not flying off into space I'm worried about. It's *space*."

"Space won't kill you fast unless something goes catastrophically wrong," the Forgemaster says, circling around me and tugging at the breach suit's seals. "If you've got a leak in your suit, it'll probably take a couple minutes for it to drain your oxygen reserves, as long as the hole doesn't get any bigger. The real challenge is moving without getting caught."

"Caught by *what*?" I yelp.

The Forgemaster points overhead. "Did you forget what's up there?"

"More . . . inner ring?" I hazard. The drum's circular, spinning around a central point to keep our feet pinned to the floor. But as I process her question, it dawns on me.

"The core," Fitz says, just as I'm about to open my mouth. *The monster's heart.* I lean back, peering up at the narrow crack of a window in the airlock's hatch, and stare into the face of God.

The *Justice*'s core is massive, spherical, and completely free-floating, positioned at the heart of the ring that forms the ship's body. A sinking feeling envelops me as I gauge just how enormous it is—and just how far away. We're out in the deep black, far from the light of any star. The core's barely a suggestion of a looming form, distinct against the far side of the ship's drum only because it occludes the running lights sprinkled across the hull surface.

This is what Hark thought we could overtake. What Hark thought it was possible to reach. But how the hell are we supposed to ford that distance?

You know exactly how you get to it, I hear the *Justice*'s construct croon in my ear.

A flicker of movement catches my eye, slipping from the core's surface like a raven's wing over a starlit night. Ham mentioned shuttles that ferry the banded faithful out from the core to do the ship's bidding. No doubt that's one of them. In the narrow window, I can't track its trajectory, but now I understand the Forgemaster's warning. If one of those things sights us, we're in deep trouble.

So we won't be carrying any lights.

I take a slow, bracing breath as the Forgemaster straightens from checking Fitz's seals. "You have the map," I mutter, tapping the polymer sheet sketched over in pen that's been strapped around my suit's right forearm. "You have the cutter," I continue, tapping the device clipped onto my belt that will carve the hullmetal free. "You've got this."

"You do," the Forgemaster says, and I stiffen as she knocks her knuckles against the side of my helmet. "You're ready, kiddo."

And oh, that's Hark. That's Hark through and through, putting faith in me that I never deserved, that only ever led to me letting her down—and suddenly I'm convinced I'm about to paint the inside of this forty-year-old helmet. I'm a second from calling the whole thing off, but before I can unstick myself from panic and shout, the Forgemaster's slipped back down the ladder, hauling the hatch shut behind her and leaving me trapped with Fitz in the airlock.

"Want to do the honors?" Fitz asks, gesturing to the overhead crank that'll release us into hard vacuum.

With my face trapped behind my helmet, she has no idea how badly I'm panicking. Maybe it can stay that way. I glance at my wrist, where the breach suit's clunky old display reassures me its seal is holding and my air supply is only just starting to eat into its first few percentage points. I think back to the moment the *Justice*'s construct pinned me to that wall in Southeast Upper, then let myself imagine how that encounter would have gone if I'd had my sword.

The sword I'm not getting unless I climb that ladder, release that hatch, and do this goddamn spacewalk.

I'm moving before I can second-guess myself.

It takes a few spins just to crack the hatch, unleashing a hiss that fades into nothing as I keep reeling the winch. My breach suit swells as the air inside it finds itself unopposed by atmospheric pressure. For a moment, I feel like a balloon—and imagine just how easy it would be for me to pop—but this suit's survived over four decades of use for a reason.

A mechanical release does the heavy lifting once the seal of the hatch is freed. As soon as it's finished, I heave the rest of the way up the ladder and crawl cautiously out onto the surface of the inner ring.

It feels like the dark side of a moonscape, all vague, craggy surfaces I can barely distinguish in the low light. I push myself into a crouch, though my instincts are screaming at me to stay curled up as tight as possible. At the scale we're dealing with, it isn't going to make enough of a difference—and yet there's a primitive part of my brain convinced I need to find cover fast. I wage war with it by holding up my forearm, squinting at the nebulous shapes of the landmarks the Forgemaster sketched as I try to match them against the surface surrounding us.

By the time Fitz has followed me up and kicked the release to seal the hatch behind us, I think I have the lay of the land. The way the Forgemaster explained it, there are certain parts of the hullmetal we shouldn't be touching under any circumstances—including most of the landscape surrounding the hatch. If we damage any critical shielding, we might be signing a death warrant for the Forgemaster or her neighbors the next time the *Justice* passes through a debris field.

But there's one place we're guaranteed to find the makings of a good sword, a place where hundreds of people have come to chip away at the metal over the years. The *Justice* was a warship once, after all, and its external surface is scattered with gun mounts.

"I think that's the nearest one," I say, pointing at a looming shape on the distant edge of the ring roughly two hundred meters away. The sight of the deep black beyond, littered with stars that slowly wheel with the *Justice*'s rotation, is so disorienting that for a moment I lose my balance completely, convinced I'm tipping over and about to plummet down into the core overhead. I cant backward, but Fitz catches me with a steadying hand. With the other, she points in the same direction I did.

If she's saying something, I'm not hearing it. A radio signal would be asking for trouble, so we've stepped out into the vacuum with no easy way of speaking to each other. I reach around her waist and tug, relishing the way she seizes up and fights me as my other hand comes up to pull down her helmet.

Our heads clunk solidly together, and I shout, "Calm down. Just trying to talk!"

She stops struggling, instead locking her hand around the back of my head to pin me in place. Beyond the scraping of our helmets grinding together, I can almost hear her rapid, adrenaline-soaked panting.

"We gotta do this the old-fashioned way," I tell her, and she jerks her head in what barely registers as a nod.

"That's the gun mount," Fitz says, pointing again.

"Yep. Stick close to me." I release her, regretting it a little, if only because I don't think I'm ready to stand freely on my own with the universe still whirling around me. I should be used to this from my years on Pearl, but Pearl's outward-facing windows were few and far between—too impractical unless they could be shielded properly from stray debris—and the stars were too often drowned out by the glow of the planet we orbited. I have to fight to ground my focus down into the centripetal force pushing up against my feet rather than the vast blanket of stars slowly moving in the corners of my vision. As long as I look down, it's like any other stroll. One foot in front of the other.

If I could see my feet.

I spread my arms wide for balance and start to ease forward, sliding my toes along the hullmetal. It's deceptively smooth—smooth until it isn't—and I nearly trip in a patch of scarring.

Fitz strides past me, weaving through the plain of the inner ring as if she's sauntering through a cocktail party. I bite back the useless urge to yell after her. The Forgemaster warned us not to trust our feet. The surface out here is littered with raw edges from centuries of debris strikes, and every last one of them is a disaster waiting to happen for our antique breach suits. I step where she's stepping, tiptoeing faster and faster as I try to catch up.

I'm almost a body-length away when I spot movement out of the corner of my eye.

Instinct takes over, my fears of tearing my breach suit tossed aside as I lunge, tackling Fitz down into the shelter of a jutting piece of hullmetal. She fights and shoves at me, but I grab her by the wrists and wrestle her into stillness, then slam my head against hers and shout, *"Turret!"*

She hitches—I can imagine her giving me a look that says, *Yeah, dipshit, that's what we're headed for*—but then I hear the faint sound of her sucking in a breath. "Moving? Sighting us?"

I let her go, keeping my helmet pressed against hers. "Think so."

"Wouldn't the Forgemaster have told us?"

"Who knows? Maybe this is part of the test of courage. Or maybe she's trying to off us."

"But Ham's done this before. It doesn't add up with what I read from them.".

"What you . . . read?"

"What do you think I do on this crew?" Fitz asks flatly. "Ham's just a do-gooder in want of some real convictions, and the Forgemaster wouldn't send some fresh-faced kid with the same problems as her out to die pointlessly. Especially not in a suit that's survived forty years. So something else has to be going on here."

I frown.

After a pause, Fitz nudges her helmet harder into mine. "Your turn, genius."

I move as if I'm going to knead at my brow, then remember the complication of the breach suit. "Maybe it's the *Justice* itself, out to get me personally." But that doesn't add up either. The *Justice* wants to seduce me. If it wanted to kill me, it could have accomplished that in far less complicated ways than waiting for me to take a fraught little stroll on its hull. And then it clicks. "Why would the ship have a gun that points at itself?"

I'm pretty sure Fitz is giving me a look that says, *Am I supposed to answer that?*

"It wouldn't," I continue. "It doesn't. None of its weaponry should have the firing radius necessary to point at the adjacent deck. But it does have automated weaponry, because of course. Because this is a big, complicated system trying to stay intact in fucking *space*."

I should have gotten it way sooner. But Pearl Station was in a stable orbit sanitized by a dedicated sweeper team. The *Justice* is an ancient brute meant to drop onto hostile battlefields—battlefields where ships would be shredded to their component parts. And those component parts wheeling around on unpredictable trajectories could spell *incalculable* damage if allowed to impact on the *Justice*'s surface.

I stand up, popping my head clear from the shelter we've ducked behind, and squint into the darkness, where the shadowy outline of a turret from the ship's automated defense array has just swiveled back to its sentinel position, its gun barrel locked neutrally out toward the stars.

"Ha!" I shout, throwing my fists up triumphantly, and Fitz startles at the sudden motion. I reach a hand down for her, and she surprises me by taking it without hesitation, letting me haul her to her feet. I reach up for the back of her helmet and draw her head down to connect again. She anchors herself with a hand at my waist.

"Debris defense array," I tell her, fighting a flush that absolutely should not be there. "Must have reacted to our movement, but it never could have fired on us without impacting the surface of the ship itself."

"So we're good?" she breathes.

"We're not going to get shot, at least. But the gun almost targeting could raise a red flag with the big bastard itself. Best to hurry now."

I let her go and bring my map arm back up, reorienting myself in the landscape. We're halfway there. Only another hundred meters to go. Before Fitz can take the lead again, I plunge forward. The incident with the turret has my heart racing, but after tackling Fitz headlong into the inner ring's surface, I'm a bit surer in my footing. The terrain is smooth panels of hull-metal, slightly slippery under the rubber of my breach suit's boots. At standard grav, it's almost like we're not in space. Just out for a very strange, very quiet walk in partial darkness.

At least, until my next step plunges through nothing but empty vacuum.

I shout uselessly, my arms pinwheeling as I tip forward over the edge. Below is sheer blackness, vast and all-encompassing, and in it I see nothing but my inevitable end.

A pair of arms snags me from behind.

The stop is ungainly, strangling, and puts the taste of oranges in my mouth as the contents of my stomach make a valiant attempt to slough up my windpipe. I choke back the bile and scrabble desperately for purchase on the cliff's edge as Fitz hauls backward with all her might. She collapses down on one knee just as I manage to hook my leg back up onto solid ground, and the two of us topple over in a heap.

The silence of the void's been washed away completely by my panicked gasping and my hammering heart. For a moment, I do nothing but try to reclaim it, biting back my heaving breaths and not daring to move a muscle. Fitz has an arm pinned beneath my back, and the connection between our suits is just enough for me to hear what sounds like a storm of swearing that gradually peters out as she, too, calms the fuck down.

I roll upright, glancing sidelong at her. When we started this excursion, I thought having her face blacked out wouldn't be an impediment in the slightest. All I had to do was imagine the consternated looks she was throwing my way. But suddenly I'm desperate. Suddenly I want to know exactly what she looks like seconds after saving my life on nothing but raw impulse.

Instead I ease to the edge of the drop-off, peering down

into the darkness. The distinction between shadow and emptiness is so vague that I have to stick my hand out just to confirm there really is nothing there.

When I turn back, Fitz is already on her feet, one hand on her hip, the other jabbing insistently in the direction of the gun mounts. Right. Wasting time. I was the one who said we should hurry. I shove upright, and thankfully my sea legs are starting to lock in, my vision tuning out the rotation of the stars as I start off once more in her tracks.

The gun mount looms over us as we approach. Unlike the turret, this monstrosity was built for annihilation, not defense, a towering monolith to Ybi expansionism. I wonder how long it's been since it last fired. These guns are part of the force the *Justice* uses to extract its tithe from settlements, and briefly I entertain the idea of figuring out how to take this beast apart with nothing more than the laser cutter strapped to my hip.

It's a useless fantasy. If triggering the automated turret might have alerted the *Justice* to our presence, tampering with one of its big guns is the equivalent of singing an aria naked in front of a sensor box. Better to save that for *after* I get my sword.

When we're close enough to reach out and touch it, I can make out the sharp, precise cuts where people who came before us carved their own little pieces out of the ship's flesh. Every one of those missing pieces is now a weapon somewhere aboard the *Justice*. The thought sends a shiver up my spine.

Manipulating the laser cutter's enough to get my heart properly hammering again. Sure, I've used one—mostly while jamming alongside Bea as she tuned up her latest demo-derby beast or hacked apart the twisted carcass of her last one—but those were always in a nice planetside garage. Here, if I slip up, I don't just lose a finger. I lose my suit's integrity and, most likely, my life.

"Y'know, maybe your hands are steadier," I comment, then remember Fitz can't hear me. She's bent backward, staring up at the mind-boggling scale of the gun, but her hand's still propped casually on her hip. She looks less like a daring spacer, more like a tourist ogling a monument, and now I'm really glad she can't hear the way I'm snickering at her.

I leave her to her sightseeing. This is supposed to be my spacewalk. My sword. My responsibility. I bend to one knee, gauge the size of the brick I want to extract, then pull the cutter's trigger before I can second-guess myself into oblivion.

As I work, I feel the prickle of Fitz's attention shifting to me. In the past, anytime she scrutinized me, it was a coin toss whether it made me sloppy or forced me to get my act together. But all of that was under the shadow of Hark's judgment—and I find that without her, I'm not any better or worse under Fitz's observation. I'm doing my part, and after all we've been through in the past couple days, I'm starting to trust that she'll do hers.

The brick comes free at last. I clip the cutter back on my belt, wedge the block of metal away from the wall, and heft it, my stomach dropping at the weight. I know the forging process will leave me with something lighter and far nicer to carry, but its mass makes it dauntingly real.

I turn to Fitz, holding out the metal. "C'mon, take it," I scoff where she can't hear. "It's gonna rip your twiggy little arms off."

Fitz shakes her head. At first I think it's because she knows this is all a ruse, a way of reminding her about my superior arm muscles, but then I realize her hand is still pinned on her hip. The gesture's no longer casual.

She looks like she's holding her guts in, but that's not quite it.

She's been keeping her hand there ever since she stopped me from plunging off the cliff's edge.

If I had to guess, that's when her suit tore.

CHAPTER 20

The hullmetal brick tumbles from my hands.

I lunge in close, but Fitz gets her free arm between us, catching me by the shoulder. Before I can argue, she flashes her wrist gauge at me. The bright "50%" there taps the brakes on my panic.

Then it slips to "49%."

We have two hundred meters to ford back to the hatch. That's assuming we can find the hatch again in the vague dark of the ring's inner surface. I glance down at the brick I've dropped. How much extra time does carrying it add? A whirlwind of calculations has replaced my rationality, meters per second doing war with liters of oxygen in our tanks.

The *thud* of Fitz's helmet against mine snaps me out of it. "C minor," she grits out.

Then she turns and starts walking.

I hate how she knows. One of Hark's keys is all it takes to cut right through my overthinking. C minor, meaning *Grab the necessities and bug out as fast as your legs will carry you.*

I could kick and scream about taking orders from Fitz, but in the end, she's left me no choice.

I stoop, heft the makings of my future sword, and take off after her.

We come back through the airlock in a jumbled mess. Fitz sags against the floor, and I throw the brick of hullmetal down, wincing at the way it vibrates all the way up to the top rung of the ladder, where I'm desperately winching the overhead door shut as fast as it'll go. The moment I have a confirmed seal, I slam the release to cycle atmo back into our environment, then drop clean off the ladder, landing in a crouch and immediately slumping back to join her on the ground.

A moment later, I hear the faint strains of her ragged breathing.

"The *fuck* were you thinking?" I snap.

Before Fitz can catch her breath—or bullshit an answer— the lower door cracks open and the Forgemaster clambers up. "See, what did I tell you? Nothing to worry about," she drawls. "I'll just take this—"

I sputter, but there's a manic glint in her eyes as she cradles the hullmetal brick close to her chest, looking for all the worlds like a mother with a newborn.

"Gorgeous, gorgeous. We'll do great things together, you and me," the Forgemaster coos. Without sparing a glance for me or Fitz, she drops back down from whence she came.

Leaving me, Fitz, and the fallout of the *monumentally* brainless thing she's just done.

"I had enough air in my tanks," Fitz croaks at long last. "The leak's not that big, see?"

She pats her hip. In the brightness of the airlock's lights, the tear is immediately evident—a four-centimeter-long ragged edge where it looks like she must have snagged against something when she fell.

When she saved me.

The danger's behind us, but my heart's still going rabbit-fast and I'm starting to feel like *I'm* the one with a suit leak, with the way my breathing just won't calm down. I don't understand it. Any of it. The echoing of my breath in the helmet is only stoking my panic worse and worse, but I'll be damned if I take mine off before Fitz does.

She doesn't get to see my face like this. Not until I see hers.

But a new sound is starting to creep past my hyperventilating, one so impossible I'm forced to hold my breath just to make sure I'm hearing things right. Fitz is *laughing,* sitting up to bend forward over her stomach as she rests her free palm against her faceplate. It's not the tittering, polite chuckle she'll let loose around a mark who needs to think she finds him charming—it's ugly, snorting, and barely rhythmic.

"Stop that," I rasp.

She doesn't.

"Seriously, what the *fuck,* Fitz?" I've never heard her laugh like this in four years of knowing her. Bea would never believe me if I told her. "You're oxygen-deprived. You're losing your mind."

She flashes her wrist gauge at me, still chuckling with her head between her knees. I can't argue with the "15%," but I'm going to need another explanation. "I'm happy," she finally wheezes. "I'm so fucking happy to be alive, and it makes no fucking sense. This is the happiest I've been in ages, and it's here, and it's with you, and it's *stupid,* so the only thing left to do is laugh about it."

I can't reckon with that. It sounds like bullshit, and with her voice muffled behind her helmet, all I can think is that it's a ruse. I'm a mark—I've never been anything more to her—and this is just another layer of artifice she's wrapped around herself like a warm blanket. Just like her saving me, it doesn't track with her previous behavior at all.

But the more I think on that, the more I remember it's not quite true.

She didn't just hand me an orange.

In the inertial shelter, I screamed, she heard, and she came running. In Southeast Stair when the *Justice* hauled me into a dark corner, I didn't scream, but she found me anyway right when I needed her most. And out on the surface of the inner ring, she couldn't hear the moment I shouted in surprise, but she caught me all the same.

And what have I done to deserve that? I've mocked her, fought her on every little thing, and forced her to come with me on a spacewalk that nearly killed her. I might be the reason she got fed to this monstrosity in the first place.

Maybe the least I can do is this. I reach up for my helmet's seals and pry them free with shaking fingers. The faint ozone smell of the airlock seeps in as I lift it clear, and I blink against the harsher cut of the lights with no filter.

Fitz has frozen. This must be as alien for her as hearing her laugh was to me. She's never seen me give up ground so easily without an explicit order from Hark before, but it's the only way I can think of to show her I'm finally catching up on what she's been doing all along.

It's agony, the long seconds I have to let her look at my waning panic with absolutely no idea what's going on behind her faceplate. It could be anyone in that breach suit. An impostor wearing the shape of her, hiding behind her brush with death to explain away the strange lack of poise in her slumped posture. But then her hands go to her own helmet's seal.

My breath stills. It shouldn't, it *absolutely* shouldn't, but I find my lungs just won't *work* until she's tipping it up off her head.

Below it, she's pink like I've never seen her before, the flush of her cheeks stark against the wisps of platinum blond hair that have come loose from her braid. Even stranger is the lightness in her eyes, the bend of a genuine smile playing across her lips. I wait for it to fade—wait for the dose of outside air to wash it away or the sight of my face unimpeded to shock her back into being the asshole I've reluctantly worked with for four years.

"This isn't real," I mutter.

And that's the thing that really convinces me, because I see the moment her eyes shutter, the moment the joy leaves them. It's something I've seen her do time and time again, that buttoning up, battening down, slamming the mask back on. I always thought it was a restoration of reality, that underneath her glittering party charm, Fitz was nothing but haughty and unknowable. But both were always pretense.

Worse, I never thought I'd be gutted to see that switch flip. I don't want to go back. We forged something new and strange out there together on the *Justice*'s hull. We proved that we could work together—maybe only because we couldn't see or hear each other properly, but still.

I see her now. And I don't want to stop seeing her. So before the flush can fade from her cheeks, I toss my helmet aside, lunge across the airlock, and seal my lips over hers.

She startles underneath me, and for a moment I fear I've gone too far. Maybe I'm desperate, and maybe she's not. But then her glove is in my hair as her other arm snares around my waist, crushing me into her as she kisses me back.

I haven't seen Fitz *want* before. She's always been perfectly compliant, pouring herself into the shape of whichever mold Hark had selected, and the only goals she ever aligned herself with were the ones that fit Hark's objective. Everything else she kept close to the chest, and I was never interested enough to pry her deepest desires free.

It turns out when Fitz has something in her sights, she grabs tight and doesn't let go.

Being that something is overwhelming. The airlock door overhead might as well have cracked open for the way my world reduces to two extremes—everything she's touching and absolute vacuum. She pulls me into her lap, breaking free to drag kisses along the length of my jaw as she works the seals on her wrists loose behind my back. Before I can get a word— a *thought*—in edgewise, she has her hands out of her gloves, one of them brushing faintly over the buzzed-short sides of my hair in a way that has me wondering how long she's wanted to do that.

My own hands have frozen, clutched around the clasps of her breach suit's seals. It feels like a boundary that can't be uncrossed—but then again, we've plowed through *several* of those in the span of a couple seconds.

"Why are *you* the one who's overthinking this?" Fitz groans against my neck.

It fucking carbonates my blood, makes me feel like we've just lost pressure. I buckled myself into my breach suit with care and caution. I tear open hers with so much reckless abandon that the Forgemaster might not get another use out of it. Beneath, she's wearing the starchy gray tank we were issued back on Gest. I've got it halfway rucked up over her stomach when I notice a patch of ruddy skin far too violent to be a blush.

It freezes me again.

"For fuck's sake," Fitz groans. Her hand goes tight in the long part of my hair, making like she's going to reel me back in, but I brace.

She looks like she's been scalded. Right where her suit tore.

My brain's been struggling to add up all the pieces, but now I have the whole picture. Fitz's face bare to me, her heavy-lidded eyes and flushed cheeks. Her arms straining to reel me in. And the vicious mark on her body where the void did its best to sear her as she held it back with nothing but a gloved fist.

Because what? Because she thought me having a sword was more important? I can't make the calculus work out to anything I deserve, anything that warrants her getting hurt like this. In all of our work together, Fitz never took hits. She'd seduce marks with far gentler tactics, leaving them pliant and ready for Hark to do her work. And if she *were* to get hurt, if someone roughed her up a bit more than she bargained for, she'd put the job first. She'd take it for Hark.

Not for me, though. Never for me.

Fitz's hand slips out of my hair and comes down to prod gingerly at her stomach. She sucks in a breath through her teeth. "Maybe a little worse than I thought," she admits, letting her head roll back to clunk against the airlock wall.

Impulse has me before rationality can have any say in the matter. I bend low, brushing my lips against the heart of the mark. I'm expecting her to shove me back, but Fitz only lets out a low groan that twists something deep inside me. She did this to herself for me. I don't know what to do with that other than putting my mouth to her wound like a penitent. My gaze slips up to meet hers, and the look in her eyes is devastating. I've ruined her. I've taken Hark's perfect little actress and torn away the curtains.

I want to do it some more.

But before I can move my mouth—higher, lower, there are no wrong answers here—Ham's voice calls up from below, "Hey, you two?"

"Yes?" Fitz replies, her voice perfectly prim in a way that makes me want to dig my fingers hard into her thighs.

"Forgemaster says the bath is yours when you want it."

HAM'S INTERRUPTION WAS A SPLASH of cold water to the face. Fitz and I untangled ourselves, shucked the rest of the way out of our breach suits, and scrambled down to the forge's main floor without so much as looking at each other.

Now we sit on opposite ends of the Forgemaster's bath, stripped to our underclothes and continuing to avoid eye contact. The water's mercifully warm and overly salty—a fact I discovered only after I plunged in and immediately got a mouthful of it. Over my hacking and spitting, I heard the Forgemaster cackling somewhere deeper in her machinery.

"Brine baths are the best for blades," she'd called over the clanging. "And it does miracles for muscles after a hard day."

I'm not about to dispute her twenty years of experience. Academically, I understood what floating in salt water would be like, but I've never experienced it for myself. I let my eyes slip closed and my head roll back, the surprising buoyancy cradling my body up to the surface. I've always dreamed of floating in an ocean, and for a moment I'm lost in the fantasy, on my back in a body of water that spans a *planet*, not a pocket of a spinning wheel flung deep in the cosmic black. My ears dip below the surface, muffling the forge's noise to a distant rumble over the ever-present hum of the *Justice*'s machinery.

But the bath's not a planet. The waves that pulse over me aren't windswept swells curated by the gravity of a moon or two. Every little disturbance of the surface is either me or Fitz.

I let my eyes drift open barely a crack, terrified she's going to sense the second my gaze settles on her. She's eased herself down to her chin in the water, her hair splaying out in a silvery fan around her. Her eyes are fixed somewhere deeper in the forge's shadows, and even though she looks like she's com-

pletely zoned out, her expression has that careful tautness to it
that tells me her mask is back in place.

It's a bit of a relief. It's what I know how to handle.

I've been trying to untangle what just happened between us,
with little success. Fitz is attractive. The whole point of her is
that she's attractive—that's how she baits our marks. Before
today, I'd been aware of this fact, but in a totally different context. Fitz's hotness was her value to Hark. It was something I
could never replicate. Sure, I'm handsome in my own way, but
not in a way that trucks with the people Hark wants to defraud.

The part I keep coming back to is the fact that I never would
have kissed her if Hark was around. Ever since I joined the
crew, I've been at war with Fitz for Hark's favor. There was no
room for anything else between us—and I'd never thought to
want it until I saw her face bare and unguarded and smiling
because of me.

And then it only took seconds for me to do something
about it.

Even more surprising was the way she rolled with it. Sure,
her options are limited aboard the *Justice,* but I'd assumed I'd be
the absolute bottom of the barrel when it came to her prefer-
ences. Fitz has always leaned toward people who can match her
glamor, not people who cut the sleeves off their shirts and crawl
through dust-choked vents without a second of hesitation. Her
genuine hookups—not the ones she strings along on Hark's
command—are nothing like me. Is she that desperate already?

I know the easiest way to sort all this out would be to ask
her directly, but I think I'd rather claw my own face off. There's
a part of me that *likes* that she's closed-off and unknowable. It
makes things easier. Why ruin it?

Because what other opportunities are there to get laid around here? a
voice in my head counters.

I draw a deep breath and curl in on myself, letting my entire
body sink below the water.

When I resurface, I find Ham crouching at the side of the pool with his hair loosened from its bun, working through the complicated process of tugging apart the ties that bind his overshirt together. He took a nap while we were out on the hull, but since our return, he's been working through a set of sword forms off in the forge's open training ground.

I watch him disrobe with far more interest than I could spare with Fitz. Clothing aboard the *Justice* seems to come in far more pieces than usual. It's clear now why the one-piece jumpsuits we came aboard in immediately mark us as ingest. Ham's overshirt is stitched together from the pieces of two separate originals, the tunic beneath it is actually two garments stacked on top of each other and padded out with light polymer armor plates between them, and his pants are the lower half of a jumpsuit, betrayed by the ragged edge he unveils when he loosens their tie and drops them.

"Scoot," he tells me, but doesn't give me any time to follow through before he's plunging into the water, sending a spray of brine washing over me. Fitz huffs as she's forced to rear back from his wave a second later. "So, how was the walk?" he asks once he's dunked his head and resurfaced with his long, loose curls flattened against his face.

"Uneventful," I reply, maybe a bit too casually. In my periphery, I catch Fitz's gaze darting to me. "Seriously, I don't get why you didn't just tell us what we were in for. Would have saved us a whole lot of trouble."

Ham shrugs, leaning back against the pool's edge and spreading his arms. "It's how I made the walk a year ago. My master didn't tell me anything. Just dropped me off at the forge and let her take it from there."

"Is your master here? Would your master know if you'd told us, *Oh hey, watch your step, don't worry about the turrets because they can't shoot you, and try not to rip your suit on a sharp edge?*"

Ham tenses. "You tore your suit?"

"*I* tore my suit," Fitz interrupts from his other side. She eases to her feet, slipping her stomach out of the water to bare the exposure wound. I decide now's a good time to become *extremely* interested in the forge machinery's workings.

Ham lets out a sympathetic hiss. "I'm sorry. You're right—I could have prepared you better. I thought because my master did it, it was the way it needed to be done. But they were training me to be a Blade-sworn. You're just getting a sword for self-defense."

Something about the way he says it has my hackles up. "What's so special about Blade-sworn training anyway?"

"It's a commitment to fight in service of others, not for one's own interests. It's a lineage of combat technique unique to the ship it was cultivated aboard, passed down from master to student. And it's . . . it's personal. I didn't think there was much I could amount to—much good I could do—until my master took me under their wing."

If I didn't know any better, I'd swear he was trying to get under my skin. "Do you think I'm selfish?" I ask.

I can't stop myself from meeting Fitz's gaze.

"I think you're misguided," Ham offers, oblivious to the electric current that's just snapped across this pool. "I think you're putting a lot of stock in this Hark person being the answer to all your problems."

"You don't know Hark," I counter. "Fitz, back me up."

Fitz scoffs.

"What?" I snap.

"Hark's been off her game for a while now. She didn't make the rendezvous at the festival, even after a clear signal. And you're still worshipping the ground she walks on even after she told you to your *face* you're the reason we got caught."

"That doesn't mean I'm going to give up on her completely," I retort.

"Hark's served me well—gave me good work and got me

plenty rich. Hark's still my best chance of getting off this ship, so I'll chase her, but I think we need to be realistic about what she's capable of."

Ham blinks. "Hang on, *off this ship*?" He glances between us, his brow furrowed.

"If we can find Hark," I clarify, holding up my hands and giving Fitz a pointed glare. "Hark *can* put together a plan to get us out of here."

Ham lets out a short bark of a laugh. "Look, I know you're both only a few days post-ingest, but I need you to understand that the words coming out of your mouth are the *ingestiest* thing I've ever heard in my entire life. Tons of people come to this ship thinking they'll be the ones to escape it. Want to know how many that's worked out for?"

"None?" Fitz sighs flatly.

"No, thousands, of course," Ham replies. "Hundreds of thousands, probably. Everyone escapes this ship eventually, but only ever in the same way. You're here until you die. Anything else is a delusion in the face of three hundred years of solid fact."

The existential dread is starting to boil in my gut—or maybe it's the heat of the pool. The truth Ham's just thrown out with remarkable clarity is too obvious to evade. What makes me think Hark can take down the *Justice*? She herself said she didn't have a plan yet. We've been struggling to pick up her trail, hoping that by the time we reach her, she'll have it all figured out. But what if Ham's right?

I need something to hold on to. Something solid and real. My gaze slips once more into the depths of the forge, drawn to the Forgemaster's ungodly echoing noise. Maybe Fitz has the right idea. Let go. Be realistic. Focus on what serves you.

I nudge Ham's shoulder. "Speaking of delusions, how much Blade-sworn training do you think I can pick up by the time she's done with my sword?"

CHAPTER 21

We start the next morning.

More precisely, we start at the moment the environmental lights begin to glow toward daytime, when Ham prods me awake. It can't have been more than a few hours since we toweled off and clambered up into the loft, where the Forgemaster's constructed a cozy little living area.

I scowl up at Ham and peel back the cup of the heavy-duty headphones that have been doing the valiant work of keeping the sound of the Forgemaster's creative fervor at bay. From the noises still echoing up from below, she's worked straight through the night. "C'mon," I groan. "You got to nap while we were risking our lives in a hard vacuum. At least let me sleep in."

Ham drops a sword on me. I jolt away from it like it's a live snake, then realize it's a blunted polymer blade, weighted with what looks like a metal rod down the middle. The motion wakes Fitz, who's swaddled in a mound of blankets on the far edge of the bed. She huffs, then yanks my pillow out from under me and crams it over her head.

"Good morning to you too," I grumble, kicking my way out of the sheets. Ever since that back-and-forth in the Forgemaster's bath, Fitz has been her usual self—which is to say her face is blank and she's trying to have as little to do with me as possible. All it took was one mention of Hark, one reminder of how differently we see her. Between that and the exhaustion from our spacewalk, we all but collapsed on opposite sides of the bed and haven't so much as made eye contact since.

"My master always said it's best to start your day with something that gets your blood pumping," Ham remarks as we amble down the stairs from the loft. "Keeps you sharp and wakes you up better than any stimulant."

"Seems both highly individual *and* something that doesn't necessitate swordplay. Well, depending on the equipment you're working with—"

Ham flicks me on the back of the head. "I know you're all riled up because you shared a bed with Fitz, but could you *please* let me get through a sent—"

"I'm riled up because you dragged me out of bed at the crack of the dawn cycle to go medieval on your ass," I interrupt, whirling on him as I reach the forge's main floor. It might be he's right about the sleeping arrangements, but I'm not about to admit that.

Not that I would have known what to do with it if there *was* a window where Fitz wasn't giving me the cold shoulder. Every time I let myself entertain the notion, my thoughts circle inevitably back to Hark. To how easily entangling myself with Fitz might destroy my usefulness to her. Might destroy *Fitz's* usefulness, while we're at it. It's an ugly thought, one I can't get to rest comfortably. Hark's supposed to be the person who opens doors, who invited me out to see the universe with her.

I've never thought of her as holding me back before.

Ham smirks like he's not buying a second of my bullshit. "Whatever you say. I woke up early and got bored."

"*Early*," I huff.

He heaves a bundle at me. I catch it and shake it out one-handed to reveal a battered-looking padded tunic. Ham shrugs his own over his head, and I follow his lead, setting down my practice sword to leave my hands free for the cinches around the waist. Midway through tying the knot, it occurs to me that this padding isn't decorative. We're not just waving our swords around—we're going to be sparring for real.

I flash back to my scuff with Ham in the potato fields and the brutal efficiency with which he tossed me like I weighed nothing at all. In the past couple days of traveling with him, I've gotten used to the soft, generous man I've come to know, not the newly minted Blade-sworn who leveled a sword at me as I fought for breath in the dirt. Only now that I'm swaddled in protective gear do I remember how easily he handed me my ass.

Ham strides out onto the training ground, his bare feet spry against the spring-loaded floor. He sets down his sword and begins easing through a series of stretches, then glances back over his shoulder. "Mimic me if you know what's good for you."

I've never once in my life claimed to know what's good for me, but I follow his lead anyway, tucking my sword in a loop on my tunic's belt as I start to sway and wheel my arms in concert with him. "Is this part of Blade-sworn training too?" I ask.

"My master says ninety percent of combat is readiness."

I frown. Violence, to me, is raw impulse. Readiness feels antithetical, a slippery slope toward overthinking and freezing in a critical moment. But then again, I've heard the same sentiment expressed by Hark, who always had contingency stacked on contingency—until the moment she didn't.

"How'd you end up with your master anyway?" I ask, my voice throttled by a backward bend that Ham's holding far steadier than me.

"They were contracted to guard the jail where the Moon Eater's held," Ham replies with a shrug, easing effortlessly out of the motion. "They got sick of me visiting the prison every day and told me if I wanted to feel safe, I ought to learn to protect myself instead of trusting the apparatus of a deck settlement to do it for me."

"Sounds paranoid."

"Nah, they were on to something. Thing is, I don't think I would have lasted another year aboard the *Justice* if I hadn't found a way to put power back in my hands. It was healing."

Hark's always told me that my gut instinct to punch my way out of trouble was base, that there was always a cleverer way. Her way, usually. But I remember how good it felt to scrap with the scavs, to tackle Ham, to feel like even in this monster's gullet with the walls themselves watching my every move, there was still something I could do to take control of a situation.

Ham's frozen, his gaze caught in the middle distance, and I realize there's something else lurking beneath what he's just confessed. "The Moon Eater really did a number on you, huh?" I ask softly.

Ham shakes his head, moving quicker than usual into the next stretch. "There wasn't much of me to do a number *on* before I met him. I was a kid."

"How much of a kid are we talking?"

"Seventeen."

I purse my lips. It's too close to eighteen, too close to the age I was when Hark swept me off Pearl Station and into a life of daring capers and fast escapes. Part of me rebels at comparing her to the Moon Eater. The Moon Eater eats fucking moons. Hark just steals from assholes who deserve it. But with far too few twists, I can imagine an inverse of our scenarios—one where Ham's fighting like hell to get back to the Moon Eater's side and I'm praying that Hark never finds me.

"Do you . . ." I start, then hesitate. Ham's been endlessly patient with my questions, but this one might go too far. "Do you feel like he made the best parts of you too?"

Ham pauses, straightening out. "I don't think he made any part of me. I think he made me do things. Things I definitely shouldn't have done. But my actions don't add up to who I am. My choices do. And he limited my options, but he didn't make my choices for me. Would I be a different person if I'd told him no the first time he offered me a gig? Sure. But I was the one who took the gig. The guy who'd choose that existed before he met the Moon Eater, and he still exists in the foundations of everything that adds up to me. The Moon Eater put choices I might have never made in front of me, but my decisions—those are me. Those are what's real."

"He didn't put a gun to your head? Force your hand?"

"He did," Ham says, a noticeable shudder pinching his shoulders. "But again, doing what he forced me to do was either a choice I made or a choice he took from me. And if he took the choice from me, it's not *me*. Make sense?"

Barely, but I'm starting to see the logic he's pieced together. I shrug, then nod.

"Your . . . Hark, you think she made the best parts of you?" Ham asks, bending to pick up his sword.

Guess I wasn't being subtle. "Well, when Mr. Self-Actualization puts it so eloquently, don't I have to say no?"

"Not necessarily," Ham replies. "You're allowed to have a different outlook. And it sounds like you do."

"I don't know." I pull my own practice sword from my belt, adjusting my hands around the grip and levering it by the pommel. It's no fine work of craftsmanship. The balance favors the blade, leaving it feeling heavy in my hands. "Before I met Hark,

I had plenty going for me, but no prospects. I would have been stuck on that shitty old station for the rest of my life, scraping data to line my mother's pockets. I don't think that person is made of the same choices I am today, if that's how we're thinking about these things. So if that wasn't Hark shaping me, what was it?"

"You shaping yourself in the company of Hark," Ham replies, like it's as easy as that. "Now do what I do."

He starts with a simple sequence, raising and lowering the sword. It feels beyond basic, but the weight of the sword begins to drag at my shoulders after only a couple sets. By the time Ham's satisfied I have the fundamentals locked in, I've started sweating enough that the brine bath is looking tempting.

As we move into the next set, my mind begins to wander. I've spent the past four years chasing the version of myself Hark wanted, the person who could hack through anything and someday write a con elegant enough to rival hers. In smoky lounges, with a drink in her hand and my knee propped up against the table, she'd tell me any day now we'd hit on *the* job. The job where she'd sit back and for the first time, I'd run point.

I'd always balked, demurred, waved my hands, and made excuses anytime she mused about it. Why fall back on *me* when we had *Hark*? But the larger issue that lay beneath all my objections was the fact that I knew I could only muster two-thirds of the crew. Hark would let me lead, since the whole operation was her idea. Bea would heckle me, but when push came to shove, she'd follow my directives.

Fitz would defy me at every turn.

I wonder how true that is now.

"Murdock?"

I snap out of my reverie to find Ham's giving me a *look*. I lower my sword and give him a sheepish shrug.

"Okay, if this is boring you so much—" He raises his blade at me. "Get inside my guard," he commands.

"You sure about that, big guy? I hear these things are dangerous."

"It's a blunted practice blade, first of all, and I doubt—"

I lunge, swinging with a hack so wide and obvious it's no wonder Ham deflects it with nothing but a flick of his wrist. As I'm spun round by the momentum of my blade getting swatted aside, he reaches out and catches me by the shoulder with a forceful stiff arm, shoving me back.

I land squarely on my ass, already laughing.

Ham glares. He knows that was bullshit. He lets his sword spin in a flashy circle, then levels it at me again. *For real this time,* the look in his eyes dares me.

I shove myself upright and lunge into the laziest feint I've ever attempted. He completely ignores the swing I choke, then catches the real one before I can dip down over his guard.

I should be trying. If I want this sword to be useful, I'd be best off learning from someone with proper training while I have the time. But I'm afraid of finding my limit. If there's a ceiling to what I can do, there's the reality that a sword in my hand might not be enough to protect myself. If I keep playing with Ham instead of committing to the fight, I don't have to face that reality.

Maybe I don't want to know the full extent of what Hark's done to me. I was a fighter before I met her, able to hold my own in any side-street scrap aboard Pearl Station. I was cocky and confident until the day she caught me by the wrist and told me I could be doing so much more with myself. She had me on a leash for four years, until the *Justice* dropped me in a pressure cooker and taped it shut.

Hark's not here to judge me. And maybe Ham's a little bit right. I get to choose who I want to be, because my choices are what makes me. And if that's the case, maybe I ought to choose better. Maybe I deserve it.

So when I drop my shoulder back, letting Ham's sword whiff past my face, I don't hesitate. My pommel's already sailing straight for his gut. He swings his free hand down to catch it, but it's already too late. His left foot steps out and back.

"If that's not inside your guard, I don't know what is," I grunt as he shoves me back hard. It doesn't matter that a slight motion from him knocks me back a full meter. I never came here to be a duelist. I came here to play tricks and win.

"You didn't hit me."

"I hit your hand."

"My guard hand."

"If my pommel had a spike—"

"Then your weapon would be way too dangerous for you to wield," Ham replies, but he's grinning. A spark of understanding lights up his eyes. "C'mon. If you think you're so clever, let me show you a real gambit."

I'M NOT GOING TO BECOME a master of the blade in a single session, but I'm already a fairly handy con, and the pivot from serious training to absurd trick-shot competition has taught me there's a surprising amount of overlap between the two. Ham and I have spent the past hour feinting around each other, trying to come up with even more clever sleights of hand, and the net result is the two of us bent over howling with laughter and the blade feeling far more comfortable in my hand than I ever thought it could be.

I wipe the tears from my eyes and glance up to find Fitz lounging against the rail of the Forgemaster's loft, watching the two of us play. Her hair is piled in a loose bun, and she wears a fitted tank with her original colors stripped to the waist. It's a good look on her—such a good look that Ham manages to poke me in the back of the knee with his sword, buckling me sideways. I commit to what I've earned, collapsing on the mat hard enough that the springs bounce me airborne for a second.

I roll on my back to find Ham flashing me an earnest grin. "Like you said. Wait for the target to pick their own distraction, let them fixate, then strike," he quips, offering a hand.

Hark's words, not mine, but I'm not about to correct him. "Maybe teaching you to fight dirty was a mistake," I grumble as he hauls me to my feet.

"That wasn't fighting dirty." His gaze slips over my shoulder. "Morning, Fitz."

I glance back, then startle as he lunges again, his sword whipping out for a strike I only barely duck.

"*That* was fighting dirty," he says. "Also, it's stressing me out that you don't block."

"I'm better at moving my body than moving this," I counter, waggling my weapon at him.

"It's gonna get you in trouble when you're up against a real blade. If that doesn't get you in trouble first," he replies, glancing up to the loft. "Not to be a gossip, but what's—"

"*Nothing* is going on there," I reply.

Ham makes an unconvinced hum and beckons me close. "Remember those lessons of surviving the *Justice* I was telling you about?" he mutters. "Got another one for you. Third lesson: savor good things while you have them."

I huff. "I don't . . . I can't . . ."

"I think that's enough for one day," he announces, so loud and obvious that I resist the urge to bury my face in my palm. "I call first dibs on the bath."

With that, he saunters off the mat, tosses his practice sword back in the barrel of battered, blunted equipment on the training area's periphery, and disappears into the forge's machinery.

I glance helplessly up at Fitz. She's still propped up on the rail, her head tilted just so as she stares after Ham. Her expression is the usual unreadable mask, and I hate the way it pinches.

Her gaze slips down to me, and something loosens in her. A sly, real smile creeps into the corners of her lips.

It's the first moment we've had alone since the airlock. Since I realized what she'd nearly sacrificed for me, the way she's been saving me ever since we got stuck together. The ruminating in the bath and the scant amount of sleep I managed last night haven't granted me any grand insights on why that compelled me to kiss her like I was drowning, but maybe Ham's got a point.

Maybe it's enough just to grab onto goodness while we have it.

Outside those forge doors, there's an intelligence bent on wearing me down that controls the very walls of this ship. Out there is Hark and Bea and all the opinions they might have about our strange entanglement. And all around us is absolute nothingness, the deep void we've been sentenced to. But here, within the safety the Forgemaster's wrought for herself, we can afford to let our guards down.

With how easily the *Justice* can rip everything away from us, we owe it to ourselves to take what we can while we can. We're thieves, after all.

I ease up the stairs, gaining momentum as I go until I'm stumbling onto the landing, my breath coming hot and heavy. Fitz looks me up and down, her lips pursed like she's fighting like hell to keep them from betraying her. "See you've worked up a sweat already," she murmurs.

I shrug, then close on her. "Your turn."

CHAPTER 22

It'd be rude to fuck in the Forgemaster's bed, but we end up there after we've had our fill of the floor. Even though the clatter of machinery makes it impossible to doze off completely, I can barely keep my eyes open. Curled on my side in a daze, I trace my fingertips gently over the fringes of the sear mark on Fitz's stomach. She trails her fingers through my hair with equal care, watching me with half-lidded eyes.

The Forgemaster's still hammering away at her work, and Ham knows to give us space. It feels like we have nothing but time, even if each thunderous noise from deeper in the forge is another tick closer to the moment we're going to have to leave this little refuge and face the *Justice*'s machinations head-on. It's the last thing I should be thinking about with a naked Fitz sprawled on her back next to me, and the past hours have given me more than a few reasons I'd rather ignore the reality of what awaits us.

But the fact of it drags at me with all the inevitability of a black hole. I keep thinking back to Ham's stark declaration yesterday. We're here until we die. Maybe we get to choose a little of how we'll live until then. We could die as scavs in the outer ring, trading violence for violence. We could die as potato farmers in the settlements, as Blade-sworn trying to atone for our crimes, or as banded faithful under the *Justice*'s command.

And yet all of that hinges on accepting a truth I just can't let myself embrace.

The *Justice* is not a god. It's powerful—probably the most powerful thing aboard—but that doesn't make it infallible. It's a machine. An ancient machine, engineered by a long-dead empire and certainly beyond my understanding in many respects, but a machine all the same. Something that can be broken down into hundreds of intertwining components, from the outer guns it uses to bully settlements into handing over their sinners to the mechanism that keeps the drum spinning.

Hark always wanted me to understand that her plans were a little bit like machines too. She was assembling components, figuring out what she could use, what she had to watch out for, and what needed to be discarded as a distraction. One loophole in a security apparatus became a diversion at the right point to slip a wristwrap off a mark. One phrase dropped casually in a conversation could become a compulsive urge to check your wallet just in case. And out of those little bits, she'd build something so grand and awe-inspiring that I'd convinced myself I could never possibly imitate it.

But I know machines. I've spent my whole life learning all the little ways you can trick them into doing your bidding. It's not quite the same as conning a mark, where you have to understand not just the reality of your scenario but how their beliefs warp it—and where best to twist those beliefs toward your own purposes. A machine's mind is grounded in all the information it's assembled over the course of its lifetime. Its evaluation of that information isn't a belief system like a person's because there's no emotion to weight it, but that doesn't mean it's fully objective. It can still fall victim to bad information. It still has its weak points.

Put like that, it almost sounds like *I* could be the one to break us out of here.

"Murdock?" Fitz murmurs. "I can hear you thinking."

"Not about you, don't worry," I reply. Then I remember the strange position we've found ourselves in and brace for disaster.

But she only smirks and whispers, "Good."

"Good?" I repeat. My hand has frozen, just barely touching the softness of her stomach.

"I don't think it gets us anywhere good, thinking too deeply about . . ." She gestures lazily down the bed. "This."

"Sure, yeah," I murmur, letting my fingers trail lower, arcing over the dip where her hip joins her thighs.

She tenses beneath my touch. "What were you thinking about instead?"

I huff, then roll onto my stomach as I ease higher up on the bed and bundle a pillow beneath me. "The thing we're supposed to be thinking about. Once we get that sword, what next?"

"You mean how are we going to find Hark and Bea?"

"Not exactly. I think you might have been right, back in the bath."

Fitz's frown gets deeper and deeper as I explain the path my mind's wandered down. It's strange to see her so loose, so open with everything she's contemplating. Part of me wishes I could keep her like this. I'm not totally convinced I'll see this side of her again once we've left the safety of the forge.

When I finish, she hums and lets her head fall back in the pillows. "Does this mean you have a plan?"

I hesitate. The last time I tried to get her on board with a scheme I hoped would save our lives, she rejected me instantly. Sure, that was before the odyssey we've undertaken together— and before several blissful rounds on the floor of this loft— but it's not enough to negate the instinct four years of working with Fitz has locked inside me. She's been the voice of my doubts more times than I can count, always there to cut down what Hark had so carefully built up.

But maybe that's not such a bad thing. If a plan of mine can't hold up to her scrutiny, there's probably a reason for it. Her judgment is a stone. Swing my weapon against it, and it'll shatter. But use it to hone the blade, and I'll be better for it.

"I have the beginnings," I tell her. "First things first, I think Hark's idea about pursuing the core might be offtrack."

I watch her chew on that with my breath caught in my chest. I've led with what has to be the worst sticking point for her— the one that requires her to doubt Hark's plan. "And why is that?" Fitz asks after a good long stare at the ceiling.

"It's way too hard to get there. You saw it when we were out on the hull. We'd have to steal a shuttle—not impossible, but incredibly difficult to do without anyone noticing. The *Justice* would see us coming instantly. There'd be no window to do anything useful even if we managed to steer ourselves there."

"And you have something else in mind?"

I nod. "We've been thinking about the *Justice* as governed by the intelligence housed in the core. We've assumed the way to strike it down is to strike there. But this is a warship above all else. We've forgotten that reality. There's a lower place to hit— one that's bound to be far easier to access *and* bound to do far more damage."

Fitz fixes me with a look I used to dread. *Go on, I dare you,* her eyes say.

"We go for the jump supply."

She opens her mouth, and I brace for the inevitable doubt, but she seems to snag on the thought before it can fully form.

"How would we figure out where the jump supply is?" Fitz asks at last.

"We need Bea. She heard it when the ship jumped from Gest. I'm sure if we get her in the right place, she could pinpoint exactly where to find the jump core."

Fitz nods slowly. Doubting me is one thing—doubting Bea's ability to finesse a ship's workings, even one of this scale, is another. "So we locate the jump core. Then what?"

"We take out the jump reserves."

"Take them *out*?"

"Destroy them," I tell her, clenching my fist emphatically. "Antimatter pellets are useless once they're destabilized. I used to watch the fuel engineers loading 'em for transport to the naval berths on the Pearl Station docks. All it took was one wrong move—one trip and they'd go inert. We do that to every jump the ship has in stock."

"Stranding the *Justice* and everyone aboard in deep space," Fitz replies with a quirk of her eyebrow.

I shake my head. "That's the thing. Out in the black like this, there's no way the ship doesn't travel with a jump locked and loaded in the core. Even if we destroy its supply of jumps, it'll still have that one remaining."

"That's worse," Fitz says. "That means the *Justice* will just jump to another settlement and take it hostage until they supply it with jumps—and probably a few more sinners for good measure."

"Sure. Unless we convince it to jump somewhere else."

Fitz purses her lips. She's radiant like this—hair a mess, sprawled naked in the sheets, working a problem side by side with me. I have to fight the urge to kiss her. "How are we going to convince it?" she asks at last.

I grin. "That, my dear, is your expertise, not mine."

I expect her to grin back, to rise to the challenge, but instead Fitz looks confused. She's never held back on speaking her mind around me before, and the sight of her opening her mouth and hesitating has me wondering if Ham might have knocked me around a little too much. "You know," she says after a harrowing pause, "Hark usually has the plan for me. Doesn't really ask for my input."

I'm terrified of reading her wrong, but she seems . . . *pleased.* Like she's been waiting years to be invited into this part of the scheming.

"Well," I reply, scarcely believing the words that are about to come out of my mouth, "I guess it's a good thing I'm not Hark."

And there's the grin I was looking for.

THE FORGEMASTER'S NOISE WANES AS the day wears long until, at last, a triumphant *"Done!"* echoes through the cavernous space.

It startles me out of the hazy half nap I'd been enjoying. I'm on my feet and down the loft stairs a second later, tying my jumpsuit off around the waist as I hunt through the looming equipment. I find the Forgemaster slumped over a workbench like a new parent fresh from delivery, her eyes hollowed by exhaustion but lit with a fervent spark at the sight of her creation.

I'm almost afraid to look at it. Afraid of the disappointment that might come from seeing my imagination made real, the instant grounding that'll happen when I'm forced to reckon with an object as it is, not as I thought it might be.

But there's no denying the beautiful work she's done. The raw block of hullmetal I carved from the *Justice*'s skin has been refined into a short, elegant blade. The size throws me for a moment—the practice sword I used this morning was almost a full handspan longer—but when my fingers close around the hilt, I feel the rightness of it instantly, the way it aligns with my body and makes the blade a natural extension of my arm.

I now understand Ham's superstition about the risk of a

blade not made for you. The practice sword was easy to ignore, because it was only natural that it be big, clunky, and hard to wield. But comparing the sword in my hand, crafted just for me, to the dagger I had before, there's no question the dagger would have only betrayed me in the end. This grip meets mine like a familiar handshake where the dagger only barely consented to being held.

I'd scoffed every time Ham fretted over the beliefs that governed the *Justice*, but I'm starting to get it. Even if they're survival mechanisms, I can't deny the benefits.

I heft the sword in a showy swing, then move through the sequence of patterns Ham drilled into me this morning. My muscles burn, but it's nothing in the face of the easy confidence the blade instills in me as I step through each movement. "This is exactly what I needed," I blurt, flushing at how sincerely the words spill from my mouth.

"Well, thank fuck for that, because you weren't getting a do-over," the Forgemaster replies with a weary grin. "Now, if you'll excuse me."

She heaves herself to her feet, grabs the hem of her shirt, and strips it off in one fluid motion. I'm torn between shock and awe, but the Forgemaster only moves past me, shedding more clothing as she goes. She trudges across the forge, kicks off her boots, shucks off her pants, and rolls headfirst into the brine bath with barely a splash.

For a moment, I'm terrified she won't surface. She's been working nonstop for the last full day cycle—I wouldn't blame her if her body gave out entirely now. But after a frighteningly tense moment, her head breaks the water and she lets out a long, keening groan that has me once again thankful for the forge's heat. "If you're still here by the time I'm done with my soak, I'm going to give that thing a hell of a first test," the Forgemaster mutters. "Tell Ham to take the back way out. There's been someone watching the front all morning."

I tense. "A redhead?"

She shrugs, mopping her hair back from her face. "I didn't take a peek, but my sensors picked up something networked out in the hall. Could be banded faithful, could be a drone, could be a construct. Whatever it is, it's talking to the *Justice,* and I'm not opening my door as long as it's out there."

The weight of the blade in my hand feels doubled, the confidence it instilled in me starting to crumble. "I'm sorry," I say. "I didn't mean to bring so much trouble."

The Forgemaster flaps a hand dismissively. "I've dealt with worse in my time aboard. Stay sharp, keep your eyes open, and drop anything you don't trust before it can turn on you. And if you use that blade to make some trouble of your own, we'll call it even."

With that, she heaves a deep breath and slips beneath the water once more.

CHAPTER 23

The sword is heavy at my hip. Ham's furnished a flexible polymer sheath from the Forgemaster's collection, and though it fits just right, the weight of it still feels ungainly—made worse by the fact that the so-called *back way* the Forgemaster told us to take was a trapdoor leading to a narrow metal ladder that plunges down an unlit tunnel.

Worse still, the sword infused me with just enough misplaced bravado that I offered to go first.

I take it rung by rung, Fitz's flashlight clenched in my teeth as I try to keep my pack from dragging my grip loose and my sword from wedging in the ladder. Fitz follows close enough that I'm fighting the urge to snap at her for hurrying me. Above her, Ham's taking his sweet time. I'm trying not to imagine the consequences if either of them slips. The beam of the flashlight is just bright enough to tell me we've still got a long way down.

Maybe it would have been better to meet the *Justice* head-on. The confrontation is inevitable, and I have the sword now. I want it to be the answer to every fear, the light against every dark corner on this ship, but it's just a sturdy piece of metal I barely know how to use. If it were Scarlett waiting for us outside the Forgemaster's door, she'd probably hand me my ass in a second.

If it were a construct—

My boot jams hard into solid ground, jolting me out of the hypothetical. I stagger back on the landing, spitting the flashlight into my hand so I can take better stock of our surroundings.

The ladder's deposited me into a cozy alcove, a space barely large enough to fit two people shoulder to shoulder. There isn't an obvious door—only a wall of intertwining metal that mirrors the forge door we came through yesterday. I turn back just in time to catch Fitz by the elbow as she steps off the ladder and sways. "Easy there," I tell her.

"I've got it," she replies tersely. The narrow landing forces us into each other's space, and I'm not sure how to handle being so close to her again. I reach up and tuck a strand of her pale platinum hair back behind her ear.

She reaches down and tugs her flashlight out of my grip.

"Really?" I huff. "I even asked politely—"

"Coming through," Ham interrupts, and before I can put two and two together, Fitz's chest is pressed against mine, crowding me back against the wall, her forearm braced over my head. Ham wedges past behind her, but there's barely space for the three of us. "Light," he grunts, and Fitz flicks her wrist to point the flashlight's beam at the mechanism on the wall.

She may be dressed in her original colors again, but my focus drops down the long column of her neck to where her jumpsuit's collar is just a tad looser than usual.

"Murdock," she warns.

"Hmm?"

"Stop that."

"Stop what?"

"Stop . . . *juddering*. You're even more anxious than you were before you had the sword."

I hadn't even noticed I was shaking until she said it. "And what about it?" I bluster.

"Wasn't the whole point of the sword that it'd make you feel safer?"

"I do feel safer."

"Then quit fidgeting."

Ham huffs. "Y'know, I thought the two of you fucking would sort your shit out," he mutters as he fusses with the Forgemaster's mechanics.

Fitz and I both breathe deep, ready to object, but it's at that exact moment he drives a pin home and the whole wall swings open. We collapse out into a hallway in a heap, blinking at the sudden wash of day-level light. Ham's the first to roll clear of our ungainly tangle, popping to his feet and wedging himself against the open wall to press it back into place. A mechanism clicks, the seams settle, and if you'd told me there was a door there a minute earlier, I never would have believed you.

There's no going back now.

Just as the dread starts to kick in, Fitz stands. She looks down her long, elegant nose at me, then bends and extends a hand.

I take it, and she hauls me to my feet.

We've stepped outside the safety of the forge, and it feels only natural that we slide back to the way things were before. But we built something new in there. We have a plan now. *Our* plan, not just mine. Now we just need our crew back.

The corridor is clear of any signs of *Justice* architecture, but it's completely unfamiliar. "Where are we now?" I ask Ham.

"Still in the upper ring, just a few floors down from the surface. Which direction are we headed?"

Fitz catches my eye. There's a part of me bristling to talk over her, to declare I know exactly where Hark and Bea would have gone, but it'd be a lie. We could try following their signal in D major to some other large gathering, but it's been days now. Hark never lets a plan get that stale.

I give Fitz a nod and tilt my palm to gesture, *After you.*

"Our only lead is that Hark thought she could figure out a way out of here if she could get to the core," Fitz says. "If that's true, they'd be somewhere in the upper levels of the inner ring. Which means we're in a good position already. What else is up here, Ham?"

"Nothing like the settlements you've seen already. Enclaves, mostly—like the people who supply the Forgemaster. Not all of them are so willing to go against the *Justice.* They live along paths where the banded faithful deploy when they come ring-side, which means they have to compromise, sometimes, to keep their peace. Also means they're incredibly suspicious. You might not get much out of them, and I doubt your Hark and Bea would have managed to convince them to grant shelter."

"Our Hark and Bea might surprise you," I reply, raising an eyebrow at Fitz.

She shakes her head. "It's a long shot, but if those are places close to the target where Hark could safely observe and plot . . ."

"C-sharp major," I murmur, nodding. In Hark's music, that key means *Find a safe place to roost and gather intel.* It's not much to go on, but at least it sounds like something she would do.

"So what, you want to go search every enclave on the inner ring?" Ham asks, his voice barbed with trepidation.

"Or we could go ask them nicely if they've seen Hark and Bea," I suggest.

"Asking nicely isn't going to get you anywhere with these people."

"You don't know how nicely Fitz can ask," I reply with a smirk.

To MY HORROR AND SHAME. Ham was a little bit right.

I thought visiting the enclaves would be more like moving from town to town, traipsing through miniature versions of the majestic settlements we saw on the lower levels. But the inner ring is a different animal entirely, a cramped network of corridors wrought in unyielding Ybi ceramic. Any advantage we gained by sneaking out of the forge the back way evaporates the moment we step into the main halls. It feels like I can't go three meters without spotting another sensor box, and the reliefs etched into the paneling are done with all the ugly assuredness of imperial propaganda.

I fight the urge to start throwing elbows and smashing the hilt of my sword into the walls. That'd have the banded faithful on our asses for certain, and while I know there's no avoiding the ship's attention entirely, I'm determined to make some real strides toward finding Hark and Bea before the *Justice* regroups for its next move.

When Ham announces we've reached an enclave, I expect to round a corner to another hacked-out open space, but instead he pulls up short in front of a heavy-looking door. Much like the Forgemaster's, its design is a deviation from the Ybi aesthetic that dominates this hallway—which, under the circumstances, is comforting.

Fitz tugs the keychain out from the front of her jumpsuit, but Ham shakes his head and knocks.

"Was it worth snatching it back?" I mutter in her ear, and she delights me with a weakly thrown elbow.

A slot in the door shucks open to reveal a squinting set of eyes. "Who goes there?" a rough voice asks.

I guide Fitz forward with a gentle hand on her lower back, and Ham steps aside to let her take point. I feel it in her spine, the way the transformation takes her—how all her tension unfurls into perfect poise. "Hi there," she says, her voice pitched a full half-octave above her usual timbre. "We're new ingest who got separated from the rest of our friends. We're wondering if—"

The voice interrupts with a scoff. "You look like ingest. Those two don't. What're you really after?"

Fitz tilts her head. "We're looking for two women. Both in their mid-thirties—"

"No," the voice announces flatly, and the slot snaps shut.

Fitz blinks, her expression dropping back into her usual blankness.

I gape. "Holy shit. I've never seen you beef it that badly before."

"*You* try laying on the charm through a gap this big," she retorts, pinching her fingers in an exaggeration of the door's aperture.

She moves like she's going to knock again, but Ham catches her by the wrist before her knuckles can make contact. "That's just going to put you on their bad side even worse," he says. "You have no idea how many people with swords could be behind that door, and you don't want to find out by pissing off whoever's guarding it. We could try this one again tomorrow, but for now, it's best we move on."

By the fifth enclave that turns us away, I'm starting to take it personally. "What are they hiding that's so important?" I grumble, resisting the urge to aim a kick at the door.

"Well, that's kind of the point," Ham offers. "Most of these places are self-sustaining capsules unto themselves, and that

takes balance. They're not going to invite some random troublemakers in to throw off that carefully won order."

I'd object to *random troublemakers* if it weren't so accurate.
"So maybe Hark and Bea didn't make it into one. Then what?
They're wandering the inner ring, looking for a way to sneak
onto the shuttle decks?"

Fitz's brow furrows. I'm pretty sure I can guess the thought
spiraling between her ears. She's missed the mark with every
enclave we tried to sweet-talk today, and if *she*—Fitz, Hark's
reliable charm incarnate—couldn't get through to anyone,
could Hark?

I clap her on the shoulder. "We need to rest and regroup.
Ham, what's the nearest settlement?"

But Ham's shaking his head. "I don't want you to waste a
whole day trekking back and forth. We can find a place to camp
up here."

A place to camp turns out to be the polite term for something
I'm almost certain used to be a janitorial closet back in the warship days, if the lingering scent of three-hundred-year-old
cleaning solvents is anything to go by. The lock has long since
been busted and the contents emptied, leaving a cozy nook just
large enough for two bedrolls.

I volunteer for the first watch. We've seen a few people on
the course of our trek through the inner ring—none of them
helpful, all of them hurrying past us with their heads down and
their eyes firmly averted. I don't know how much of that to
attribute to the general sense of mistrust in the inner ring and
how much to blame the daylight, but Hark would tell me to
take no chances. I crouch in the door of the closet with my
sword laid over my knees as behind me Ham and Fitz settle
down for whatever sleep they can manage to grab on thin blankets and hard floors.

From my position, I can see a few sensors. Part of me is
tempted to stare them down, to make sure the bastard knows I

see it, too, but we've managed to go the whole day without provoking the *Justice*. I keep a lid on my impulses—if not for my sake, for the sake of Fitz's beauty sleep—but as the ship's environmental lights begin to slip toward full night, my dread starts to simmer. The corridor's brutal architecture has bled into murky shadow, and the intricate Ybi designs carved into the tiling almost seem like they're moving.

Maybe I should have grabbed some sleep first.

The night wears long, stiffness settling into my limbs—until a faint whirring noise from somewhere down the hall evaporates my exhaustion in an instant. My hand goes tight on the hilt of my sword as I lurch onto numb legs and drop my breathing shallow.

The noise is getting closer.

I glance back over my shoulder to where Ham and Fitz are sleeping peacefully. It would be better to wake them, if only to prove this isn't in my head, but I'm not ready for that answer. I squint into the corridor's gloom, trying to pick out real movement among the swirling Ybi murk.

Then the noise shifts, the whirring's uniformity perturbed by something that almost sounds like a whisper.

Almost sounds like "*Murdock.*"

"Took you long enough," I murmur.

"I think it's time we had another chat," the *Justice* replies.

I should shout. I should wake them up. But a part of me knows it wouldn't make any difference. We've passed enough sensor boxes over the course of our search. The *Justice* has known exactly where to find us since the moment we started pressing into the inner ring, and whatever it's doing now is inevitable. I want to keep Fitz and Ham out of it for as long as I can.

I square my shoulders, lift my sword, and ease out into the corridor to find a hovering observation drone no bigger than my fist. A pit of tension in my stomach uncoils at the realization this isn't another construct. I wonder if this is what was waiting for us outside the forge, or if the ship has switched tactics once again. "Fine," I whisper. "Chat away."

"I see you've made an acquisition," the *Justice* says, its voice emanating from the drone. "That's fine craftsmanship."

"Would you like to get acquainted with it?" I ask, circling the tip in the air.

The *Justice* lets out a purring noise, a snarl of a laugh. "No need to sound so defensive. I'm thrilled for you, my dear. You've already started your transformation into exactly what this ship needs from you. You're armed with a proper blade. You've discarded your original colors. You're starting to accept your reality. Soon you'll be ready to accept the truth at the heart of my domain. Do you know, I think you hold a new record for the shortest time from ingest to taking up a blade? It's like you were made for this place."

"Is that it?" I ask through my teeth. "Did you just come here to try to convince me I'm made for you again? Because I've had a long couple of days, and the only thing that's changed is that now I can take my terrible mood out on you with my cool new sword."

The *Justice* gives another purring chuckle, but this time it seems to reverberate from both ends of the corridor. My grip goes sweaty. The drone was a ruse—a way to bait me into entertaining the conversation by making me forget the truth of our circumstances. The halls are still lined with sensor boxes. We're surrounded on all sides. We've never been anything but that.

"No, Murdock." The *Justice* sighs. "I told you before. You'll come to me when you're ready. But I have some information for you that couldn't wait. It seems your dear Hark is in danger."

It pauses, savoring the silence as much as I dare imagine a machine is able.

"Would you like to know where she is?"

CHAPTER 24

I shake Fitz awake first, then move on to Ham before she's finished blinking her confusion away. "Now, now, we've gotta move now," I mutter, grabbing her pack and shoving it into her arms.

"The hell is going on?" she asks, her voice husky from sleep.

"Hark and Bea are in trouble. I know where they are. But that could change, so we have to move fast. C'mon." I start trying to pull her bedroll out from under her, shunting her upright as I go.

"You know where they are?"

"I know how to get to them."

"And how do you know?"

Hark trained me to be a good liar, but I can't lie about this. "The *Justice* told me."

Fitz glances at Ham, who's already half-packed. "You're just going along with this?"

"Fitz, look at me," I demand, and instantly regret it. She's fighting every instinct baked into her over the past four years, everything we've started the fraught process of unraveling, just to hear me out. "It could be a trap, I know. It's the ship playing games, I know. But look at me and tell me we're going to get any closer on our own. The ship wanted us separated. Now it wants us together. I'm not going to miss out on the moment our objectives align."

"Murdock," she murmurs, and fuck do I want to kiss her like this. She's too soft, too vulnerable, too *much*. "If this *is* a trap—"

"If this is a trap, give up on me. Never do another damn thing I say—I'll understand. I'll do whatever you want, you'll have me on my knees—but . . . we have to try."

She's slipping away. I'm losing her. I can see it in the way her mask eases back on, her expression locking into a flat, dead stare that I've never been able to read. The trap is obvious, and springing it is possibly the worst idea I've ever had. Asking her to follow me into it was too much too fast.

So when she whispers, "Okay," it takes the wind out of me completely.

"Yeah?" I blurt.

"Yeah." She lifts a hand to my cheek and lets her knuckles skim it, but before I can *do* anything with that utter slap of tenderness, she's tugging her bedroll out of my hands so she can fold it the right way.

It's another few minutes of frantic scrambling to pack up the little camp we pitched, and then we're off. I lead, counting doors as I go, one hand on the hilt of my sword, the other tapping against my side to help me keep focused on the *Justice*'s instructions. Fitz is right on my heels, like she can't bear the thought of me reaching Hark first, and Ham brings up the rear, moving in a shuffling sidestep to make sure nothing can surprise us from the shadows we leave behind.

We're playing right into the *Justice*'s hands. I know it has some deeper machinations at work, something that will become clear when we reach Hark. Maybe it wants us reunited just for the satisfaction of having the banded faithful ambush all four of us at once. Maybe that closet we camped in was more important than we thought and it needed us out of there as soon as possible. Maybe this is all a lie and it just wants to see me run.

But after a day of going from enclave to enclave, getting absolutely nowhere, after *days* without Hark and Bea, the *Justice* knew I'd be getting desperate. And while I'm trying to resist the urge to grant it the omnipotence it so clearly wants, I can't help giving it this small scrap.

So I follow its directions through the looming halls of the inner ring with a single mind, blowing past enclave door after enclave door, sidestepping huddled bundles of people camping in whatever nooks will shelter them, charging recklessly over threshold after threshold with no fear that the ship's about to slam another door in my face. I slow for nothing until we reach the final turn and hear the sounds of a scuffle around the corner.

My sword's out before I know what's good for me. I hurl myself around the bend and into the low glow of a lantern. By its light, I take in the torn-up remains of a camp much like the one we pitched and the equal parts balm and terror of seeing Hark and Bea scrapping hand to hand with three other people.

I let out a yell that echoes down the tight corridors, and all five of them freeze in confusion. One man has Hark's wrist locked behind her back as she grapples valiantly with the dagger he's trying to lay against her throat. The other two are in the process of wrestling Bea to the ground, but she's managed to get ahold of one of their batons and she's not giving it back for anything.

"This is our find," the guy holding Hark snaps. "Back the

fuck off." No headbands crown them, and their clothing is rougher than anything I've seen in a settlement. They look more like the scavs who greeted us on the *Justice*'s outermost ring, but that can't be right. Even if what Ham said is true, even if sometimes people fight the *Justice*'s gravity, their presence feels . . . ordained.

Before I can dwell on that too much, Ham rounds the corner to join me, sword drawn, and all three attackers straighten as the calculus shifts.

"Let me guess," I drawl, holding my head high as I give my sword a showy little flourish. "None of you folks bothered to make introductions before you started clobbering these two. Bad manners. Very bad hospitality. I'll start. I'm Murdock. This is Ham, Blade-sworn to . . . well, what do you know? He's Blade-sworn to me at the moment. And since I'm certain you didn't bother to ask, that delightful specimen of a woman *you* hold is wanted by at least seven names across seven systems, but her friends know her as Hark. And that beautiful nightmare *you two* are wrestling is Bea, three-time Grand Champion of the Galgothian Demo Derby."

That last bit of math finally adds up. The scavs stiffen as they realize they're outnumbered.

I charge.

Hark takes the moment of distraction to do what she does best, slipping the scav's hold so easily I wonder if she was just playing with him before. He staggers back, waving his knife wildly as I choke back my swing to keep from slicing his hand off. I glance right to confirm Ham's got the other two handled— I'm rewarded with the sight of him heaving one of them off Bea and throwing her clear down the corridor as Bea kicks the other one away, sending them crawling on hands and feet to regroup. I heft my sword into one of Ham's stances, hold my other hand up as a guard, and pray it looks professional enough to stave off any second thoughts from this group.

"Nice friends you've made, ingest," the man with the knife spits. "Better be sure to keep those Blade-sworn close."

"I'll keep it in mind," Hark replies smoothly, cutting me off from blurting a correction.

I keep my sword up until the scavs have retreated completely. They melt back into the darkness of the hall, disappearing around a bend, and I let out a sigh of relief that turns into a strangled yelp when a pair of arms snare around my torso.

"I thought we'd lost you," Hark mutters into the back of my shirt.

My guard goes completely, my sword clattering to the ground as I wrestle myself around in her grasp to hug her back with everything in me. I can't hold her tight enough to convince myself this is real. "Just took the scenic route," I choke out.

Over Hark's shoulder, I catch Fitz slipping around the corner, catch the flash of something I hate to see in her eyes as she takes in me and Hark. I wasn't ready for *this* to be real either, for the two of us to reckon so suddenly with how much has changed over the time we've been separated from them. There's no going back to the crew as it was, but maybe that's not so terrible. That was the crew that got caught.

This could be the crew that makes it out.

Hark shoves out of my grasp to hold me at arm's length, looking me up and down. "I'll be damned, kid. I didn't recognize you for a second."

I glance down at my clothes hewn on settlement looms, my boots bartered from my prison shoes, my slick polymer sword belt strapped around my hips. It's not *too* far flung from the Murdock she left behind three days ago, but now that I get a moment to take her in, I realize Hark is still suited head to toe in her original colors, looking like she's fresh through the airlock—if not a little weathered. Same with Bea, whom Ham is helping chivalrously back to her feet. And Fitz, now that I think about it—Fitz dressed in her original colors when we plunged back out into the *Justice*'s body. Fitz was taken for ingest at every enclave we approached today.

I wasn't.

The *Justice*'s voice is in my head, telling me I was made for this ship. I try to crowd it out, try to summon a grin as Bea grabs Fitz around the middle, lifts her off her feet, and twirls her, as Hark pulls away from me to snare both of them in a hug. I'm left standing side by side with Ham, who stoops to pick up my blade and offer it to me hilt-first.

But the smile won't come. There's only the cold comfort of the sword I had forged in record time as my fingers close around it.

"How the hell did you find us?" Bea asks, her eyes watery in the dim light of the lantern. "We didn't make it to that music festival in time—we tried, but we kept getting turned around."

Fitz, frozen up like a cat ambushed by puppies, catches my eye. I give her the slightest shake of my head. It shouldn't be a test, but I feel the tender edge it presses against my throat, having to wait to see if she follows my lead now that we're back with Hark at the helm.

"It was Murdock," Fitz says.

I flinch.

"She knows how Hark thinks," she continues. "Knew you'd be somewhere in the inner ring, trying to find a way to the core. Good thing I listened to her, huh?"

Hark stares in naked disbelief. "First Murdock's waving a sword around, now you're saying you listened to her? Did I get hit on the head?"

"Been an eventful couple days," Fitz says, holding my gaze. I swear she's keeping a smile down, trying to maintain the veneer of professionalism she always holds around Hark. "By the way, the big guy's name is Ham. He's a Blade-sworn we contracted as our guide. Ham, this is Bea and this is Hark," she continues with a tip of her chin toward each of the women hugging her.

"Ham's the one you have to thank for this, not me," I add, clapping him on the shoulder as he gives the two of them a bashful wave. "Without his guidance, we'd never have found our way."

"Just doing my part," Ham says with a stiff bow. "It's wonderful to meet you. Murdock and Fitz have told me so much about you."

A sour taste blooms at the back of my throat. Yeah, I told Ham plenty about Hark. Told him I was scared she made the best parts of me. All of a sudden, all I want is to pull him aside and ask what he sees when he sees her. Is she as great as I believe? Am I enough to stand next to her?

I think I know the answer already.

"Well, you have my thanks, Ham," Hark says, stepping back from Bea and Fitz to come clasp his hand. She's absolutely dainty next to Ham's bulk, but with the confidence of a seasoned con, she makes that difference look like nothing, greeting him with the same unshakable posture that blended her effortlessly among the galaxy's rich and famous as she swindled them. I've tried to mimic that straight-backed confidence so many times and always drawn up short. I do my best to sink into it now as I step in close and mutter in her ear, "Can I talk to you?"

"Always, Murdock, always."

"One-on-one," I clarify. Ham catches my eye, plainly worried, but I wave him off with a twitch of my fingers.

Hark seems thrown, but she nods and lets me usher her to the edge of the corridor, where there's a seam between the coverage of two sets of sensor boxes embedded in the walls. If I box her in and talk low, I can prevent the ship from picking up what we're saying or reading my lips. Hark gives me a quizzical look as I position myself.

"Eyes in the walls," I clarify under my breath, but something about it raises my hackles. Hark's been on the *Justice* just as long as I have. Has she not built up an awareness of its gaze?

"Miracle we survived this long without you," she says, abruptly voicing the sum total of my concerns.

"Did you figure out that plan?" I whisper urgently.

"Who do you think you're talking to?" Hark replies. "Plan's right on track. Find this thing's heart and fucking eat it. We're going to keep moving inward, tracing the embedded tech—which is going to be *vastly* easier now that we have you—and that'll lead us to the ship's core."

I shake my head. "I've seen the ship's core. I walked on the inner surface of this ring, and I saw it free-floating above me. It's not contiguous with the rest of the *Justice*'s body. The only way to reach it is through a shuttle, and those are guarded by the banded faithful. No one gets to the core who isn't loyal to the ship."

"So we steal one of the shuttles. Bea can fly anything. I'm still not seeing the problem."

"You don't see the problem with getting past the banded faithful?"

Hark grins. "Why do you think we keep Fitz around? She'll talk her way through them."

I hate how I hear it instantly—the way she angles the two of us against each other at the first opportunity. Part of me wants to snap at how dismissively she talks about Fitz, but the rest knows she wouldn't be doing it if I hadn't been proving it worked for the past four years. I grit my teeth. "The faithful are religious. Devoted. The *Justice* is a god. I don't think Fitz can compete with that."

Hark lets out a short scoff. "The *Justice* isn't a god. Where's my logical little tech-head?"

"Look, *I* know it's not a god, but it runs on belief all the same. Even if it's a machine that can be hacked, it has a hold on the minds of these people. That *belief* is real, and unless you treat it as real, you're never going to be able to leverage it. Isn't that what you've always preached? To use belief instead of denying it?"

The look in Hark's eyes is tearing me in half. "I also taught you not to get taken in by the irrational. Look at yourself, Murdock." Her fingers come up to play with the rough edge of my sleeve. "Dressing like one of them. Waving around a sword. Telling me the *ship* has a stronger hold on people than Fitz's wiles. I know you've always butted heads with her, but if you're going to help me get us out of this, I need you to put that aside."

Heat is starting to flood my cheeks, and suddenly I'm twelve years old again, listening to my mother spin her bullshit about what is and isn't for my own good. "Fitz has been right there with me every step of the way these past few days," I whisper vehemently, biting back the urge to tack a vindictive *unlike you* at the end of the sentence. "She's learned what does and doesn't work when it comes to this ship, and she'll tell you the same as me. Which is why the two of us have come up with our own plan."

"Murdock," Hark says, and I can't help but marvel at how such a gentle tone can be such a forceful stop. "I appreciate that you're trying to help, I really do. But this isn't the place for your first op, and I think you know that. When we get out of here, I've got several little games in the cooker I'd be *happy* for you to take the reins on, but for now—"

"Nothing you try will work," I tell her flatly. "Not unless you accept the reality of the ship. I have something that will. A little number in F minor, if we want to use your vernacular."

Hark's eyes sharpen. "*Really?*" she asks.

"Really. But you've gotta dance my steps, or we're never getting out of here."

"Murdock, you've been back for all of two seconds. Can we sit down and talk about this? No great plan is born on a whim."

"This isn't a whim. What do you think I've been doing for the past three days?"

Hark looks me up and down, giving me a face that says, *Fuck if I know.*

"I know this ship better than you. I've learned how it works while trying to find you—things you didn't even bother learning because you don't think we'll be here long. But I promise you, if·you don't hear me out, you're going to have plenty of time to catch up with me." *Please,* I have to fight to keep from begging her. *Please, just let me earn my forgiveness.*

"We've traversed the same ship over the same amount of time. What makes you think you know it better?"

"Because I've been *speaking to it*!" I shout.

The others' heads snap toward us in alarm. "Murdock's already causing a ruckus?" Bea asks, her eyes narrowed and her grin sly.

"It's what I do best, huh?" I retort, fighting the anger threatening to boil over inside me. I don't make the plans. I cause the diversions. I'm not at the center of the party. I'm in a dusty vent, pulling plugs, deadening alarms, clearing the way so the rest of the team can shine. I could never be the one who made the plan that saves us.

Hark's studying me like a mark. Like she's getting ready to pick me apart and put me together again. "You've been talking to it?" she asks levelly.

It's the last drop of doubt I can take. "The ship wants me," I croak. "Says it has use for me."

"How . . . How often have you been speaking with it?"

I lower my eyes. There's no coming back from this. No hiding anything from her. Hark's always been the person who saw clean through me, from the moment she first grabbed my wrist. Might as well make it fast.

"It told me where to find you," I confess to my feet. "And I think I'm starting to understand why."

We were never going to be the crew that makes it out. The hope I'd carried—the hope that we'd changed—is nothing but ashes in the stark light of the *Justice*'s truth. And if the reality I have to accept is one where I spend the rest of my life on this ship, then there's only one choice left for me.

It's Fitz I find when I finally lift my gaze. Beneath her flat affect, there's something brewing that looks dangerously close to anguish. Fitz fought for me. Crawled through the vents when she heard me scream. Picked me up when the *Justice* left me crumpled in an alleyway. Braved the void to fetch hullmetal for a sword that would make me feel safe again. Fitz doubted when I told her the *Justice* had pointed us at Hark, but she went along with it anyway.

She's always seen right through me, seen me down to my bones. I think she knows what I'm about to do.

I step away from Hark and up to her side, raising a careful hand to trace my thumb over her cheek, returning the feather-light touch she gave me with all her misplaced faith. "Smile, Fitz," I murmur. "One last time. For me?"

Before I can see if she does, I turn away, sheathe my sword, shrug my pack higher on my shoulders, and stride across the nearest threshold.

I don't even flinch when the *Justice* slams the door shut behind me.

CHAPTER 25

"Are you happy?" I ask the dark.

"Emotions like *happy* are constructs of an endocrine system I lack, Murdock. You should know better."

"You don't get any sort of . . . I don't know, *reward* when something executes exactly as planned?"

"If I planned it and it executed to perfection, then expectations were met. There is no reward necessary for performing within parameters."

"This was perfection?"

"Perfection would have been achieving this state about seventy-two hours ago, but I rolled with the punches, as you say. Now, come. We can make up for lost time."

A hand finds mine, and I resist the urge to jerk away from it, to scream, to marvel at how easily the *Justice*'s construct snuck up on me. The fluid motion it uses to draw me forward couldn't be anything but a body it's piloting with total control.

In the cavernous darkness, I can pretend it's nothing but the hand of a friend, guiding me to the fate that's been waiting for me ever since I came aboard.

I follow its winding path until my next step lands, improbably, in dampness. The *Justice* gives me a moment to balk. I bend and feel the liquid, draw it up to my nose and sniff. It's water, the scent cut with a raw metallic edge—at least, that's my best guess.

The construct pulls me forward again. My next step sinks deeper. The next even deeper. Up to my knees, then my hips, then the limbic squeeze as its chill crosses my heart.

I sink back into my heels, but the construct's grip on me tightens. All at once, I understand. The *Justice* knows that I could be fucking with it, that maybe my defection wasn't genuine. This is a test of faith. Either I trust where it leads me, or I prove I never truly chose it over Hark.

"Good girl," the construct murmurs as I take a slow step forward. "Deep breath now."

I let out a long sigh, bottoming out my lungs, then breathe from my belly with so much force that I nearly choke. With the chill of the pool hugging me tightly, it feels like it's nowhere near enough, but the construct is already tugging me under.

I let go. Of every ounce of resistance that could drag me back. Of any expectation, whether it's resurfacing safely side by side with the construct or staying twined with it as it sinks me to a watery grave. Of any hope that I'll see Hark again. See Bea, see Ham.

See Fitz.

This is my only future. The only one I'm suited for.

I feel the fluttering pulse of the construct kicking, so I kick too, letting it guide me through darkness so complete that cracking my eyelids open does nothing. I've lost track of what's up and what's down, but when I stick my hand out toward my best approximation of overhead, I meet a wall. The thought sends a clench of panic into my gut that nearly costs me some of my air. If we're not just underwater but enclosed overhead, the only way I'm getting out alive is with the construct's guidance.

I have no trust for the *Justice*—I think I understand it well enough to know how it'll behave, and at the end of the day, that's close enough to the same thing. But as we swim deeper and deeper, I feel that sureness waning. My lungs are beginning to ache enough that I have to let out a slow stream of bubbles. The cold is pulling at me like a physical weight. And through it all, the construct powers ahead unbothered.

I know the *Justice* can't feel. The construct's response to the cold and the oxygen deprivation is nothing but a series of signals it's interpreting, and the way the construct responds is nothing but signals the *Justice* sends. If that's the case, it's feasible the *Justice* can force it to stay submerged for far longer than I can manage.

It's like null, I try to tell myself. *Like crawling through a vent.* I have to make this anything but the reality, the way I might be enclosed on all sides, the way my lungs are starting to burn with the need to inhale. If I can just imagine the sensation of floating without gravity, I can imagine myself safe and free. If I can picture myself squirming through a vent, I can picture the light at the end getting closer. But the one thought that cuts through my panic like a molecular edge is the knowledge that if I fight, if I flail, if I do anything to make the construct let go of me, the *Justice* will decide that's a choice.

This, too, is a behavior I can anticipate. If this is a test of faith, I have to believe the *Justice* will guide me through it.

But I'm not fighting the part of my brain that chose to walk over that threshold. I'm fighting a million years of base human survival instinct that knows no loyalty. Its only allegiance is to my continued existence, and no amount of rationality can combat that. All at once, I understand that I might not be enough for this machine—not by virtue of failing to live up to the faith it requires but simply by being human.

I've already failed to live up to Hark's expectations today. Maybe it's no big loss to fall short of a god's.

I can't hold the water back any longer. My lungs convulse, and my throat burns as I lose control of my lips. My kicks get more frantic, thrashing in the construct's wake as I try to force both of us to get wherever we're going faster.

It keeps its same steady, unbothered pace.

My eyes slip open to find a glow ahead, but I can't differentiate it from the pulsing flashes of my own brain betraying me as more and more water scorches down my windpipe. This isn't a vent crawl. It can't be null either—I'm far too heavy to float, so heavy that it's starting to feel as if I'm yoking back against the construct's grip.

This is it. The moment it releases the deadweight and casts me aside because my faith wasn't enough and my body couldn't make up the difference.

But then I lock onto the lights overhead. The pull is guiding me upward. I'm wanted. Needed. A last spark of fight snaps through me and I kick for the surface with everything I have.

I break free into crisp, cool air and immediately vomit a slurry of my half-digested dinner and all the water that seared down my throat. The construct guides my hand to its shoulder and lets me use it to keep myself afloat as I struggle not to choke back any of the upsetting liquid coming out of me. The convulsions wrack me like a towel being wrung out, and by the time they're done, I can barely keep my head above the water. The construct loops an arm around my torso, maneuvering me onto my back as it kicks us into motion again.

I stare up at the vaulted ceiling, feeling like I've just been reborn. The stippled Ybi arches are awash in swaying specular threads, the reflection of lights off the water I'm being bodily dragged through. It sends another shudder of nausea through

my gut, but I don't think I have anything left to hurl. I squeeze
my eyes shut.

The construct shifts from swimming to walking, the water
growing shallower around us as it heaves me up onto a sloping
metal beach. More hands find me—constructs, I think with a
twinge of helpless revulsion, until I realize the dancing lights
beyond my eyelids are the halos of other faithful. They pull me
out of the water, rolling me on my side to rub my back and
make sure my airways are clear. Through the hazy slits of my
eyes, I watch a pair of faithful tending to the construct, easing
an aspirator into its nostrils and peeling down the soaked coverall it wears to wrap a blanket around its shoulders.

Careful hands pry me up to my knees, and before I can
croak that I, too, would like a blanket, I'm suddenly swathed in
warmth. They've wrapped a cloak around me—brilliant white,
like the ones they all wear.

Mine. This cloak is mine, because my faith is sufficient, because I made it through the waters, because that was all the
Justice ever needed from me. I pull it tighter and glance up at the
person who placed the cloak on me.

Scarlett winks. Of course it's her. "I knew you'd come
around," she says.

My throat's far too sore to risk a retort, but I shoot her a
look I hope she understands means *That makes one of us.*

The construct is back on its feet already, the blanket hanging loose around its frame like a ceremonial robe as it holds out
its hands. Another faithful steps up and presents it with a pale,
flexible circlet.

A prickling awareness dances over my goosebump-ridden
skin as the entire chamber turns its attention to me. "Welcome,
Murdock," the *Justice*'s voice announces. It comes not from the
headpiece of the construct but from every headband surrounding us, as omnipotent as its gaze. "You've chosen to walk

the path of the faithful. To serve as an agent of true justice to enemies of order. To be initiated in this ship's holy mission."

I nod weakly. "I have." My voice comes out in a strained whimper.

"You join the ranks of generations of faithful, a lineage that stretches back to the very foundations of the Ybi Empire. For three hundred years, my beloved followers have kept the flame of this ship burning bright, and you will add to that wondrous light. Every one of them started as humble sinners, brought aboard to remove their scourge from the greater galaxy, but through their service, they have made themselves into saints. Today, you take up that splendid torch."

I sway unsteadily on my knees as the construct steps up to me, lofting the band with one hand and smoothing back my dripping hair with another. Under its careful attention, I feel myself shaped into order, ready to receive its blessing. My gaze stays fixed on the circlet like it's an anglerfish's lure at the bottom of the deepest ocean trench.

I can't help but lean up into it when the *Justice* sets it on my head.

The wearable connects, drawing the initial boost of power it needs from my body as it tightens to mold into the shape of my cranium. The band warms, and ethereal light spills from it. A hum kicks to life under its gentle pressure, and a voice croons directly into my skull, "Now you're perfect."

Tears well in the corners of my eyes. The construct bends to offer a benevolent hand, and I take it without hesitation, letting the ship itself put me back on my feet. I'm bedraggled and radiant. Wrung out and saintly.

Wrecked and finally enough.

CHAPTER 26

"You're gonna love it coreside," Scarlett says as she settles in next to me.

The shuttle is idling, waiting for the rest of the faithful making the crossing to strap into their seats. The *Justice*'s voice guided me to the bench I've deposited myself on. I wonder if it also told Scarlett to stick to my side.

"That's fine work," she notes, eyeing my sword. I stowed the rest of my gear in the overhead bins, but I couldn't bring myself to part from my blade. Neither, it seems, could she, because she pulls her own out from between her knees and holds it up to mine to compare. "It took me four months aboard before I got mine, and I was already banded. This was made by one of the core forges," Scarlett says, easing her blade partly out of its sheath to give me a better look at it. "I've always admired the work done ringside, though. There's something about the pressure of it all—the wildness, I suppose. Makes for a more interesting blade than one that might as well have been printed."

I tug my sword a few centimeters out of its sheath to match, and instantly I see what she's talking about. While the Forge-master's work is beautiful, the blade I'm comparing it against is so perfect it could be a render.

"I'll trade you," I croak. Scarlett laughs, but the joke goes down like a swig of liquor, burning my already-abused throat. Fitz put her life on the line for me to have this sword. It de-serves more respect than that frivolous quip. I snap the weapon back in its sheath and swing it down to rest between my knees.

"Final safety check. Launch in one minute," an intercom overhead announces. The hold fills with the sounds of buckles clipping into place, and the pitch of the shuttle's hum shifts as the outer door seals and the air starts to cycle. I settle deeper in my seat, wishing there were a window to offset the claustropho-bia of being locked in. It's a little too much too soon after my underwater adventure.

"Launch in ten," the intercom declares. My knuckles whiten around my sword's hilt.

There's no countdown, only an escalating whine that cre-scendos into a deep rumble as the engines fire behind us. The thrust kicks me hard into my cushion as the shuttle accelerates down the launch tube. The amount of rattling is a grim re-minder this vehicle's no younger than three hundred years, the same as the rest of the ship, and my breath goes still in my chest.

Until we break free. The moment we're spat from the launch tube, the noise drops so dramatically that for a moment I fear the void's crept in. The thrust cuts, leaving us floating up against our restraints, and I relax into the comfort of null.

At my side, Scarlett's taking a turn white-knuckling her sword, her brilliant red curls puffing out into a wild spill as she squeezes her eyes shut. It's more evidence in favor of my initial read on her, and it has me curious. "Not much time in null?" I rasp.

"No more than necessary," she replies.

"Grew up planetside?"

"For the most part. The occasional off-world vacation, of course, but you can sedate those away."

I note the *of course*. "How'd you end up here?"

Scarlett chokes back something with a surprising little snarl. "The usual unfairness. My family's stake went sour, and the workers blamed us. Like we had anything to do with the viability of the soil when *they* were the ones who should have been bringing it to a baseline. Said we lied to them, sold them bad investments, and decided in whatever law book they'd pulled out of their asses, that meant they could imprison us. Then the next day, the *Justice* showed up in orbit."

There are about three hundred things wrong with what she just said, but my curiosity gets the better of me before any judgment can take hold. "You were a homestaker? What was your settlement called?"

Scarlett scoffs. "Hardly matters now, does it? No one's ever heard of it." She blows out a long sigh. "Vestal."

The shuttle sways into its approach, giving me the perfect excuse to blanch. Fact of the matter is, I *have* heard of Vestal. Mainly because a few years back, I helped Hark orchestrate its collapse and siphon the spoils. We never once set foot on the rock—before Gest, we did all our work from the galactic core, wining and dining the corporate lords into dubious boilerplate and vanishing before the consequences caught up.

My gaze drops to the sword Scarlett showed off to me. Maybe now isn't the best time to be sharing our tragic backstories.

Fortunately the landing sequence smothers any further attempts at small talk. I recognize the thrust pattern as the one used to bring a ship in for docking on a surface rotating to approximate grav. The trick is to hit the apogee of your approach parabola at precisely the moment the landing lines lock in, magnetizing against the hull to winch the ship into the cradle of its rotation. The ride is far rockier than I'm used to in a way that makes me miss Bea's flying.

And you gave that up. The voice in my head might as well be the *Justice*'s for the way it gets me right between the ribs. I didn't even say a proper goodbye to my crew—just touched Fitz's face like a weirdo and catapulted myself into the *Justice*'s arms. Now I'm palling around with a woman who'll probably gut me the moment she learns what got me onboard this ship and seconds away from walking into the very heart of the monster.

I have to let that hurt, because it's the truth. Because it's what I deserve. But equally, I have to let it be behind me, because this is what I chose. Ham was right. The reality of me is that I made this decision, and it'll only hurt me to sweep it away under a delusion. If this is the truth of who I am, then this is the only future left for me.

Gravity settles back under our feet as the landing lines pull us flush with the hull above us, latching onto the core like a remora onto a great whale. It's the gravity of a smaller rotating body, a little more angular than the slower progress of the ship's outer ring, and it feels like Pearl Station's.

Feels like coming home.

SCARLETT HOOKS ONTO MY ELBOW the moment I'm clear from the airlock ladder. I'm far too worn-through to protest, but when she guides me out into the core proper, I end up grateful. For a hot second she's the only thing keeping me on my feet.

I'd brushed off the rumors of the command core's splendor. At worst, I figured it would match the grandiose Ybi architecture I'd gotten sickeningly familiar with in the *Justice's* main body. But I'd forgotten that above all, the *Justice* is about hierarchies, and a pinnacle isn't a pinnacle if it looks just like everything else.

We emerge into a cathedral. Support struts arc overhead, wrought in pearlescent engraved polymer, converging on the blinding glow of a computing core, the heart of the *Justice* itself. Its light falls on us like a sun, illuminating the hyperbolic bend of the concourse around us in the buttery glow of dawn. The massive, hollowed-out shape of the core peeks through gaps in the struts, and if I look carefully, I can see clear through to the other side, where people go about their business inverted. When I squeeze my eyes shut against the brightness, the patterns that dance against the dark are the stippled pinpricks of a thousand eyes.

"Sure is something, isn't it?" Scarlett murmurs from my side, her head bent back with the same reverence. "First time I saw it, I fell flat on my back."

If she weren't keeping me upright, I think I'd do the same. I don't feel worthy of these sights, but there's something about it that puts a hollowness in my chest. I've traversed the entire hierarchy of this ship, from its lawless outer decks to the seat of its power. There's more to explore out in the ship's main body, but I doubt any of it could surpass the miracle of mind-warping architecture that is the command core. If this is the peak of what the ship can offer, where do I have left to climb?

I suppose that's up to the ship now.

As if it heard my very thoughts, the band around my head goes warm. "That's enough gawking," the *Justice* murmurs into my skull. "Right now, I need you rested."

Scarlett's got her head cocked to the side. At first I wonder if the *Justice's* vibrating voice is projecting loud enough for her to hear, but then she nods subtly and I realize it's having a concurrent conversation with her. The thought is dizzying. On an academic level, I'd understood that many religions put forward the notion of a personal dialogue with God, one thread in a tapestry of interconnected exchanges, but it's another thing entirely to know I have a place in it.

My gaze settles on the computing core overhead, fighting to pick out its details through its radiance. That's *it*. That's what's speaking to me now.

That's what Hark wanted to destroy.

She's never been the type to change her mind over a pretty face, but hell, I dare her not to get seduced by the sight. A three-hundred-year-old gem of gorgeous engineering that's survived the collapse of an empire and maintained continuous operation. The part of my brain raised in my mother's shop quivers at the thought of what I could achieve with that kind of computing power.

The part of my brain forged by Hark wonders what that kind of computing power could possibly need with me.

"All things in their time, Murdock," the *Justice* says, and again I worry it's reading my mind. "Come."

A prickle on my headband guides me like the brush of a hand, turning my head to direct me toward a path. Scarlett's hand slips from my elbow, letting me take the first steps forward on my own. I feel like a sheep being herded, but after the weird night I've had, all I care about is that the path I'm on ends with a dormitory. We trudge along the lanes that wind perpetually up the gentle slope of the core's bend until the *Justice*'s guidance pulls me down a set of stairs and into a long, narrow hallway.

"You'll be training with my squad," Scarlett says as we approach a door. "That means you'll share our suite. Don't worry—plenty of room for everyone in these quarters."

The door sweeps open automatically, and it startles me like

I'm new to the ship all over again. I've come to expect the *Justice* slamming doors in my face, but never opening them. Scarlett makes an *After you* gesture, and I step through to discover a cozy, well-appointed atrium. Skylights open overhead, letting light from the computing core spill into the spacious dwelling, painting over luxurious couches and unmissable Ybi molding.

"Like I promised," the *Justice* says through my band. "These were once the quarters granted to my upper echelon of officers."

"So this all used to be for one person?" I mutter, my gaze flicking sidelong to where Scarlett's throwing down her sword and toppling onto one of the couches. Sure, this is far more spacious than most of the hotel rooms Hark would run our jobs out of, but my exhaustion demands a victim and it might as well be the roommate situation.

"There's a private room for you this way," the *Justice* says with another pleasant brush of tension along the band. "Right now, all I need from you is your body rested."

With the *Justice* wrapped around my head, there's no true privacy within reach. But I follow its guidance anyway to a door I can close and mechanically latch behind me, a bed so soft it's almost uncomfortable, and a sleep so deep I nearly forget about the warmth of it pressed into my skull.

THE *JUSTICE* GIVES ME A full cycle to recover, and by the next morning, I'm starting to realize it was deliberate. I've gone from exhausted and wrecked to so eager for something new to do that I practically throw myself at Scarlett when she reenters the suite.

"Murdock, hey," she says, smirking at the way I've come bounding out of my room. "Wanted you to meet the rest of the squad before we get started."

She's trailed by three people who look vaguely familiar. I suppose if I'd paid more attention to anyone but the brilliantly redheaded young woman talking my ear off at that tense East Deck dinner party, I might recognize them better.

"This is Allen," Scarlett starts, nodding to the hulking man on her left. He has a mean-looking longsword strapped across his back, and between that and the fact that he's easily bigger than Ham, I instantly decide he's the one I'd least want to tangle with head-on. "The *Justice* brought him on as muscle, but he's been training as a backup tech-head in his spare time. Maybe you'll be able to teach him a few tricks."

"Only if he teaches me a few in turn," I reply, tapping my fingers on the hilt of my sword as I reach out for a shake with my other hand.

Allen takes it, revealing a gold-toothed grin.

"This is Soren," Scarlett continues, gesturing to her right. "They're our best duelist by a light-year."

The slender whip of a person shrugs their shoulders bashfully. I take the hand they offer next, my eyes settling unsubtly on the elegant hilt of the rapier belted at their waist. Now that I know what to look for, I can see that this weapon was forged ringside, much like mine. I'll have to get the story behind it later.

"And this," Scarlett says, stepping aside to beckon the third squad member forward, "is Sumiko. She's been on this ship for twenty-five years, so you won't find a better navigator in all of the faithful."

Sumiko rolls her eyes at the praise but takes the hand I offer with surprising sincerity. She doesn't look threatening at first glance, built short and heavy, but if my time training with Ham has taught me anything, it's that heaviness is a weapon of its own in well-trained hands—and if this woman's survived twenty-five years aboard, she must know a thing or two about using the shortsword at her hip.

"So, muscle, duelist, navigator, tech-head—and what do you do?" I ask, eyeing Scarlett.

She quirks her lips. "Public relations."

I know exactly why that twists my gut, but if I think about it too hard, I'll combust. "What brought you all to the *Justice*?" I ask, swallowing back the bitterness.

Sumiko shakes her head. "That's ingest thinking. Unfaithful thinking. Don't worry—you'll get over it. Whatever I was originally, I was remade when I was initiated into the *Justice*'s service. As were you."

I have to suppress a shudder. My near-drowning in the wee hours of the morning yesterday has taken on the texture of a fever dream, but the reminder brings back an unsettling mixture between the vivid sensation of water forcing itself down my throat and the sheer relief of my subsequent rebirth.

Allen offers me a sympathetic smile. "Trust me. You'll be happier leaving the life you knew behind."

I resist the urge to glance sidelong at Scarlett. "The *Justice* didn't tell you about the life I lived before?"

Soren cuffs me on the shoulder. "Doesn't matter. You're at the most exciting part right now—the part where nothing matters but the shape you can fill in the ship's grand plan."

THEY SEEM HAPPIER IN THE core.

The thought strikes me as we emerge into the brightness of the cycle's afternoon and I see the way our god's light puts a smile on each of my squad mates' faces. Scarlett beams outright, stretching her hands up over her head as she leads the way down a meandering path that winds through spiraling trellises of flowers. I search for fruit on the vines, but these gardens seem to be purely decorative. Purely for pleasure.

The *Justice*, I'm starting to realize, never lies.

The faithful we pass seem equally cheerful, free from the hassle of tracking down errant ingest or battling their way through unruly scavs. Under the *Justice*'s brilliant sun, in the turn of its steady gravity, everyone looks healthy and relaxed. Is this what awaits redeemed sinners under the ship's mercy? Is this what everyone in the inner ring is refusing to strive toward?

Now, *that's* an ugly thought, the idea that everyone on this ship who isn't here has missed out due to some personal failing. I was lucky enough to draw God's attention from the moment I came aboard, inevitably crowned as one of its chosen. But I can feel the temptation, now that I've walked these gorgeous streets, lined with blooming greenery, to accept my own redemption—and to go back out ringside to tell everyone what they're missing out on.

We arrive at the rim of a green-coated bowl of a field, a half-domed dent pressed into the core's inner surface. In it, I see an echo of the computing core overhead, a space where the massive sphere could have once docked for repairs, but in the intervening centuries it must have been cultivated over. I bend to a knee to confirm my suspicions. It's real grass, soft and cool beneath my fingertips. "You have some good gardeners, huh?" I ask, eliciting a purring chuckle from the *Justice*.

"I have good everything," it replies, its voice pure honeyed confidence.

The shove catches me off-guard, tipping me over the edge and sending me rolling down the steep slope of the sides into the center of the bowl. I tumble to a halt and peel my face off the grass to discover Scarlett looking down on me with a sly grin tugging the edge of her lips. "The *hell*?" I shout, but she only shrugs and starts pulling her brilliant red curls back into a tie.

I surge to my feet, panic sparking through me as our other three squad mates begin to fan out around the edges of the bowl. My knees are grass-stained, but the deep black of my new sleeveless jumpsuit hides the green markings better than any of my other clothing ever could.

"Welcome to the Dip," the *Justice* says, its voice projecting from every headband but my own. "Your task is simple. Escape it."

As one, my squad mates draw their swords.

CHAPTER 27

My breath freezes on a choke. My fingers fumble on the hilt of my sword, strapped in its sheath at my waist.

"Relax," the *Justice* croons in my ear. "Their objective is to stop you, not kill you. Get that heart rate down and show me what you can do."

Sure. One person against four on the high ground, all of them clearly experts with their blades where I've had mine for a couple days. Those odds don't shake out. But Ham did his best to teach me—and when that failed, gave me a handy bag of tricks to pull from. I suck in a deep breath and draw my blade, glancing at each of my opponents as they settle into their places on the Dip's horizon.

And Ham's not the only one who's taught you a trick or two, I remind myself, sinking into memories of quick escapes, clinging to safety bars as Bea rocketed recklessly through a tightening

net. *You're never surrounded,* she always used to tell me. *You're just
at the center of a balanced system. Identifying it is step one. Step two?*

Knock it over. It's what I do best.

The Dip is about two meters deep, thirty across by my reck-
oning, its slopes asymptotic in a way that's going to severely
hamper any attempt to climb out of it, even if I weren't cor-
nered. Scarlett's shove has rolled me a good ways toward the
middle, but she's still my closest opponent. I glare up at her and
get a cheeky wave in return. Her sword's held loose at her side.
If I had more confidence in my abilities and less conviction the
Justice could throw me out an airlock for doing grievous harm
to one of its precious faithful, I'd pitch my sword at her and see
where it got me.

But I'm trying to be clever here. So instead I return the
wave with a flirtatious wink and set into a brisk walk angled
toward the gap between her and Allen. She follows me, forced
to lengthen her strides to keep up with my pace, but slows as
we start to close in on him. I keep up my speed, unbothered, as
Scarlett falls off and Allen noses in to match me.

With his size, he has a far easier time matching my strides,
but I edge faster, forcing him into a jog to keep up. I feint at
doubling back, trying to see if I can get him to trip, but he's
ready for it, swinging his longsword with expert grace to coun-
terbalance the maneuver.

After a few more paces, he trades off with Soren and things
get trickier. They're faster, lighter on their feet, and keep their
rapier's tip pointed at me unwaveringly. If I weren't a full body
length below them, I could use that to my advantage, letting
their guard wear them down until I had my opening, but the
Dip's forcing me to be a little more creative than that.

When Sumiko takes over, she has to jog from the get-go,
her shorter legs doing double the work to keep up with me.
The shortsword she carries is well matched to mine, but by the
way she carries it, I know a one-on-one duel with her would

only have one outcome. I let her follow me instead until we close in on Scarlett and she falls off to let the redhead pick up the task of guarding me.

"Having fun, are we?" the *Justice* asks by the time we've finished our second circuit.

"Oodles," I deadpan, glancing back over my shoulder to clock the positions of my squad mates. "At least, I think geometry is fun. Don't you?"

"I don't," it replies. "You think you can tire them out, get them sloppy, and make your break."

"Smart, right?"

"Smart, I'll give you that. But it's not what I was looking for."

Before I can conjure the appropriate curse, all four of my squad mates move as one, stepping over the edge of the rim and sliding down the side. With one hand braced on the wall, they loft their weapons with the other, all moving toward me.

I bolt. Rabbit. Run for the nearest edge, throw myself at it, and try with every bit of strength I can muster to haul myself over the top. It doesn't do me an ounce of good. I had the misfortune of being closest to Allen, and it's his hand that latches around my ankle and drags me back down into the Dip with a heave so mighty, it sends me rolling clear to the middle. By some miracle, my sword stays in my hand.

By an even greater miracle, I get it up in time to parry Scarlett's swing.

"You said they weren't gonna try and kill me," I snap, shoving her off and getting my feet under me.

"Then don't get killed," the *Justice* replies with all the indifference of a machine.

Scarlett moves in for another teasing strike, this time a thrust I sidestep easily. I may not know what to do with my sword, but my early life on Pearl Station gave me both the sea legs necessary to handle myself in a rotational-gravity situation as tight as the *Justice*'s core and the ability to dodge like no other. Her next swing forces me to get my sword involved, and she dances around my block into another strike that I barely catch on my guard. I try to shove her back, stepping in close and shouldering all of my momentum behind the hilt of my sword, but she steps out, lowers her sword, and lets me run straight into her knuckles instead.

The blow crunches hard into my jaw, whiting out my vision for a second, and I lash wildly with my blade, forcing her to jump back. Scarlett takes a leisurely circle, swishing her own perfectly wrought weapon back and forth as I probe the spot where her fist made contact. "So we're fighting dirty?" I grind out.

"We're seeing what you can do," Scarlett replies. She nods over my shoulder, and I leap sideways just in time to duck Allen's swing. The other three faithful have closed around us, their swords up and ready, and my stomach drops.

This isn't a real fight. If it were, I'd be dead in seconds. It's just a test.

Doesn't make it any softer.

They take their turns with me. First Allen, whose heavy swings are easy to dodge—a small comfort against the fact that his reach is impossible to penetrate. Past a certain point, he seems to get tired of playing, swats my sword aside so hard I nearly lose my grip, and drives his pommel into my gut with so much force, it takes me a full minute to recover my breath.

Soren taps in next, and at least they do me the courtesy of waiting for me to beckon them in once I'm back on my feet. Doesn't do me much good. With their nimble footwork and a well-aimed kick, they have me on my knees barely three moves into our bout. I stagger back onto my feet just in time for Sumiko to charge me with the ferocity of a boar, forcing me to dive to the side to avoid her swing.

By the third round, I'm starting to suspect this isn't even a test. Each person takes their turn, has their fun, and tags out when they score a blow. If it were about assessing my skills with the sword, they wouldn't be hitting me. If it were about assessing my endurance, they wouldn't be hanging back politely every time I need to catch my breath. The *Justice* croons soft encouragements every time I flag, and I hold back the urge to ask it what it wants, what it can possibly gain from having them beat the shit out of me.

It's Scarlett who finishes it, Scarlett who slams a whirling kick into my sternum that knocks me flat on my back so hard it shreds any illusions I have about getting up and going for another round with Allen. I stare up at the brilliance of the *Justice*'s computing core, choking on my own spit, desperately searching for a part of my body that doesn't ache, wondering if this is when one of the faithful will finally put me out of my misery.

"Good girl," the *Justice*'s voice murmurs against my skull.

I have no retort for it, nothing to offer beyond my continued hacking wheezes.

"That's given me the data I need to calibrate my assessment of your physical skills."

"And?" I manage.

"And it's certainly going to be a while before you're any good with that sword."

"Because I'm untrained, or because you just had me beaten?" The only mercy I can take solace in at the moment is the fact that none of the blows seem to have broken bone.

"The former. I expect you to walk off the latter. You're capable of standing, aren't you?"

Goaded, I roll onto my side and drive the tip of my blade into the turf, using it to lever myself back to my feet. The moment I'm upright, Scarlett lunges forward. I stagger back, trying to get my blade up to counter the attack, but she only swats it aside and catches me by the shoulder, grinning brightly. "Well done, Murdock," she crows.

I startle under three more hands that come to pat me on the back, the other three squad mates murmuring words of congratulations.

"Fuck all of you," I snarl, and they laugh. "I'm not kidding," I add, and they laugh harder.

"You lasted a lot longer than most initiates," Soren says, which I'm guessing is supposed to be a compliment. "You've got great control. Most people call it by the fifth or sixth blow."

I can't handle the way they've closed around me, the way any one of them could lash out and strike me at any moment. I catch Scarlett's eye, and she seems to recognize that panic's closing around my throat like a vise. "Give her some space, c'mon," she says, waving the other three off.

I make for the edge of the Dip, and Scarlett follows, stowing her sword at her hip and offering her hands as a stirrup. I take the boost, letting her lift me up over the edge. Once clear of the lip, I roll onto my back, rubbing my hands over my sweat-soaked face and basking in the warmth of the computing core's light. When I finally crack my eyes open again, Scarlett's seated next to me, her legs dangling over the Dip's edge.

"Was the hazing really necessary?" I mutter.

"It was a calibration and an introduction to your squad's capabilities," the *Justice* replies.

"Wasn't asking you. Scarlett, you answer me."

Scarlett glances down. Some of her electric energy has bled away, and I take the sight of her exhaustion as a little victory. "Maybe it could have been different," she hazards. "You came in with a sword already forged. I . . . didn't realize you weren't a fighter. I would have pulled my punches a bit more if I had."

I want to rage that I *am* a fighter, but I know it's a lie. Maybe I could have been a fighter in another life, one where Hark never caught me trying to mug her, never scolded me for using violence over cleverness, never shaped me into a worshipful little shadow of her brilliance. Maybe it's possible I could be a fighter now, wielding my brand-new sword for the *Justice*'s agenda. Like Ham said, reinvention is the name of the game here.

"I broke an arm during my evaluation," Scarlett says. Her gaze is pinned on Allen, who's climbing up the opposite side of the Dip to retrieve his cloak. "Took me a full month before the *Justice* could put me out on assignment."

"And it didn't make you want to quit?" I ask. "This exercise doesn't inspire loyalty, if I'm being honest." I'm too worn out to be anything but bold with what I say in earshot of the band on my head.

"All loyalty is fear, anyway," Scarlett says, and this time her eyes drop to her knees.

A quiet moment passes. Quiet enough that I can pick up the faint hum of a conversation the *Justice* is drilling into Scarlett's skull. It's surprisingly tolerable, knowing it must be talking about me. I'm used to the uncomfortable itch of seeing Hark bending close to Fitz's ear as Fitz's gaze locks unsubtly on me—but Hark's attention was always a finite, rare resource. The *Justice*'s is as abundant as air.

At long last, Scarlett pulls her feet under her and rises. "Come with me," she says, not bothering to look back as she heads toward where she dropped her cloak.

"What are we doing?" I call after her. If it's not good, I'm not getting up.

"It's time you met God face-to-face."

CHAPTER 28

There's no way in hell Hark's plan ever could have worked.

I decide this about halfway up the ladder to the computing core, fumbling with the twin carabiners lashed to my safety harness. The climb is completely unsubtle, a ladder straight up along an exposed support strut in plain sight of the entire core's interior.

I thought it was impossible when we started out. The computing core is hung so high above us, and the beating I took less than twenty minutes ago wasn't doing me any favors. But as we climbed, I realized I'd forgotten to account for one thing.

The *Justice* itself is suspended at the exact center of the command core. The command core that's rotating to mimic a gravitational force.

The higher we climb up the ladder, the more the effects of gravity wane beneath my feet.

It's still precarious—still necessitates that tedious process of clipping my way up the rungs. A fall from this height is going to be disastrous, even if at the moment it feels like I'm on the edge of floating. The rotation generating the gravitational force is pushing me into the ladder, but if I lose my footing, there's plenty of room to accelerate into a nasty landing. I advance my clips one by one, grumbling as Scarlett's progress gets slower and slower.

By the time we make it to the platform at the top, she's looking noticeably wan, bobbing at the end of her tether like a queasy red balloon. Her eyes are blacked out behind the thick, dark lenses of the goggles we both wear to filter the brilliance of the core's light, but now that we've climbed past the panels that generate it and into the heart of the computing core itself, I dare to slip mine down around my neck.

It feels like I've crawled into the heart of an alien beast— warm, dark, and strangely constricting after the terrifying open-air climb. I let myself float in a slow turn, tracing the pathways of systems I recognize. Coolant lines twine through processing units like veins furrowing into organs, and though everything is built with elegant Ybi angles and harsh corners, there's something uncannily organic about all of it. I look at it and I see flow. Purpose.

I look at it and understand why someone would call it divinity.

And here I am, utterly unworthy to float in its center. I'm still coated in dirt from my little adventure in the Dip, my body barking reminders of my painful humanity with every little adjustment I make to keep myself oriented in null. Even though I can see the protective covering that shields the machinery from my greasy filth, I feel like I've just stormed into an art museum and only my careful balance in null is keeping me from smearing my hands all over the exhibits.

"Welcome, Murdock," the *Justice* purrs, its voice humming from every direction with equal force.

"What is this?" I mutter. "A reward for taking my beating?"

"I'm flattered that you see this as a reward, but no," the *Justice* replies. Scarlett's head perks up, and she unclips her tether, fumbling along a series of handholds with the null sense of a Pearl Station five-year-old until she reaches a panel that's slid out of the ground. She guides it farther out of its slot, easing it into bloom.

It isn't until I spot the keys that I realize what she's just unpacked is a terminal.

"I've brought you here to evaluate your skills," the *Justice* says. "Your reputation for hacking preceded you aboard this ship, of course, but I find it's sometimes necessary to observe and form my own calibrations."

"Which is why you had my so-called squad mates beat the shit out of me," I deadpan, my gaze drilling warily into the back of Scarlett's head. From her utter lack of reaction, I'm hoping this means the specifics of my reputation haven't reached her ears.

"She doesn't need to know," my circlet buzzes into my skull. "At least, not until I decide she needs to know."

Sweat prickles over my palms as I hazard a glance back to the aperture we crawled through and the long way down beyond it.

"If I'm to make use of you, I need to know how useful you can be," the *Justice* says aloud.

"Couldn't the technical part have come first?" I groan, but I can't deny the way my curiosity is starting to perk up. Ever since I first came aboard, I've wanted to get my hands on the *Justice*'s processes, to delve into the architecture that sustained this ship for three centuries. With an open terminal in sight, it's starting to gnaw into me like a hunger, making all my aches and pains fall away.

"See what you make of this," the *Justice* says, and Scarlett pushes back from the terminal, leaving it wide open for my approach.

I might as well be floating toward an altar. I wipe my hands desperately on the sides of my jumpsuit, as if that's going to be enough to make me worthy of touching this relic. The configuration of the input keys is unfamiliar, but at least the *Justice* has done me the favor of translating its screens from Old Imperial to modern language.

It's presenting me with a crash log. I skim the readout until my attention snags on a line that points so obviously at the culprit that at first I think it must be a trick. "That's just badly formatted input," I announce, and the band around my head warms.

"Correct," the *Justice* says. "Next."

The difficulty escalates with each challenge it throws in front of me, but there's a comfort to it. This isn't a job interview. I've already passed the only test that matters. This is the *Justice* gathering the data it needs to wield me—and me gathering the data I need in turn to understand how best to serve it. Past a certain point, it becomes a conversation. The *Justice* will present a new problem, and instead of hunting for the issue immediately, I let my curiosity guide me, picking my way through the underlying structure of the *Justice*'s systems.

As I do, a larger realization starts to creep in. I'm at the heart of the computing core, working on a terminal with direct access to the ship's most critical systems. It's intimate, almost as intimate as the construct crowding me back against the hab-fabric wall in Southeast Upper, but this time I'm the one pressing in close. The fixes I'm implementing imply that I've been granted permissions to make nearly any modification I can imagine.

And suddenly I'm imagining less what the *Justice* has in mind, more what Hark hoped I could achieve if I made it to the core.

It's terrifyingly possible. Not only because I have the permissions necessary but because I know exactly how to make it sound like I'm doing something else. It's a perverse fusion of my mother's training and Hark's, coaxing a customer—a *mark*—into thinking I'm doing everything in their best interests while I steal right out from under their nose.

Would it work on the *Justice*? It could. Machines can be fooled just as easily as people if you know the trick to it.

I can do it. Every part of my history was built to do this. But just as I know it's possible, I also know the consequences. Hark would tell me to forget them. *Consequences are for people who look back, and people who look back get caught.*

The *Justice* is a god. Not just in the sense of its planetary-scale ego, but in its function. It's a fixed point of worship for the faithful to organize around, and just as strongly it's a pole for the rest of the ship to diametrically oppose. In the course of my hours untangling the workings of its architecture, I've come to understand just how deeply entwined it is with the ship. Much like any other megastructure intelligence, it keeps the lights on, the drum spinning, the air pumping steadily through the recyclers. The *Justice* is a universe unto itself, and as god, it holds the fabric of its reality together.

Without it, that all goes away. I picture those kids on the playground outside Southeast Stair screaming in terror as the ship's running lights plunge not to the familiar low glow of twilight but to a darkness deep enough to rival the void outside. I imagine the pulsing, joyful noise of Southeast Upper Limits going silent as hundreds of bodies packed in close together breathe themselves into oblivion. I'm sure if I pulled aside any of the people in the settlements who call this ship home and asked, they'd tell me this place shouldn't exist. Everyone aboard it should be freed.

But pulling the plug on the *Justice* isn't freedom. It's hastening the only escape that's ever been available to us in the first place.

I think I understand now. Why we came all this way when surely there are terminals like this scattered all throughout the core. This is the real test—the *Justice* pulling my gun to its head, looking me in the eye, and goading me to shoot. I understand, too, why the beating came first.

There's no fight left in me. The *Justice* has hollowed me out from the inside, and the only thing left that makes sense is filling that void with the one thing I'm good at. It's not swinging my sword around. My bout with the faithful has proved that much. But these challenges are proving another thing entirely. Even with every muscle in my body aching, dirt and grass stains coating my uniform, bruises patterning my skin, I can still waltz through a computer system and figure out every issue plaguing it. In the past, I've only ever used that skill to steal. To break.

The *Justice* wants me to use it to build.

So I take the redeeming hand it offers, and I throw myself into the work.

CHAPTER 29

On the morning of my first assignment, one full week after my arrival coreside, I stand before the mirror in my quarters and allow myself to imagine what Hark would think if she saw this.

I'm dressed in a clean black jumpsuit, my bare shoulders sheltered under the mantle of my shimmering white cloak. My newest accessory sits snug around my waist just above my sword belt—a sturdy tool belt packed with every bit of hacky trickery I could ever ask for. Everything I wear was gifted by the *Justice*, from the military-issue boots molded to my feet to the glowing band that crowns my slicked-back hair and casts my eyes in deep shadow.

If Hark was put off by the sight of me in settlement clothing with a sword on my hip, she'd probably shit herself now.

Or assume it was part of some elaborate con, because of course that's the first thing her mind would go for. With Hark, there's always a ruse, always a second level the rest of us might not know she's maneuvering on.

I'm battling a lingering guilt over how much of a relief it's been to set all that aside. No more plots. No more schemes. Just God's great plan for me.

Knuckles rap on my door. "Shuttle casts off in thirty," Scarlett announces from the hall. "You miss it, it's gonna be a hell of a walk to get ringside."

Leaving the core feels oddly mundane. We pack onto the shuttle with all of the other faithful deploying today, and it might as well be a public bus in a core world, some people chatting with their neighbors in low tones while others doze in their seats. The flight is quick, the landing surprisingly smooth, given the physics of bringing in a small craft to match speed with the massive rotating drum of the ship's main body, and before I know it, we're hustling out of the landing bay and into a familiar chamber.

Now that I'm not half-drowned, I can appreciate the elegance of the architecture around the water's edge, but I can't help the dread that rises in me at the sight of it. Even watching other faithful wade in without hesitation, I balk at the memory of being dragged underwater by the *Justice*'s construct.

"Hey." Scarlett hip-checks me, handing me a plastic bag to seal my gear in. "You know exactly how far it goes now. Just stick close to me and we'll be out in no time."

"More important," the *Justice* hums against my skull, "you have my guidance." As I strip and stuff everything into the bag, I feel it feathering over my headband, urging me gently toward the water's edge. "Anywhere my network reaches, you can never be lost. Anywhere it doesn't reach, well. That's why we have you."

I go willingly into the water.

My squad regroups once we've all emerged on the other

side, drying ourselves under the heat output from a massive piece of equipment Allen tells me is part of the air circulation. The plan for today is to stick to repairs in the inner decks, where I can get the hang of the workflow without worrying too much about needing the sword on my belt. There's a busted transponder somewhere in the North Upper region, a dead zone that needs fixing.

Once we're dried out and reequipped, we start the hike.

Traversing these corridors by daylight is only part of the gaping distance I feel from the last time I was here. The people we pass step out of our way without hesitation. Eyes peer from slots in enclave doors, but their wariness takes on a different timbre with a pack of four other armed faithful at my side. Doors yawn open for us like old friends, the ship itself laying out our path, and part of me feels downright guilty for the luxury of it. For most, traversing this ship is an ordeal. For us, it's a breeze.

It takes us no time at all to reach the edge of the *Justice*'s signal range, the deadened gap in the network where something's been torn out. All of us feel it in our bands, the way the *Justice*'s presence starts to slip away. I ease out ahead of the rest of the crew, scanning the sensor boxes wired into the wall. After the *Justice*'s training, it's almost second nature to follow the seams where panels cover the wires leading to the transponder.

I'm about to round a corner when Sumiko's hand latches onto my shoulder, yanking me back. Before I can make a noise of protest, she crams a hand over my mouth. "We're out of our depth with a network dead zone," Sumiko whispers in my ear. "No eyes in the corridor. Let the advance guard clear it."

She and Scarlett take point, drawing their swords in practiced synchrony as they ease around the corner and into the next hall. Allen and Soren wall up behind me, but when I drop my hand to my own sword hilt, Allen shakes his head. "We cover your back. You do the job," he says with an encouraging nod.

Scarlett beckons me forward, and I slip around the corner to crowd in at her heels as the two of them advance. I spot the damaged transponder immediately. The mechanism has been hacked apart, long gouges torn in the polymer casing to wrench it back and expose the guts of the device.

Now I understand the caution. Someone came after this with intent, and whoever it was might be just as intent on keeping their work in place. One tech-head isn't enough to fix the damage, because no matter how good I get with that sword, I'm never going to be able to defend with one hand and repair with the other.

I clamber up the wall's ornamentation, using Allen's proffered shoulder as a brace, and get to work as the rest of the squad fans out into defensive positions. It takes only a few soldered-in wires to get power running to the device again, and not long after I've got the base functionality repaired. The relief of it washes over me in the way the band around my head warms with the *Justice*'s presence, and with its voice crooning encouragement and advice in my ear, I finish restoring the connection to each sensor array this transponder governs.

I sag back, but the *Justice*'s band tightens, a reminder that even though the functional repairs are done, the work's not finished. I pull the damaged housing free, slip off Allen's shoulders, and unclip the polyprinter from my belt. If it were up to me, I'd have one of the coreside recycling shops whip up a brand-new casing—a much simpler one, not beholden to the strange, overwrought design sense that plagued the Ybi Empire.

But the *Justice* insists. So I lay the tip of the printer's pen against the scars torn in the housing and let it ooze fresh polymer into the wound.

"It's not just about restoring functionality," the *Justice* says in that quiet, personal register that feels like it's beaming the words directly into my brain. "We're fighting to unify this ship, and that goes all the way down to the very look of it."

"You think you're saving souls with these aesthetics?" I ask as I finish filling in the first gap, then pull a scalpel off my belt to carve out some of the excess and refine the detailing.

"Aesthetics are a surprisingly essential part of authority. It's something the Ybi know well. If we're to remake the galaxy in our image of perfection, we have to have a firm agreement on what that image is."

I purse my lips, fighting the urge to note that slip of present tense.

Our second repair is a sensor box that's been outright smashed on the fringes of East Deck. For this one, there's no salvaging the original function—it needs to be completely re-placed. My squad mates' packs are filled with new parts manu-factured by faithful engineers in the core or shipped in as part of the demands made with tithes, all planned according to our itinerary. Fortunately the *Justice*'s network is still present, and its memory of our loadout has my hands reaching for Soren's pack before I myself remember that's who has the new sensors I'll need.

I'm halfway through pulling it out when a man appears on the far end of the hall. At a glance, he looks like recent ingest—the lower half of his clothing is too new to be anything but his original colors. From the twisted scowl on his face, I'm guess-ing I have him to thank for this patch job.

"You banded fucks," he snarls.

I straighten, my hands going to my sword, but the *Justice* whispers, "Leave it, Murdock. The others will handle it."

Scarlett takes point against the man, her sword held loose at her side. "Haverson, right? Nice to meet you."

"I didn't tell you my name. That *thing* did, didn't it?" Haver-son says. So far, his hands are empty of weapons, but he carries himself with a nervous energy I've seen start fights with barely a wink of provocation.

"Murdock, focus," the *Justice* demands.

I force my eyes to drop back to the new sensor I've laid out, but my heart is hammering. The *Justice* wants me to be a component, performing its assigned function while the other faithful perform theirs. I try to tell myself it's like any other job—like Hark in my earpiece, delicately threading herself through a tense conversation while I worked to reroute security footage from a nearby vent. But the net result of that tricky hobnobbing was never someone getting punched.

And in my periphery, I hear the sounds of a scuffle.

"In your training, you typically made this kind of repair in twenty minutes," the *Justice* comments blithely an hour later.

I scowl, snapping the last part of the sensor box's housing into place.

The deeper we delve into the *Justice,* the more frequently we encounter pushback. Passersby scoff at us, muttering about brainwashed lapdogs and entropy. Another busted transponder has a knot of people guarding it. Soren takes them on single-handedly and sends them running—a healthy reminder that I'm never crossing blades with them again if I can help it. The damage, too, is growing more frequent, stagnating us in the region around East Deck. The farther we get from the core, the less of a hold the *Justice* has. When I first came aboard, I understood that—the base urge to reject authority and forge a life independent of the entity that stole you.

But the deeper I get into the repairs, the more I see how precarious it is. There are corridors that have become dead zones, filled with stale, uncycled air because the wrong systems got damaged. Places that could end up like that shelter packed with bodies that Fitz and I stumbled upon, simply because they got separated from the *Justice*'s care. If enough of the *Justice* gets eroded away, this whole ship could become a death trap.

It gnaws away the scraps of any sympathy I have for the people trying to protect the damage they've caused. By the time the environmental lights are fading and Allen and I are working on our last scheduled repair, I catch myself smirking as Scarlett sends another person scrambling away from her whirling, gleaming blade.

Once we've snapped the last bit of freshly printed housing into place, I expect the *Justice* to shepherd us back up to the shuttle deck, but instead it leads us through a hidden door that opens at its signal, into a narrow passage lit only by the glow of our bands, and out into an open space that's shockingly familiar.

I stare up at the green, overflowing tiers of East Deck, a bitter wash in my throat.

Fatima greets us as we approach the outermost archway into the settlement. It's a relief to see Heeseok behind her, kitted out in his scary armor, though less of a relief when the slash of his mouth visible beneath his helm twists into a distinct scowl as Scarlett steps out to take point. I'd wondered how their encounter during my escape went, and I guess that sums it up.

Fatima's gaze slips over to me and she stiffens. Is that guilt? I wonder. She didn't do a damn thing to stop the faithful when they crashed our little welcome dinner. Is it any surprise I ended up in their number?

"How can the *independent* settlement of East Deck help you," she asks Scarlett primly.

Scarlett gives her a shitty grin. "We'll be quartering here for the night."

There's no fresh ingest to play nice for this time. We're granted the rooms we request from the settlement's available space and invited to take whatever we'd like from the nearest community table, but it's all done in strained voices, through gritted teeth, or with at least two meters of healthy distance between us and our purportedly gracious hosts.

The rest of my squad doesn't seem bothered by it. They praise the quality of the food, heaping their plates high, and offer nothing but cheerful smiles to every wary stare we get. They act like they might as well be celebrities, soaking in the attention, happy to be cleaved from the ranks of the ordinary.

For me, the sensation is utterly alien. On Pearl Station, I was a nobody, noticed only by the one woman who could keep her wits about her when my fake grav-out struck. Under Hark's care, I became an expert at slipping undetected into places I didn't belong. I was never supposed to be the kind of person whose presence commands the attention of an entire settlement.

Like a shark sensing blood in the water, the *Justice*'s awareness bumps up against my own. "There's nothing to be worried about," it whispers to me, its voice somewhere in the uncanny space between a lover crooning sweet nothings and a parent soothing a squalling infant. "I know you're not used to people noticing how exceptional you are. Your Hark never saw it. Now you're crowned, ordained in my favor, and no one's able to look away. Let them look."

"They look like they're afraid," I murmur back.

"Fear and respect walk the same path as good friends," the *Justice* replies. "They're correct to be wary of my chosen, but they'll come to associate their fear with the good works you do when they begin to reap the benefits of the repairs you've made today. All of this is in service to our higher purpose—making this ship fit to serve the glory of the Ybi Empire."

"The Ybi Empire that crumbled three hundred years ago."

That gets me a sharp glance from Scarlett. She makes a little no-no gesture with her fork, but I can't help my curiosity.

"How did it come to this?" I ask. "To you stealing people— *sinners*, sinners, I know," I add as the *Justice* attempts to interrupt. "You give us something to build, but how did this ship ever fall from its original glory in the first place?"

I wait for the answer from my band, but it comes from Scarlett. She sets her utensils down, swallows her last bite, and says, "The Ybi Empire was at war."

I remember that part from history lessons in crèche. The collapse of the old empire was spectacular, fought on hundreds of fronts as its components dissolved into feuding states that would take another hundred years to settle into what we now call the Known Harmony.

"A battle left the ship stranded in the deep black, too badly damaged to make its next jump and far outside the comms radius of anyone who could come to its aid. Repairing itself became the only priority, superseding all other directives. The soldiers it had aboard were just enough to get it moving, get it jump-capable again. In the Ybi mode, the next logical step was to acquire laborers to finish the repairs. The galaxy was rich in small settlements that were enemies to the empire, and the first tithes were gathered from those."

The history lessons I grew up with were painted with the broad brush of hindsight, cynical almost to the point of parody about the empire's cruel methods. It makes it easy to picture the *Justice* wounded but awash in imperial fervor, clawing entire settlements off planets to serve its ends.

Scarlett tips her head, examining my expression with a thoughtful pinch of her eyebrow that I don't like. "Resources grew scarcer, and enemies of the empire grew more powerful," she continues. "The repairs wore long, and the original officers began to age past the point where they were willing to manage the difficulties of keeping their laborers in line."

"So, sinners," I mutter.

I see it from the machine's point of view. Raiding entire settlements was too much work. Too much ammo fired, too many additional repairs if some of them managed to fight back, and too much resentment built up in the workforce for an aging class of overseers. Why go through all that trouble when instead you could convince a settlement to give you the people you need for free? Just point a bevy of imperial firepower at them and demand they hand over everyone they'd rather be rid of.

That's the ugly truth the *Justice* built its system around—the weight a society is willing to sacrifice for their own sakes.

It took those unwanted, and it gave them redemption in a new purpose, the infinite project of building this ship back into its original glory. All of it adds up to the band around my head and the endless cycle it represents, raging against the entropy of this little kingdom the *Justice* has wrought from its defeat. As long as the *Justice* is programmatically unable to accept the Ybi Empire's downfall, the loop continues.

"Do you think it can be done?" I ask, then realize Scarlett's missed out on the tangent my mind's wandered down. "How many days like the one we just had could bring the ship up to full function?"

"Feels like building sandcastles right next to the ocean, doesn't it?" Scarlett chuckles. I wouldn't know, but I'll take her word for it. "It's all a matter of numbers and power. The power's always been on our side," she says, brushing the pads of her fingertips fondly over the band on her forehead. "The numbers? I believe they'll come. You did, after all."

I SAVE MY BIGGEST QUESTION for the dark of my borrowed room, late in the night. The *Justice*'s band glows warm around my brow, and if it were capable of such a thing, I imagine it holding its breath. "When the work is done, when the ship is back to its original configuration, what happens to us?" I whisper at last.

"You will have fulfilled your obligation. You will be redeemed by your great works. Those of you who wish to join me on my crusade will remain by my side, but the rest can go forth, fit to live under the auspices of Ybi glory."

As easy as that? I think, but then I remember the scale of the
backlog, the kilometers of ship, and the impossibility of holding all of that in my head at once. An irrational part of me
wholeheartedly believes it could be done in my lifetime, the
same part that looks into the deep black of space and thinks I
could see it all. The goad of it sticks in my side like a spur. If
we could just convince everyone else aboard to fall in line under
the *Justice*'s directive, freedom could be in sight for all of us.

I chase my tail on the *how* of that problem into an uneasy
sleep.

It doesn't last. In the dead of night, my band goes taut
around my skull, shocking me awake as its light flares so bright
the room seems lit by daylight. "I have a new directive for your
squadron," the *Justice* announces, its voice cast loud and unmissable.

I rub my eyes against the brightness, muttering a litany of
oaths I picked up from Bea.

"A group of four sinners are attempting to break into my
jump storage. *Your* band of four sinners. Report to North Deck
and put a stop to it immediately."

CHAPTER 30

There isn't room to think in the tumult that follows, in the haste to dress and crash out of my room and find my squad mates doing the same. All of them are just as wild-eyed with confusion, but none of them are looking at me like I'm the reason the *Justice* is yanking us out of bed and driving us toward North Deck.

It doesn't register that I *am* the reason until we're running, the bouncing glow of our headbands lighting the way as we tear through the ship's corridors. Sumiko has our heading, Scarlett's gnashing her teeth about how night watches are supposed to handle this kind of thing, and finally it clicks.

The jump supply was *my* plan—back when I had a plan, back when I thought maybe I could figure out a way off this ship. The *Justice* called the perpetrators my band of sinners. Hark. Bea. Fitz. Possibly Ham too. Everyone I left behind when I realized Hark would never listen to me and that only left a single future in my path.

I never told her about the jump supply. If she's going for it . . .

A tightness forms in my chest that has nothing to do with the running, and I push myself to keep pace with the rest of my squadron. I can't assume anything until we get there.

I hear the hum of machinery before I see it, the same music Bea tuned into when the ship last jumped. We sweep through a wide set of doors as they snap open to admit us into a chamber nearly as towering as Southeast Stair, lined with massive, piston-like jump capacitors. At the core of the enormous cathedral lies a dome that houses the cryochamber where the antimatter pellets that power the jumps are stored.

Perched on top of the dome, kicked back with her legs crossed casually, is Hark.

Her eyes snap to me, taking in my banded glory. Crown on my head. Sword on my hip. Black jumpsuit, no longer a twin to the original colors she wears without modification. Shining white cloak clasped at my throat, ready to be torn off the moment I'm called into action.

Then her gaze drops to the arched entrance of the dome beneath her feet as she whistles a tune in A-flat minor.

Out of its shadows steps Fitz.

Hark, I was ready to face. I'd taken the time in the mirror yesterday to imagine the moment she saw me, to categorize every inch of what I was throwing in her face. Hark rejected me. Our parting was clean.

Fitz strides down the walkway, her platinum hair aglow in the cyan cast of the jump chamber's lights and her expression sly and haughty. The sight of her might as well have reversed the ship's spin. I left Fitz with nothing more than a few shaky words and a brush of her cheek. Whatever she wants to do next, I deserve.

"Hey, Murdock," she says. "I like the new look."

I've spent four years reinforcing my immunity to Fitz's wiles, but all that has come apart since we came aboard this ship. With her vibrant green eyes on me, I feel like I can't move, like I'm back in that airlock, wondering how we're both still breathing.

"Ah, yes," the *Justice* says in my ear. "The girl who hates your guts. Whose guts you hate in turn, if your heart rate has anything to say about it."

The hammering in my chest catches up to me, and I realize all at once how much the *Justice* missed when we were holed up in the Forgemaster's workshop. My squad mates have pulled up short behind me, no doubt held back by a command from the ship. It dragged all of us out of bed to sort this out, but it only ever wanted me to take point, to prove once and for all that I belong to it.

"Murdock?" Fitz asks. I've never heard her so uncertain, and part of me wonders if it's an affect she's playing up to stall for time. Ham and Bea must be inside the cryochamber behind her. Once again, Hark's called Fitz in to be the cavalry—and she herself is sliding down the dome to retreat into the darkness.

I watch her go, choking back simmering anger rising to a boil. She's just proved every point that shoved me into the *Justice*'s arms. She won't hear me out, and she's left Fitz to take the heat. Consequences are for people who look back, and Hark won't even face me.

"They cannot be allowed to access the jumps," the *Justice* murmurs urgently. "It could set our progress—your progress, the progress we've all worked so hard to achieve—back by *decades*."

There's only one thing I can do. Only one thing that will keep the four faithful behind me, that will please the *Justice,* that will put a stop to the irreparable damage. I drop one hand to my belt, the other coming up to the clasps around my neck.

Fitz takes a step forward, her hands still raised—close

enough that when I draw my sword, its tip lands perfectly beneath her chin.

"Ah," she says, her smile so silky I want to throttle her for
not taking my threat to her life seriously. I could cut her throat
with a flick of my wrist, and that's all she has to say? Worse, she
lowers one hand to my sword, running the back of her nail
delicately along the flat of my blade, like she knows there's not
a power in the universe that could convince me to hurt her.
"So, no to the plan then?"

The plan. Our plan. It was my idea to go for the jump core.
The fact that we're here now can only mean that Fitz convinced
Hark to abandon her original notion of going after the *Justice*
itself. That even after I gave up and handed myself over to the
ship, Fitz still believed in the scheme we came up with
together—believed in it enough to turn her most potent weapons against the woman whose orders she's followed unques-
tioningly for the past five years of her life.

I gave myself to the *Justice* because I realized I could never
go back to the way things were under Hark's direction. And
maybe it's true that Hark won't change—but I'd missed that
Fitz could. That she had. And that all we needed for the plan to
succeed was for *her* to fight for it.

And suddenly I'm grinning too—grinning like an absolute
devil, feeling so light I might as well be floating. Which could
be because of the button I've just pressed on my belt, the one
wired to do nothing but send a simple signal to the network
I've spent all day restoring, a signal that triggers the work I
threaded into the *Justice*'s core processes on the day it let me
into its heart of hearts.

I couldn't betray it. Couldn't kill it from the inside. But in
the midst of its tests, I built myself a secret advantage. A bit of
glass to break in case of emergency.

A backdoor that triggers the *Justice*'s system of engines and
counterweights and tells it to kill the grav.

The change is subtle. Massive things in motion need massive amounts of time to slow, and the friction of the rings against the counter-spinning outer deck is less of a hard stop, more of a steady erosion. I feel it coming on like a song rising in my bones, whistled in the key of F minor.

"The fuck is going on?" Scarlett shouts from over my shoulder.

"A Murdock Grav-Out Special, baby," I holler back, whirling on one lightening heel to level my sword at the other four faithful.

"What have you done?" the *Justice* snarls against my skull. The band tightens punishingly, its light flaring harsh and bright. I try to tear it off, but it's latched on with a python's ferocious strength.

"I'm having second thoughts about some things," I grind out against the pressure.

"You are *mine*. You are *sworn*. You are—"

"A sinner and con," I reply, drawing a soldering pen from my belt and ramming it against my band. With a flip of my thumb, a surge of electricity fries the wearable, hitting my brain like a static shock.

Next thing I know, I'm sagging in Fitz's arms, barely held upright despite the waning gravity. She's giving me a *look,* and before I can open my mouth, she snaps, "Did you really just electrocute yourself?"

"Worked, didn't it?" I shrug, prying the loosening band from my skull. Now if the *Justice* wants to talk to me, it's going to have to do it out loud.

Scarlett stares at me in naked horror, her face stuck somewhere between outrage and utter confusion. She's got her head cocked to the side, a giveaway that she's listening to whatever the *Justice* is whispering in her ear.

If I had to put money on it, I'd wager it's something along the lines of "Stick her with the pointy end."

"C'mon, babygirl," I simper with a crook of my fingers. "Let's get this over with."

"Murdock, it's four on two," Fitz hisses in my ear.

"Four on one," I correct. "So Ham had better be with you."

"He is, but Hark said she needs him for the heavy lifting in there."

Scarlett's swishing the tip of her sword back and forth, her fingers playing impatiently with the snaps on her cloak.

"Is this our plan or is this Hark's plan?" I whisper urgently.

Fitz's lips go thin. Something too complicated to be anything but genuine flashes across her face. Even in this new world, even after all we've been through, it's no small thing to ask her to go against Hark's orders.

"*Fitz,*" I plead.

"I'll see what I can do." She turns tail and retreats into the cryochamber on unsteady legs, leaving me filled with a growing lightness that's only partly to blame on the shifting gravity.

I hop from foot to foot experimentally, smirking at the easy thirty centimeters of clearance I get with each bounce.

Scarlett lunges, the other three faithful hot on her heels.

Thanks to the *Justice*'s brutal little hazing ritual, I know exactly how fucked I'd be in other circumstances. Four against one is a death sentence no matter how skilled a fighter you are, and unlike the last time I fought these four, no one's taking turns. But the faithful are used to nominal gravity. Apart from short-range shuttle rides or the occasional trip up to the core's heart to talk to God face-to-face, they've never had a break from it in their time aboard.

Me, on the other hand—I grew up on Pearl Station. Shitty Pearl Station, where it seemed like every other day, something would gum the drum and leave us floating. It was regular enough to become a game in my crèche, a competition of aerial tricks that drove our chaperone out of her mind trying to keep a pack of spinning six-year-olds from breaking their necks. Null is the ocean I've been swimming in my entire life.

So none of the faithful are ready for my first feint. A pinion of my arms gives me the momentum I need to wheel under Scarlett's first swipe. I tear my cloak from my neck and whip it around like a bullfighter, snapping it wide to catch Allen in a tangle. From there, I kick off the ground, vault clean over Soren's thrust, and—just for fun, just to make Ham happy— actually parry Sumiko with my blade.

It happened so fast that I don't begrudge the moment of blinking disbelief as I push Sumiko back, using the force to give myself a solid two meters of space. No one's forgotten that just a week ago, they collectively beat the shit out of me. I've still got the bruises to prove it, and a day of trekking through the *Justice* and making repairs has done me no favors. But this isn't a fight. It's a dance, the same steps I'd practiced when I triggered grav-outs back on Pearl Station and used them to knock over rich travelers passing through.

I learned how to be untouchable. And as long as I can stay untouchable now and keep these four assholes occupied, my plan has a chance of succeeding.

So I whirl into the dance, tamping down the urge to shout in outright glee as the muscle memory of skipping through lowering gravity comes back so easily it's almost like I never left Pearl. Like I never left all the cruelty and violence and injustice of my upbringing, like all the things that made me uniquely suited for the *Justice* were really just the tools I needed to fight its chokehold. I may not be an expert with the sword I'm swinging, but like Ham taught me, it's an extension of my body, and in this circumstance, knowing exactly how to move my body is enough.

Fast like a rat. Fast enough to survive. The gravity is trickling away bit by bit, stealing a little of my opponents' maneuverability with every passing second. All of them learned the sword in a reliable standard grav environment. I never learned the sword at all, but I learned to be slippery no matter what forces were acting on me.

Unfortunately one of those forces is my own exhaustion. Each leap drains me a little more, each tumble giving them an extra centimeter of ground toward the door to the cryochamber. My grip on my sword is loosening, and my jaw is starting to tighten as I clench my teeth against the ache wearing into my muscles. I've committed myself so wholeheartedly to holding the line that I can barely remember what's supposed to come after, much less save my strength for it.

Sumiko and Soren close on me as one, and I know my luck's run out. I twist away from Sumiko's blade, but even as I move, I see the flash of Soren's rapier out of the corner of my eye.

The blow never comes. Instead, a hand latches around my wrist, pulling me back as another sword comes up to parry.

"Ham?" I croak in a haze. But Ham never could have snuck up on me in null. Only one person has ever been able to get inside my guard like that.

I sneak a glance over my shoulder to find Hark standing over me, her teeth gritted, Ham's sword clutched in her hand as she shoves back the blow that would have ended me. "Hey, kid," she grunts, her dark eyes fixed on Soren as she reestablishes her guard. Her hair is loose, the inky sheets rippling in the low grav as she steadies me on my feet.

The four faithful give us a wary pocket of distance, sizing Hark up. She's certainly not a swordfighter, and even if she were, she's wielding a blade crafted for a man easily twice her size. But their hesitation gives her an opportunity to size them up in turn, and I've been on enough jobs with her to know what a horrible mistake that is. Hark's eyes dart among them, and God, what I wouldn't give for a readout of the tactical assessment she puts together in a matter of seconds.

"Nice work," she mutters, squeezing my shoulder.

"I *did* almost get my head taken off just there," I reply sheepishly.

"I mean the scheme, Murdock," Hark says, still scanning the faithful. "The jump core was clever. It was the right call."

I feel like someone's knocked me upside the head, like my null sense has slipped away all at once. "Would have been nice to hear before I went and surrendered myself to a delusional god," I hiss between my teeth.

"I'll admit, that didn't speak well to your rationality at the time," she replies with a sly smile. Before I can get genuinely pissed at her, her eyes drop from our opponents' to mine, taking all the air out of my retort. "It was my fault. I didn't know what I was saying. Or what I was giving up by saying it. Fortunately for both of us, Fitz talked some sense into me."

"I'm starting to realize she has a way with that," I mutter, hoping the sweat I've worked up in the fight is covering the blush rising in my cheeks.

"If you'd told me a week ago that you and Fitz would be working in perfect harmony, I'd have thought there'd been an atmo leak somewhere. And if you'd told me all it took was the two of you being stranded together, I'd have kicked you out on your own myself. When Fitz told me you came up with a plan, the thing that made me listen wasn't the plan itself—it was the fact that she was still following your directive, still believing in your vision, even after you'd given up. You'd become the very thing I'd been pushing you toward all along, and I just hadn't seen it in time."

It's not the perfect forgiveness I crave, but it's the closest thing I'm going to get under these less-than-ideal circumstances. "You sure there's not an atmo leak right now?" I croak.

"Just your sneaky little grav-out, kid. Now, keep your head on straight." She whirls Ham's sword in a showy circle that only pulls her off-balance, and I swallow back a swell of nerves.

"You know that's what I do worst," I reply, just to see her fierce grin.

The faithful lunge.

CHAPTER 31

Hark puts her back to mine, locking her free hand at my waist to keep us joined. Gravity's close to an afterthought at this point, and I use it to my full advantage, squatting low and leaping with all the force I can muster as Hark mirrors me. We take off sailing, arcing high over our opponents as they scramble to throw themselves after us.

All except Allen, who realizes the opening we left behind. The door to the cryochamber is sealed, but after working with him all day yesterday, I know he has enough tech-head training to get through it fast.

Can't have that. "Hark, throw me!" I grunt, leveling my blade at Allen.

All that fast-talk she spun earlier could have been con shit, but this is the true test. Hark twists in midair, plants her feet firmly against my back, and shoves with all her might, sending me sailing down toward Allen like a missile.

She took my direction. Without hesitation, without inserting her own grand scheme, with nothing but raw trust.

I hit Allen like a goddamn shooting star, my blade plunging into his dominant shoulder hard enough to keep me from bouncing right off him. He roars, scrabbling at me in an effort to tear me off, but I cling hard, my free hand taking root in his flaxen hair. I can feel the vibrations roiling off his band, and I'm just close enough to pick up the faint strains of the *Justice* berating him for not blocking me. Allen heaves, trying to throw me off, but the push sends both of us into the air, pinwheeling over and over as he swings his blade wildly back at me.

I give in to instinct, sinking hard and fast into the feral kid I was before Hark found me, the one who could take the upper hand in any fight the second gravity went out the window.

She welcomes me back with open arms.

I switch my grip from his hair to his arm, bracing myself against it to keep his sword from making contact. There's a telltale tremor in his muscles, and when I wrench my own sword sideways, driving it harder into the meat of his shoulder, his grasp on the hilt slips. I dart in before he can regain it, prying his blade from his hands, then plant my boot in his neck and strain, tearing my own weapon out of him and sending him hurtling back down with a lethargic, arterial gush.

We're almost at true null. I can see it in the way his blood burbles in the air, forming ellipses that are dangerously close to spheres. He's going to have a hell of a time getting that wound to clot properly, but I've got more important problems at the moment.

My trajectory has me sailing toward the pinnacle of the jump core, into the thicket of its cathedral-like ceiling. Hark's still keeping one step ahead of the faithful up here, using every strike they try to levy at her as momentum to propel her even farther away, but as I approach, I notice that Soren's starting to get their null sense—and that Hark's still treating each fighter with equal disdain.

I set my sights on them next.

Allen's larger sword trails behind me, and I use its mass as a rudder, levering against it as I twist myself around to face Soren. Their eyes go wide as I sail past with nothing but a teasing smack of my blade against their own, then kick off one of the spires in the jump core's ceiling to drive myself right back at them. They twist their rapier around, their body shifting naturally into a dueling stance, but it's something they always practiced with solid ground beneath their feet.

There's nothing for them to brace against when my strike hits and sends them spinning. We sail for the floor of the jump core with Soren fighting for distance, trying to wrestle their rapier tip back into the gap between our bodies. I deflect it again before they can get it around, then aim my own sword point over their shoulder.

Soren's brow wrinkles in confusion a half-second before their back hits the ground.

The strike's enough to stun them, and the root my weapon takes in the floor panel is enough to keep me from bouncing right off onto another trajectory. Before Soren can get their breath back, I leave Allen's sword to float and drop my hand to my belt.

Their eyes flare wide in panic as I wheel my dagger back.

Then their brow wrinkles in confusion as I drive it not into their stomach but into the loose fabric of their jumpsuit waist and the polymer paneling beneath it.

They make another swipe at me with their rapier, but I twist out of the way, snatching Allen's sword again as I go. Another solid kick uproots my sword and sends me sailing away, leaving Soren to flounder against the dagger staking them to the floor.

If I ever see that scav again, I'm going to thank him for the tip.

Up above, Hark's still bouncing between Scarlett and Sumiko. Her moves are getting more sluggish as she tires, and Ham's heavy-ass sword is doing her no favors. My eyes ricochet through possible paths I could take to get up there and defend her, but before I can settle on a course, I catch a streak of platinum out of the corner of my eye.

"We got them," Fitz shouts triumphantly as she hurtles out of the cryochamber. "All jumps are totally destabilized. All that's left is the one primed in the chamber."

Ham and Bea are fast on her heels, and a grin breaks over my face as the simple numbers tip in our favor. Four of them. Five of us.

Except they're not just four—a fact made horrifically clear by the way Sumiko and Scarlett both tilt their heads and then beat a hasty retreat to the jump core's doors. A simple numbers advantage isn't going to do anything when the resident deity has also picked a side.

Hark comes hurtling in from above, catching me by the shoulder. I look her over for wounds, but it's like I forgot who taught me how to be properly slippery in the first place. She grins at me, panting, clutching Ham's sword like it's a lifeline. "See that, you big bastard?" she shouts, her voice echoing against the jump core's prismatic architecture. "That's a little tune in the key of F minor."

The radiant glow of her pride in me barely has a chance to settle before I notice the way Scarlett's stiffened at the jump core's entrance. "You know," she says, swaying queasily as she brings her sword up again. "I never found out who defrauded my family. Who tore the legs out from under us and ensured our settlement would fail. They disappeared into the black. Never heard from them again. But my father told me one thing about his dealings with them. They always had a tune going. Always paid special attention to the key."

Her band flares brilliant white, and Sumiko lunges for her, no doubt spurred by some command from the *Justice*. Scarlett kicks hard off the wall behind her, ducking Sumiko's swipe for her arm and hurtling herself straight at Hark, her sword cocked back for a vicious swipe.

I yank Hark's sleeve, throwing myself out in front of her to intercept Scarlett's blow. "Get everyone out of the core!" I grunt as our blades clash.

"Everyone?" Hark shouts, but in the corner of my eye, I see Fitz already moving toward Soren, pointing Ham and Bea to where Allen's drifting, clutching his shoulder wound.

Above us, the cyan light of the core shifts, growing ever so slightly more intense. I didn't hear the hum Bea tuned into just minutes after we came aboard, but now it's unmissable, starting as a low tone that cants up and up and up in pitch until it's rattling my bones.

The *Justice* is wasting no time. It's staging its last jump.

And none of us want to be here when it fires.

"Scarlett, hey. Let's be rational now," I yelp, ducking another wild swing. Rationality looks to be a long walk away for her at the moment. Her band is searing white, and close up I can see how tightly it's winched around her skull. The *Justice* must be trying to rein her in, but its godly command can only do so much against the righteous fury that's seized her. Even the nausea of her weak null sense isn't enough to crack through it.

"She ruined my life! She ruined my family! I wouldn't be fucking *here* if it weren't for her." Her face crumples suddenly, and I know the *Justice* must have broken through with something, but just as quickly she snarls it away.

"Look, we're all sinners here," I mutter, levering Allen's sword between us before she takes my head off. "The *Justice* wouldn't have picked us otherwise. But can we have this conversation somewhere that's *not* about to get bathed in antimatter backwash?"

Scarlett only wheels in midair, reorienting herself to drive her feet against the wall she's fast approaching. She's so pissed, she might have cracked right through her shitty null sense, and the net total is a punishing trajectory she locks onto as she throws herself headlong at Hark again.

"Just go!" I shout. The whine of the jump drive's song is building toward a peak. Bea and Ham are already at the door, Allen slung between them. Sumiko's thrown herself over to where Fitz is still trying to uproot the dagger staking Soren to the floor.

Hark bolts for the door, tucking Ham's sword into her armpit as she checks back over her shoulder and discovers how fast Scarlett's closing on her. My heart leaps into my throat, but before Scarlett can catch up, Hark feints to the side with a kick off the jump core's doorframe.

Leaving Scarlett sailing straight into Ham.

He has her by the wrist before she can react, wrenching her sword arm behind her as he grapples her into submission. The flutter of relief that passes through me barely has a chance to settle before I hear Bea scream, "*Murdock!*"

Now or never. I hurl myself at the door, fast on the heels of Sumiko, Fitz, and Soren. We pile out into the corner just as Allen jams something in the door controls, snapping them shut behind us with a decisive *whumph*.

The howling scream of the jump drive's windup goes suddenly silent. Nothing feels any different. It's a stutter-step, a blink, and suddenly we've popped out in a completely different corner of the universe. In the eerie quiet, there's a moment of stillness. Bea hovers over Allen, her hands bloodied against the wound on his shoulder. Ham has Scarlett locked in a hold, quivering with barely restrained rage. Fitz and Sumiko flank

Soren, who seems to have lost track of their rapier in the scramble to evacuate the core.

And in the middle of the corridor floats Hark, looking at complete odds with the sword she's clutching, eyeing Scarlett warily. "Vestal, right?" she says.

"Fuck off," Scarlett snarls back. "You knew," she spits, her gaze snapping to me. "Shouldn't have pulled my punches in the Dip."

"Scarlett—" Sumiko starts, but Scarlett thrashes.

"You think this is all fine because we ended up in the same place, huh? Well, my family ended up here too. We came aboard together."

The *Justice*'s old threat echoes in my ears. *The ones that come as a set? They never stay that way.*

"Scavs hit us the second we were out of the ingest chamber," Scarlett grits out through her teeth. "We fought back against them, but we weren't ready. Never could have been ready. I think the Envoys know that. I think that's why they wait—just to see who's worth rescuing. Turns out it was just me."

Tears are starting to well in the corners of her eyes, and she flinches suddenly. The *Justice*'s band is still wrapped tight around her skull. It must have said something she didn't like.

"*You were going to do the same fucking thing a second ago,*" she spits, and the rest of the faithful tense in alarm. "You didn't have to stage the jump right away. You could have waited for us to clear the chamber."

"It was a calculation," the *Justice* says out loud from all four bands simultaneously. "And as you can see, I totaled the sums correctly. With no jump supply remaining, I had no choice but to bring us to a new source immediately."

"And where, exactly, is that?" I ask.

Like I don't already know. Like I don't believe the precepts that have been carved into the intelligence's core systems. *Swift justice to enemies of order,* it promised—and I've made myself public enemy number one.

"Somewhere bound to have an ample jump supply," the *Justice* replies, its voice like a blade on my neck. "Somewhere worth taking from you."

The logic is too neat. The ship feels its lack of jump charges like a hunger, like a wild animal knowing by the rumble in its gut that it's time to hunt. It's heard my history and plucked Pearl Station from that data—a transit hub bound to be full to the brim of ships with charges to spare. The perfect vengeance for me cutting its belly open in the first place.

There's just one problem.

"Been a little while since you came to this corner of the galaxy, huh, bud?" I simper, unable to keep the shit-eating grin from spreading over my face.

Pearl Station is ancient. A wheezing relic, doomed to faulty architecture that'll never get better as long as elected officials are using it as nothing but their next empty campaign promise. Ancient enough that the *Justice* knew its position, even after three hundred years hunting the galactic fringes. But in the three hundred years since, the galaxy has kept spinning. Borders have been redrawn since the Ybi Empire collapsed and the Known Harmony stitched itself together from the pieces. And what was once a little outpost orbiting a sad nothing of a planet is now home to one of the grandest military bases in the galaxy.

My wager was that they wouldn't be too happy to see us.

The distant *boom* of a weapon impact tells me I was right.

CHAPTER 32

A siren flares to life, bright lights flashing up and down the corridor. "All hands, all hands," the *Justice* announces, its voice thrown unmissably loud. "Report to battle stations."

"What battle stations? What *hands*?" I shout back. "Are any of you trained for ship-to-ship combat?"

Sumiko shakes her head, glancing nervously at Soren. "We repair whatever takes hits, but the *Justice* usually does the hunting itself. It's never called us to battle stations before."

If I had to wager, it's never been this badly outnumbered in the twenty-five years Sumiko's been aboard.

She stares down at her sword, and I wonder if she's feeling something similar. With Scarlett restrained, Allen wounded, and Soren disarmed, Sumiko's the only one left still capable of doing any damage. I'm not about to put her out for the count, not when she's spent over two decades in the *Justice*'s thrall, but if I've learned anything during my time aboard this ship, it's how a sudden change of circumstance can rearrange your priorities in a blink. Like Ham once said, reinvention is the name of the game.

"What's out there?" she asks.

I open my mouth to answer, but she cuts me off with an emphatic flick of her sword. Her head tilts, and I recognize that classic banded faithful listening face I've come to know so well.

"And you have it handled?" she asks after a long moment.

My heart sinks. It doesn't matter that the base berths three capital ships with batteries to rival even the *Justice*'s excessive firepower. I've seen enough of how the *Justice*'s mind works to know how deeply rooted the delusion of empire is. The *Justice* believes victory belongs to it by right, that the natural order of history follows the logical progression written out in its archives that paints the Ybi Empire as inevitable.

Worse, that language is its natural tongue. No doubt Sumiko's band is pouring those empty promises into her skull with all the religious flourishes it's spent decades priming her to receive. With no sight line to the reality of the battlefield, she's helpless to dispute it.

So it takes the air out of me completely when she reaches up for the band.

It tightens immediately, fighting her efforts to pry it off. Sumiko's face twists in pain, and my hand drops to the soldering pen on my belt. Lightly electrocuting myself was one thing—safely disengaging Sumiko's band while she twists and thrashes in null is something else entirely. Before I can lunge across the corridor, her sword blade flashes up, the lethal edge clawing deep into the circlet's polymer flesh. The strike is panicked, imprecise, and immediately sends a spurt of blood burbling out into the air, but the glow of her band goes dark as it slips limply from her skull.

"Twenty-five years on this ship," Sumiko mutters, clutching at her temple as she probes the severity of the wound, "and

I've never heard a hit scored on it like that—that quickly, that easily. Whatever's out there, it's something worse than anything we've faced before. You want to fill me in on what that is?"

By the time I've finished talking, Soren's wrestled their band off too, then helped dislodge Allen's. Even Scarlett's given up on her fruitless struggling against Ham's grip, though trying to pry her band away from her head is just asking to get a finger bitten off. Her face has gone ashen, and I'd wager her nausea's finally catching up to her. "Well if that's the case, we're fucked," she warbles. "What did you think this would accomplish?"

"I thought the Harmonic Forces could subdue the *Justice*. It's out of jumps. There's nowhere to run."

"You think the *Justice* can be subdued?" Scarlett asks. For a moment, I think it's that religious fervor talking, but the hollow panic in the stare she fixes me with tells me it goes a little deeper.

"They just have to take out all the batteries, then knock out the core once they can get close enough."

To my horror, Hark shakes her head. "You've been on this ship too long, kid," she says.

"I've been on this ship just as long as you." I can't take her doubt. Not now, not when I thought I'd finally pulled off my first grand plan.

"Murdock, what's the key to a successful con?" Hark asks. "You gotta live in both realities at once. The one you understand, with the full picture of everything that's happening, and the one you've created in your target's mind."

"Can we cut the shop talk with"—I hitch my thumb at Scarlett, who's starting to tense in Ham's grasp—"her listening in?"

Hark shakes her head. "We know what the *Justice* is. The people doing *that*?" I don't know how she knows a distant, muffled explosion will punctuate her perfectly, but it does. "All they know is a fuck-all big warship just dropped into their space and started firing. They aren't going to differentiate between the ship taking shots at them and the people who happen to be on it."

I stiffen. "Not unless we tell them."

SUMIKO LEADS THE WAY. BUT the *Justice* fights her at every turn. No doors whoosh open for us, no lights come on, and by the time we make it into North Stair, I can tell it's starting to put a panic in the faithful. They're used to sweeping through this ship unimpeded, used to always having a path lit by the glow of their circlets.

Then again, I'm not far behind them. As we follow the tenuous beam of Fitz's flashlight, the distant rumble of intermittent shelling striking the outer hull is a reminder that at any moment something could break through and vent this space. Rising up the spoke of the massive support at the center of the settlement, the empty air around us fills with the uncertain noise of people sounding off with their neighbors as they try to figure out when they should anticipate the grav coming back. A few thin, higher noises pierce the general murmur—the sounds of children crying.

I did this. I took this place they made into a home, stalled it into null, and threw it to the wolves. I did it to spite God, but all I hear is how I've once again flung everything into chaos to serve my own whims.

I have to fix it.

But there's an obstacle ahead of us we can't traverse by hacking through a door or simply taking the long way around. Past the inner decks, past the enclaves, we reach the water's edge.

In null, it's transformed. Without gravity to pin the body of water down, surface tension has rendered it a vertical wall molded against the sides of the corridor. It's shifted slightly from the last time we crossed it, migrated a little bit farther down the hall.

Hark, Fitz, and Bea stare at it in naked confusion. "We . . . have to go through?" Bea asks.

"How far through is through?" Fitz adds.

Hark gives me a grim look. "So I guess I see now one of the reasons the core plan was going to be a little harder than we thought."

I toss her a plastic gear bag, already unclipping my tool belt. There's no time to strip completely, so only the essentials get packaged for travel through the water. The faithful work with us to make sure everything's sealed, driven by the same dire urgency.

There's no *Justice* to guide us through the waters, and with the way they've shifted down the corridor by the force of the drum slowing to a halt, I can't totally trust the map I remember. Worse, null has scrambled our spatial awareness, and even with my body reoriented in the corridor to approximate, the sensation is totally off.

The faithful seem just as uncertain. They may know the ship better, but they're strangers to null, and the physics of swimming in water without gravity is daunting.

"Everybody pair off," I call, gesturing from my crew to my squad mates. "Allen with Bea, Soren with Ham, Sumiko with Hark. I'll take Fitz, which just leaves . . ."

Scarlett scowls at me, floating next to Ham like a pissed-off crimson kite. He's bound her hands behind her back with a strip of fabric, and Fitz has commandeered her sword, but I know she's probably just as dangerous without it. The faithful wouldn't let us leave her behind, and now that she's overheard where we're planning to go and what we're planning to do, I'm not too keen on it either.

"We brought her back to the inner decks," I mutter to

Sumiko. "Can't we just tie her up here and let someone else pick her up?"

Sumiko's gaze goes to the towering wall of water ahead. "The ship's not fighting all-out yet, but if it does, that could mean high-G maneuvers. Ones everyone needs to be in an inertial shelter for. If that call goes out, Scarlett's dead before she can get those ties off. Maybe even faster, if the water here shifts."

I blow a long sigh through my teeth, then beckon to Ham and Soren. "You two are the least likely to set her off. Scarlett'll go with you."

Soren looks uneasy, but they give me a quick nod.

"Without grav, you're fighting surface tension at first," I announce, swinging to the front of the group. "There's nothing to kick off for momentum until you're fully immersed, so we're going to need to hit the water at speed."

I turn to Fitz and offer her a hand.

"On my mark," I murmur. Out of the corner of my eye, I catch the worried glance Hark and Bea exchange. It's one thing for them to hear that Fitz and I collaborated on the plan that's brought us to this moment, another thing entirely to see her slip her palm willingly into mine without protest. I line us up against the wall, flex my knees and wait for her to mirror me, then mutter, "Deep breath in three. Two." On one I hold up a finger and fill my lungs to bursting.

We leap together, my hand tight in hers, pushing off the wall on a trajectory that sends us sailing into the water's center. A hand up over my head breaks the surface with a strange, rippling splash, and then I'm fighting the shock of the cold as the rest of my body submerges.

With Fitz in tow, I kick down the corridor, praying I remember the twists and turns after just two trips. The darkness is all-encompassing, and I can feel Fitz starting to balk as she realizes this goes on for longer than she anticipated. I give her what I hope reads as a reassuring squeeze. There's no faith to guide us—only me.

Just when the panic starts to grip me from the bottom of my lungs, my fingers break abruptly into empty air. I tug hard, sending Fitz out ahead of me, then delve forward with a forceful kick. My head breaks the surface with another ungainly ripple, and I nearly choke on the bubble of water that congeals over my mouth when I try to take my first breath. I'm twice as drenched as I've ever been in my life, the lack of gravity letting water cling to me that otherwise should have dripped, and I run my hands over my eyes to clear the pools that have lodged in them.

Fitz is breathing hard, wringing water out of her steely sheet of hair. She catches my eye, and suddenly it's all too familiar. Suddenly we're back in that airlock and I'm wondering how she could possibly trust me enough to let me drag her through something so dangerous—and she's smiling that rare, *real* smile because she knows how badly she's gotten into my head.

I know there's no time for it, but I can't help myself. I reach out and snag her by the belt loops, reeling the two of us together so I can clamp my knees on either side of her hips and seal my lips over hers.

We stay like that as long as we're able—up until we hear the ripple of someone else breaking through the water. I can feel her mouth firm up beneath mine as the impassive mask locks back in, and I can't resist kissing the corner of her lips, just to see her fight to keep it in place.

"Oh," I hear from the water's edge. I glance back over my shoulder to see that both Bea and Hark have emerged, side by side with Allen and Sumiko. Bea's grinning. Hark looks like I might have finally surprised her. "Well, that explains more than a few things," Hark says.

"Pay up," Bea says, nudging her with an elbow.

"I assure you, the *second* we're off this hell ship—"

"You bet on this?" Fitz mutters flatly.

"*You* won a bet?" I direct to Bea. I'm waiting for the moment Fitz shoves me off her, and my flustered grin is only getting wider every second she doesn't.

Sumiko's worried glance over her shoulder shatters the moment, and I realize it's taking a little bit too long for Ham, Soren, and Scarlett to come through. I suck in a breath, loosening my knees to let Fitz free as I paw for my gear bag and draw a flashlight out. The light is blindingly bright in the looming darkness of the cavern, and the beam barely cuts into the water. With the way we've recently perturbed its surface, it's hard to tell if the twisting shapes are the figures of the final three approaching or just our own reflections thrown back at us.

Sumiko's lips set in a grim line. "She's our problem. We'll deal with it. Allen, you go on ahead with the four of them."

Allen's looking worrisomely pale, but he gives the other two faithful a nod. "Shuttle deck's not far from here."

The distant sound of a muffled impact vibrates down the chamber, sending a shimmering ripple across the water's surface. The strikes are growing more and more frequent—likely as more and more ships deploy against the *Justice*'s surprise appearance. We're running out of time.

With the rest of the ship battened down for battle, the shuttle decks are empty. It's child's play for Bea to pop the door of the nearest one berthed, and the five of us pile into it, Allen hovering back near the entrance to keep an eye out for any danger—or Sumiko, Ham, and Soren. There was a reshuffling of the swords, and Hark's ended up with his. Nobody's figured out whether we should give it back to him or not.

There's a relief in crossing the shuttle's threshold, one I never noticed in my first couple rides because I'd had the *Justice*'s band locked around my skull. The shuttle interfaces with the ship's systems, but it's a separate entity, and without a single banded faithful aboard, the intelligence has no presence here. But because of that separation, the shuttle needs comms tech—and if I'm guessing correctly, that tech wouldn't have been altered that much since the warship days.

Bea works side by side with me to override the shuttle's comms. She's the expert here, but she's used to working with contemporary tech, so I fill in the gaps to help her trick her way around the outdated system. "I don't think the radius on this thing is going to be very big," she warns, squinting at one of the readouts. "It'd be easier if we could launch, but . . ."

Not exactly an option, given the conditions outside. "Whoever we manage to hail, we're going to need to be extra convincing."

I glance back over my shoulder to where Fitz and Hark are standing guard, Hark with her wary eyes locked on Allen and Fitz frowning as she tries to puzzle out the chaos of Bea's hotwiring job.

Two weeks ago, I'd have done anything to make sure it was me. To make sure I was the one at the heart of the call that would save our skins, to make sure Hark *saw* that I'd been paying attention to her teaching all along. But if it's me, I *haven't* been paying attention.

I reach out and slip my fingers carefully around Fitz's wrist, reeling her in to join me at the terminal. "I think you should do the honors," I announce.

IT FEELS LIKE NOTHING AT first. Like screaming into the void. We blast Fitz's voice on every frequency we can manage as she desperately pleads for someone to understand the facts. That there are ten thousand hostages aboard, all trying to survive the onslaught, and the real enemy is the intelligence at the core. I'm not even sure our receiver can tune into the frequency the Harmonic Forces are capable of broadcasting back at us, but Bea and I keep fussing with it until finally, *finally* someone responds.

From there, it's all Fitz. All that incomparable charm as she talks circles around the comms officers, sounding less like a young woman begging for her life and more like a schoolgirl sprawled on her bed, kicking her heels up as she gossips. Hark's moved in at her side, listening intently, ready to fill in anywhere she might slip.

I can feel a rankling instinct tugging at me, urging me to draw her attention away from Fitz. It's a habit four years in the making. Hark made herself a reward for good behavior, then acted surprised when we fought over the ever-scarce resource of her admiration.

But then Hark catches my eye sidelong, and I realize how pointless it would be. This is the real magic she's been trying to get me to seize all along. I don't need the galaxy spinning with me at the center. I need the galaxy to spin exactly as I've ordained it.

The shuttle rocks suddenly from a nearby hit, and I brace against the nearest bulkhead for stability. Fitz keeps talking, and again I feel the brush of old instinct, the thought I would have had a week ago. *Perfect Fitz, thinks she's so above it all that even in the face of a nearby missile strike, she's unfazed.* Now all I feel is admiration—both for her unflappability and for the choice I made to put her there, knowing she wouldn't falter on the mic.

It's hard to home in on the absence of something, but as the minutes wear long, I realize the distant rumbles of weapon strikes are becoming less frequent. I nudge Bea. "I think it's working."

Allen stiffens, and my hand slips to the hilt of my sword.

"Something wrong with that?" I ask.

Allen casts a nervous glance out to the rest of the shuttle bay. "If the attackers are shifting their strategy to a more effective one, that means the ship's going to have to redouble its efforts to protect itself. Could mean going all-out. Could mean—"

The intercom cuts him off as the *Justice*'s voice blasts terrifyingly loud. "All hands, all hands, report to your nearest inertial shelter."

CHAPTER 33

It could be worse, I try to tell myself. *At least there were no corpses.*

Which is cold comfort when I've been locked in an over-padded coffin. Whatever material the Ybi used to construct these shelters is porous enough that you can *sort of* breathe through it, but the overall effect is still suffocating. The needle beds are cocked back from my skin at the moment, but if my thumb twitches the wrong way, I might end up dosing myself with three-hundred-year-old blood thinners, and no risk of stroke-out is worth that.

But worst of all, my splendid little tomb is networked, wired with a microphone and a set of speakers. In principle, everything is there for a good reason, meant to let me know when the danger's passed and I'm safe to resurface from my swaddled-up hell.

In practice, it's yet another avenue for the *Justice* to have its way with me.

I'm pinned in place by the cushioning, rattled by the choking high-G maneuvers the ship's throwing itself through with wild abandon, and forced to listen to every little thought it wants to jam into my head. With a disgusting, ancient mouthguard jammed between my teeth, I can barely get a word in edgewise.

"I gave you a chance to build something glorious, and this is what you did," the ship croons in my ear. "Would you like to know how many people your little maneuver has killed so far? I have tallies for everyone internally. When the engagement is over, I'll update the number to account for the crew manifests of the naval birds I've struck down."

"Go ahead," I grunt. "Your bullshit's on its last legs. You're not going to steal any more lives after today."

"*Last legs?*" the *Justice* crows. "Oh, my dear, I'm only getting started."

Despite the fear, the uncertainty, the sensation of being stuffed into a chip tube and shaken, pity overwhelms me at the sound of its delusions. If I had years, a full team, and maybe a doctorate, I might be able to unwind the programming that made this poor ship utterly incapable of change, locked in a reality it could only sustain by pillaging. On my own, I'm just a hacker and a con, and the only fix I have for these endless cycles and the crushing force of their gravity is breaking them.

It's what I'm best at.

"You know what?" I grit out against the mouthguard. "Tell me how many ships you've downed. I'm curious."

"Three light fighters and a support carrier," it answers without hesitation.

"So none of the capital ships, huh?" I reply, trying my best to sound nonchalant as yet another crushing maneuver grinds me deep into the padding.

I wonder what part of its programming makes it choose not to answer. There's no tactical advantage lost in telling me the score—only pride. The *Justice* has spouted enough propaganda to make it clear that its service to the glorious Ybi Empire motivates it. It's spent three hundred years scooping up easy pickings, riding its absurd firepower to scrape its continued existence off the galaxy's fringes.

Now it finds itself faced with three hundred years of technological progress and a superior force, all because it followed exactly what it was programmed to do.

"Want to know the worst part?" I goad it.

Intelligences love answering questions too much to let obvious bait like that hang. "What's the worst part?" the *Justice* asks.

"You had absolutely *nothing* to gain from targeting Pearl Station. There's never been anything left for me there. You picked it because it sounded like it was the most important place in the galaxy to me, based on the data you'd collected."

At that, a rumble shakes my coffin so forcefully that I brace for another high-G maneuver before realizing the strange, vibrating sound is the *Justice*'s best imitation of laughter.

"You're a liar and a con, dear Murdock, I'll give you that much. Enough so it seems you're capable of fooling even yourself."

I frown. The *Justice* fell for my scheme without an ounce of hesitation. It's believed every lie I've fed it so far.

Unless this is another one of its nonsense psychological tricks. A manipulation designed to create dependency, a new way to dictate my reality. There's nothing for me on Pearl Station. Nothing but the memories of the kid I used to be, the sucker falling for the first, longest con of my life until Hark caught me by the wrist and tore me free from the ties that had trapped me there.

No, everything I love is stored in the inertial shelters lined up next to mine. If the *Justice* wanted its vengeance, it should have started with them.

With Hark, who saved me, who condemned me, who latched on one day and never let me go. With Bea, who took me on the wildest rides with the steadiest hands, whose rotten luck has never extended to the bets she made on me.

And with Fitz, because there's a thing or two we need to sort out if we live through this.

A strange, muffled clunk sounds from somewhere in the shelter. Almost as if someone's unlatched their coffin.

But that would be madness, with the unpredictability of the way the ship's spinning through this fight. I think back to the corpses Fitz and I found, crushed into oblivion because they weren't packed safely away for the high-G maneuvers. No one in their right mind would risk that.

Unless we're locked in this shelter with someone who's not in their right mind. Someone whom the *Justice* could have told about a perfect little window between maneuvers. The *Justice* may only dole out vengeance as a logical sum, but that doesn't mean it's not capable of harnessing someone else's craving for it.

My fingers hesitate on the trigger that will unfurl my own coffin's padding and let me free. I don't have the *Justice*'s guarantee— or any faith that the ship will hold off on its next movement if I intervene.

Now I'm desperately trying *not* to think of those corpses.

I pull the trigger. My coffin makes its own clunk as it un-latches, a signal stiffening the padding to force it open. I spring out into the cradle of null and slam headlong into Scarlett where she's crouched over Hark's bed.

She shrieks, lashing out. Something collides with my thigh—a punch at first, but a searing, shocking burn follows.

I almost recognize the shape of it. Almost laugh out loud when I look down and see the dagger Ham kept insisting would someday betray me lodged in the meat of my leg.

I brace as we hit the ceiling and punch Scarlett before she has a chance to yank the blade back out. "Fucker," I seethe.

The force is enough to knock her back, to give me the space I need to reorient, but it also gives her time to draw her sword. Somehow she's gotten it back.

I didn't think to pack mine in the shelter with me.

I can't move like this—can barely think with the way the pain is starting to overtake my brain. Scarlett grins, the light of the circlet crowning her pushing the expression skeletal. She knows she's just won herself the upper hand, cutting my null sense out from under me in a single strike.

She throws herself at Fitz's coffin.

I lunge for her sword arm. I can't stop her like this, but I can delay her, and with the *Justice*'s next maneuver inevitable, maybe that's all I need. Maybe it wasn't entirely my fault we got into this mess, but I'll be damned if I don't get my crew out.

Scarlett fights me like a wildcat, clawing where she can't quite maneuver her sword as I struggle to leverage it away from me. The sharp burn of the dagger is starting to transform into a deeper ache that only worsens with every movement.

I'm listening for the rumble, for the firing of the drives, the music Bea always hears that she's never been able to teach me to appreciate.

Instead I hear something even more beautiful. A silence, an absence, something I notice only because I'm listening so closely.

Only an act of God was going to save me—but in the end, it's just the opposite. I hear the moment God leaves us. The lights flicker, the pitch of the humming machinery shifts, and the band locked around Scarlett's forehead drops to darkness.

Her expression crumples, suddenly a thousand times softer without the stark light. I can't stop myself from pitying it. Scarlett's been aboard the *Justice* for years, in its thrall for most of that time. She's forgotten a world where she doesn't have a higher power to serve, and the starkness of its absence can't do anything but hurt.

I know a bit of that feeling.

I give the shock of it a moment to settle. Then I redouble my grip on her and shout, "The *Justice* is offline! It's safe to come out!"

"ATTENTION ALL RESIDENTS OF THE rogue ship *Justice*," a stately voice announces over the intercom. It's surreal to hear a human, not the *Justice*'s slightly artificial intonation, ringing through the halls with all the authority of a deity. "Triage efforts are under way to evacuate the ship. Please proceed to the nearest shuttle dock on the outer ring, where Harmonic Forces will direct you through screening and egress."

Hark's eyes narrow at the word "screening." She's bent over my leg, carefully winding a bandage around the coagulant patch as its anesthetic bite finally sets in.

It's only natural that the navy's going to try to establish identities for the thousands of people it's discovered trapped on this ship. When they realize the percentage of those that line up with a criminal record, I have no doubt the tune's going to change a little bit.

But Hark's starting to get that *look,* the one I've been searching for ever since the airlock door closed behind us. It's the spark in her eyes that once convinced me that a galaxy of adventure was ahead, that I could leave Pearl Station behind and strike out into the unknown, chasing the light of her brilliance.

"You know, I've been thinking," I grit between my teeth as she finishes taping off the bandage's end. "I don't think it really matters who got us into this mess."

Hark softens, glancing up at me.

"What matters is that *I* got us out of it."

She lets out a short laugh, a flash-bang of a grin cracking across her face. "We're not all the way clear yet, Murdock."

"So what's the key, then?" I ask. On the far side of the inertial shelter, the ex-faithful are arguing over what to do with Scarlett, who's now thoroughly trussed up between them.

"Little number in C minor," Hark replies.

My focus narrows on Ham. He's hovering near the door, looking unsure of himself. His contract with us is complete— and his reward for it has been rendered utterly useless in the wake of the *Justice*'s destruction. "Mind if I improvise on that?" I murmur.

Hark smirks. "Show me what you've got, kid."

CHAPTER 34

"Hey, big guy." I grin as I slip into Ham's airspace, and he startles. The motion jars the chain around his neck, drawing my eyes inevitably to the key floating there. "Wanna get out of here?"

Ham's brow furrows. "Isn't that the idea now?"

"Oh, you mean the slow way? Sure, that's one option. You heard them though. *Screening*." I sneer. "Something tells me a facial scan that matches me up to an ident isn't going to work out in my favor. Same probably goes for you."

"So much for second chances, huh?" he says with a dark chuckle, but I can't miss the relief that flickers over his face when his eyes drop to the key floating in front of him. If the navy's evacuating everyone on the ship, at least that means the Moon Eater's going to stay locked up where he can never make good on his vow.

Thing is, I think I can offer him something even better. "Do you want to come with us?" I blurt.

Ham's brow lifts. "Are you saying your . . . Hark—"

"Finally has a plan, yeah. And I've thought of a way to improve it, but to do that, I'm going to need your help. If you're up for it, of course."

He glances back to where Hark's got Bea and Fitz folded under her arms, their heads pressed together as she fills the two of them in on what we've just plotted. "Your crew's been together for a while. Sure I won't ruin the dynamic?"

I laugh out loud, drawing startled looks from the faithful and a grin from Hark. "You traveled with me and Fitz for *days*. You know the dynamic's already in shambles. But we're going back out into a galaxy that's caught us once before. Might be good to add a little extra muscle to the team." I offer a pathetic flex, a sheepish grin. "And I think you could use someone watching your back too."

He's already floating, but there's a spark in Ham's eyes like he's just gotten even lighter.

"There's just one snag," I add before he can get too carried away. I flick the key floating between us, sending it spinning on its chain. "We're gonna need to make a little stop on the way."

HARK'S GOT A THEORY WHEN it comes to audacity. In moderation, it'll sink you. It'll get you feeling overconfident enough to make all the right missteps, and before you know it, your plan's gone to ashes. The only way to make audacity work is to do it in excess.

I think this plan counts.

I sort of wish the *Justice* could see how easily we waltz through the people who conquered it. With a few tricks I learned from studying its systems, I'm able to pick off soldiers one by one as they move through the corridors, slamming doors shut the moment one of them falls back from the rest of the group, until we've collected the uniforms and badges we need.

We make our run at the next shuttle deck over. Hark takes point, looking whip-smart with her sleek dark hair folded up in a strict bun and her brassy officer patches on full display. "Holy fucking shit," she announces giddily as we sail into view of the checkpoint. "You'll never believe what we found."

I'm a little impressed with how quickly the Harmonic Forces have put together a slice of bureaucratic hell. They've wrangled all the desperate *Justice*-dwellers into an orderly line, soldiers with shock batons floating up and down along it to make sure everyone filters through the facial-scan station before they even stand a chance of making it to the shuttle deck.

But for the struggling man Bea and Hark hold between them, no facial scan is necessary, even with the gag stuffed in his mouth. I'm honestly astonished his jailers got him into an inertial shelter in time—and more so that they didn't just leave him to take the G's. It's been three years since the Moon Eater vanished under mysterious circumstances, but it's done nothing to wean away his notoriety. Guess that's what you get when you eat fucking moons.

"Captain Brandt says we've got to arrange special transport for this one," Hark says. "They're already on the line with a tribunal in Igol that wants him jumped to them immediately."

The targets have picked their distraction, and boy are they fixated. Every Harmonic Forces soldier is gawking at the Moon Eater too much to notice the places where we've had to pin the uniforms in to fit our bodies or the way Fitz is subtly gripping me by the elbow, covering for the fact that I can barely move my left leg. No one's going to comm Captain Brandt—a name Fitz picked up as the hastily appointed head of this operation while she was convincing the Forces to switch their targeting from the *Justice*'s body to its core.

In seconds, we're waved through the checkpoint.

Everything past it is a foregone conclusion, from the breach alarm I trigger to send the entire deck into a panic to the speed

with which Bea hotwires a shuttle, overriding its intelligence as
Ham tosses the pilot out the back to join the Moon Eater where
we've left him struggling fruitlessly against his bonds. Hark
whistles her little tune as she straps herself in the copilot's
seat—C minor, but with a few variations in it that are all me.

No hesitation. Not until the moment we scream down the
launch tube and into the void, falling out and away from the
Justice's mind-warping curvature. In the blazing, unforgiving
light of the inner solar system, it's lit up like a halo fit for a god.
It sends my heart racing. I've never broken something this big
before. Even if it deserved to be broken, even if the galaxy is
better off without its cruelty, I can't feel anything but devasta-
tion at the sight.

Until a cautious hand finds mine and squeezes. "It worked,"
Fitz murmurs—and the smile teasing the corners of her lips is
real.

ACKNOWLEDGMENTS

It took a lot of back-and-forth conversations, several bouts with a Markov chain, and an overly complicated spreadsheet to finally nail down a title for this book, but in the meantime, I called it Lucky Number Seven. *The Salvation Gambit* is my seventh published novel, after all, and it feels outright miraculous to still be doing this strange little side job after all these years.

So obviously I've got a lot to be thankful for.

Thank you to the whole team at Del Rey for falling for this delightful little con—first and foremost to Sarah Peed, my editor, who saw the vision for this scheme when it was nothing but a single-page pitch. Thank you to Scott Shannon, Keith Clayton, and Alex Larned in publishing, to editor in chief Tricia Narwani, to Ashleigh Heaton, Sabrina Shen, and Tori Henson in marketing, to David Moench, Jordan Pace, and Ada Maduka in publicity, and to Cindy Berman and Jane Haas in production. All of your incredible work has shaped this book, and I'm so grateful to continue working with such a dedicated team.

The gorgeous package around these words is thanks to the outstanding illustration work by Mojo Wang and the slick art direction by Ella Laytham. Thank you both for the perfect visualization of the weird, wild landscape of the *Justice* and the one little con woman out to fuck it up.

This book would not exist without the tenacity of my agent, Thao Le, champion of champions. Thank you for being in my corner, no matter how many pitches it takes. Thanks to the whole Sandra Dijkstra Literary Agency team, especially Andrea Cavallaro and Jennifer Kim, for supporting my career with all your dedicated work.

Thank you to my critique partners, Tara Sim and Traci Chee, who've weathered every high and low of this business side by side with me. Tara, thank you for indulging all my worst impulses (especially calling Scarlett "babygirl"). Traci, thank you for indulging all of my craft geekery (and giving me any excuse to fly across the state and have dinner with you at the drop of a hat). Thank you to all the writer friends who have supported me over the years—none of us does this alone, and for that, I'm so grateful.

Thank you to everyone who gives me a vibrant life separate from the thorny warrens of publishing. Thank you to my co-workers, for making earning my living a joy. Thank you to my climbing partners, D&D co-conspirators, and all my friends who get me out of the house. Thanks to Wop House for every virtual hang and yearly vacation. Thank you to my family—my parents, whose science continues to fuel my fictional nonsense; and my sister, Sarah, whose artistry was key in visualizing these characters. And to Mariano: you know.

I wouldn't be seven books in if it weren't for the support of the book community. Thank you to every reviewer, bookseller, librarian, bookstagrammer, booktoker, booktuber, book blogger, and everyone who's ever recommended my work to a friend. Your love for my stories is a gift I can never repay, and I'm eternally grateful that I get to keep telling them thanks to your work.

And if you haven't yet been encompassed by any of the above, thank you to you, dear reader, for falling for my cons. I hope I get to take you on another adventure soon.

EMILY SKRUTSKIE is six feet tall. She lives and works in Los Angeles. Skrutskie is the author of *Vows of Empire, Oaths of Legacy, Bonds of Brass, Hullmetal Girls, The Abyss Surrounds Us,* and *The Edge of the Abyss.*

skrutskie.com
Instagram: @skrutskie
Twitter: @skrutskie